T0031119

the darkest child

The Darkest Child

DELORES PHILLIPS

Published by
Soho Press, Inc.
227 W 17th Street
New York, NY 10011

Library of Congress Cataloging-in-Publication Data
Phillips, Delores, 1950–2014
The darkest child / Delores Phillips.
Introduction by Tayari Jones

ISBN 978-1-61695-872-5
eISBN 978-1-56947-749-6

1. African American families—Fiction. 2. Mothers and daughters—
Fiction. 3. African American girls—Fiction. 4. Single mothers—Fiction.
5. Teenage girls—Fiction. 6. Georgia—Social life and customs—20th
century—Fiction. 7. Domestic fiction. I. Title
PS3616.H455 D37 2018 813'.6—dc23 2017037341

Printed in the United States of America

10 9 8 7

To my sister, Linda Miller, my
brothers, Lennie Miller and
Gregory Green, and my
daughter, Shalana Harris.

Introduction by Tayari Jones

I read *The Darkest Child* for the first time upon its publication in 2004. At the time, I was a new writer myself. I read the entire novel on a cross-country flight. I recall thinking that one day I would meet the author—after all, we were both black women writers from Georgia. Surely our paths would cross. People say that it's a small world, but it's a very small black world, and the black writing world is even cozier. I asked around, but no one I knew had ever met her. She didn't haunt the book festivals, artist colonies, or reading series where writers gather. Nevertheless, Delores Phillips maintained a quiet, steady presence in the hearts of anyone who had read her astounding first novel. In our new digital world, where artists are expected to interact with readers, pitching themselves along with their work, *The Darkest Child* has endured by the strength of its artistry alone.

The title may lead a reader to approach the story as a companion piece to Toni Morrison's classic *The Bluest Eye*, but this would be a misdirection. *The Darkest Child* is more suitably compared to Maya Angelou's *I Know Why the Caged Bird Sings*. Both works cover the fraught terrain of coming of age against the backdrop of Jim Crow in the rural south. Both women write candidly about lynching, sexual abuse, servitude, and other injustices of the day. However, *The Darkest Child*, published twenty-five years after Angelou's groundbreaking memoir, is its own singular accomplishment.

The throbbing heart of this novel is Tangy Mae Quinn, one of Rozelle Quinn's ten (or so) children. She is not the oldest, nor the youngest. As the title indicates, she is the darkest, and she is also the smartest. She is an irresistible narrator—observant, quick-witted, and compassionate. Her challenges are many and her suffering is immense. Yet Phillips uses Tangy Mae's unique perspective to relay brutal turns of events without creating a novel that is, itself, brutal. This is the sort of literary sorcery that leaves me—as a reader and a writer—in open-mouthed awe.

The entire book is populated by unforgettable characters. Rozelle, the matriarch of the Quinn family, is beautiful, violent, insane, but in Phillips's skilled hands, she stops short of evil. Tangy Mae's younger sister Martha Jean is deaf, mute, and deeply passionate. Her older sisters, Tarabelle and Mushy, practice everyday resistance. All the women struggle to live their lives with dignity although they are preyed upon sexually, emotionally, and financially—mostly by men. Yet Phillips imagines a small cohort of heroes—the schoolteacher who spreads the good word about racial equality, the brother-in-law who struggles to protect his wife and daughters, and even a no-count father who rises to the occasion in a startling plot surprise. There is a world on these pages reflecting the vast range of human complexity.

One of the benefits of the late twentieth century publication date of this novel is that Phillips is free from drawing characters that represent some fundamental truth about the African American female experience. The Quinns are not stoic and unyielding in the face of adversity. They are by turns mad as hatters and mad as hell. They love each other like crazy and they love each other like they are crazy. At the root of their sadness and fury lies the legacy of slavery that has left them warped, but also strong.

This story is intriguingly idiosyncratic. While the Quinns are steeped in the details of the place and time, they are not like anyone else you will know in real life or in fiction. Tolstoy was right: every unhappy family follows its own rules of discontent. The

Quinns are products of a breathtaking imagination and their experiences reveal a novelist who is a master of plot. This novel comprises grand occurrences—both in the lives of the Quinns and in the course of history. But at the same time, the quiet daily markers of ordinary life propel the story to its dramatic (and deeply satisfying) conclusion. Tiny pieces click into place with every chapter up until the very last page.

Delores Phillips is a heartbreaker and a heart-mender. In the days of Zora Neale Hurston, the folks who sat on Southern porches spinning yarns were said to be "lying." So in that vein, Phillips is a liar who can clobber you with the truth of a young girl's heart.

When I learned that she passed away in 2014, I regretted that I had never met her. I was also weighted down with longing for the other books that she would never write. But perhaps this is selfish of me, and even disrespectful of the great accomplishment this—her one, brilliant novel. *The Darkest Child* is a great gift, a timeless American treasure.

Tayari Jones, 2017
Atlanta, Georgia

one

PAKERSFIELD, GEORGIA 1958

Mama washed the last dish she ever intended to wash. I alone witnessed the event, in silence. It was on a Friday—a school day—but instead of sitting in a classroom, I was standing in unfamiliar surroundings, the home of my mother's employers, stunned by the wealth around me. As I watched my mother through unwavering peripheral vision, something in her glances at me seemed to say, "Tangy Mae, this will be your life. Grab an apron and enjoy it."

Domestic servitude was not what I desired for myself, but she had only to speak and I would do anything she asked. It was my obligation to obey her, though I did not want to be like my older brothers, Harvey and Sam, who seemed to breathe at our mother's command. They were men, and so their lack of initiative disturbed me, although I knew they could not just *leave* our mother's house. Departure required consideration of consequences and a carefully planned escape.

At the age of thirty-five, our mother was tall and slender with a head of thick reddish-brown hair. Her face, with its cream-colored skin and high cheekbones beneath dark gray eyes, was set off by a gleaming white smile accented by dimples. I thought she was beautiful, despite my acquaintance with the demon that hibernated beneath the elegant surface.

She had worked seven years cleaning house for the Munford family. Now she stood at their kitchen sink, holding a dish under running water longer than necessary before handing it to me to wipe. She finally dried her hands on her apron, took a seat at the table, and waited for her pain to subside. She had spent most of the day complaining of her misery while instructing me on the proper way to make a bed, scrub a floor, polish silverware, use a washing machine, and so on.

According to Mama, her pain—something like gas—had begun during the wee hours of the morning. It balled up in her chest, rolled through her stomach, between her thighs, and into her knees. It did a slow dribble in her swollen ankles, then just like that—her finger snapped—it bounced back to her chest and started all over again, taking her breath away.

On the table, beneath a crystal saltshaker, was an envelope. She picked it up and fanned it before her face. "Fifteen dollars," she said indignantly. "I don't care what I do 'round here, it's always the same fifteen dollars. Never mind that I stayed late on Tuesday evening when Mister Frederick's mother came for dinner. Never mind that I walked to the Colonial for flour that Miss Arlisa forgot to pick up. Week in, week out, always the same fifteen dollars."

She removed the bills and tucked them inside the pocket of her dress, then slid the envelope and a pencil across the table. "Sit down," she said, "I want you to write me a note to Miss Arlisa."

My obedience, as always, was swift.

"Dear Miss Arlisa," Mama started as soon as I was seated across from her. "Tangy Mae can do just as good a job as I can. She is my child and I learned her good. She can start work for you on Monday. I will be dead."

My hand trembled slightly, but I wrote the note exactly as she dictated. She snatched the envelope from the table, scanned the words, then passed it back to me. "Sign it, Rozelle Quinn," she said. "Miss Arlisa probably won't even know who that is. All they know 'round here is Rosie. Rosie do this and Rosie do that."

I sat there, dumbfounded. Loss traveled through my body, pulsed at my temples, and numbed my fingertips. I wanted to wail, to one-up her moans, believing my pain to be more severe than anything she could be feeling.

"You got something you wanna say?" she asked.

"No, ma'am," I answered, forcing myself to look at her. There was plenty I wanted to say. The words were choking me. I covered my mouth with my hand so they would not seep out. *Mama, you promised Mr. Pace that you would let me go to school one more year. You promised me the ninth grade. You promised! Mr. Pace thinks I'm smart. Please, Mama, let me go to school!*

But I had nothing with which to bargain, and I knew it. Already I had attended school longer than any of my siblings. I was in ninth grade, which in itself was miraculous, considering I had never set foot in an eighth-grade classroom. Academically, I had surpassed my peers, but at home I was a complete failure. At the age of twelve, my mother's children were expected to drop out of school, get a job, and help support the family. I fell short of expectations.

"We gotta get on home," Mama said. "Put me a bit of coffee and sugar in some wax paper. And Tangy Mae, don't make it noticeable."

"Yes, ma'am," I said, and thought how calm my mother appeared for a woman who planned to be dead come Monday morning.

Holding onto the table with one hand and supporting her back with the other, she heaved herself to her feet, then removed her apron and hung it in the broom closet. She checked the house one last time to make sure everything was in order, retrieved yesterday's newspaper from a basket beside the trash bin, and ushered me out by way of the back door.

The bitter cold January afternoon seemed to freeze my mother's face into a mask of disdain. "They done seen the last of me," she grumbled. "They don't give a damn if I freeze to death. They don't care nothing 'bout me, and I don't care nothing 'bout them."

I knew she was talking to herself, so I walked along beside her, keeping my mouth and my coat tightly closed. Sometimes Mama would come home from work and talk about the Munfords for hours. Miss Arlisa, she opined, was a fat, lazy white woman who had no idea how to keep house or satisfy a man. Mr. Frederick was a show-off who drove his automobile around town, honking the horn, and bragging about everything he possessed, including his ugly wife.

I had seen them only once, the time they brought Mama home with a load of old clothes they had given her. The only things I knew about the Munfords were that they owned the hardware store in town and that Mrs. Munford was not nearly as ugly as Mama had described her. She was not nearly as pretty as Mama, either.

"I been watching you," Mama said as we walked along the paved street that led out of East Grove and toward the Cherokee Creek Bridge that would take us into Stump Town. "You think them Munfords is rich white folk, don't you? Well, they ain't rich. If you wanna see rich, you gotta go up there on Meadow Hill. That's where the really classy white folks live. They got mansions up there that take from morning to night to clean, and that's wit' five and six people working. These East Grove whites bow down to them on Meadow Hill, and you better believe it."

I had long been familiar with the Pakersfield hierarchy, which ranked Meadow Hill supreme. Everybody bowed to somebody, but, all in all, Pakersfield was a decent place to live. The Negroes had Stump Town, the flats, and Plymouth, while the whites had Meadow Hill, East Grove, and North Ridge. There was never any trouble, as long as everybody stayed where they belonged. We usually did.

Miss Janie Jay's house was the first house on the Stump Town side of Cherokee Creek. Mama didn't care much for Miss Janie— claimed she was highfalutin and put on airs—so it surprised me when she strolled through the gate and up to Miss Janie's porch. I hesitated for only a second before following.

"Knock on that door and tell Janie I'm dying out here and I'd be much obliged for a drank of water," Mama said.

Miss Janie taught Sunday school and sang in the choir at the Solid Rock Baptist Church. She was old, probably about sixty or so. She wore her hair parted down the center with a thick gray plait on each side. On Sundays, she covered the plaits with one of her many fancy hats, and when the spirit moved her, she would wave one hand in the air and hold tight to the hat with her other hand.

"Tangy Quinn," she said, opening the door and staring out at me. "Shouldn't you be at school?"

"Mama's real sick, Miss Janie," I said. "She's out here on your porch and wants to know if you can spare her a drink of water."

"I'm dying, Janie," Mama groaned. She had positioned herself on Miss Janie's porch swing, slumped over, with her head resting between the chains, looking as if she might die at any second.

"Rosie, what is it?" Miss Janie showed alarm at the sight of Mama. "Just hold on, honey. I'll get you some water."

While Miss Janie went for water, I kept a close watch on my mother. Her eyes were closed and her arms rested against her abdomen with one hand clutching the newspaper. She moaned, shook her head as if disapproving of the sound, then moaned again. She did that several times, changing the pitch and depth of each moan, before it dawned on me that she was rehearsing her suffering, exaggerating her misery.

By the time Miss Janie returned, Mama was trembling all over, tears streaked her cheeks, and her hair was loose and tangled about her head. She was in such a state that it took me and Miss Janie both to get her into an upright position. Miss Janie held the glass and Mama took a few sips of water before slumping over again.

"Rosie, maybe you need something hot," Miss Janie suggested. "I can get you some tea."

"No, Janie. I'm going home to my children," Mama whispered. "This is a terrible way to die, but I need to be wit' my children. There's things I need to tell 'em before it's too late."

Miss Janie's eyes brimmed with tears. "Oh, Rosie, I'm so sorry," she said. "Just remember, Jesus saves. Put your trust in Jesus."

Miss Janie tried to get Mama to come inside to warm herself and offered to call the doctor, but Mama refused. Miss Janie helped her to her feet and walked us out to the gate, saying we should pray, that God answers prayer.

Mama held tightly to my arm and used my shoulder to support her weight as we made our way slowly up Oglesbee Street. My knees were so cold that I knew if one touched the other, I would fall to the ground, taking my dying mother with me. As we turned the corner onto Chestnut Street, Mama loosened her grip on my arm. She straightened her back, smoothed and pinned her hair in place, then smiled and winked at me.

Painfully, I parted my frost-chapped lips and returned a smile. I loved her with all my heart, but if she did not die by Monday morning, I was determined to discover from the pages of my schoolbooks how to break the chains that bound me to my mother.

two

Our house stood alone on a hill off Penyon Road, about half a mile outside the city limits. It was old, crippled, and diseased—an emblem of poverty and neglect. Nature had tried to cure it by embracing the rear frame with herbs, roots, and a jumble of foliage which spilled over from the surrounding woodland. Nature had failed, and in frustration she sought to destroy the house by eroding the very foundation on which it stood.

Erosion had left the house slanted at an odd angle, held up on the east side by thick, round poles lodged into tilted, unstable earth. Occasionally, huge chunks of brown earth shook loose, skirted around the poles, and rolled down the slope into a waiting gully.

All of my life, home had been these three drafty rooms under the same rusted tin roof. The house swayed in the wind but still stood. It absorbed its fill of rainwater and stood. It groaned under the weight of celebrations and sorrows and did not crumble. But for how much longer? I thought we might wake up one morning—or fail to wake up—in the rocky, muddy gully below. Or maybe we would simply blow across the dirt road and get lost in the overgrown field of weeds. I could not predict what would happen, but I feared we were destined for disaster.

Mama stood at the foot of thirteen sagging, rickety steps that led up to a wide, shaky porch. All pretense was over. She was gasping for breath as she placed one foot on the first step and began, gingerly, to climb. She had almost reached the top when her knees buckled. My arms shot out instinctively, ready to break her fall.

"Tara! Tarabelle!" I screamed.

"Be quiet!" Mama snapped, regaining her balance and resuming her climb. "Ain't no need to wake the dead."

The front door, which was as much cardboard as plywood, swung open and my sister, Tarabelle, appeared on the porch. "What is it?" she asked irritably. "Why you calling me like that?"

"Mama's sick," I answered breathlessly, my heart pounding in my chest.

Tarabelle was sixteen and almost as tall as Mama. She had long, jet black hair, a copper-colored complexion, and the cold, black eyes of a corpse. I had never seen the eyes of a dead person—in fact, I had never seen a poker game—but I had heard that poker faces were expressionless, and I knew that dead people showed no emotion. That was Tarabelle. She stepped back, regarded our mother with those cold eyes. Her mouth twitched as if she might smile, but I knew better.

"She ain't sick," Tarabelle said, still staring at Mama. "She 'bout ready to have that baby. That's all."

I had been ignorant in my innocence, but I was wiser than my sister in that I had learned to study Mama as diligently as I studied my books. I watched our mother as she squeezed the collar of her coat. I heard her sharp intake of breath. I saw the frustration and pain leap from the core of her soul and surge the length of her arm, down to the delicate hand that struck my sister's face.

The blow sent Tarabelle reeling back. She bounced off the porch wall and landed less than an inch from the drop that would have taken her down into the gully. She lay there, those cold, black eyes boring into the equally cold, gray eyes of our mother.

"I'm dying," Mama said with calm finality.

Tarabelle gripped the splintered boards at the edge of the porch and nodded her head. "Yes, ma'am."

Edna Pearl and Laura Gail, who were only four and five, stood in the doorway, staring in fascinated fear. I watched as Edna stole back into the shadowy gloom pierced intermittently by daylight filtering in through cracks in the walls. It was our only source of illumination until dusk, when we were allowed to light the kerosene lamps. I knew Edna had gone to alert Martha Jean to our mother's presence.

My next eldest sibling, Martha Jean, was a defective replica of our mother. She could not hear and had not spoken one coherent sentence in her life. There but by the grace of God went I, for only eleven months separated her silent beauty from my articulate homeliness. My imagination ran rampant when I thought of our births. I would fantasize Martha Jean stubbornly refusing to leave our mother's womb until I was conceived. We would blend together, and my thick nose would become thin; my coarse, tangled hair would become silky and straight, and I would have deep dimples in my cheeks. And, in turn, Martha Jean would be able to hear and speak. We would come rushing from the womb fused together, yelling at the top of our lungs, and no one would know that there were two of us. We would be smart, beautiful, and white, and Mama would love us with all of her heart.

Mama swept through the doorway of her castle and plopped down on her throne—the only bed in the house. Laura and Edna immediately knelt, removed her shoes, and began to rub her feet. Martha Jean brought in the customary cup of steaming water, and I produced the stolen papers of coffee and sugar from my pocket. Tarabelle, having pulled herself together, came to stand beside me.

"Mama, you want me to go get Miss Pearl?" she asked.

"No, I don't want you to go get Pearl," Mama snapped. "I want you to get outta my sight, Tara. How the hell you gon' go get Pearl when she at work way up there on Meadow Hill? I swear, I got the dumbest children in the world. Sometimes I wonder if all y'all belong to me."

I wondered, too. Sometimes I even prayed there had been a mistake, and that somebody would come along, take my hand, and say, "Rozelle Quinn, I believe this child belongs to me." Mama would push me into the arms of the stranger and say, "You're right. I knew all along that she was your child, but I loved her so I just couldn't bear to let her go. You take her, though, because she rightfully belongs to you." I would go off to my new home where there would be a bed from the Griggs furniture store, a dress for every day of the week, a change of underpants, and two pairs of shoes with good hard-bottom soles. I would have an electric light to read by, and rows and rows of all sorts of great books.

Most of the books I read belonged to the colored library, and the selection there wasn't great, but I would read anything, even when I had to ask Mrs. Jordan, the librarian, to pronounce words for me. Winter months are bad for reading, but during the summer, I sat out on the porch, or in the woods behind the house, and read until God dimmed His lights and called it a day.

"Tangy Mae, don't you hear me talking to you?" Mama barked, and I jumped because I had not heard her. "I told you to write a letter to Mushy." That was my oldest sister. "She needs to know her mother is dying. And you go straight to the post office and mail it off. Take the dummy wit' you and don't y'all be gone long."

The command was barely out of her mouth when she took a sip of coffee, gave a short cry, and doubled over in pain, as if she had been poisoned. Five of her nine children stood at her bedside watching and waiting.

She breathed in and out through pursed lips, then her eyelids fluttered and opened, and she turned glassy eyes on the five of us.

"You sick, Mama?" Laura asked.

Mama placed her coffee cup on the floor and gathered Laura and Edna in her arms. "It's all right, baby," she said. "Mama's just dying, that's all."

"Humph." Tarabelle snorted so quietly that only I could hear it.

"Tell the dummy to fetch the tub and warm me some bathwater," Mama said. "I don't intend to die smelling like a white woman's kitchen." She stretched out on the bed, settling Laura and Edna beside her, while I stood there miming a bath to my deaf sister.

It was uncanny the way Martha Jean understood the crude signs we dangled before her eyes. My hands had barely cleared my armpits before she was off to the yard with the water bucket. Tarabelle followed after her and returned shortly, carrying the round, tin bathtub by a single handle. She placed the tub on the floor at the foot of the bed.

I retreated to the front room. There, I settled and wrote a most convincing letter of suffering, pain, and impending death. I begged Mushy to return to Penyon Road. Mushy, whose real name was Elizabeth Anne, had been gone for four years. One summer evening, just after her eighteenth birthday, she had left for Ohio. She had not returned, not even for a visit.

The house still mourned her absence. It had taken on a coldness that no amount of coal or kindling in the stoves or fireplace could penetrate. Life seemed to have drifted out through the chimney in gray whiffs of smoke. And yet, for some reason, we continued to exist.

three

Martha Jean wore a brown and purple plaid dress that was at least three sizes too large. It had once belonged to Miss Arlisa. Mama had given it to Martha Jean, saying how it didn't matter about the size since Martha Jean wasn't going anywhere anyway.

It was true. Martha Jean did not go to church, school, or anywhere much else, except up to Miss Pearl's house on Sundays. There were times when I would take her with me to the colored library in Plymouth, or to the Colonial store in town, but mostly she just stayed at home and watched over Laura and Edna.

She walked ahead of me, exploring the world as though for the first time. She wore white knee-high socks, and I watched as her heels bobbed up and down in a pair of hand-me-down Buster Brown loafers that were also too large. She was not wearing a coat because she did not own one, but she wore, one on top of the other, two wrinkled, navy-blue sweaters, each of which had seen better years.

We walked past the familiar: small shotgun houses with tin tubs hanging from hooks on side walls, outhouses beyond rows of

winter-bare trees and empty clotheslines, chicken coops, wood-
piles, coal bins, the standard black cast-iron washtubs, and the
ever-present water pipes snaking up through the ground like
bronzed pythons.

We crossed Buford Street—the area of Stump Town modern-
ized by electricity, indoor plumbing, and telephones. It was the
street where Frank and Pearl Garrison lived. Mr. Frank was one of
five Negro men who had been lucky enough to get a job at the
Pakersfield carpet mill. In our eyes, the Garrisons were wealthy.
Miss Pearl just happened to be Mama's best friend.

Martha Jean slowed, then stopped. She raised her right arm
above her head with the palm of her hand turned down—her sign
for Mama. She then crossed both arms over her chest and leaned
forward, her brows drawn into a frown.

I nodded. She had asked if Mama was sick. I wanted to tell her
what Tarabelle had said, but I didn't dare. It was possible Tarabelle
was wrong, and I did not want to confuse Martha Jean.

Mushy could make Martha Jean understand anything. She had
spent long hours, many days, teaching Martha Jean to read and
write simple words, and coming up with different signs which she
made the rest of us learn. Mama had refused to participate, called
it a waste of time, but within a matter of months Martha Jean could
write and sign all of our names.

Martha Jean's most profound lesson had been learned through a
curriculum of intimidation and pain. In fact, we had all been students in that classroom with our mother as our teacher. Although
I had been only six at the time, and Martha Jean barely seven, it
was a day that we were not likely to forget.

Late evening. Mama saunters in from one of her many excursions car-
rying a metal box. It is slightly larger than a cigar box and has a thin
sheet of tin covering the bottom. She makes my brother, Harvey, pull up
one of the floorboards in her room. She nails the box to the underside of
the board, then she demonstrates how the tin slides in and out. We are
fascinated. It is like a game to us, although we do not understand the sig-
nificance of the box.

Mama tears a strip of newspaper and crumples it into a ball. Her gray
eyes sparkle with delight. "As long as y'all live, don't ever touch this box,"
she says.

Mushy speaks up. "Why you showing it to us, Mama?"

Mama shoots her a cold stare, but Mushy repeats the question. "Why you showing it to us if you don't want us to touch it?"

We are sitting on the floor in a circle. It is warm and cozy, all of us together like this, with a fire on the grate heating the room and making shadows dance on the walls, swaying to the crackle of burning kindling.

Mama drops the crumpled paper into the box, then she touches Martha Jean's arm, and points. Martha Jean reaches for the wad of paper, but before she can grasp it Mama slaps her hand. Martha Jean draws her hand back and studies our mother's eyes. Mama is smiling.

Again Mama nudges Martha Jean and points. Martha Jean is hesitant, but she reaches for the paper because she has been bred to obedience and has not been able to hear our mother's warning.

Mushy's head rocks from side to side. No! No! No! Her hands are pressed against her chest, one over the other. Tears spill from her eyes and roll down her cheeks.

Martha Jean misses the sign. She holds that ball of print-covered paper and offers it to our mother as if it is a sweet-smelling bouquet of roses.

I am witnessing it all, every movement in this room, from the shadows on the walls to the shift of my mother's dress as her hand sweeps down and shoots up again, tightly clutching the handle of an ice pick.

She seizes Martha Jean's wrist with one hand, but her other hand is wrapped into a fist of thunder that flashes a spike of lightning through the flickering shadows. The ice pick pierces the flesh of my sister's hand and stands there, the handle sways back and forth as if it might fall, but we can all see that it is not going to fall. It is embedded in Martha Jean's hand.

Mama grips the handle, and deliberately rips flesh as she wrenches the ice pick from the tiny, trembling hand that rises with the motion. A dark crimson oozes from the wound and begins to spread across the skin and down onto the paper bouquet that has fallen to the floor.

Martha Jean opens her mouth. "Baahaa! Baahaa!" Over and over she wails, twitching as she scoots away from our circle, across the floorboards, back against the wall. Her eyes are wide with terror and pain.

"Baahaa! Baahaa!"

I cover my ears with my hands but cannot silence those terrible inhuman wails issuing from some place deep within my sister's soul, shrill and dull, long and halting.

For a moment we do not move, do not dare to move. Mushy, Harvey,

Sam, Tarabelle, Wallace, and I sit on the floor in a circle, afraid to move. Wallace is sucking his thumb, and I forgive him his pleasure because he is only four.

Mama is wearing a brown dress with a wide white collar and buttons all the way down the front. Her hair is hanging down her back, and her lips are painted to perfection with ruby red lipstick. And I am so afraid.

Mushy is the first to move. She wraps her arms around Martha Jean and pulls her to her feet. We all begin to move, fetching water, tearing bandages, pouring our love onto a wound that will never heal. We work as a silent, defeated army, beaten down by our mother, tending our wounded. We do not retaliate, for our victory is inconceivable.

In less than five minutes, our mother had taught us to never touch her metal box, and the true meaning of fear. I wondered that day if I was the only one in the room who knew that there was something terribly wrong with our mother.

Martha Jean and I approached Market Street, the widest and busiest street in all of Triacy County, where stores and office buildings stood side by side both east and west of the railroad tracks. We passed the Colonial store and the Greyhound bus depot, then entered the business district. The Griggs furniture store took up most of the block on the right side of the street, adjacent to that were the offices of the town's doctor and dentist plus a bicycle shop. Past that, closer to the tracks, were the fashion dress shop, the newspaper office, and the drugstore. On the side of the street where we walked were the Munford's Hardware, the five-and-dime, the picture show, and a lawyer's office. A center divider separated Rockside from the train depot.

Poor planning had placed the white library, Pakersfield's city hall, and the courthouse on Rockside Street, where they were disturbed by the noise of the trains. The courthouse ended at Barley Street, which ran parallel to Market. The Negroes in our town seldom went to Barley, and we called Rockside "white man's row" because we had very little use for the street. We were denied entrance to the library, we could not drink from the fountain or sit in the gazebo at the courthouse, and very few of us could afford to deposit funds at the bank, nor were we welcome to do so.

Automobiles were parked at meters along both sides of Market

Street and on the courthouse side of Rockside. People scurried in and out of buildings; it was always like this on Fridays and Saturdays. On Wednesdays the stores did not open, and if anyone passed through town, the only people they were likely to see were the Negro men sitting or standing about on the platform of the train depot. Every day except Sunday, these men would come into town and wait around for some form of labor to be offered.

It was late afternoon, and only six would-be workers were left loitering about the depot. My brother, Sam, was one of them. He wore overalls and a plaid shirt. His hair was cut in the high-right, and low-left style that most of the young men wore. He was neither the tallest nor the shortest on the platform. What set him apart from the others was his light complexion and the sandy-brown color of his hair. He looked like, and was often mistaken for, a white man, although everybody in Pakersfield knew he was Negro. Probably the only person who did not know he was colored was our mother. She took pleasure in categorizing her children by race. Mushy, Harvey, Sam, and Martha Jean were her white children. Tarabelle, Wallace, and Laura were Indians—Cherokee, no less. Edna and I were Negroes.

"Hey, Sam," I said, approaching the platform where my brother sat with Maxwell James and Junior Fess, rolling cigarettes from a Prince Albert tin. Behind them and across the platform stood three older men, talking and staring out at four free-standing buildings: the Market Street Café, Pioneer Taxicab Company, Western Auto, and our red-brick jailhouse.

Sam glanced up. His gaze traveled from me to Martha Jean. "Why you bring her out looking like that?" he asked.

"We're going to the post office," I said. "Mama's sick. She wants me to mail a letter to Mushy."

"How sick?" Sam wanted to know.

"Real sick. She thinks she's dying."

"Is she?"

"I don't know," I answered truthfully. "She might be. Where's Harvey?"

"Who knows?" Sam shrugged his shoulders. "Truck rolls in, truck rolls out. Big boss sit in the cab, point out the men he want. Never say a word—just point. Never say what the job is, never say what it pay, and nobody never ask."

"Depends on how well a man knows you," Maxwell said.

"Yeah?" Sam questioned in obvious disagreement. "There ain't a man in Pakersfield, black or white, don't know every other man. Getting hired out depends on how low you cast yo' eyes, bow yo' head, and bend yo' back. You know that as well as I do, Max."

"Nah, man," Maxwell disputed. "You been listening too much to Hambone. Man, that nigger gon' get you in all kinds of trouble the way he carry on. That's the reason the sheriff all time watching yo' ass as it is. He waiting on y'all to start something." Maxwell tilted his head toward the First National Bank and rolled his eyes, indicating that Sam should take notice.

I glanced over and saw the sheriff, Angus Betts, sitting in his cruiser, watching us. Even seated, the sheriff was an intimidating figure. He was over six feet tall, with a tightness about him that seemed to start at his waist and move up across his chest, into his neck and jaws, and he had a nose that was exceptionally thick for a white man's. I guessed him to be in his late thirties or early forties because of the way his hazel eyes stared out at the world with what appeared to be boredom, as though he had seen it all before and would not be surprised by anything or anybody.

Sam stared across the divider and mumbled something under his breath. He finished rolling a cigarette, licked the edge of the paper, then said, "Hambone ain't so bad once you get to know him."

"I do know him," Maxwell countered. "Maybe you think he ain't so bad, but he be trying to handle them white folks and they gon' kill 'im or run 'im outta town. You mark my word. He keep running his mouth, and they gon' do something to 'im."

"I agree with Max," Junior said. "Hambone's back from Chicago like he's ready to kill somebody. They're not going to let him get away with that. We do need change, but he's going about it all wrong. We need to organize like they're doing in other cities, bring in the NAACP. We need to be in agreement on what we're going to do and how we were going to do it. You can't beat a man down with your fists and not expect retaliation, but that's just what Hambone thinks he can do. I, for one, think we should solicit help from the outside. We need laws to enforce the law, if you know what I mean. Take Chad Lowe, for instance. He's not a sheriff, deputy, or policeman, but he carries a gun and patrols the Negro sections, and we allow it. That's the first thing we need to put a stop to."

They were quiet after that, maybe thinking about what Junior had said. It was rumored that Chad Lowe, the name run together as one word by most, was the sheriff's cousin, but I didn't think that gave him the right to arrest people. He did it all the same, and people seemed to accept him as law in Pakersfield, although we knew him to be the proprietor of the Market Street Cafe and not a lawman.

"Tangy Mae, the post office gon' be closing in a bit," Sam said.

"Yeah," I said, agreeing with Junior rather than Sam. I liked listening to Junior. He had completed two years of college, and our principal, Mr. Hewitt, sometimes called him in to teach when one of the regular teachers was absent. Sometimes Junior talked about earning enough money to go back to college, but mostly he talked about the plight of the Negro. Junior was a lanky young man with a dark complexion like mine, and one day he had told our class that life was hard for Negroes, but harder for those his color. He held us riveted with his tales of the Ku Klux Klan, Jim Crow laws, and injustices taking place right in our own town. We never opened books when Junior was our substitute teacher, except old copies of *Jet* magazine that he distributed to the class and collected at the end of the day. Though Junior never told us so, we knew Mr. Hewitt was to remain ignorant of the lessons he taught us.

If Junior had continued to speak, I might have stayed and listened until the post office closed. He didn't, though. He stepped down from the platform with his appendage—an old, tattered brown satchel that he carried everywhere—and joined me and Martha Jean on the sidewalk.

"I'll catch up with you later, Sam," he said.

I took Martha Jean by the hand and began to walk alongside Junior. As we cleared the tracks, I glanced at the satchel he had tucked beneath one arm. "Do you carry your lunch in that bag?" I asked.

He smiled at me, a closed-mouth smile that lifted his cheeks and slightly widened his nose. "I guess you could call it lunch," he answered. "This bag is filled with nourishment for the mind and soul. What I have here, Tangy, are promises and hopes, as well as scattered disillusionments. It's like filling your plate with ham, green beans, and potato salad, only to have someone come along and spoon lumpy, dried-out oatmeal on the side. Wouldn't that spoil your appetite?"

"I guess," I answered, "but you're talking in riddles. Tell me what you mean."

"Some other time," he said. "Right now I'm going home to find something to do to make the hours pass, so I can go back to the train depot tomorrow with renewed determination to find work."

"You can make time pass by walking to the post office with me and Martha Jean," I suggested.

"That's one way to do it," he said lightly, "but I'm not up for battling with Mr. Nesbitt today. I'll walk with you as far as Pately's."

As we walked, I kept glancing over at Junior. There was an oily substance smeared around the edges of his neatly trimmed hair. It was always there, giving a sheen to his hairline and a glow to his forehead. Had he been one of my brothers, I would have reached up and rubbed the shine away with my thumb. Since he was my brothers' friend and sometimes my teacher, I did not.

Martha Jean let go of my hand, stepped in front of me, and touched Junior's bag. It seemed for a moment that she was going to snatch it from him. I pulled her back, shook a warning finger at her, then apologized to Junior.

"It's all right," he said. "She's probably curious. Most people are."

He stopped and leaned against the wall where Peggy Ann's dress shop connected with Billy's shoeshine parlor. He unbuckled the straps on the satchel, then held it open so that Martha Jean and I could look inside. We saw a newspaper, magazines, loose-leaf papers, and two first-grade reading books. Everybody knew that Junior traveled the rural areas teaching people to read and write, so I wasn't surprised by the books, and nothing else in the bag intrigued me. Martha Jean, however, reached into a side compartment and brought out a pencil. I took it from her and returned it to Junior.

"It's all right. Let her have it," he said, passing the pencil back to my sister. "And you take one of these magazines. Read it, and explain it to her. There's a lot of information here."

I took the first magazine my hand touched. It was old—a March 1954 *Jet*. I glanced at the cover, then tucked it away inside the pocket of my coat. I was more interested in listening to Junior talk than I was in reading a magazine.

"Tell me about the lumpy oatmeal," I said.

He fastened his satchel and glanced back toward the depot. "No, I don't think so," he said. "I'm pretty much worn out from talking all day to your brother and Max. Sam could be a leader, a good one, if he wasn't afraid."

"Sam's not afraid of anything," I said.

"He's afraid of a lot of things, responsibility and commitment being two of them. Max could have worked today, but he wouldn't go out because no one hired Sam. Max will do anything your brother tells him to do, or die trying. Most of the young men in this town will. I thought I had Sam on my side, thought I had him seeing things my way, but then Hambone came back. Hambone is bitter, full of hatred. The way things are going now, I don't know if we'll ever get anything done."

"You don't consider yourself a leader?" I asked.

"No. I've never been. I'm older and wiser than Sam, but I lack his magnetism. I'm a talker, but that doesn't necessarily make a leader. And I'm a gentleman, like my daddy."

We were nearing the Pately shoe store, and I was getting nothing from Junior that made any sense. As we reached the front of the store, I tried one last time to get him to explain what he was talking about.

"What is it you want Sam to lead?" I asked.

"The Movement," he answered. "You must know about the Movement, Tangy. We're going to change some things in this town. We're going to change some things in this country. You'll see."

I stood there perplexed, staring at his back as he crossed Market Street and made his way toward the flats. What a ridiculous statement, I thought. *They* can't change anything. My entire life had been spent in Pakersfield, and I knew. I didn't know about the rest of the country, but I knew that nothing was going to change in Triacy County.

four

"You people always wait to the last minute," Charlie Nesbitt drawled irritably as he glared across the counter at me. "What you want, gal?"

I placed my envelope on the counter. "I'd like to mail this letter to Cleveland, Ohio, and can you see if there's any mail for the Quinns on Penyon Road?"

He regarded the envelope as though it was a dead mouse in a trap, unable to decide which end to touch, or whether to touch it at all. Finally he turned from the letter and began a half-hearted search through the mail slots behind him.

"Nothing here," he informed me, returning to the counter, "and I hope you know you have to pay to mail that letter."

I was already holding the pennies in my hand, having been to the post office a hundred times and knowing full well that I could not send a letter for free. He had waited on me the same hundred times and was well aware that I knew the price of a stamp. I offered the coins, but he refused to take them from my hand, playing the game he so often played with Negro customers, letting us know that he'd rather we did not enter the United States Government's post office.

"Drop 'em on the counter," he said roughly, rapping the countertop with his knuckles.

For a second or two, I stood there staring down, knowing it would be considered impertinent of me to make eye contact.

"Niggers," he mumbled, slowly shaking his bald, melon-shaped head in a gesture of disgust.

As I clenched my fist, then opened it to surrender the coins, I found that I no longer commanded Mr. Nesbitt's attention. He was busy waiting on a plump, white woman in a blue wool coat.

"Charlie, I'm so glad I caught you," she said in a rush. "I simply must get these invitations out today. You know how it is, don't you?"

"Yes, I do, Mrs. Simmons," Charlie answered. "How's Mr. Simmons? I haven't seen him around in a month of Sundays."

"Oh, Gus is about the same," she said, placing a bundle of envelopes on the counter and peeling white gloves from her hands. "Amelia is the one you ought to be asking about. She insisted on having a February wedding, and we can't seem to talk her out of it. I've pleaded with her to wait until June. There's nothing like a June bride, wouldn't you say?"

"Yes, ma'am," Charlie agreed.

I groaned inwardly and turned from the counter to check on Martha Jean. The lobby was no larger than our kitchen at home, and I had left Martha Jean standing beside the entrance, but she was no longer there. I glanced toward each corner of the small space and did not see her. Finally I caught a glimpse of her sweater through the window in the top of the door. She was standing out on the walkway, and some man was wasting his time talking to her.

I had started for the door when it occurred to me that Charlie Nesbitt might close the post office before I mailed my mother's letter. Returning to the counter, I kept my gaze on Martha Jean's back, silently willing her to stay put.

Charlie was in a better mood after his chat with the woman in the blue coat. He waved to her as she left, then turned back to me. It took all of thirty seconds for him to produce a stamp, and for me to place it on the envelope.

Outside, the sky had grown darker and the temperature colder. I buttoned my corduroy coat up to my neck, then stepped up beside Martha Jean. The man who stood facing her glanced over at me as I approached, and I glared at him. He was a dark, wiry-looking young man with processed waves in his hair. I had apparently caught him by surprise, in the middle of speaking. He was missing a tooth at the top, on the right side. His nose was short and wide above a thin mustache, and he barely had eyes to mention, just narrow little slits below angular eyebrows. He stood about five-ten, give or take, tall enough to look down on me and Martha Jean.

"Mister, why are you bothering my sister?" I asked.

"Your sister?" he questioned, glancing back at Martha Jean.

"My sister," I repeated defiantly.

He flashed a lopsided smile. "What makes you think I'm bothering her? She don't look bothered to me."

It was a statement of fact. Martha Jean was studying him the way she studied the images on Miss Pearl's television screen, with interest and something akin to appreciation. She did not seem bothered; in fact, she seemed unaware that the temperature had dropped, although I could plainly see she was shivering.

"She can't hear a word you say, so you're just wasting your time," I said.

"It's *my* time," he countered.

Anger rippled through me. My armpits itched and burned the way they do when I'm nervous or ashamed. "Who are you?" I demanded.

"I'm Velman Cooper. I work here at the post office, and I'll be getting off in a bit. Y'all wait for me! I'll be right back."

"You must be crazy!" I said, astounded by his arrogance. "We are not about to stand out here in the cold waiting for you. We don't know you, and don't want to, and anyway, we've got to get on home."

"Where's home?" he asked, stepping between me and Martha Jean, and reaching for the door.

"None of your business."

Much to my surprise and dismay, he stopped, turned, and once again faced Martha Jean. He pointed to his watch, then put both hands up. "Wait!" he said, and entered the post office.

I stared after him, then grabbed my sister's hand and started for the street. Martha Jean freed herself from my grip. Her gaze was glued to the post office door. I blocked her view with my body. I raised my right hand with the palm turned down. I leaned forward, crossed my chest with both arms, and twisted my face into a frown. I made walking and running gestures. I mimicked the worst beating imaginable, but none of that swayed my sister.

Suddenly, I was afraid. There was always talk in Pakersfield about voodoo, and I wondered if the stranger had worked some kind of spell on Martha Jean while I had been inside the post office. I knew nothing of spells, but it would have to be a strong one to make Martha Jean risk the wrath of our mother.

Finally, in desperation, I shoved Martha Jean as hard as I could. Her shoulders rocked back, but her feet remained firmly planted. "Let's go!" I yelled, my arms flailing in the air, trying to make her understand that I was not going to take a beating for her or anyone else.

Martha Jean's fingers snipped and circled the same air as she waved a number-two pencil in my face, too close to my eyes for comfort. We were like two stubborn, competitive conductors presiding over invisible orchestras.

"Hey, what is all this?" The voodoo man came strolling back, shoving his arms into the sleeves of a black jacket, pulling a chain of keys from his pants pocket, and making it all look graceful.

"It's all your fault," I blurted out. "What did you do to my sister?"

"Nothing. I just asked y'all to wait, and I'm glad to see you did."

"Well, we're certainly not waiting for you," I said, trying to sound mature and in control, but even I could hear the whine in my voice.

"Just thought you might want a ride," he said. "It's getting kinda cold out here, and I noticed your sister there ain't got on no coat."

"What's that to you?" I challenged.

"What's that to me?" the man asked. "Ain't nothing much. And I can see it ain't nothing to you. You got on that nice warm coat, but your sister there, she chilling and shaking like a leaf on a tree. Don't guess you mind she be cold long as you nice and warm, huh?"

I was silent for a moment, thinking how it had not bothered him that Martha Jean might be cold while she was standing out here waiting for him. I started to say as much, but changed my mind. "Where are you from, mister?" I asked.

"Dalton."

"Georgia?"

He nodded, swinging his keys around on one finger and watching me with a look of triumph on his face.

"How old are you?" I asked.

"You sho' ask a lot of questions for somebody don't wanna know me," he said. "I'm twenty-two. How old are you? And is there anything else you need to know before your sister freezes to death?"

"I'm thirteen, and it's not cold enough to freeze," I retorted, although it was.

"Not for you. You got on a warm coat." He took Martha Jean by the hand and led her toward an old, green Buick that was parked just a little way from the building.

I followed, wondering how I had allowed him to make me feel guilty for something that was not my fault. He was right, though. Martha Jean had to be freezing, but I wouldn't give him the satisfaction of admitting it.

"Hey, you ever heard of the Quinns?" I asked. "Everybody around here knows the Quinns."

Maybe I imagined it, but it seemed to me that he loosened his grip on Martha Jean's hand and slowed his pace just a bit.

"I ain't from around here," was all he said.

"Martha Jean is only fourteen. You can't court her if that's what you think," I continued.

"Martha Jean," he echoed. "So that's her name?"

"Yeah, that's her name," I answered, and quickly stepped forward to block his path. "And my name is Tangy. We're Rozelle Quinn's children, so you'd better leave us alone."

"Martha Jean sho' is a pretty one," he said admiringly.

"And I guess I'm the ugly one!" I snapped.

"Oh, no, little sister," he answered. "There ain't nothing ugly 'bout you, not that I can see anyway. You 'bout the prettiest little dark-skin girl I ever seen. Now, I got a problem with that mouth of yours, but other than that, I don't reckon there's an ugly spot on you." He stepped around me and opened the door of the Buick.

Martha Jean made a move toward him, but I stopped her by throwing an arm up in front of her. The man slid onto the front seat of the car, shook his head slowly, then closed the door. I breathed a sigh of relief that was barely out when he rolled the window down and stared at me.

"Little sister," he said. "I didn't mean y'all no harm. I just thought Martha Jean might be cold, that's all."

I nodded, wanting to believe him.

"I'm Skeeter Richards' nephew," he said. "You know Skeeter?"

"Everybody knows Skeeter," I answered. Skeeter ran the concession stand in the colored section of the picture show.

Martha Jean shivered again, rubbed her hands together, then pointed to Velman Cooper and ran a finger across her chest.

"What's that she's doing?" he asked.

"She wants to know your name," I said, spreading my middle and index fingers apart to form a V, and pointing the V toward the ground, then bringing it up to my head like horns on a devil.

Velman seemed puzzled, but Martha Jean smiled and mimicked the sign I had made.

"What is that?" Velman asked.

"A V straight up from Hell," I answered.

He laughed, stepped out of the car, and made the sign himself. "A V straight up from Hell," he said. "I like that. Come on. How about I give y'all a ride home?"

"Okay," I agreed reluctantly, admitting to myself that Martha Jean should not have been out without a coat, "but you can't take us all the way." I knew Mama would skin us alive if she knew we had taken a ride from a stranger.

"All right. Halfway," he said.

Martha Jean scooted across the seat and sat next to him. I crawled in next to her and shut the door. I told Velman how to get to Penyon Road and where to let us out, and for the rest of the ride I stared at my sister's head, trying to find a way inside. I wanted to know why she had been willing to trust this stranger, why she had not waited for me inside the warm post office, but had waited for him out in the cold. I needed to know what went on in her silence.

five

Saturday morning dawned bleak and dreary. I longed to pull the blanket over my head and curl back into a cozy ball of sleep, but I could not. There were so many things to do. The coal stove stood as a gloomy reminder of the chores that lay ahead. I rolled over on my pallet and touched the bottom of the stove, feeling only a hint of last night's warmth. My right side, from the waist down, was soaked with urine, and my gown clung to my legs as I crawled up from the floor. My teeth chattered in the morning chill, and I cursed Laura for her weak bladder, or kidney, or whatever caused her to routinely ammoniate my body.

As my eyes adjusted to the semi-darkness, I could make out the two brown armchairs guarding the small, round table where the kerosene lamp stood. They were the only pieces of furniture in the room, except for the cedar chest that stood beneath the front window and the wooden crates where we stored our clothes. The table and chairs displayed a pleasing silhouette in moonlight, but in the light of day they were hideous monstrosities—gutted and stripped—with coiled springs sprouting from the backs and seats. The makeshift chair covers were useless in disguising the hateful springs that ripped our clothes and tore at our skin.

The dress I had worn the day before was draped over one of the chairs. I moved cautiously across the room, avoiding the curled forms of my sisters, and retrieved my dress. I held my breath and quickly pulled the wet gown off over my head.

When I was dressed, I tipped out to the kitchen where my brothers slept. Harvey and Sam were gone. Their blankets had been rolled into neat bundles and were stored in a far corner of the kitchen. Wallace was sitting up, his back against the wall, a blanket pulled up to his chin.

"Wallace," I said, surprised at finding him awake and idle.

"Morning," he said in a voice hours removed from sleep.

It was not so chilly in the kitchen. The coal stove, which was identical to the one in the front room, had been lit and was making a feeble attempt at warming the room. The pipes of both stoves elbowed at about the same angle and met at a junction between the walls. Smoke from the stoves came out on the gully side of the house. The entire house should have been warm with the two stoves back to back, and the fireplace in Mama's room, but somehow a draft of cold air always found its way inside.

"How long have you been up?" I asked, sensing that something was troubling my younger brother. Wallace, at the age of eleven, was not one to linger, not in bed or anywhere else. His store of energy did not allow for much in the way of idleness.

He shrugged his shoulders. "What time is it?" he asked. "I been woke since Harvey and Sam left. Told Mr. Frank I'd come around today, help him fix his fence. He's gonna give me a dollar."

"Don't tell Mama about the dollar," I warned. "Don't tell anybody."

"I ain't stupid," he said indignantly.

"You told me."

"Yeah, but you don't never tell nothing."

I lit the kerosene lamp, placed it on the kitchen table, and knelt down on the edge of Wallace's pallet. "Why are you sitting here like this?" I asked.

"Like what?"

"You know. Like something is wrong."

He was silent for a moment, his gaze avoiding mine. He glanced around the kitchen, toward the back door, up at the ceiling, and finally at me.

Wallace was frail, and small for his age. His eyes were large and round with thick, long lashes. He had the same silky, black hair as Tarabelle, and his thin face seemed to shrink beneath the mane of hair and those wide eyes that took up so much space.

"Tan, I think I been sitting here sinning," he whispered. "Tarabelle says Mama is gonna have another baby. She said it hurts awful bad and sometimes people die."

"That has nothing to do with you, Wallace. It wasn't you who sinned."

"I ain't told you yet what I been doing," he said.

"What? What were you doing?"

"I was thinking how Mama might die, but that ain't the worst of it. I was thinking how that might not be so bad. I heard Mama tell Miss Pearl that every time a man look at her she gets knocked up. If that's true, there could be a hundred of us in a few years."

"Wallace, nobody gets knocked up just because somebody looks at them," I said.

"I don't know, Tan," he said, shaking his head.

"Just think about it," I said. "Mr. Frank has been looking at Miss Pearl for years, and she doesn't have a baby. It doesn't happen just because you look at somebody. And anyway, Mama is always saying something that's not true."

Blasphemy!

Simultaneously, we gasped and stared at each other, waiting for the roof to cave in, or the ground to rumble and open and suck us in. I had overstepped my boundaries, and poor Wallace was guilty by association.

Wallace slowly shifted his gaze from my face to the doorway from which I had entered. My pulse quickened, and I hunched my shoulders, waiting for a blow to the head. Mama was standing there, had heard every word I had said. I just knew it by the terror in Wallace's face. Mama was taking her time, preparing for the slaughter, making me squirm and suffer.

When I could take it no longer, when I knew that the pounding of my heart had awakened everybody in the house, I turned to face her.

No one was there.

I finally exhaled. "I shouldn't have said that," I whispered, "but it's true. Remember when she used to tell us we were rich, and how we'd never be hungry as long as we lived in Georgia? 'Too many trees bearing nuts and fruits. Corn and bean stalks running out to the road for the taking. Bushes of berries and vines of grapes. No way to be hungry.'" I said, quoting my mother.

Wallace smiled. "Yeah, I remember," he said. "I believed that all the way to the second grade."

"Me, too. I'd be sitting in school with my stomach making all sorts of noise, and everybody looking. I'd keep telling myself how it couldn't be hunger because people in Georgia don't get hungry. At lunchtime, I'd go off by myself so I wouldn't have to smell the food."

"Tan, do you ever wish you'd been born in another family? I mean . . . like Shaky Brown's, or somebody like that. You know, where you don't have to worry 'bout things so much."

"Wallace, it's time for you to get up," I said. If I could help it, he would never know how often I wished for that very thing.

He rose from the floor, pulled on a sweater and a pair of blue jeans over dingy underclothes, then made his way to the front hall to get the night bucket. It was his responsibility to empty it each morning and wash it out, then bring it back in at night. While he was getting the bucket, I rolled his blankets and placed them next to the other bundles.

Martha Jean was with Wallace when he came back to the kitchen, both of their noses twisted from the stench. Martha Jean handed him the water bucket and watched as he stepped outside, then she took down two pots from the open shelf, one to heat water for Mama's coffee, and the other to cook grits.

I returned to the front room to find Laura and Edna sorting clothes that Tarabelle and I would have to wash. Tarabelle was holding a handful of newspaper and a few sticks of kindling.

"I'll start the fire in Mama's room," she said.

"Try not to wake her."

Tarabelle took a deep, weary breath. "She already woke. Don't you hear her in there howling like some ol' kicked dog? I hope we ain't gotta listen to that all day."

I listened and heard the moaning come to an abrupt halt. It was followed by a loud, strong voice that I knew so well.

"Where's my damn coffee?"

"What you reckon we'll burn in Hell?" Tarabelle asked as she hung a sheet on the clothesline and clamped it in place with wooden pins. We worked in silence as a Krandike dairy truck rounded the bend below us and moved westward toward the farmland.

I turned Tarabelle's question over in my mind, then asked, "What do you reckon?"

"I reckon we will." She leaned over the washtub, tossed a couple of shirts into the sudsy water, and began rubbing one up and down against the rub board. "Just think, Tan, all we do is fool around fire. First thing in the morning . . . fire. Last thing at night . . . fire. I think the devil getting us ready. We gon' be the ones keep the fires burning in Hell."

It was a cold morning and the clothes froze almost as fast as we hung them up. They stood on the line, stiff and glazed in a thin layer of ice. We hung as many as the line would hold, then we went back inside to warm our hands and wait.

Around noon, curiosity and goodwill brought Reverend Nelson and half of the women's choir down from the Solid Rock Baptist Church. They were about a dozen or so, bearing gifts of prepared meals, bumping into each other as they scrambled for a position near Mama's bed, slipping white handkerchiefs from patent leather handbags with gloved hands, dabbing at dry eyes, but mostly protecting their nostrils as they discreetly surveyed our cramped, odorous accommodations.

"Count you blessings, sisters!" Reverend Nelson bellowed. It was the first time he had been a guest in our home, and apparently he had just noticed that our ceiling offered an excellent view of Heaven.

The women burst into song, their voices combining and reverberating in the small confines of the house. I could not see my mother from where I stood, but every now and then I would hear her moan or scream. Reverend Nelson had brought God into our house, and Mama was deathly afraid of God. She was so afraid, in fact, that she would not go near a church. She sent us, instead, to collect her blessings and bring them home. I think she had convinced herself that God could not see her evil deeds if she did not go near His house.

I felt overwhelmed by miracles. Our little house was still standing under the weight of Reverend Nelson and the women's choir. They had braved our rickety, old steps to pray over Mama, and just when it seemed they would be the death of her, God opened the door for Miss Pearl.

She poked her head in first, her short, kinky hair sparkling with Royal Crown hair pomade. Her large, brown eyes took in the scene, then she pushed the door wide and brought too much of everything into the house—too much laughter for a death room, too much swearing for the reverend and the women's choir, and too much weight for a woman of forty. Miss Pearl was like a huge, chocolate Tootsie Roll Pop on a broken stick. Her feet, the smallest part of her entire body, padded across the floor as her pudgy arms swung back and forth, clearing a path from the front room to Mama's room.

"What's going on here?" she demanded.

"Pearl," Mama cried out. "I'm dying, Pearl."

"The hell you say." Miss Pearl roared with laughter. "Rosie, you ain't bit mo' dying than the man in the moon. You done had these people come out here thinking you dying. That's a damn shame."

"Well, I feel like I'm dying," came Mama's sulking voice.

Miss Pearl turned to Reverend Nelson, a short, stocky-built, handsome man in a dark blue suit. "Y'all can leave now, Reverend," she said. "I'll call y'all back if I have to kill 'er for being a jackass."

Reverend Nelson seemed flustered for a moment. "What's going on here?" he asked. "Sister Janie informed me that . . ."

Miss Pearl put up a hand to silence him, and then apologized for the misunderstanding. She told him that Mama was in labor, but she probably wasn't going to die. The reverend nodded, and his nod ended in a bowed head. He clutched his Bible to his chest with one hand, raised the other, and prayed for my mother. When he was done, he said, "Sister Rozelle, you send these little ones to church every Sunday. God loves them, and He loves you, too. Why don't you join us one Sunday? We'd like to see you there."

"Amen!" the women chorused in unison before they began backing along the short hallway toward the front door, spilling out onto the porch, and descending the steps.

Reverend Nelson glanced at me and smiled sadly as he left. I felt a lump in my throat, and I felt sorry for him. He had put on a suit on a Saturday, and had come all the way down from Plymouth to the outskirts of town to pray for a woman who was not dying after all. God was surely frowning down on the whole lot of us, and Tarabelle was right. The Quinns were going to keep the fires burning in Hell, and Miss Pearl was going to be right there beside us.

"Okay, we got work to do," Miss Pearl said, rolling around to face us. "We gotta get something up to this door. Where them boys?"

Tarabelle answered, "Harvey and Sam out working, and Wallace . . ."

"I know where Wallace is," Miss Pearl said. "He up to my place helping Frank tear the house apart. Look like we gon' have to do this ourself. Let's get a sheet up."

Tarabelle pulled a sheet from the cedar chest beneath the window. She stretched it out, gave one end to me, and we hung it over rusted nails that were already sticking out around the doorframe. Miss Pearl stepped up and tugged at the sheet to make sure it would hold, and just as she did, a soft, angelic voice whispered from beyond. "Tan. Tan, come here, baby."

My pulse quickened, and I looked at Tarabelle, whose placid face could have belonged to a statue. She shrugged her shoulders, and I pushed the sheet aside and entered my mother's room.

Mama raised her head from the pillow and reached a hand out to me. Her eyes were glassy, and beads of perspiration covered her face. "You see, Tan," she said between deep breaths. "You gotta tell the right person."

"What, Mama?" I asked. "Tell them what?"

"You have to tell Janie," she said, winking one glassy eye at me. "What they bring?"

"They brought potato pie."

"What else?"

"Black-eyed peas and collard greens."

"They bring any money?"

"No, ma'am." I shook my head, and Mama let go of my hand.

"Guess it's too late to fix that," she said. "Pearl done run 'em outta here." She sighed. "Leastways we'll eat good for a day or two."

A car horn blared in front of the house, and I was relieved by the distraction. I silently prayed it was not the reverend returning with money for my mother. As much as we needed it, I would not have been able to attend the Solid Rock Baptist Church again. Already I did not know how I was going to face the congregation after word got around that Mama had been pretending to die.

Miss Pearl pushed the sheet aside and stood in the doorway. "That's them Munfords out there," she said. "They wanna see Tangy Mae. Say they can't have no girl working for 'em they ain't never seen."

I took my coat from a nail in the front room and went out to face the Munfords.

They were standing on the road beside a shiny red automobile. Mrs. Munford stepped forward as I approached. "You're Tangy?" she inquired.

"Yes, ma'am." I nodded.

She studied me closely, starting at my black oxfords with no shoestrings, my ashy knees, my worn-thin cotton dress, my corduroy coat, and my uncombed hair. I was sure she could smell Laura's urine which had probably soaked into my pores.

"How old are you?" she asked.

"Thirteen," I answered, and did not bother to tell her that I was within spitting distance of fourteen.

She stepped back, consulted her husband, then faced me again. "You tell Rosie that I'm sorry, but you're too young. We can't use you." She was preparing to climb back inside the car, and I should have been relieved, but I knew I could not let them drive away, for surely then my mother would yank me into her deathbed and drag me to the depths of Hell with her.

"Wait!" I pleaded. "Please, wait just one minute."

I rushed up the steps and burst into my mother's room, pausing only a second to catch my breath. "Mama, they don't want me," I cried out, shifting from foot to foot in my anxiety. "They said I'm too young. What you want me to do, Mama? They gon' leave."

"Damn!" she exclaimed. "Did they ask about me?"

"Yes, ma'am," I lied. "They wanted to know if you were feeling any better, and I told them no."

"Good. You tell Tarabelle to go out there and talk to 'em. We can't afford to lose that money."

I watched from the safety of the doorway as Tarabelle made her way slowly down the incline and onto the road. The Munfords looked her over and questioned her the same as they had done me, and I could tell from her slumping posture that they were accepting her, and, unknowingly, giving me a reprieve. Though no one knew as well as I that Tarabelle would make me pay for my freedom.

six

"Get it out, Pearl!" Mama screamed. "Get it out!"

"Rosie, I'm doing the best I can. You gotta help me."

Something horrible was taking place behind the sheet-curtain we had mounted over our mother's doorway. For hours, Mama had been making hooting owl sounds, and Miss Pearl's voice had fluc-tuated between low coaxing and high swearing. They would not allow anybody in that room, except Tarabelle.

"Kill me, Pearl! Just take something and knock my brains out. Oh, Lord! Sweet Jesus. Kill me, Pearl!"

"I declare, Rosie, you ain't never carried on so. You just having a baby, and it sho' ain't the first one. You know we can't rush this."

In the front room, Harvey paced the short distance before the coal stove, back and forth, stopping every now and then to warm his hands, or just to stare at the forbidding curtain. Sam knelt beside the stove, smoking a cigarette and flicking ash into the opening of the grate. He was still wearing his work overalls even though it was close to midnight. The overalls were clean, which meant he had spent another idle day.

"You think Miss Pearl know what she doing?" Harvey asked.

"She know," Sam answered, blowing a string of smoke toward the stove.

Harvey continued to pace, changing directions several times, coming within touching distance of the better of the two armchairs that Martha Jean and I shared. We had left the other one for him, but he seemed unable to sit. In contrast to Sam's overalls, Harvey's would need two days of soaking before going into the wash. They were frayed at the hems, patched at the knees, and dotted with greasy stains that were visible even in the dim light of the kerosene lamp.

"I wish Mushy was here," he said, nervously running a hand through his short, auburn hair. The hair curled around his fingers, and for a moment he stood massaging his scalp.

"What?" Sam asked. "Mushy done went to Ohio and learned how to deliver babies?"

"Nah, man. I just wish she was here."

"If I was Mushy, I wouldn't never come back here," Sam said. "When I leave, don't none of y'all look on me coming back."

"Why don't you leave, Sam?" Harvey's deep, baritone voice was laced with frustration. "What's stopping you? You ain't doing nothing to help out, and I'm getting tired of working to feed you. You don't give a damn 'bout nobody but yo'self. Why don't you leave?" He glared down at Sam, who refused to be intimidated, although Harvey, at the age of twenty, was two years older and at least twenty pounds heavier.

Sam inhaled the last of his cigarette, flicked the butt into the stove, then stood to face Harvey. "I don't leave for the same reason you don't. I can't." His voice, though not as deep or angry as Harvey's, seemed to convey just as much strength. "Yo' mother," he said, bowing slightly at the waist and sweeping a hand toward the curtain. "Yo' mother won't let me go."

"What you mean she won't let you go?" Harvey asked. "She ain't stopping you. She didn't stop Mushy."

"She couldn't stop Mushy," Sam countered.

"Man, if you wanna go, just go."

Sam stuck his hands into the pockets of his overalls and brought them out empty. "Wit' what?" he asked.

Harvey's jaw stiffened, but before he could respond, Miss Pearl stepped from behind the curtain. "I can't do this by myself," she said breathlessly. "You boys gon' have to run and get the midwife."

We stared at her in disbelief. We were forbidden to even approach Selman Street where the midwife lived, and Miss Pearl knew it.

"Nooooo!" Mama yelled, as something in her room crashed to the floor.

Wallace, who had been quietly studying us from the doorway of the kitchen, turned and pulled the flashlight from the kitchen shelf and placed it in Harvey's hand. Harvey and Sam, without a word to each other, left the house together, united in their decision to get Mama the help she did not want.

"You know better, Pearl!" Mama exploded when Miss Pearl went back into the bedroom. "She ain't coming in my house. That shriveled up, rheumy-eyed, snuff-dipping ol' bitch. I'd rather die a hundred deaths than let her touch me."

I glanced at Wallace, who grinned and shook his head. "They sleeping through all this," he said, indicating Laura and Edna who were lying on the kitchen floor. "I don't know how they can sleep through this."

"It's nice somebody can," I said. "I think I'll curl up in this chair and try to get a little sleep myself. It could be a long night."

I nudged Martha Jean and pointed to the other chair. She stood and stretched, and while she was doing so, Tarabelle strode across the hall, brushed past her, and slumped down in the unoccupied chair.

"Po' Mama," Tarabelle said in a voice void of sympathy. "She done had her whites, her Indians, and her coloreds. This one must be Chinese or something 'cause it sho' don't wanna be born in this house."

"What they doing in there?" Wallace asked.

"Nothing," Tarabelle answered. "Ain't nothing they can do."

Martha Jean knelt on the floor beside the stove, and I said, "Martha Jean is scared. She doesn't understand what's going on."

"You the one scared," Tarabelle snapped. "Martha Jean know all about it, a lot more than you. I tol' her about having babies—how it tears yo' insides out. How you bleed like a hog, and pieces of yo' body come rolling out on the bed, all slimy and smelly."

I could feel her watching me, but I kept my eyes averted and said nothing.

"Tan, I bet you don't even know how a baby is made, do you?" she whispered, and did not wait for a reply. "Takes a man and a woman to do it. You take off yo' clothes and let him pee inside you. That's all there is to it."

It was too disgusting to be believable, but Wallace, intrigued by Tarabelle's nonsense, stepped closer toward her. "Is that true, Tara?" he asked.

She nodded.

"It is not, Wallace," I said. "She's making that up."

"Takes days to get all that pee out yo' body," Tarabelle continued, enjoying herself. "That is, unless you know how to wash it out. One day, Tan, I'm gon' tell you how to wash it out. Sometimes you can't get it all, and some of it gets in yo' belly and mixes wit' food and makes a baby."

I began to laugh. It was a high-pitched, humorless laugh, bordering on hysteria. My mother was a clean woman. Never would she allow a man to do the number one in her. Tarabelle should have known better than to say such a thing, and anyway, babies did not grow in bellies; they grew in wombs.

My laughter brought Miss Pearl back into the front room. She stood over me and shook my shoulders. "Child, ain't nothing funny here," she scolded.

I struggled to regain my composure, to become once more the calm, sensible Tangy that she knew so well, but each time I opened my mouth to explain, shrill laughter erupted. My jaws ached, and my stomach cramped. I was so consumed by laughter and tears that Miss Pearl stepped back and just allowed me to ride it out.

At first, I could not identify the sharp pain in my left arm. I thought it was just another symptom of my hysteria, like the aching jaws and the cramping stomach. But as the pain intensified, I tried to move my arm and found that I could not. Tarabelle had a grip on me. She was pinching the skin above my elbow so hard that she had bitten down on her bottom lip.

"Stop it, Tara!" Wallace shouted. "You hurting her."

It was an understatement. Tarabelle probably would have ripped the skin away from the bone of my arm if Miss Pearl had not intervened.

"That's enough of that," she said, gripping Tarabelle's wrist. "Let her go!"

Tarabelle gave one last, long twist before releasing my arm. "It's all yo' fault I gotta go clean somebody's house. Ain't no telling what you went out there and said to them Munfords wit' yo' uppity ass," Tarabelle lashed out at me. "I do mo' 'round here than anybody, now I gotta do even mo'. It ain't fair."

In my opinion, Tarabelle did less than anybody in the house. She did not go to work or to school. She did not watch over Laura and Edna. She did not scrub the outhouse, dump the night bucket, lug the water bucket, chop wood, haul in coal or kindling, sweep or mop the floors, wash dishes, cook meals, clean the ice box, nor run errands. She helped wash clothes on Saturdays, and as far as I was concerned, that was all she did.

I expected Miss Pearl to remind her of that, but Miss Pearl sat on the arm of Tarabelle's chair, gave my sister a hug, and said, "It's awright, chil'. Thangs got a way of working out. C'mon now, let's go check on yo' mama."

Okay. So maybe now Tarabelle could add delivering babies to her list of chores which consisted of washing clothes, hanging clothes, and letting the air take care of drying.

Thus far, Miss Pearl had done all of the delivering in our house. From Mushy to Edna, she had delivered all of Mama's babies, and had a long tale to tell about each birth. I had grown bored over the years of hearing how my mother did not trust the midwife or the hospital, and of how young and scared Miss Pearl had been when she had delivered Mushy.

The springs in the seat of my chair cut into my bottom, but I did not want to move. I was angry, hurt, and scared. I lowered my head to the armrest and stared at Wallace, who stared back at me. Martha Jean stood and began shifting coals in the stove with the poker.

That was the way Harvey and Sam found us when they returned with the midwife, Miss Zadie. She was indeed shriveled. She was a high-yellow colored woman who wore thick-lensed, brown-frame glasses. Her back was stooped to an angle so that she appeared to be searching for something on the floor, and when she held her head up, she resembled a turkey in the act of gobbling. Her bottom lip was unmistakably packed with snuff.

Miss Pearl stepped out into the hallway, greeted the old woman, then rushed her into Mama's room. I turned my attention back to the curtain. For the longest time there were only whispers and flickering light, but then Miss Pearl's huge frame formed a silhouette against the sheet. She pushed the sheet aside.

"Go get Frank!" she ordered. "Right now! Tell him to get the car out here as fast as he can."

"Mr. Grodin's out front in his car," Harvey said. "He brought us back wit' Miss Zadie."

Miss Pearl nodded her head impatiently. "I know," she said, "but he won't take yo' mama nowhere in his car. Go on and get Frank like I tol' you."

"Look here, Miss Pearl," Sam said. "I wanna know what's going on in there."

"She bleeding awful bad, and we ain't got no choice but to take her to the hospital. I think she done lost that chil', and if you boys don't get a move on, we might lose yo' mama, too."

"Mr. Grodin can take her," Sam insisted.

"Yeah," Harvey agreed. "Tan, you go on out there and tell Mr. Grodin we coming out wit' Mama."

As Harvey and Sam stormed past Miss Pearl and into Mama's room, I stayed in my sanctuary. I felt warm and secure in the chair, and I had no idea what the darkness outside held. What type of man would refuse to take a dying woman to the hospital? I did not know, but I was not going out alone to face him. Nothing made any sense. Mr. Grodin had brought his wife to our house to attend to Mama. Surely, that showed he was a kind and neighborly man.

"You going, Tan?" Wallace asked. "If you ain't, I'm going."

"No, Wallace, don't!" I said quickly. "If you warn him, he might drive off."

"He ain't gon' leave his wife."

"He might," I said. "You don't know."

Wallace thought about that for a second, then he snatched up the flashlight from the round table where Harvey had placed it, and started for the door. "I'm gon' tell him," he said. "If he drives off, I'll just keep going till I get Mr. Frank or somebody else."

"I'll go with you," I said.

We were stopped by the old midwife before we even reached

the door. "Ain't no need to go out there," she said. "John ain't gon' take her nowhere, and that's all there is to it. No need troublin' a ol' man that's set in his ways."

"Okay then," Harvey conceded, stepping around Miss Zadie and taking the flashlight from Wallace's hand. "I'm gon' run on and get Mr. Frank."

"I'm gon' wait right here," Sam said. "If Mama gets any worse, I'll *make* Mr. Grodin take her. If she dies, I'll kill him." To seal his threat, he walked into the front room, snatched the poker from Martha Jean, and glared at Miss Zadie.

Harvey was well on his way before Miss Zadie chuckled and responded in an old woman's patient voice. "He still wouldn't take her," she said.

A knowing glance passed between the two midwives, something I did not understand, but that aroused my curiosity. They did not return to Mama's room, but instead sat, like a fat woman and a dwarf, in the twin armchairs.

Sam, Martha Jean, and I stood beside the stove with Wallace squatting at our feet, as our guest silently observed us. Miss Zadie, with her stubby little elbows braced on the armrests, fanned her hands and waggled her fingers. "So this is it?" she asked in a dry tone. "It ain't fit for chickens."

"Now, Miss Zadie, don't you go starting on nothing," Miss Pearl warned. "These chilluns don't know nothing 'bout you. This ain't the time."

The old woman's head inched upright on her neck with such an effort that I found myself straining my own neck in order to assist her. When she had it as far up as it would go, it bobbed unsteadily a few times, then settled. "When is the time?" she asked.

Miss Pearl said nothing, and the old woman seemed not to expect an answer. She screwed her head around and stared at Wallace. "Come here, boy," she said, as snuff oozed across her lip and rolled down her chin.

"Nooooo!" Mama screamed, and I could hear Tarabelle in the next room trying to soothe her.

Miss Pearl rose from her seat and padded back across the hall, and Wallace rose from his squat and stood watching Miss Zadie.

"I said, come here, boy," the midwife repeated, and when Wallace did not budge, she asked, "You scared of me or something?"

"Ma'am," Sam said, taking a step toward her, "we brought you out here to help our mother. If you can't do that, I don't see no sense in you wasting yo' time or yo' husband's."

Miss Zadie grunted and wiggled into a standing position. With her back stooped and her head lowered, she made her way across the floor toward the four of us. She stopped in front of Martha Jean, went through the painstaking effort of lifting her head, then raised a vein-rippled hand and stroked my sister's face.

Martha Jean did not draw back, but I flinched enough for the both of us. Martha Jean drew a short line across her chest with a finger. "Name?" she signed, oblivious to the weakening moans coming from the bedroom.

The midwife seemed not to hear them, either. She dropped her hand from Martha Jean's face, surprise registering behind her thick lenses. "So, this is the deaf one," she said. "I heard Rozelle had a deef and dumb. Looks just like her mama, too, don't she?"

Sam stepped in front of Martha Jean, pushing her back slightly. "Miss Zadie, I don't know you," he said, "but I always heard you was a pretty decent midwife. Everybody say so. They say you delivered half the babies in Pakersfield. How is it you can't help Mama?"

She did not look at Sam. She took two awkward steps toward the stove as her tongue sank beneath her lower lip, and then, as if it were the most natural thing in the world, she spat a mixture of saliva and snuff right onto the belly of the stove. "Yo' mama can't be helped," she said. "Ain't nobody in the world can help yo' mama."

With that, she turned her back to us and left our house. The gob of snuff sizzled in her wake and became a permanent stain on the stove. For some reason, I felt it was a stain on me as well.

That stain, scorching into the iron, held me captivated as Harvey and Sam carried our mother, moaning weakly, out to Mr. Frank's car, which had finally arrived. And for the first time, I wondered if my mother could be helped, or if she were truly going to die.

"One or the other, Lord," I prayed aloud. "Help her or take her."

seven

In the absence of our mother, gluttony threatened to be our downfall. Martha Jean, encouraged by Sam, cooked a huge pot of grits and fried over a dozen thick slices of bologna. We gathered in the kitchen and ate until every grain and morsel was devoured. We were undaunted by the prospect of repercussions, even as we consumed the last of a loaf of bread. We sampled, savored, and digested the sweets of freedom.

We were quiet—too busy eating to worry about talking—which is probably why I did not miss Wallace until Tarabelle asked where he was.

"Gone," Edna answered, pointing toward the back door.

"Probably went up to Mr. Frank's," Harvey said. "When did he leave?"

Nobody answered; no one seemed to care. We had not dressed, washed our faces, brushed our teeth, or done any of the other things our mother required of us in the morning. I wasn't sure Wallace had even dumped the night bucket.

It was Sunday and we should have been in church, but we had gone to bed late and awakened late, and I guess that was our excuse.

I went into the front room, draped my coat over my damp nightgown, stepped into a pair of shoes, and went out into the backyard. I followed the foot-worn trail past the outhouse and deep into the naked woods. Frosted brown leaves and twigs crunched beneath my feet as I walked. Above me, through the bare branches of birch trees, a gray sky mirrored my mood.

The woods stretched southward for about a quarter mile and ended at a barbed-wire fence that protected Mr. Nathan Barnwell's property from niggers. There was a sign to that effect nailed to a fence pole. Over the years we had used the sign for target practice, had thrown rocks at it, but we had never considered removing it. Harvey and Sam had ignored the sign several times, breaking through the bottom wires and coming home with their arms loaded with corn, beans, or tomatoes, and once with two chickens. Mama had said it was all right since they weren't niggers anyway.

As I returned to the house, I saw Wallace pass the washtub and dart beneath the clothesline. We reached the back steps at about the same time, and entered the house together.

"Miss Pearl say Mama had a girl," Wallace announced excitedly, and if he had expected a celebration, he was sorely disappointed. Not even Laura or Edna, who were sprawled on the kitchen floor coloring the printed pages of a newspaper, responded to the news.

"You think you grown, boy?" Harvey asked. "You just gon' leave outta here and don't say nothing to nobody?"

"I wanted to see how Mama was doing," Wallace said.

"How is she doing?" I asked, before Harvey could lash out again.

"Miss Pearl say she had a hard time of it, and she'll probably be in the hospital for a while."

"What's a while?" Sam wanted to know.

Wallace shrugged his shoulders. "I don't know—just a while. That's all Miss Pearl said. Ain't y'all glad about the baby?"

"Yeah, Wallace, we're glad," I answered.

"Speak for yo'self," Tarabelle snapped. "Tangy, you always glad about something. Where we gon' sleep a baby? What we gon' feed it? Martha Jean gon' spend her whole life looking after Mama's babies. Shit! I ain't glad."

"Me neither," Sam said. "It ain't that I got nothing against no baby, but something just ain't right. Why this time Mama try to hide it, acting like she gon' die and carrying on? Why she make it such a big secret?"

"Mama's no stranger to secrets," I said. "We should all know by now that she has a private life, and she does not feel obligated to share it with her children. And that is what we are—her children. She has a right to . . ."

"Shit!" Sam hissed.

I stopped. Mr. Pace undoubtedly would have been proud of my rhetoric, but my siblings were staring at me as though I had grown an extra head.

Tarabelle flicked a hand in my direction. "Y'all see," she said. "That's why I can't stand her."

"Tangy Mae, you oughta quit," Sam said. "What you trying to say anyway?"

"Don't matter how she say it, man, she right," Harvey said. "Long as I can remember, Mama been hiding things from us. Far as I know, she didn't tell nobody 'bout me, or you, or any of the rest of us. She got fat, and we just sort of knew it, but I don't remember her coming right out saying nothing."

"Yeah, but did you ever hear her talking 'bout dying like she was doing?" Sam asked.

"Don't matter," Harvey said. "Tan is right. Mama ain't never told us much of nothing."

Harvey had given me the encouragement I needed to speak again, and this time I intended to be heard. "Ain't nobody got no daddy," I said, "except Archie Preston claiming to be Harvey's. How come?"

There was silence. I had broached a subject that was taboo, and they all stared at me again. "Tarabelle says it takes a man and . . ."

"Don't worry 'bout what I said," Tarabelle snapped.

"You did say it," Wallace interjected.

"That's why people don't tell children nothing. Children got big mouths," Tarabelle said.

"You didn't say it was a secret," Wallace responded in a wounded tone. He was big on keeping secrets.

"What did Tarabelle say?" Harvey asked.

Wallace glanced at Tarabelle, twiddled his thumbs for a second, then allowed his arms to swing at his sides as he began to repeat, verbatim, what Tarabelle had told us the night before.

Harvey and Sam roared with laughter when Wallace was done telling. I stared at Tarabelle, expecting to see her seething with anger or squirming with discomfort, but her expression was as stoic as ever.

Sam, carried away, jumped up and down on the floorboards which caused Laura and Edna to cease coloring, and Martha Jean to stare at him quizzically. "Pee?" he said between bouts of laughter. "She said it was pee?"

Had they been just a bit more subdued, they might have heard what I heard as Tarabelle turned to leave the kitchen.

"It feels like pee," she mumbled.

Sam pulled himself together first. "C'mon, boy," he said to Wallace. "Let's walk over to Logan's store. We gon' get us some Nehi and celebrate our new sister."

And I was relieved because I knew Sam was going to tell Wallace what went on between men and women, Wallace would tell me, and eventually I might share it with Tarabelle.

eight

My dread of leaving Martha Jean alone, with only Laura and Edna as her ears, was shared by Wallace. "What if somebody comes in? She wouldn't even hear 'em. She can't hear if somebody knocks on the door," Wallace protested. "I ain't going to school. It ain't gon' hurt nothing if I miss one day."

"Martha Jean gon' be awright," Harvey assured him. "Ain't nobody coming out here. You going to school, Wallace, so you might as well shut up and get dressed."

Sam leaned against the back wall behind the stove, grinning at the exchange and smoking a cigarette. He wore the same overalls he had worn the week before, and they were still relatively clean.

"I'm trying to think, Wallace," he teased, "who gon' come out here and bother Martha Jean? Who you think?"

Wallace did not have to think about it. He was ready for the question. "A stranger," he said, "or the insurance man, or the ice man, or Mr. Poppy, or dirty ol' Mr. Harper who brings the coal."

"Why they coming?" Sam asked. "You done went and ordered ice and coal, and didn't tell nobody?"

"Get yo' clothes on, Wallace," Harvey said. "You talking 'bout people don't wanna come when they got to."

"Bang, bang," Sam teased, pointing a trigger finger at Wallace. "You gon' shoot all them people wit' yo' cap pistol, Wallace? Make me wanna stay home and watch. I can just see it now. Mr. Poppy come to the door and ask for his rent, and you shoot him through the heart wit' yo' cap pistol. They put you on the chain gang for shooting people, boy, and that's worse than any school I know of."

Wallace stood up under Sam's taunting, but finally went back to the kitchen and made a show of getting dressed.

After Harvey and Sam left, I poured warm water into the washbasin and began my morning bath. Tarabelle came from Mama's room where she had slept for the past two nights. She didn't say anything, but as she swept by me on her way to the kitchen, she purposely shoved my arm, and water sloshed from the basin.

I turned to stare at her and saw that she was wearing her white, cotton dress—the one with the tiny rose pattern and short sleeves. It was more suited for spring, but no one was going to tell her that.

"Grits," she grumbled, coming back into the front room. "I'm sick and tired of grits. Oughta be something else in the world to eat besides grits all the time."

"I want grits," Laura said.

"You would," Tarabelle snapped. "You always want something. I'm glad I'm getting out of here today. Never nobody to talk to but a dummy and two whining brats."

"There won't be anybody to talk to at the Munfords', either," I informed her.

"Huh," she snorted. "That's what you think. Might not be nobody after today, but today *you* gon' be talking to me. Don't tell me you thought you was running off to school."

"I am going to school. Harvey said we have to go to school."

"Wallace might be going, but you ain't. Who you think gon' show me where these people live? I ain't never been to no East Grove. You just expect me to walk up to some house and start cleaning? Tangy, you gon' show me the house, where they keep things, how they like things, and how to do things. I ain't working today, sister. I'm gon' be watching you."

"Come on, Tara," I pleaded, "I missed school on Friday. Mr. Pace is gonna be upset with me."

"So?" she asked, moving in to stand nose to nose with me. "Who you think you are? You think 'cause you can read a little bit better than the rest of us that it makes you special or something? You ain't special, Tangy. Ever' time you gotta do something, you whine. You just like Laura and Edna, whining all the time 'bout everything."

She grabbed the undershirt that I was about to slip over my head and tried to yank it from my hands. "You think you special, Tangy?" she repeated, tugging and stretching the shirt.

"Yes!" I shouted, and pulled the shirt with all my strength.

My beautiful sister chose that particular moment to loosen her grip. I stumbled backwards and fell to the floor, bringing the basin of water with me, soaking the undershirt.

Edna began to cry, and Laura shrieked for Wallace who came rushing in from the kitchen.

"I don't need Wallace," I croaked from beneath a black oxford that was firmly planted atop my naked chest. Tears sprang to my eyes. "Mama said we don't fight each other," I whimpered, and the heavy shoe was immediately replaced by a gob of saliva. I could feel it oozing across my ribcage, and I used the wet shirt to wipe it off.

"Silly," Tarabelle said, as she turned on her heels and marched across the hall.

"I'm gon' tell Mama on Tara," Laura said with such sympathy for me that I felt ashamed for myself and for Tarabelle.

"Ain't nothing to tell," Wallace said, helping me to my feet, although I did not want his help. He refilled the basin with warm water, then turned his attention to Laura and Edna. "C'mon," he told them, "Martha Jean's got breakfast ready." On his way out, he stopped long enough to whisper, "Tara's just a bully. You'll get her one day."

Alone in the room, I thought about bravery and common sense, exploring the thin line that separated the two. I was not a brave individual, and common sense told me that my strength would be no match against Tarabelle's, but I was not afraid of her, either. Not really afraid.

Fear was a thing I understood all too well. It was a malignancy that had spread throughout my body until my mother, in her godly wisdom, had diagnosed and cauterized it.

I stared at my reflection in the basin of water, remembering that day vividly, and shuddering from the memory.

I am ten, sprinting the miles between Plymouth and Stump Town with sticks and stones pelting my thin winter coat, being chased by four girls who are no bigger or older than I.

"Pee baby, cry baby, pee baby, cry baby," they yell from behind me, and I run even faster.

"You'd better run."

"Ugly, stinky, tar baby. You'd better run."

Their words hurt worse than the rock that draws blood from my scalp, and the stick that bounces off my leg and does not draw blood. I run with fear pumping through my veins. My notebook and pencils are scattered somewhere miles behind me, and I am trying desperately to reach the safety of my mother's arms, screaming her name in my flight.

I round the bend, running from Fife Street to Penyon Road, and I see my mother. She is standing on the front porch, staring down past the field and directly at me. She turns her back and opens the front door. I think she is going inside, deserting me in the presence of my enemies, and I scream for her again.

"Mama! Mama!"

Martha Jean and Tarabelle emerge from the house. My mother rushes them toward the road, and they obey. My warriors charge the battlefield without armor, attacking my predators, pulling clothes, and hair, and skin, drawing blood and screams of terror, as I fall to the dirt, panting and crying.

Above the noise of my pounding heart and panting breath comes the distinct sound of bone cracking. I turn my head slowly and see three of the girls running back toward Fife, and the unlucky fourth sitting on the road, holding her right arm with her left hand.

Tarabelle circles the girl once, then turns her cold eyes on me, and before I can blink, she rams a knee into the girl's face. Martha Jean, a long red welt running from ear to chin, helps me to my feet and delivers me into the waiting arms of my mother.

Mama makes herself comfortable in an armchair and pulls me onto her lap. She strokes my hair, then wraps an arm around my back, drawing me closer to her heart. With her other hand, she motions to Tarabelle, and my sister steps away from us. Mama brings her arm around and under my thigh, pinning my body to hers. "You a Quinn, baby," she says softly. "We don't run from nobody. Nobody! Do you understand that?"

"Yes, ma'am," I mumble against her breast.

"You gotta fight. Don't take nothing but swinging yo' fist. You understand that?"

"Yes, ma'am."

"I'm gon' make sho' you understand it," she says, loosening her grip on my thighs. "Hand me that poker and hold her feet, Tarabelle."

Tarabelle clamps down on my feet, immobilizing me. There is no time to cry out as my mother brings the searing fire iron down onto my leg. I swoon from the pain, and my mother's voice trails me as I enter into a darkness that is death and float deeper still into Hell. "I done branded you a Quinn, girl. Don't you ever run from nobody else long as you live."

Much later, the next day or the day after that, my mother's face comes into focus before my eyes. She opens her mouth, and the strong smell of onions assaults my nostrils. "It wouldna burned you so bad if you'da been still," she says.

I remembered wanting to fade back into the darkness, but being unable to. I will forever wear a brand on my lower left leg that I am able to hide beneath a sock. Sometimes when I am most afraid, I touch my scar to remind myself that I am not a coward. I am a Quinn.

nine

Velman Cooper was standing beside the flag pole when I came out of the post office, empty-handed, on Friday afternoon. "Hey, little sister," he called when he saw me. "I was kinda hoping you'd come by today. Where's Martha Jean?"

"At home," I answered irritably. "She doesn't go everywhere with me."

"Stop trying to be so mean," he said, smiling and exposing the gap between his teeth.

"What happened to your tooth?" I asked.

"Got it pulled out. Something you don't ever wanna have is a bad tooth. Had me walking the floors. Felt like somebody was hammering away at my mouth and my head at the same time. I was crying like a baby. That was years ago when I was still in Dalton, but I ain't never gon' forget that pain."

"Oh, is that all?" I asked flippantly. "I thought somebody knocked it out."

"Ain't nobody bad enough to knock my teeth out, little sister."

"I bet one of my brothers could," I said, and immediately

regretted my remark, because I had the feeling he was not being arrogant now, but was only trying to get a smile out of me.

"Maybe, and maybe not," he said with a smirk. "I been asking around 'bout yo' family. People say you got some pretty tough brothers, but I don't know that they could knock my teeth out."

"What else do people say?"

"Not much."

"Liar."

"Yeah, you right, I am lying," he admitted, "but what people say ain't hardly worth repeating."

"How about worth believing?" I asked.

"You can't believe everything you hear, either," he said. "People had me dead once. Said I had been struck by lightning under Miss Thatcher's peach tree. I musta been about eight or nine. Me and some mo' boys was out there stealing peaches, 'cause Miss Thatcher had the biggest, healthiest peach tree in Dalton. All of a sudden the sky got just as dark as night, and Gabriel commenced to calling my name, 'Velman. Velman.' He wadn't blowing no horn, but his voice was howling out my name. He had done seen what we was up to and he knew it wadn't no good.

"I looked up and saw him standing there in midair, swinging his horn in his right hand and staring down at me. Gabriel is a Negro, little sister. Don't let nobody tell you he ain't. He's a big fat black man, darker than soot, and he was standing on a cloud. Every time he opened his mouth the wind howled. He raised that horn, and rain fell on us like rocks, and lightning zoomed 'round our heads. We didn't know whether to run or just stay put, so we did a little bit of both. Some of us took off running, and some of us stayed under the tree waiting for the rocks to stop.

"All of a sudden—whack—something hit me upside my head and I fell to the ground. Wadn't nothing but a peach done got shook loose from the tree, but by the time I got back on my feet, I was the only one under that tree. Them other boys had done took off and told my mama I was dead, done been struck by lightning."

"You're making that up," I said, trying to keep from laughing. "You're just trying to change the subject."

"No, I ain't, either. My mama come running through that yard wit' tears and rain mixed on her face, crying that her boy was dead. That ain't nothing to lie about."

He'd ended his story, and I realized that I wanted him to continue. I enjoyed the sound of his voice and the way his hands occasionally swept though the air to place emphasis on some of his words.

"Why you staring at me like that?" he asked, and I averted my eyes, but did not deny what was obvious.

"I've got to go," I told him.

"Wait a minute," he said, placing a hand on my arm to detain me. "I got something for Martha Jean. It's in my car."

"What is it?"

"You'll see."

I followed him to his car which was parked in the same spot as when I had first seen it a week ago. He opened the passenger door, reached into the back seat, and withdrew a large, brown paper bag.

"Here, take a look," he said, handing the package over to me.

I opened the bag and was surprised to see a brand new, navy blue cloth coat. I stared at the dark fabric until Velman took it from my hands.

He held the coat up by the shoulders and peered over the collar at me. "You think it'll fit her?" he asked.

"Velman, you can't give that to Martha Jean," I said. "Mama will have a fit."

"Trust me, little sister. Yo' mama ain't gon' have no fit. I found that out before I went and spent my money."

I did not know how to respond to that. Before me stood a man who had seen my sister, to my knowledge, only once. He had never seen nor spoken to my mother, and yet he thought he knew them both. My jaw tightened and anger escaped from my nostrils in little whiffs of frost.

"What have people been telling you about my mother?" I snapped. "And about my family?"

"What you think they been telling me?"

"Can't you ever just answer a question?"

"Depends on the question," he said, taking the bag from my hands and placing the coat inside. "I guess I'll have to find out where you live so I can take this coat to Martha Jean."

"She doesn't want to see you," I said quickly. "She doesn't even like you. She thinks your hair is a mess, and you talk too much."

He laughed. "She told you all of that, did she? Well, she can tell it to me when she sees me this evening. I'm gonna take this coat to her just as soon as I get off work."

I snatched the package from his hands. "I think you already know where we live," I said angrily. "You also know that our mother doesn't take kindly to visitors."

"Yep. I know all that, but I also know yo' mother ain't there right now. I hear she's in the hospital."

Velman Cooper had asked questions about my family, and he had gotten answers. Someone had warned him not to come to Penyon Road, though, or he would have done so by now. I was certain of that.

With the package tucked under my arm, I stepped out onto the sidewalk, and heard him say, "Next time you come, you bring Martha Jean wit' you."

As I spun around, I saw him leaning against his car with his hands shoved into the pockets of his gray uniform pants, and a grin on his face. "I'm not bringing my sister to see you," I hissed. "You're a grown man. You should find yourself a girl your own age."

"A girl my age is called a woman," he countered, "and that's just what Martha Jean is—a woman."

He stood there with that idiotic grin on his face, and I thought for just a second that I was bad enough to knock his teeth out.

"I don't like you," I said, "and if I tell my brothers that you're chasing after Martha Jean like some old dog, they'll break your neck. Maybe I won't even give her this coat. Maybe I'll drop it in a ditch on my way home."

"Yeah. That oughta be easy for you to do since you got a nice warm coat," he responded. "And by the way, there's something in that bag for you. It's a red scarf to tie around your beautiful hair."

I didn't know what to say, so I rushed off down the sidewalk toward home. At the bend on Penyon Road, I reached into the bag and found the scarf at the bottom beneath the coat. I took it out and tied it into a bow around my ponytail.

Harvey and Sam had both put in a full day of work. They were dirty, tired, and hungry when they arrived home at a little before dark. When they were done eating, they stood side by side in the front room by the coal stove while Martha Jean cleaned the kitchen. It was their secretiveness, their whispering, that caused me to close my schoolbook, stare at their backs, and strain to hear what they were saying.

"You think Hambone gon' come?" Harvey whispered.

Sam shrugged his shoulders. "I doubt it, but we'll see."

"I don't think I want no parts of this."

"Ain't gon' hurt you to listen to what Junior gotta say, Harvey."

Harvey slowly shook his head. "I don't know 'bout this, Sam. I think we asking for trouble."

"We already got trouble. If you don't know that, maybe you don't want no parts of it."

It was about an hour later when I saw my brothers, all three of them, carrying our milk crates, kitchen chairs, and their bed rolls out to the back porch. I could no longer pretend that I did not know something was going on.

Laura and Edna were asleep, and Tarabelle was stretched out in Mama's room. Martha Jean was finally taking a rest in the armchair beside me, and I was clutching my history book and staring toward the kitchen. Wallace came inside, took the kerosene lamp from the kitchen, and was on his way back out when I sprang from my chair and intercepted him.

"Wallace, what in the world are y'all doing?" I whispered.

"This is man stuff, Tan. We got some people coming out here tonight, some important things to talk about."

"Who's coming out here?"

Wallace was moving toward the back door as he answered. "I don't know, but I gotta go. Sam wants me to stand out front and show them to the back when they get here."

The kitchen was now bare, except for the table and the icebox, and I couldn't even see them since Wallace had walked out with the lamp. I stood in the dark room for a few seconds, then began to pace. I nearly bumped into Wallace when he returned, anxious, rushed, and talking fast.

"Tan, Sam says to keep the lamp burning in the front room."

"How are we suppose to sleep with the lamp on?" I asked. "And, anyway, that's wasting kerosene."

"Just leave it on," Wallace said impatiently, and then he was gone again.

I went to the front door, cracked it open, and stared out into the night. After a few minutes, I heard Wallace call out, "Back here! Back here!" Then I saw the first two men climb up the bank and into our yard. I counted seventeen heads before I saw the one that was Junior's. I knew it was him because he was carrying a satchel.

As a girl, I was excluded from the gathering, but there was nothing to prevent me from eavesdropping. I decided to sit on the kitchen floor with an ear pressed against the door. I would listen to every word they had to say. There was the possibility that someone might open the door and bang it against my head, but I didn't think they would. Everything they needed and then some was already outside.

I eased into the front room and saw that Martha Jean was asleep on her pallet. Leaving the lamp burning, I pulled my coat from a nail, tipped into the kitchen, and took my position on the floor. I blocked the cold draft that was seeping in from beneath the door with my coat, sat perfectly still and listened.

At first everybody spoke at once. They kept their voices low, but I could hear them clearly. After a few minutes of chatter, Sam's voice rose above the others.

"Awright," he said, "let's get started. It's cold out here, and I know everybody wants to get home. Junior, you the one wanted this meeting. Say what you wanna say, man."

"Everybody knows why we're here," Junior said, and his voice rose up to me. "Since you're here, I'm going to assume that there's something you want to change. This is not about me, so when you leave here tonight, I don't want you mumbling about how Junior thinks he can change the world. It's true that I have a long list of grievances against this town, but I'm not the only one. I think every man here should have his say, and we can move on from there. We'll change what we can, and get help with the rest."

As I listened to Junior I wished I could see his face. I thought about moving to the kitchen window, but I did not want to risk being seen.

"I'll start with the one injustice that has caused me the most sorrow," Junior continued. "I think you all remember my uncle, Nathan Fess, my daddy's only brother. You all know that he was murdered. But why?" He paused, giving the others time to think about it. "He was murdered because he and my daddy decided to start a taxi service. Your mothers, neighbors, and maybe some of you, used their taxi cabs. They were pulling business away from the white taxi company, and they were warned to cease what was called illegal activity. That was four years ago, and I haven't been able to talk about it until now. I couldn't speak about the way they intimidated my daddy, threatened our family, and used a shotgun to demolish a car we had worked years to buy. Daddy's decision was to give in, keep his family safe. Uncle Nathan, however, was an optimistic and determined man who felt he had just as much right as the next to earn a living. He paid for his beliefs with his life."

"I remember when that happened, Junior," someone said. "They never found out who killed him, did they?"

"They never even tried. Which brings me to another point," Junior said bitterly. "Chad Lowe was the spokesman for the white cab company. How he got involved, I'll never know, but he was the one who threatened my daddy."

"He got involved because they all stick together like that," Sam said. "That's what we've gotta start doing."

They were quiet for a few seconds, and I assumed they were nodding in agreement.

"In my heart, I believe Chad Lowe murdered my uncle," Junior finally said. "I don't know about the rest of you, but I have a problem with that evil man riding around this town with a gun on his hip. I've complained about it. I knew I couldn't go to the sheriff, but I wrote a letter to the mayor, and I went to the other policemen in that clubhouse they call a jail. They laughed at me. One of them told me that the United States Constitution gave Chad Lowe the right to bear arms." Junior paused. "I asked him if it gave me the same right. He stopped laughing then, told me to try it and see."

"Man, they'd shoot you down real quick," Greg Henry said, "and you right about that damn Chadlow. That mothafucka is in everybody's business, but ain't nothing we can do about that, Junior. I'm here tonight 'cause I wanna know if anybody got any ideas about some jobs."

"You one of the few of us got a job, Greg," Sam said.

"I know, Sam. I know," Greg responded. "I know y'all probably think I'm lucky 'cause I get to clean slop out them toilets at the bus depot. But it's a thousand times a day I wanna walk off that job. I would, too, if I didn't have Darlene and our baby to think about. You say they laughed at you when you went to the police, Junior? You ain't heard no laughing. Them fools that run the bus depot, they some laughing hyenas, man. Ain't but two of 'em, and they gotta be the worst two clowns ever wore britches. One day they took the lock off the colored toilet and jammed the door just for fun. The one, Mr. Lester, say he heard niggers shit like monkeys. The other one, Mr. Samuels, say he had to see that for himself. Then Mr. Lester say, 'Be careful! Monkeys throw their shit, you know.' Boy, did they laugh about that. It took a whole week before they let me fix that door. But they still do all kinds of lowdown dirty stuff."

"Well," Sam said, "seems like I can't even get a everyday job like a man s'pose to have. People think I don't wanna work, but that ain't it."

"Nah, what it is, Sam, you be asking them white folks too many questions," Harvey said. "They ain't gon' have no colored man questioning them."

"See, Harvey, you just climb on them trucks and go wherever they take you. I can't do that no mo'," Sam said. "I know I make it hard for myself, but, hell, Max can tell y'all some of the things we been through. We went out wit' Mr. Butterfield one time. I asked him before I got on his truck, and he told me he needed cotton pickers at three-and-a-half cents a pound. I sweat my way through a hundred and fifty pounds of cotton. It was dark when we finished, and he gave us seventy-five cents apiece. Said we had done put rocks in our sacks."

"I remember that," Max said. "Sam, man, you cried like a baby all the way back into town. The whole truckload of us was scared to touch you or say anything to you."

Sam laughed. "I didn't cry, Max, but I know I was mad enough to kill that bastard. I wanted to kill 'im, but I always heard that nigger time in a jail is worst than death."

"I believe it is," Andy Porter said, "and that's what everybody's scared of. Don't nobody wanna go to jail, but if you added up all the law in Triacy County, it would total nine white men—ten, if you wanna count Chadlow. I think there's enough of us to beat 'em down."

"And what would that accomplish, Andy?" Junior asked. "Don't you know they have politicians in this town who would appoint somebody else before you could blink your eye?"

"They can appoint me," Andy asserted. "What's wrong with a Negro being sheriff around here. Shit. I can crack a nigger's skull as well as the next man."

There was laughter, and then the conversation turned serious again, with each man telling his story, justifying his reason for taking his place in their gathering on a cold winter night. Some of the voices I recognized, others I did not.

"It's the schools," Harvey said. "I thought a law had done passed that said all the children can go to school together. Archie Preston say the Plymouth School is falling apart, and he oughta know, being the janitor. He say one of them children gon' get hurt up in there."

"Well, Harvey, that's nothing new," Junior informed him. "That school was falling apart when you and I were in first grade together. The state of Georgia has a governor, Melvin Griffin, who has stated that there will be no mixing of the races during his administration. I don't think there's anything we can do to change the man's mind, so we'll have to make do for a while longer. Things are changing, though, and some of that change is bound to spill over into Pakersfield. I keep writing letters, that's all I know to do. I've written to the NAACP and to some of the larger newspapers in this state. I've also talked with a reporter at the *Pakersfield Herald*."

"Junior, you can't trust no white man," someone said.

"They're not all bad, Homer. You have to trust somebody."

Then Homer's voice said, "Hambone and a few of us believe in an eye for an eye. I admit I get mad enough sometimes to kill 'em all, but I ain't figured out yet how to best use my switchblade against them rifles and shotguns they got."

There was laughter before Sam said, "You ain't never gon' figure that out, Homer. Can't be done."

"The best way to get them is through education," Junior countered. "What good are laws that cannot be read or understood, or a tongue that spews only hatred and ignorance? What good is the written word to an illiterate man?"

Complete and utter silence followed. I imagined the other men must have been staring at him with the same perplexity that I sometimes felt when Junior spoke.

Finally Sam said, "Shit, Junior, we ain't out here to listen to no . . ." He paused. "What the hell you talking 'bout?"

"I guess I believe in education as a weapon in our fight. That's why I walk those roads out through the country every week. I want to help people learn to read and write. I know knives and guns are not the answer. Once we get a fight like that started, who will have the power to stop it? How many deaths will be enough?"

"I ain't got no gun to shoot at nobody, and I don't want nobody shooting at me," Skip Carson said. "But getting back to this thing Sam was talking 'bout. I think we just ought not go out in them fields no mo'. Just let them crops stand out there 'til they shrivel up and die. Don't hoe, plant, or pick nothing else for 'em. That'll teach 'em."

"And while the crops are dying, what will you be doing, Skip?" Junior asked.

"I been thinking 'bout something," Skip said. "We don't have to stay here. Hambone say they got good jobs for Negroes up north, like in Chicago where he was staying. I say we move to Chicago."

"Nah, Skip," Harvey said. "Man, you talking crazy. We can't all just pack up and move nowhere."

"Some of us can," Junior admitted wistfully. "But some will have to stay and fight this battle the right way."

Their voices grew louder as they divided over the issue of fight or flight. I allowed myself a yawn, more from sleepiness than boredom. I was not bored; I was waiting to hear what they intended to do.

Finally, Sam, who Junior had termed a leader, spoke. "There's one question I done asked myself more than a hundred times," Sam said. "If the grass is greener everywhere else, how come people always move back to Pakersfield? Seems like they can't make it nowhere else. I can't stop nobody from leaving here, and I wouldn't even try. All I gotta say is good luck. I wanna leave here myself. But when I leave, whether it's on a bus or train or in a pine box, somebody gon' know I was here. They still think I'm a boy, and they don't ever have to know I'm a man, but one day they gon' know that Samuel Quinn was here."

"What are you planning to do, Sam?"

"I don't know that I got no plan, Junior. It's just these times we living in, man. The times say I gotta do something. You gotta do something, too. You all time writing them letters and talking 'bout education, but what good is that? We just a small town, and ain't nobody coming here to help us do nothing. Education ain't nothing but words, man. We gotta show 'em that we mean business."

"Yeah," Andy agreed. "I'm all for that."

"I'm with you, too, Sam," Junior said, "but you have to know what you want, what you're trying to accomplish, before you make a move."

"Okay," Sam consented. "I want what everybody else want. I want a job. I wanna drink from that fountain down at the courthouse. I want Andy to be a sheriff if that's what he wanna be. I'm tired of being on the back end of things like I just don't count. I wanna be able to move my mama outta this house, move her to East Grove or Meadow Hill. I wanna see Chadlow brought down, and I wanna feel like a man in this town. I want a whole lotta things, Junior. And if I can't get 'em, I wanna take one of them pencils of yours and erase this town off the face of the earth."

When Sam finished speaking, it was so quiet in the yard it seemed the others had left, but then Junior said, "All right, Sam. Let's start with the water fountain."

eleven

I t was the first Thursday in February, and I had lit the kerosene lamp and settled in an armchair to read a novel when I should have been doing my chores. I was no more than five pages into my reading when the sound of pounding against the exterior wall of our house startled me. The sound came again—an object striking rapidly against wood.

The boys were not home, and Tarabelle was asleep in Mama's room. I tipped out to the kitchen. I got Martha Jean's attention, and signed to her that someone was outside.

Keeping Laura and Edna close to her, Martha Jean followed me to the front door. I opened it slowly and peered out. The first thing I saw was an old, banged-up, brown car parked down on the dirt road. There was a man sitting behind the steering wheel, but I could not make out who he was.

As I turned my head to the left, I came face to face with a dark, stocky man who had a bushy beard and mustache surrounding thick, pink lips. He was about three steps away from the door, and I jumped back before I realized it was Harlell Nixon who owned the barbershop in the flats. Behind him, at the foot of the steps, was my mother. She did not look like a woman coming home from the hospital. She looked younger and healthier than she had appeared in months. In her arms, wrapped in a white blanket, was the newest addition to the Quinn family.

"Where's the dummy?" Mama yelled up to me. "Tell her to come out here and get this baby, and tell Tarabelle to get on out here, too."

Tarabelle ignored me when I tried to wake her. But when I told her Mama was home, she sprang from the bed, turning circles, and nearly tripped over her own feet. She was sleepy and confused, but alert enough to know that she was camping out in forbidden territory. She raked her fingers through her hair as she surveyed the room, then quickly straightened the bedcovers and stepped into her shoes.

I paused long enough to slide my book beneath the chair, and extinguish the kerosene lamp, then I went down to the yard.

Martha Jean was already holding the baby in her arms and a bottle in her hand. Harlell Nixon stood beside Mama, blatantly appraising Tarabelle, gripping a bag in his fat fist.

"Give that stuff to Tangy Mae," Mama said, and Harlell extended the bag in my direction. I took it, and stood there waiting for instructions until it became apparent that my mother had no words for me.

The man in the car rolled the window down. "Hey, Harley, y'all coming?" he asked.

"In a minute," Harlell called back, exposing large, tobacco-stained teeth. "You ready, Rosie?"

Mama nodded, and when she spoke her voice sounded weary. "C'mon, Tarabelle. I need you to go wit' me."

Tarabelle, who was still standing on the bottom step, shook her head slowly. "Mama, I can't go," she said. "Don't make me go."

"You got to," Mama said, in a tone that sounded apologetic.

"But, Mama, I done worked all day. Miss Arlisa say I'm doing good. I waxed the floors today, and I . . ." Tarabelle paused. "Mama, please . . ."

"Rosie!" Harlell barked when it seemed Mama was about to succumb to Tarabelle's plea. "You done had me running all 'round town today picking up thangs for you and that baby. I done lost customers 'cause of you. I come out to that hospital and brought you home just like you asked. Don't you go starting no stuff wit' me."

"Nah, Harley," Mama said, a forced smile on her lips, "we going."

She moved toward the car, and the man on the front seat got out and opened the door for her. Harlell stepped around the car and slid onto the front passenger seat. Tarabelle stood on the step and watched them until, without glancing back, Mama said, "Tarabelle, get in the car."

"Mama, please . . ."

"Get yo' goddamn ass in this car, now!" Mama ordered, and Tarabelle jerked from the force of the command. Her body seemed to convulse in a series of twitching motions before she stiffened her back and walked down to the car, her head high, her eyes staring straight ahead, and her face resembling chiseled stone.

The car pulled away in the direction of the outlying farmland, and I wondered where they were going. As I watched, the car suddenly braked and reversed along the road until it reached its original starting point. Mama lowered a window and stuck her head out.

"Her name is Judy," she said, as the driver shifted gears and the car sped off.

The bag Harlell had given me contained a blanket, four diapers, a card with two safety pins attached and two missing, two cans of Carnation milk, and a bottle of Karo syrup. I gave the bag to Laura and, without a coat or a clue, went in search of my brothers to warn them that our mother had been home, but I couldn't find them.

Footsteps disturbed my nightmare. I lay in darkness with my eyes closed, listening to my brothers sneak into the house, though there was no need for caution.

Less than an hour later, Tarabelle and Mama came home and undressed without a light. Tarabelle, after three weeks of sleeping on a bed, was back to her old spot on the floor; I had already prepared her pallet. She settled down, and I listened as her soft breathing changed to muffled sobs. In the distance, over on Fife or Canyon Street, someone's dog grieved with my sister.

When it seemed she would never stop, I tossed my blanket aside and stretched a hand across the inches that separated us. Tarabelle's back shuddered beneath my palm, but she did not pull away. I moved closer until I was sitting next to her. She raised her head and settled it on my lap, and I stroked her hair as tears rolled down my cheeks.

From the straw basket beside Martha Jean, little Judy pledged her solidarity by issuing a cry of her own, and in midnight darkness, I swam the stream of tears that connected me to my sisters, my ears ringing from the first cry I had ever heard from either.

twelve

Pots, pans, and bowls had been arranged throughout the house to catch the flow of a cold, steady rainfall. The rain had brought Sam and Harvey home early, just behind me and Wallace. Tarabelle was already in, her white dress soaked and her hair plastered to her head.

Someone, Martha Jean I assumed, had placed the three kitchen chairs and four of the milk-crate seats in the front room, making it almost impossible for us to stand by the stove to warm and dry ourselves.

Our mother, in a faded pink housedress, sat in an armchair, her feet bare and her legs crossed, a startling contrast from the day before. Her hair was pulled back in a ponytail and her lipstick was smeared across her left cheek. She held the wind-up clock that usually stood on a shelf in her room. She wound it and placed it on the round table beside the kerosene lamp, then she told us to be quiet and to sit down.

"Satan's in here," she said in a hollow voice, her gaze darting about the room. "While I was gone, one of y'all let Satan in my house. Who was it?"

No one spoke.

"Don't sit there like idiots. I wanna know who did it. Ask the dummy if she let him in here."

Harvey, who was sitting closest to Martha Jean, moved his fingers before her face, and she shook her head in fear and denial.

Mama rose from the chair, walked over to the wall of coats, and took down the one Velman Cooper had bought for Martha Jean. She flung it through the air and it landed on the floor in front of the armchair where Martha Jean sat holding Judy. Martha Jean curled over, shielding the baby with her upper torso.

"Satan's in here," Mama repeated with mounting fear in her voice.

Edna started to cry, and Mama spun around to face her. "Shut up. You want him to hear you?" she whispered, easing back to her armchair, glancing over one shoulder, and then the other.

She sat on the edge of the chair, poised to move quickly, and we followed her gaze to the leaking ceiling, to the corners of the room, and to the doorway that led into the hall.

"Mama, you awright?" Harvey asked.

"Shut up," she whispered, tilting an ear toward the hall. "Y'all done let Satan in here. I can't trust none of y'all." Her back stiffened, and she stared around the room at each of us. "What the Bible say, Harvey?"

"Honor thy mother." Automatically, Harvey gave the correct response. It had been instilled in him.

"What it say, Edna Pearl?" Mama asked.

"Honor thy mother," Edna whimpered.

"That's right, and y'all don't honor me. Y'all done brought Satan in my house just as sho' as I'm sitting here, and we gotta get rid of 'im." Her voice became conspiratorial. "We gon' sit here real quiet so he'll think there ain't no bodies to get into."

And the silence began.

And the sound of silence was frightening. Rain pounded the tin roof like a thousand demons marching for their master, and the roof yielded. Liquid curses splashed down upon our heads and into the waiting vessels. In the gray shadows of a rainy dusk, the clock on the table ticked rhythmically, but the hands never moved. They were stuck.

The angel Gabriel called to me, "Tangy, Tangy." His voice rattled the windowpanes. It whispered above and below the doorframes and through cracks in the walls. I could not answer him aloud but I thought, *Satan is not going to leave. The only way to get him out is to invite God in, and God is not welcome in my mother's house. I am going to die sitting on this milk crate in wet socks and slushy shoes.*

We shifted slightly and silently on our seats, we sighed, we sat.

Darkness filled the room until I could no longer see Sam or Tarabelle sitting on their chairs. It fell heavily over Wallace, Laura, and Edna.

Tick . . . tick.

My fingertips vanished.

The coal stove belched to the grumble of my empty belly and digested the last of its evening meal, then from the darkness came an angry voice that I recognized as Sam's. "Look here, Mama . . ."

There followed the sound of an object sailing through the air. It crashed against the back wall and shattered. And the sound of silence was missing a tick.

For hours we sat, until the beam of headlights rounded the bend down on the road. Judy began to cry, and suddenly the kerosene lamp illuminated the room. I blinked and saw my mother, milky-wet stains encircling her breast, glaring at the baby with pure hatred.

"Satan," Mama hissed. "He done crawled in that baby. Gotta get 'im out my house."

It was then that the front door opened and closed. Footsteps sounded in the hallway, and the angel of mercy appeared, wearing a wet, beige halo on her head, and carrying a dripping suitcase in her hand. She dropped the suitcase and leaned against the door frame, then shook her head, making no attempt to conceal her disappointment.

"Mama, you ain't dead yet?" Mushy asked.

Mushy removed her coat and searched along the wall for a place to hang it. She was wearing a light brown, tight-fitting skirt with a matching sweater, and a beige scarf tied around her neck. Her sandy-brown hair was tucked beneath a beige tam, and she wore small, white earrings clipped to her ears.

"What's going on here?" she asked, raising her arms and leaning back. "I don't expect all y'all to come running at the same time, but where's my hugs and kisses? I know y'all ain't forgot who I am in four years. Come on, Tan, give yo' big sister a hug."

At that moment I wanted to touch Mushy more than I wanted to breathe, but Mama gave no sign to release me from my crate. She sat back, grunted, and stared at her long lost daughter.

Mushy laughed nervously. "What *is* going on here?" she asked.

"We waiting on the devil to leave," Sam answered.

"Honey, the devil just got here," Mushy joked, winking at Sam. "Here I am in the flesh." She snapped her fingers and twirled around in the small space of the doorway.

"He ain't joking, Mushy," Harvey said. "We glad to see you, though."

"Oh, Mama," Mushy groaned, "you still up to that ol' stuff?"

Mama cupped a hand over her nose and let the tips of her fingers slide down across her lips and chin. She threw her head back and worked her fingers along the smooth skin of her neck, then she swallowed hard, and I knew that the devil was gone. My mother had swallowed him whole.

"It's a darkie, Mushy, darker than Edna, as dark as Tangy," she said sadly. "They say I can't have no mo'. It broke something inside me they can't fix. Had to take it out. Took everything out, said I couldn't have no mo', and all I got was a darkie."

For a moment, Mushy seemed lost in confusion, then her expression of bewilderment changed to one of amusement. She stepped from the doorway and into the crowded room, around pots and pans, until she stood over Martha Jean. She stooped down and picked up the coat that Mama had tossed there hours ago, then she reached out and touched Judy.

"So, she's dark, Mama," Mushy said, smiling down at the baby. "So what? You oughta kiss her little, black ass and be glad you can't have no mo'."

"You're drunk," Mama said angrily, and the spell was broken. We all knew it. We could feel recognizable anger replace incomprehensible insanity, and we began to move tentatively on our seats.

"I ain't too drunk to know you need to feed this baby," Mushy said. "This a hunger cry if I ever heard one."

"You so smart, you feed her," Mama shot back.

"I'll get her bottle," Wallace said, leaping from his crate before my mind or feet had a chance to respond to freedom.

We began to stand, stretching arms, rubbing rear ends, and waggling fingers. We crowded in on Mushy until she had touched us all. When we finally released her, she opened her suitcase and took out a white, silk blouse. She knelt beside our mother's chair.

"Look, Mama," she said, "I brought you something."

Mama examined the fabric, trailing her fingers along the small, pearl-shaped buttons, then she stared into Mushy's eyes. "Yeah, you brought me something," she said solemnly. "Did you mean to bury me in it?" She balled the blouse in her fist and walked stiffly toward her room, leaving Mushy to stare after her. After a moment, Mushy slumped into the chair Mama had vacated, and reached her arms out for Judy.

"She ain't nursing this baby?" Mushy asked.

"Wit' Carnation evaporated," Sam answered, stretching his arms and yawning.

"Mama don't touch her," Tarabelle said. "I ain't seen her touch her since she brought her home. That's Martha Jean's baby."

"I can't believe it," Mushy said, cradling Judy in her arm to feed her. "Mama always been big on saving things. Y'all mean to tell me she wasting all them gallons of free milk and buying milk from the store? It don't make no sense."

"Lotta things don't make sense," Harvey said. "Mushy, you let Tangy Mae feed the baby. You need to go in there and talk to Mama. Can't none of us do it. We didn't know 'til now that she can't have no mo' babies. You go on in there and talk to her."

"Okay," Mushy agreed reluctantly, "but when I come back, I want something to eat, and I wanna sit someplace where water ain't dripping on my head."

I gave Judy her bottle, and Mushy went in to talk with Mama, while the others moved crates and chairs from the front room, mopped rainwater from the floor, picked up the pieces of the broken clock, and prepared a late supper of sausage and rice.

thirteen

Mama was the first one awake the following morning, and gradually we all began to rise. We washed our faces over the waterbasin and tried not to get in each other's way. The rain prevented Harvey and Sam from going to the train depot, and me and Tarabelle from washing clothes, but Wallace, complaining that someone else should have to do it sometimes, still had to dump the night bucket.

I sat on my pallet and held Judy while trying to determine my mother's mood by the style of her hair. It was hanging loose down her back, and I figured, *Keep quiet, stay out of her way, we'll be all right.*

To my surprise, Mama appeared pleasant enough as she sipped her coffee and chatted with Mushy. "How long you gon' stay?" she asked. "I hope you ain't gotta run right back. It's been so long since you been home."

"I know, Mama," Mushy agreed. "I'll be here a week. That all the time I could get off."

"Mushy works in a hospital," Mama shared with the rest of us. "Just think, if I'd been in Cleveland, Mushy mighta been the one took care of me."

"Do you know how to deliver babies, Mushy?" Wallace asked, coming in and hanging his jacket on a nail.

"No," Mushy answered, and as she spoke she made an effort to remember her signs so that she could include Martha Jean in the conversation. "I work in the dietary kitchen. Biggest kitchen you ever wanna see, Wallace. No thermometers and bedpans for me."

"What's a bedpan?' Laura wanted to know.

"Well, it's kinda like the night bucket, only it's flatter, and it's for people who can't get out of bed," Mushy explained.

"Ugh," Wallace said, "I'd rather be in that big dietary kitchen, too."

"Mushy's a nurse," Mama insisted. "I can't wait to tell Janie Jay. She all time bragging 'bout that daughter of hers went off to New York to sew clothes for movie stars. I just bet that's what she doing. I can't wait."

"I ain't no nurse, Mama. Tan's gonna be our nurse," Mushy said, steering the conversation away from herself. "You still getting A's, Tan?"

"That's all she do is read," Tarabelle said. "She oughta get A's."

"That girl think she gon' spend the rest of her life in school, but I got news for her," Mama said. "She gon' get off her lazy ass and get a job."

Mushy gave me a look that said, sorry I got you into this, then she stood. "I'm gon' get outta here for a bit, Mama, and say hey to a few people."

"In this rain? Who you think want you tracking mud in they house in all this rain. You act like you ain't got no sense."

"I ain't got none, neither," Sam said, pulling his coat from the wall. "I'll walk wit' you, Mushy."

"Mushy, I thought you came to spend time wit' me," Mama said.

"I did, Mama, but I'll have time to spend wit' you. I'll be here all week."

Mama began to sulk even before Mushy and Sam left the house, and when they were gone, she kicked a foot in Tarabelle's direction. "You and Tangy Mae, get on up and go wash them clothes," she said. "Little bit a rain ain't gon' hurt nothing. It'll just rinse the clothes cleaner."

We worked in a relentless downpour and, during the entire time, Tarabelle never spoke a word. Mud covered our shoes, socks, and legs, and the area around the tub was slick from our tracks. At one point, Harvey stuck his head out the back door and told us to come in, but I didn't because Tarabelle refused to.

We pinned the clothes to the line, but the weight of extra water caused the line to sag and the blankets to drag on the ground. Tarabelle pulled the blankets down and washed them again. This time we folded them into thirds, and the pressure of the thick folds snapped the wooden pins, but we finally managed to hang them up, then we went inside to dry our hair and warm our bones by the kitchen stove.

About an hour later, Mushy returned. She entered through the back door, kicked off her muddy shoes, then rushed through the rooms to see where our mother was. Satisfied that Mama was napping, Mushy huddled us together at the kitchen table and told us we were going to a party.

"Tan, I'm gon' help you fix yo' hair," she said excitedly, "and y'all can wear something from my suitcase. Sam's gon' get us a ride, and we getting outta here and gon' have us a good time. We going to Stillwaters. Just don't say nothing to Mama."

My mouth dropped open and I glanced at Harvey. He was sitting with an elbow resting on the table, and he stared at Mushy as she spoke. Not once did he attempt to reason with her, so I assumed he wanted to go, and I knew I wanted to.

"Mama gon' kill us," Harvey said finally, a wide grin on his face.

Mushy stepped around the table, draped her arms over his shoulders, and kissed the top of his head. "So we have a good time before we die," she said. "The way I figure it, we'll . . ." She stopped mid-sentence.

We could hear Mama coming through the house. She paused in the front room to tell Laura and Edna to get their newspapers and crayons away from the stove. "I can smell that crayon melting, y'all so close to the damn stove," she scolded. "Y'all gon' end up setting this house on fire."

We could hear the crumple of the newspapers as Laura and Edna moved their coloring away from the leaking water and the stove. Then Mama appeared in the doorway of the kitchen.

"Mushy, was that you just come in my room?" she asked.

"Yeah, Mama, but I thought you was sleep. I didn't wanna wake you," Mushy said, transforming in the blink of an eye from scheming and conniving to sweetness and innocence. "I didn't get far before I thought about how you was right. I came to spend time wit' my mama, and that's just what I'm gon' do. Them other people can wait."

If Mama was aware that Mushy had been gone for hours, she didn't mention it. She settled in at the table and began to ask Mushy question after question about Ohio. A short time later, Sam stepped in through the back door and nodded at Mushy. He hung his coat, then pulled up a crate and sat between Harvey and Wallace to listen to Mushy's fabrications. Martha Jean worked at the stove, and I slipped away to join my younger sisters in the front room.

A little after dark, Mr. Frank's car pulled up outside and Miss Pearl struggled up the muddy bank, then rolled into the house breathing heavily. She held Judy for a second, used one edge of the baby's blanket to wipe rain from her face, then handed her back to Martha Jean. "You ready, Rosie?" she asked. "Time to get you outta here. Time for you to celebrate making it through that birth. For a minute there, it didn't look like you was gon' make it."

"What you thinking 'bout doing, Pearl?" Mama asked.

"I thought you might wanna come up to the house for a bit. Frank's got a fifth of gin, and Belinda and Calvin gon' drop by later, maybe a few mo' people. We can put on some records and let you get the shake back in yo' hips." Miss Pearl stuck her elbows out, tooted her rear end up, and began to shake her heavy hips.

We laughed.

Mama laughed, too. "Pearl, you know you a mess," she said. "Don't you shake my house down."

"Well?" Miss Pearl asked. "You coming or not? I got Frank waiting out in the car."

Mama massaged her abdomen through the pink housedress, and her tongue circled her colorless lips as she contemplated the invitation. Finally, she said, "I don't know, Pearl. Mushy just got here. She done come all this way to see me."

"Oh, shit, Rosie!" Miss Pearl exclaimed. "I ain't talking 'bout keeping you all week. Ain't gon' hurt nobody for you to get out for a bit. C'mon, girl."

"Okay. Just let me change my dress and put on a little lipstick," Mama said, and rushed across the hall.

Miss Pearl leaned toward Mushy, and whispered, "I'm gon' do the best I can, but I don't wanna get in no trouble wit' yo' mama. And who gon' be keeping a eye on this baby while y'all up there running wil'?"

"We already got that figured out," Mushy lied.

"Humph," Miss Pearl grunted. "You better have it figured out." She stepped away from Mushy, and as she did, her foot bumped a bowl of rainwater, spilling it onto her foot. "Goddamn!" she shouted, looking down at her feet. "Harvey, y'all need to do something 'bout that roof. Next clear day, y'all need to climb up there and fix that thang."

Standing against the wall behind the stove, Sam grinned. "It ain't our roof, Miss Pearl. This house belong to Mr. Poppy."

"Well, he ain't gon' fix it," she said. "That white man don't care if y'all drown in here. Can't you see that? He'll just rinse y'all out and rent to the next po' niggers come along."

"I heard that, Pearl," Mama yelled from her room. "The one thang we ain't is po', and the one thang we ain't never gon' be is niggers."

"Shit," Miss Pearl said, rolling her eyes toward the ceiling. "C'mon, girl. Frank out there waiting on us."

As soon as they were out the door, Mushy seemed to be everywhere at once. She opened her suitcase and removed several items of clothing, she stuck the flat iron on top of a stove eye, she examined my hair and pulled a comb through it several times, then she reached into her purse and withdrew two dollars. "Wallace, I'm gon' give you these two dollars to watch Judy and the girls," she said. "You think you can do that?"

"How come I can't go?" he asked, eyeing the bills, but not reaching for them.

"You ain't going, Wallace, so don't mention it no mo'," Harvey said.

"I'll watch 'em," Tarabelle said. "I can't go wit' y'all to Stillwaters no way."

"What you mean you can't go?" Mushy asked incredulously. "All day we been planning this, and now you say you can't go. You ain't gotta worry 'bout Mama. Miss Pearl gon' keep her up to her place 'til we get back."

"I ain't worried 'bout Mama. I just can't go up to that place."

She spoke with such loathing that it momentarily squashed my enthusiasm, but Stillwaters was a place for adults, and I wanted desperately to feel grown, if only for one night. I intended to stroll into the place feeling special and looking pretty in the nylon stockings and red sweater Mushy was allowing me to wear. I would be with Mushy, and nothing bad ever happened when she was around.

We were ready and waiting when our ride pulled up. I tipped through the muddy yard and down the bank to the car, trying to keep my shoes clean and the rain from kinking my hair again.

"Y'all remember Hambone?" Sam asked, after we were settled in the car.

The young man turned on his seat and greeted us with a nod. I returned his nod, then sat back and stared up at our house where the kerosene lamp exposed paper-covered windows, barely visible through the rain and darkness. For a moment the guilt of disobedience washed over me, then the car began moving, bearing me away from Penyon Road, and I made myself relax.

fourteen

Stillwaters Café was a long, wooden, T-shaped structure, ten minutes up the four-lane highway and five minutes down a narrow, dirt road that turned left onto a graveled drive. It stood at the far edge of a clearing, flanked by tall pine trees.

Hambone, showing expertise in maneuvering the car, had brought us here safely, pulling to the edge several times to allow other cars to pass, not once landing us in one of the wide ditches that saddled the road. He pulled into the lot and parked between two dark-colored pickup trucks.

Loud music drew us inside. Left of the entrance was a dim yellow light, illuminating a pool table, a jukebox, and a short, circular bar that enclosed a cooking area. To the right, under a red light, was a scattering of tables and chairs, and against the back wall, a platform where a band entertained the crowd with a rendition of "The Great Pretender." Deeper into the darkness, under a blue light, was a dance floor where several couples slowly swayed.

Mushy scanned the hall and waited for the music and applause to end, then she called out to a man behind the bar, "Fox." Once again in a louder voice, "Fox!"

A powerful-looking man, who could have been about fifty, craned forward trying to locate her voice. "Mushy?" he shouted in surprise.

Mushy shimmied out of her coat, revealing a skintight, V-neck, sleeveless black dress with tiny black bows stitched in at the hips. "It's me," she said, spinning around, "yo' Georgia peach back in Dixie, packaged and handled wit' care just for you, Fox."

"My God, girl," Fox grinned, stepping from behind the bar, a dirty white apron bunched around his waist. "Mushy, girl, you looking good." He embraced her in a hug that seemed to swallow her up, and she returned his hug and stepped away smiling.

"Don't you get that chit'lin' fat all over my dress," she teased.

"Nah, nah," Fox said. "We ain't having no chit'lins tonight. What you want, girl? I'll go back there and get you anything you want."

"Let's see," she said, pretending to think about it. "I want a ocean of gin, Fox. That's what my belly's calling for."

"Be right out, Mushy. Don't you go nowhere."

We settled at a table near the bandstand just as the band began to play a Chuck Berry tune. A few couples moved out onto the dance floor, and I watched them as my feet tapped the wooden floor beneath the table.

"You wanna dance?" Hambone asked, and I nodded. He was short, only an inch or two taller than I. He had a dark brown complexion, a square, hairless chin, and a flat nose. His appearance, I noticed, had not changed that much during his absence from Pakersfield. He, and his voice, were heavier, and that was all.

We danced, and when the song ended, he leaned toward me and said, matter-of-factly, "You're the smart one Sam is always talking about."

It pleased and surprised me that Sam had spoken of me to his friend. I smiled foolishly, not knowing how else to respond. When we were back at our table, Hambone sat next to me and stared until I began to feel uncomfortable. Fox had set our table up with bottles and glasses, and I toyed with an unopened bottle of beer.

"Tell me," Hambone said finally, "how does it feel to be smart and pretty at the same time? That must be an awful lot for a little girl like you to handle."

"I do all right," I answered, blushing.

Harvey, beer in hand, wandered off toward the pool table, and Mushy restlessly shifted on her seat, searching the room for familiar faces. Sam poured drinks from a gin bottle for everybody at the table, except me and Martha Jean.

Hambone swallowed the liquid in his glass and followed it by draining a bottle of Black Label beer. "You remember me?" he asked. "Your brother ever tell you anything about me?"

"I've heard him mention you."

"I know it was something good. You know, Sam is all right. He knows how to think." Hambone jabbed a finger at his head. "I like to be around smart people—people who can think."

I groaned inwardly, then reached out and swiped an open bottle of beer from the table. It was my first attempt at being an adult, and I wanted to have fun, not talk about being smart.

The band counted off for another tune, and a man appeared at our table to ask Martha Jean to dance. He stood there with a hand extended, and Martha Jean glanced at Mushy. Mushy pointed to the dance floor and moved two fingers swiftly about in circles. Martha Jean rose, took the man's hand, and followed him to the dance floor.

I nearly choked on the beer I had swallowed. "Mushy, she can't even hear the music," I shouted across the table when I was able to speak.

Mushy waved a hand in dismissal. "Let her dance, dance, dance," she said, raising her arm higher with each word. "She can feel the vibrations. She's done it before, Tan. You know that. She'll be awright."

"At Miss Pearl's house," I said, "but never in public."

Mushy paid me no attention. She moved out to the dance floor, leaving me staring after her, and I hadn't even seen who'd asked her to dance.

"Guess I'd better find me a partner," Sam said, pushing his chair back, and I was left sitting alone with a man who wanted to talk to me about being smart.

"You ever drink beer before?" Hambone asked, lifting a bottle and pouring the contents into a glass.

"No."

"I didn't think so. You let it set too long and it goes flat on you. Nothing taste worse than flat beer."

"Is that so?" I asked in an uninterested tone.

"You don't have no business in here drinking beer anyway," he said. "How old are you?"

It was a question he should have asked before he drove me to Stillwaters, so I did not bother to answer. I reached across the table, seized Mushy's glass and swallowed down a piney-tasting beverage, then fought the urge to retch.

Hambone watched with amusement. "Not what you thought, huh?"

I turned the glass up and swallowed down more just to shut him up, and to quench the burning sensation in the back of my throat.

"I've been wanting to ask a smart person about Pakersfield," Hambone said. "What do you think about this town?"

"I like it."

"Well, yeah, I know you like it. You don't have anything to compare it to, but that's not what I mean. What do you think about the way these white people treat you?"

"Mostly, they treat me all right."

"How's that?"

"Well, they give us a school. They supply our library with books, and they give us vaccinations in their library."

"Yeah, they do," Hambone agreed. "In the basement of their library. I remember that. You ever wonder why they give Negroes shots in the basement of a library?"

"It doesn't matter. We get the shots free, and that's what counts."

"You're not smart," he said coldly. "You're pretty, but don't ever let anybody tell you that you're smart again. You think they're doing so much for you? Why don't you try reading one of them damn books in that library, see how far you get."

He was right. I stared down at the table and could think of no response.

He touched my chin with a curved finger, and said, "Don't look so sad. It's all about what you can and can't do. Take your brother, Sam. Junior got him thinking he can make some changes by drinking from a damn water fountain."

"When?" I asked.

Hambone shrugged. "Sometime soon."

"Will you be with him?"

He stared at me, then said, "Probably. But if I'm gon' get my head busted, I want it to be over something more important than a drink of water. It ain't gon' work no way. The ones in positions to help them out, like the reverend and Mr. Hewitt, are too scared of these white people to lift a finger. That's where we have to start. We've got to bring the young and old together."

I was nodding my agreement when the music ended and Mushy returned to the table. "Did you see Martha Jean?" she asked breathlessly. "That's Walt Jones she dancing wit'. You remember him, Tan? Look at 'im standing over there trying to talk to her."

"Mushy!" I cried, springing to my feet and experiencing a wave of light-headedness. "You left her out there?"

"Sit down, Tan," Mushy said. "We out to have a good time. Let Martha Jean do whatever the hell she wanna do. It ain't gon' hurt nobody."

I did not make a fool of myself by charging the dance floor as I had intended, but I did not sit down, either, not until I saw Martha Jean emerging from the blue light into the red.

"Where's my drink?" Mushy asked, eyeing the empty space on the table in front of her, then the glass in front of me. "Girl, you done sit here and drunk my drink?" She laughed. "Tangy Mae, I don't wanna have to carry you outta here."

The band had fallen silent and they were now packing up their gear. Mushy turned on her seat and faced the platform, then she poured herself a drink, stood, and held her glass up toward the band. "Hey, where y'all going?" she called out. "I ain't heard no blues yet."

One of the band members, a chubby man who had done most of the singing, stepped to the edge of the platform and stared out at Mushy. "You got the blues, little mama?" he asked with a wink.

"I sho 'nuff got the blues, big daddy," Mushy answered, swaggering toward the platform.

"Your sister is something else," Hambone said, shaking his head in what I thought was disapproval.

Mushy stepped up onto the platform, and the band members unpacked their instruments and repositioned themselves. Mushy smiled down at the expectant crowd. "Y'all waiting on me to sang?" she asked, and a cheer of affirmatives rolled through the three degrees of darkness. "Well, I can't sang." She took a sip from her glass and held the glass up as if she were toasting the world. "I never could, but I got a sister out there can sang her little ass off. Come sang for these people, Tan."

Mushy was drunk or pretty close to it. For a moment I shared Hambone's sentiment, then I stood, tugged my black skirt up an inch, pulled the red sweater down over the rolled band of the skirt, and straightened, as best I could, my on-loan, sagging nylons.

"Sang 'God Bless the Child,' Tan," Mushy urged as she stepped down from the platform and I stepped up. "Sang it, Tan, 'cause I need God to bless me."

As the music began, I felt a warmth spread through me and I stared out at faces I could barely see, then I opened my mouth. My two dynamic voices fused. I sang with my own strong voice—the voice that made people shout at the Solid Rock Baptist Church, and I sang with the voice Martha Jean had left in our mother's womb—the voice I had stolen. I harmonized those voices perfectly, and I crooned for the love of my sister, "God bless the child that's got his own."

When the song ended, there was silence in the hall. I could see the people again, staring out and up at me. Sam stood just below the platform, and behind him was Harvey. I had done something to these people, but I wasn't sure what until Mushy raised an empty glass and said, "Didn't I tell y'all?"

The applause was thunderous. The chubby band member winked at me and asked if I would like to sing another song. I shook my head and floated back to my seat on a cloud of sinful pride as people praised my talent. I refused to feel guilty or afraid, even though I knew that I had brought attention to myself, and someone in the hall would probably tell my mother what I had done.

"Okay," Hambone said, after I was seated. "You're pretty and you can sing, but you're still not as smart as I thought."

"What you mean by that, Hambone?" Sam questioned. "Tangy Mae 'bout the smartest person at Plymouth school."

I knew what he meant, but the others waited for him to answer. Before he could get his first word out, though, Martha Jean leapt to her feet, knocking over two glasses, and startling us all. A voice from behind me said, "That was some real good singing, little sister."

I turned to see Velman Cooper. His processed waves had been replaced by a neat haircut. He was wearing blue jeans, and a sweater that appeared deep purple under the red light. Shamelessly, Martha Jean strode up to him and gripped his hand in her own.

"Hey, wait a minute, man!" Sam barked, as Velman leaned over and kissed Martha Jean fully on her lips. "Who the hell . . . ?"

"That's Velman Cooper," I answered. "He works down at the post office."

"And why is he all over Martha Jean?" Sam demanded.

I shrugged my shoulders.

"Take yo' lips off that girl and grab a seat," Mushy said lightly. "Last thang we need is you and Sam tearing the place up, and knocking over all the liquor. You start whupping Sam, Harvey'll have to jump in. And Lord have mercy if you start beating 'em both. I'd have to jump in, and as you can see I ain't in no shape to fight nobody tonight. So please, just sit down—right here next to me."

Velman pulled a chair from another table and placed it between Mushy and Martha Jean. Sam scowled at him, while Harvey watched with quiet amusement.

"So you work at the post office?" Hambone asked.

"That's Hambone," I said in response to Velman's questioning gaze, then I made introductions around the table.

"Andrew Freeman," Hambone said, giving his birth name and extending a hand across the table. "I'm interested in smart people. You must be pretty smart if they let you work at the post office?"

"Smart enough, I guess," Velman answered.

"Let me ask you, and this smart one over here," Hambone gestured in my direction, "what you would do if you worked all day for one of these rednecks in this town and they refused to pay you?"

"That depends," I said.

"On what?"

"On why they didn't pay me."

"Okay. They didn't pay you because they didn't want to, and because they don't have to. What would you do?"

"I wouldn't work for them again," I said. "I'd find myself another job."

"But you already worked," Hambone said bitterly. "You already earned the money that you didn't get. Don't you understand what I'm saying here?"

"You mind?" Velman asked Harvey, as he reached for the gin bottle on the table. Harvey shook his head, and Velman poured himself a drink. "Ain't nothing you can do about it," he said to Hambone.

"I'd expect a woman to say something like that, but you're suppose to be a man, nigger. You mean to tell me you'd just go out and work all day for nothing?"

"Not intentionally," Velman answered.

"What you want him to do, Hambone, if he don't get paid?" Harvey asked. "It's done happened to people before. And why we talking 'bout this shit anyway?"

Fox came over and placed another bottle of gin on the table. "Band chipped in and bought this for the singer," he said, and I noticed, for the first time, that the band was gone and the music was coming from the jukebox.

Mushy stood, somewhat unsteadily. "Dance wit' me, Fox," she whined. "They depressing the hell outta me at this table, and after I done come all this way to have some fun."

"Mushy, baby, much as I want to, I can't come out here and dance wit' you," Fox said. "What people gon' say when they thirsty and I'm out here dancing wit' you?"

"I'll dance with you," said a man who was sitting at the table across from ours. He stood, and I saw that it was Peter Swift. He was at least twenty years younger than Fox, and could probably dance a lot better. Mushy stumbled, regained her balance, laughed, then allowed him to guide her toward the dance floor.

"It's a damn shame," Hambone said, glancing around the room. "White man run us a hundred miles out into the boondocks just so we can dance and drink the liquor he makes. Colored man get caught making whiskey and they throw him in jail. He might not ever get out, and y'all know I'm telling the truth. This is the fucking wilderness. We have to go to the back doors of their cafés for a damn cheese sandwich, the back of their movie house to see them lily-white movies they make, and to the back of the line in their goddamn stores to buy a motherfucking bar of soap."

"You right, Hambone," Harvey agreed, "but that's life, man."

I was listening to the conversation, but I was also watching

Martha Jean. Her head was resting on Velman's shoulder and she was making signs with her fingers. She formed his name the way I had shown her, and to my surprise, he signed her name in return. A thought occurred to me, and I found it horrifying because I knew it had to be true. Martha Jean had been sneaking away from Penyon Road and going to the post office to meet with Velman. She must have done it while Mama was in the hospital and the rest of us were at school or work. They were too comfortable with each other for a single encounter.

"When I lived here before," Hambone said, "I thought this was the worst goddamn place in the world. Never dreamed I'd come back and be carrying suds buckets through town, washing the white man's windows."

"You doing better than me and Harvey," Sam said. "We working fields whenever we can get work." He turned to face Velman. "Man, you ever chopped cotton or hoed potatoes? You ever took a sling blade to a field where the weeds stand taller than any man alive, and the fields stretch clear 'cross Georgia, from sunup to sundown, and walk away wit' two dollars and a quarter in yo' pocket?"

He did not mention the part about turning the two dollars and a quarter over to his mother, but the unspoken words lay deep inside his brown eyes and the down-turned corners of his lips.

"I can't say that I have," Velman answered, easing Martha Jean's head from his shoulder. "But, you know, I just got here. I ain't planning on leaving no time soon, and the white man ain't causing me no trouble that I can't handle. When and if he does, I'll deal with it. I ain't gon' run."

"I'm wit' you," Harvey said. "I ain't going nowhere, either. Sam, I don't know who cheating you, but if I was doing all that work for two bucks, I wouldn't tell it. I ain't starting nothing, and I ain't going nowhere."

"Sam, you need to talk to you brother," Hambone said disapprovingly.

Sam grinned and slapped Harvey's back. "Hard to reason wit' a man in love, Hambone," he said. "That's Harvey's problem. He blinded by love."

"Who's in love?" Mushy asked, returning to the table and dragging Peter Swift along with her. "I'm glad to see y'all talking 'bout happy things, but y'all too late for me. I'm going over there to sit wit' Pete."

"How come Pete can't sit over here?" Sam asked.

Mushy smiled and glanced at Pete. "Awright," she said, "if y'all promise not to talk ugly. Who's in love?"

"Harvey," I answered. "With the undertaker's daughter."

"That makes sense," Mushy said. "Look at him sitting over there all cold and stiff, scared to laugh, and scared to dance." She stepped over to Harvey's seat and placed a kiss on his forehead. "Leastways you ain't scared of women. I remember his daughters. Which one you in love wit'?"

"Carol Sue," Sam answered. "But she don't want him to do nothing. I couldn't be bothered wit' a woman like that."

"That's why you ain't got no woman," Harvey said, and we all laughed because the girls in Pakersfield were forever chasing after Sam.

Mushy and Pete squeezed in between Sam and Hambone, and Mushy immediately reached for a drink.

"Ain't you had enough, Mushy?" Sam asked. "How much you gon' drink?"

Mushy placed an empty glass in front of Pete and poured him a drink, then she held her own glass out to Sam. "I'm gon' drink 'til I ain't got nothing in my pocket 'cept cab fare," she said. "Then I'm gon' drink 'til I can close my eyes and don't see my mama's face watching every fucking move I make. That's how much I'm gon' drink, Sam. I'm gon' drink 'til I can't feel shit. Hell, I might even drink myself to death. So what?"

The jukebox was silent and so were we. Laughter drifted through the smoke-filled room and dissipated over our table. The crowd was thinning, and I began to worry about the time. Mushy had said we would have to honk the horn four times as we passed the Garrisons' house to let Miss Pearl know it was safe to bring Mama home. What if Mama was already home?

Velman stood, walked over to the jukebox, and made a selection. He came back to the table and took Martha Jean's hand, and she rose to meet him. The voice of Little Willie John flowed from the jukebox as Velman and Martha Jean moved together under an orange glow where the lights met.

Mushy sipped her drink and watched, then she shook her head appreciatively. "Damn. Martha Jean done caught herself a dancer. Look at that boy move." She stood. "I'm gon' get me some of that."

"Leave 'em alone, Mushy," Sam said quietly.

"Come on," Pete offered, and led Mushy between the tables toward the jukebox.

"How about you?" Hambone asked. "You wanna dance?"

I did not want to, but I danced anyway because the song was too nice to waste.

fifteen

Storm clouds hung low over our heads, making the world much darker than it should have been at six o'clock in the evening. It was my fourteenth birthday, and it had not rained all day because that had been my wish early this morning upon awakening. We sat outside on the damp steps, huddled together against a chilly wind, eating Johnnie Cake cookies and discussing our mother's metal box.

"Money," Sam said. "I always thought it was stacked full of money that she was saving to buy a house. That's why I didn't mind giving my money to her. But it don't look like we ever gon' move outta here."

"Not if you waiting on Mama to get you out," Mushy said seriously. "I always thought it was full of cocks. I thought she castrated men and put their cocks in that box."

"Box wadn't big enough," Tarabelle mumbled.

"What box?" Wallace asked.

Tarabelle sighed. "Just a empty box, Wallace," she said. "Just a empty ol' box to hold over our heads. Wadn't never nothing in it. That's what I always believed, and I still do."

"I couldn't never think of nothing she coulda kept in it," Harvey said, twisting the top off a Mason jar of corn whiskey. He took a swallow, then passed it over to Mushy.

Mushy took a swig and looked out over the wet field of tall weeds across the muddy road. "Mama know Martha Jean courting that dancing man?" she asked.

"Martha Jean ain't courting nobody," Sam said.

"Yeah, she is," Mushy said.

"Tangy Mae all time putting her up to something," Sam accused, "but Martha Jean ain't courting nobody. Mama hear something like that, she'll skin 'em both."

"Why would I put her up to liking that ol' snaggle-tooth man?' I asked. "I can't stand Velman Cooper."

"It don't matter that you can't stand him, Tan," Mushy said with a laugh. "Time gon' come when you'll understand that it don't matter 'bout no teeth, no feet, no nose, no nothing. You gon' see some man and yo' heart'll try to jump outta yo' chest. You gon' feel like cotton inside, all soft and fluffy, and floating." She slapped Harvey's knee. "Ain't that right, Harvey?"

"Why you asking me?" Harvey asked shyly. "I ain't never felt nothing like that."

"I thought you was in love wit' Carol Sue."

"I ain't never once said I loved her. That was Sam talking."

"Well, I know love when I see it," Mushy said, "and Martha Jean is in love. Y'all think 'cause Mama walk around calling her a dummy that it makes her one. Martha Jean ain't no dummy. If she could hear, I bet she'd be just as smart as Tan."

"Y'all make me sick!" Tarabelle snapped. "Martha Jean ain't smart, and Tangy ain't either. Mama call 'em the dummy and the darkie. She say ain't neither one of 'em gon' ever get married. They gon' be right here. She gon' have to take care of 'em the rest of her life 'cause ain't no man gon' ever want 'em."

I was in the most dangerous spot in Pakersfield—on the top step of our porch, at the outer edge, next to Tarabelle. Sam and Wallace occupied the third step down, while Mushy and Harvey shared the fifth. I drew myself into a tight ball and wrapped my skirt and arms protectively around my knees.

Mushy took another swig from the Mason jar and glanced back

at us. "All y'all gon' be here the rest of yo' life," she said. "Mama gon' keep y'all here making you be whatever she wants you to be, long as you bring money in this house. She tried to keep me here, but I musta took after my daddy, whoever he is, God bless him. Mama had me screwing in every hayloft, field, and back room she could find. I never even knew what I was worth. One day I thought, screw *you*, Mama. I went out on my own and screwed my way right on outta Georgia."

Harvey, uncomfortable with Mushy's confession, lowered his head and asked, "Do you have to talk so nasty in front of Wallace?"

Mushy tilted her head in mock surprise. "Hell, he got a cock, ain't he? What's so nasty about screwing?"

"What if Mama hears you?"

"Harvey, I'm grown. Ain't you noticed I'm a full-grown woman?" She reached into the paper bag on her lap and brought out a large, round cookie. "Last one," she said. "Pass it up to the birthday girl."

I accepted the cookie and nibbled around the edge like a small child trying to make it last. Mushy tossed the empty bag into the air and I watched it drift. There was nothing to see on the road below. No pedestrians or vehicle had passed during the last hour, except Junior Fess walking from the farmland with his satchel tucked beneath one arm, and that had been more than an hour ago.

Mushy had called down to him, and he waved, then came up to the yard.

"Hey, Mushy," he said. "I heard you were back in town. How long are you staying."

"Not long. Where you coming from, out here at this time of evening?"

Junior turned and momentarily studied the road he had traveled. "People live out through there," he said. "It's hard to believe, isn't it? But there're colored people living out there, Mushy. The houses are so many miles apart that the people seldom visit each other, and they don't come into town that often. About six miles to the first house, three to the next. I go out once a week to let them know what's going on in the world."

"So what is going on in the world?" Mushy asked.

"I think you might know better than I do, Mushy," Junior

teased. He shifted his satchel from one arm to the other. "Well, I've got to make it on home," he said. "I'll catch you all later."

As the paper bag drifted, drifted, and finally landed silently in the mud, I found myself wishing that Junior had stayed longer with us. We could have used some stimulating conversation, something to draw us away from the metal box, and who's sick of this or that, and who is grown. When I glanced up again, Mushy was leaning against Harvey with her knees on the step, trying to kiss Sam.

Sam turned his head. "That stuff stinks," he said. "Mushy, you ought not drink that stuff."

"I know, and I ain't gon' drink no mo'. I think Harvey trying to kill me." She attempted once more to kiss Sam, but her elbow slipped from Harvey's shoulder and she wavered in a lopsided bow. Wallace and Sam held onto her while Harvey made a protective show with a hand against her back. His other hand held the Mason jar.

Mushy settled herself on the step. "Damn! I forgot about these steps," she said. "They move right along wit' you, don't they?" She was quiet for a moment, then said, "Sam, you'll be glad to know that I don't drink that much when I'm in Cleveland. As a matter of fact, I hadn't had anything for months, but when I stepped off the train and looked around Pakersfield, something said, 'Girl, go get you something to drink.'"

"Mushy, did you really think Mama was dying?" I asked. "Is that why you came home?"

"Nope. I knew she wadn't dying. She ain't never gon' die. She got too much to do. Mama gotta make sho' her pretty boys become proper, respectable field hands. And she ain't gon' rest 'til she turns Martha Jean into a meal-cooking, diaper-changing, mop-slanging ol' maid."

I fed off of Mushy's bitterness as I sat there thinking about trading in my books to make somebody's bed when I didn't even have one of my own. "She wants me to be a maid," I said angrily. "She wanted me to work for the Munfords, but they didn't want me."

"You gon' be a nurse, Tan," Mushy said, reaching for the Mason jar. "You gon' wear a white uniform and a cute little cap on yo' head, and you gon' come work wit' me." She took a drink. "What Mama gon' make you be, Tara?"

Tarabelle did not speak immediately. She stared down the rows of steps at Mushy's back, then she said, "Why don't you go back to Cleveland? We don't want you here. All you do is drink, and cuss, and laugh at everybody."

Her anger startled us all, and in the ensuing silence, her words hung in the misty air. Mushy stiffened, then turned slowly to face Tarabelle.

"Ain't no call for all that, Tarabelle," Sam said, but Mushy placed a hand on his knee to silence him.

"What's Mama making you do, Tara?" Mushy asked, her voice angry, her words slurred.

Tarabelle stood, backed up onto the porch, then reached for the door. Her hands fell to her sides. She turned from the door to the steps, and back again. She clenched her fists and looked over the porch and down into the gully. She was caged. Even I could see it. She wanted to flee, but there was no place to go.

"Oh, sweet Jesus, no," Mushy groaned. "Please, no."

"What is it? What's wrong?" Sam asked, reaching out for Mushy as she squirmed up the steps between him and Wallace, and past me. She reached the top and balanced herself against the porch wall, then extended a hand toward Tarabelle.

"Don't touch me!" Tarabelle snapped.

Mushy's hands dropped, then joined below her abdomen and began to claw as if trying to get at something too deep inside to reach. Her body seemed to fold over and shrink into the wall as she bitterly sobbed.

I did not understand this exchange between my sisters, but Sam stood and embraced the one who could be touched, until Mushy pulled herself together enough to say, "Tara, I'm gon' get you outta here."

For the longest time, we held a pose of untouchable, unspeakable confusion until it became apparent that we could not spend eternity on the front porch. One by one, we filed into the warmth of our mother's house, a silent, solemn troop.

Martha Jean stood in the doorway between the hall and front room. She held a finger to her lips, then cradling Judy in her left arm, she raised her right hand over her head, palm down. She cupped the hand over her ear, then pointed first to the front door and then to the kitchen.

"Oh, shit!" Mushy groaned.

Rank and file, we clumped off to the kitchen where we were willed to come. Mama was working dough between her fingers, staring down at a wooden bowl. Streaks of flour covered her arms and the dirty, pink housedress she had seen fit to wear once more, the one with the now crusty milk stains. Her hair stood up on her head like a ruined bird's nest teetering on a branch.

She began to speak without glancing up at us. "I done worked all my life for y'all. Never asked nothing in return, 'cept a little respect. I done put food in yo' mouths, and clothes on yo' backs. Done everything a good mother s'pose to do, and now y'all turn against me. I heard y'all out there talking 'bout me."

As she spoke, she scraped the sides of the bowl with one hand. She gathered the ball of dough into her palm, studied it for a long while, then dropped it back into the bowl, and brought her fist down. The dough gave a little pop as she knocked the air out of it.

"I never dreamed it would come to this," she said, "not when I nearly died trying to give y'all life. I fed all of y'all from my body." She tapped her chest for emphasis, leaving floury fingerprints across the milk stains. "I done went without so y'all could have shoes on yo' feet, just so y'all could be warm. I done spent many nights walking these floors wit' sick babies, getting ol' befo' my time. Long befo' any of y'all could walk or talk, I went out and washed clothes and cooked for the white folks, then come home and done the same thang for y'all. Now y'all turning against me."

Our mother stood at that rickety, old table, kneading guilt that she would later bake and feed to us in bite-size pieces. And I was determined to swallow mine without gagging or choking, although guilt has a stringy texture, like strands of hair in a bowl of Cream of Wheat.

"What the Bible say, Mushy?" Mama asked.

Mushy inhaled deeply and exhaled slowly. "Honor thy mother, Mama."

"Do you honor me?"

"Where the Bible, Mama? I ain't never seen no Bible in this house."

"Do you honor me?"

"Where's the Bible?"

"I'm yo' mother. I gave you life. Now, I ask you again, do you honor me?"

Mushy shook her head slowly, as if in resignation. Her chest heaved and her jaw tightened. Finally she deflated with a soft sigh and a bitter laugh. "Yes, ma'am," she said, and strode from the room with her eyes downcast.

Later, Sam and I found her sitting outside on a step, shivering, humming an old blues tune, and clutching an empty Mason jar.

Our somber mood seemed to bring out the gaiety in our mother. She washed the flour from her skin, brushed her hair, and changed into her new blouse, a plaid skirt, and high-heeled shoes, then she herded us along the dark, muddy roads to the Garrisons' house. We did not want to go, but we were given no choice.

There was a light on at the back of the Garrisons' house, and Squat, Mr. Frank's old sooner, stood in the backyard and stared out at us through a wire fence. He did not bark, probably because we were as familiar to him as the scraggly patches of grass covering his terrain.

Mama, seemingly contented with the world, sauntered over to the fence. She knelt down and poked a finger through an opening. "Hey, boy," she cooed, "you lonely back here all by yo'self?"

Squat took a step back, cocked his head to the side, and watched Mama's finger waggle inside the opening.

"No wonder you lonely," Mama said. "You ain't friendly enough. Come here, boy. Come here." She tapped a hand against her thigh and snapped her fingers, only to have Squat turn tail and lope across the yard.

"You lucky he didn't take that finger off," Mr. Frank said, opening the screen door and stepping out onto the porch. "Squat don't like cats, Rozelle, especially alley cats."

"What you mean by that, Mr. Frank?" Sam asked. "That's my mama you talking to."

Mr. Frank stared down at Sam, saw his clenched fist and heard the anger in his voice. He had no way of knowing that Sam's irritation stemmed more from swallowing guilt and being forced out into the cold, wet weather than from anything he had said.

"Just joking wit' her, son," Mr. Frank said, probably remembering, as I was, how Sam had opened Chester Riley's skull with an axe handle over a derogatory remark made about Mama. He would never do that to Mr. Frank—I hoped.

"Watch yo' manners, Sam," Mama said, stepping away from the fence and toward the porch. She placed a hand on the rail and tilted her head up to face Mr. Frank. Her back was to me and I could not see her expression, but something she did caused Mr. Frank's eyes to soften momentarily. He stared down at her, then chuckled softly.

"You know what I want, Frank," she said, "but you just like that ol' dog of yours. You oughta try to be mo' friendly. Where's Pearl?"

"In the house resting up for work tomorrow. Something you don't know nothing about."

"I work," Mama said lightly. "You just done forgot how hard I work. You so busy trying to be mean that you done forgot."

The muscles in his face twitched. His bushy eyebrows and mustache seemed to target then surround his short, thick nose as his eyes narrowed and grew dark under the shadows of his brows. He turned away from Mama, stepped down from the porch, and marched across the yard to stoop beside Squat.

"Nah, you don't like cats, do you boy?" he said, placing a hand on Squat's head.

Mama was smiling when she turned to face us. "My babies," she said. "My beautiful babies." She hugged Sam, then took Edna by the hand. As she led us around to the front of the house, I stared down at her heels and saw them break the mud with each step she took. I could never have walked so far on wet earth in high-heeled shoes. I would never have tried. That was one of the differences between me and my mother.

Miss Pearl was sitting in the living room on three-fourths of her sofa. Her feet were propped on a footstool, and she stared at a small television screen. "Hey, y'all leave that mud out there!" she shouted, after Mama had pushed the door open. We removed our shoes. Mama did not.

"Pearl, do you know yo' husband sitting out there in the mud wit' that ol' dog of his?" Mama asked. "I'm gon' yell out the kitchen door and tell 'im to come on in here wit' the rest of us."

We parted our huddle and allowed her to saunter by, her heels clicking across the hardwood floor, and her hips swaying. We could hear her opening the back door and calling to Mr. Frank.

Sam, his anger abated, apologized. "I'm sorry, Miss Pearl. I don't know what's wrong wit' Mama. We knew it was too late to be coming out here, but she wouldn't hear nothing we had to say. Made us all come."

"Hush, boy." Miss Pearl waved a hand to silence him. "You ain't gotta explain nothing to me. I been knowing Rosie since befo' you was born. I know how she is."

"I wish you'd tell me," Tarabelle said. "I don't ever know what Mama gon' do. I'm so sick of her, Miss Pearl, I could just scream."

"Now, girl, you watch what you saying," Miss Pearl warned.

"I know what I'm saying," Tarabelle snapped. "I'm sick of her. We all sick of her. She won't touch Judy. I ain't never seen a mother won't touch her own child."

"Maybe that's 'cause y'all don't give her a chance," Miss Pearl said, getting to her feet. She went out to her kitchen and left us to stare at each other and ponder her remark.

I lowered myself to the footstool and changed Judy's diaper, then I turned her on my lap where her head was resting against my knees so that I could gaze at her face. Sometimes I would gently squeeze the tip of her nose, trying to shape a point out of flatness. Miss Pearl had said that a baby's head and nose could be shaped if it was done early enough, before the bones formed. She had also said that the color of the baby's ears determined the color of the child. Judy was going to be black, maybe even a darker shade of black than I was.

"I got a big pot of pinto beans in here," Miss Pearl called out to us. "Y'all welcome if you want some."

We did not.

When she came back into the room, she was followed by Mama and Mr. Frank. She had a red package tucked beneath her arm, and a bowl of beans in her hand. She stood over me for a minute, looking down over my shoulder at Judy.

"Y'all hold that baby too much," she said, her mouth filled with beans. "After while y'all ain't gon' be able to put her down. I like babies, but you ruin 'em if you hold 'em too much."

"I try to tell 'em, Pearl," Mama agreed, "but you can't tell 'em nothing. They think that child a doll."

"She is a doll," Mushy said. She was sitting on the floor beside the coffee table, sweating corn whiskey and looking thoroughly miserable.

"You awright, Mushy?" Miss Pearl asked, reclaiming her seat on the sofa and handing the red package to me.

"I'm fine, Miss Pearl," Mushy answered, attempting to hold her head up and to smile, and failing at both attempts.

"It's the weather," Miss Pearl said. "It's done rained just about every day since you got here. You gotta eat if you gon' stay healthy in this weather. Here." She dipped her spoon into the bowl of beans and offered it to Mushy. "Beans warm you up from the inside out. This just what you need."

Mushy closed her eyes, then tried to get to her feet. "Open the door, Wallace," she managed to say before bumping the table and crawling for the front door.

"Um huh." Mama nodded her head. "That's what happen when they think they grown."

"Good Lord!" Miss Pearl exclaimed. She leaned forward, her spoon poised in the air, as she watched Mushy crawl through the doorway. "What's wrong wit' her, Rosie?"

"Ask Harvey."

Harvey, who had been keeping his distance from Mama all evening, leaned his head toward Mr. Frank's chair. He was sitting on the floor with his knees up and his hands cupped over them. He tried to speak, stammering over one word and slurring the next, "We . . . we . . . I, it was just . . . Mama, it was just . . ."

Miss Pearl dropped her spoon into the bowl and shoved the bowl toward Laura. "She's drunk?" Miss Pearl asked. "Rosie, we gon' have to give her some cast'oil and turpentine. Work that poison out befo' she get back on the train."

Mama chuckled. "Pearl, Mushy ain't no child. She probably got half it out already." Mama kicked off her shoes. "Tarabelle, go out there and make sho' Mushy awright," she said as she picked up one of the shoes.

Harvey's debilitated reflexes held him immobile as the shoe flipped, heel over toe, the distance of the room. Drunken sobs of relief escaped him as the shoe sailed past its target and struck Sam, who was sitting against the wall behind Harvey. Sam touched his fingers to his head.

"Stupid!" Mama accused. "Sam, you mean to tell me you ain't got sense enough to move when something flying at yo' head? I shoulda threw the damn thing at you."

"Rozelle, you gon' hurt one of these children one day, you keeping acting like that," Mr. Frank admonished. "And don't be throwing stuff in my house. You coulda hit that baby."

"Tangy Mae, go on and open yo' present," Mama said, ignoring Mr. Frank.

I handed Judy to Martha Jean, and ripped the red paper from my gift.

"How you like 'em?" Miss Pearl asked.

Every year, for birthdays and Christmas, Miss Pearl gave us the same thing—a pair of white socks wrapped in red crepe paper—and we always appreciated them. I had a suspicion that someone on Meadow Hill gave them to her, and she held on to them for these special occasions.

"I like them," I answered, as I did every time she asked that question.

"Like what?" Mushy asked. She stepped through the doorway looking disheveled, but walking upright. She took a seat on the arm of the sofa while I held my socks up in answer to her question.

"That's the one thing we could always count on, Miss Pearl," Mushy said affectionately. "No matter what the day was like, we always knew you'd have us a present. I miss that."

Miss Pearl reached out and touched Mushy's hand. "You awright, girl?" she asked. "I thought we was gon' have to give you cast'oil."

"Come on now, Miss Pearl," Mushy said, glancing over at Mama. "I'm my mama's child. If I can't hold a little liquor, I ain't got no business calling myself a Quinn."

"What's that s'pose to mean?" Mama asked.

"Means you a good teacher, Mama," Tarabelle said from her stance in front of the door.

Up came the other shoe but too slowly to catch Tarabelle as she side-stepped. It smacked the door, then fell to the floor with a light thump. Harvey belched something resembling a laugh, and Laura giggled. Mama eased to the edge of her seat. She was preparing to strike but in which direction I could not tell.

"Mama," Mushy said, moving over to kneel beside our mother's chair, "when I was outside, I was thinking 'bout that winter when everything froze up. You remember? We couldn't get down the steps 'cause they was covered wit' ice."

"Get away from me, Mushy," Mama snapped, then she turned toward me, but spoke to Miss Pearl. "Pearl, did you know our quiet, little birthday girl can sang. I hear she sangs the blues like an angel." Her voice became harsh. "Stand up and sang for us, Tangy Mae!"

"Cut it out, Rozelle," Mr. Frank pleaded, but Mama ignored him again.

"Tangy Mae, I hear you sang right pretty for a bottle of gin. Is that right? Did you go out and shame me for a bottle of gin?" Her head appeared disembodied, floating toward me until I could see the dark circular outline of her throat. "Get yo' black ass up and sang. Now!" she barked.

I stood, my mouth so dry I could not swallow the lump in my throat that was threatening to choke me. I opened my mouth and began to sing the first song that came to mind. It was a Clovers' tune that I butchered unmercifully, but Mama had no shoe left to throw and I was safe for the moment.

When I finished, Miss Pearl was the only one in the room looking at me. "Y'all shoulda tol' me if y'all wanted to hear some music," she said. "We coulda put on some records 'cause that sho' ain't how that song s'pose to go."

sixteen

"It's a shame," Mama said, as she stood in the doorway and watched Richard Mackey drive off with Mushy. "That boy got a wife. Ain't no telling what people gon' say."

I couldn't see how it mattered since Mushy would be on her way back to Cleveland by this time tomorrow. But I respectfully listened to my mother rant, finished my homework, then stretched out on my pallet and fell asleep feeling depressed and already missing my sister.

At some time during the night, rain fell from the sky and awakened me with a constant and annoying drip against my face. I sat upright and heard a muffled giggle from the center of the room.

"Mushy?" I questioned.

"It's me, Tan," she answered. "I was just sitting here wondering who was gon' wake up first. I had my money on Edna. That rain's giving her a bath over there, and she sleeping right through it."

I couldn't see Edna or Mushy, but I stretched my arm over to where I knew Edna slept, and felt rain splash against my wrist in heavy drops. "What time is it?" I asked.

"It ain't no time, Tan. It's just almost time," Mushy answered.

"You ever notice that—how it's always just *almost* time? It's almost time for Harvey and Sam to get ready for work, only they can't work in the rain, can they? It's almost time for you and Wallace to get ready for school. It's almost time for Tarabelle to go to work, and it's almost time for me to leave, but not quite." She laughed. "To tell the truth, Tan, I don't know what time it is. It's just morning and that's enough."

Mushy was talking in riddles, which made me wonder if she had spent the night drinking with Richard, and if they had gone out to Stillwaters. I scooted forward to escape the drops of rain that pelted me. Laura stirred, then yanked at the blanket I was dragging away from her. Mushy laughed again.

"I'm not going to school today," I said. "I want to be here when you leave."

"What's Mama gon' say?"

It was my turn to laugh. "Mama doesn't care whether I go or not. She thinks I'm too old to go to school."

Mushy was silent for a moment, then, in a dispirited voice, she said, "Tan, we need some light. I'm gon' scream if I don't get outta the dark. I can't stand it. Listen to that rain. I used to like that sound, but I can't stand it now. Rain and darkness. I need some light, Tan."

There was a quiet desperation in her request that saddened me. I could not stop the rain, but I crawled over to the table and felt around, then with the flick of my wrist and the lift of a glass cylinder, I brought light into the darkness.

Tarabelle's head rose from folded arms. "Go back to sleep," she mumbled angrily. "What time is it anyway?"

"It ain't no time, Tara," I answered. "Mama broke the time last week, don't you remember?"

"Silly," she said, and pulled the blanket over her head.

Mushy covered her mouth and laughed. I slipped out of my wet gown and into a dress, then together we went out to the kitchen carrying the kerosene lamp.

While I pulled out pots and pans to place under leaks, Mushy made herself comfortable on the floor between Harvey and Sam. She was still wearing her red dress, but her makeup was gone, and she looked younger and more innocent than the night before.

"Bring Judy in here," she said. "She can't move outta the rain by herself."

With Judy and her basket in my arms, I returned to the kitchen to find Harvey up and building a fire in the stove, and Mushy in his spot between the blankets.

"When it rains in Cleveland," she said, "I find myself somebody to sleep wit'. I don't like being by myself."

"We know that," Sam teased. "Mushy, you'd talk to a rattlesnake if you thought he'd talk back."

She ignored him. "There's this boy in Cleveland wants to marry me. He been asking for two years, but I keep telling him to wait."

"Now, Mushy, you know that's a lie," Sam said with a chuckle. "Ain't no man gon' chase after the same woman for two years."

"His name is Curtis," she went on. "He works at the hospital, too. I like him, but sometimes I feel like I want somebody different."

"I know what you mean," Harvey said.

"You tired of Carol Sue?" Sam asked. "She's a pretty girl, but I can see how you'd get tired of her. She don't want you to do nothing."

"I ain't tired of her," Harvey said. "It's her daddy that bothers me. Sometimes I wanna see her, but I don't wanna go up to that house 'cause I know her daddy gon' be there asking me what I'm gon' do wit' my life—like I'm s'pose to know—like I got some choices in this world."

Mushy sat up. "Tell him to go to Hell. You ain't courting him. You courting Carol Sue."

"Same difference," Sam said, and winked at Mushy.

"You know what," Mushy said. "If I had twenty dollars to spare, I'd buy Sam some sense, and I'd buy you a backbone, Harvey. That ain't to say you won't stand up to a man, 'cause I know you will, but you let women run all over you. Take Mama for instance. You ain't never been able to stand up to her."

"What would you buy me, Mushy?" Wallace asked.

Mushy leaned across Sam's outstretched form and kissed Wallace on the tip of his nose. "I wouldn't buy you nothing, Wallace. You perfect just like you are. Maybe you can talk to these brothers of yours."

"They won't listen to me."

"Harvey, think about this," Mushy said. "If Mr. Dobson didn't want you seeing Carol Sue, then you wouldn't be seeing her. All he gotta do is say the word, and she'd roll over and do whatever he say. That's the kinda girl she always been. You marry Carol Sue and you gon' screw on Tuesday nights wit' the lights out, around the crotch of cotton bloomers, and you'll know ain't nothing else coming for a week."

"Hell, that'd be a treat for Harvey," Sam laughed.

"Mr. Dobson see something in you he likes," Mushy rushed on. "It ain't money and it ain't smarts. Maybe he like yo' looks and think you can make pretty grandchildren for 'im. Maybe he like that you already trained. Don't get mad, Harvey, but you know what I mean. You already henpecked. You the type of man would bring yo' money home and give it straight to Carol Sue. That's all you know."

Harvey wiped a hand across his forehead, leaving a thin line of coal dust on his skin. "They want me to come work at that funeral home," he said. "That's what her daddy wants, but Archie wants me to work wit' him. He say the government making 'em build a new school for Negroes. He wants me to work wit' him when it's built. He says they're gonna need two janitors, and he can get me on."

"Nah, Harvey," Mushy whined. "I want you to come to Cleveland. I want all y'all to come. I'm gon' send for Tara first, then the rest of y'all. Archie Preston ain't nothing but a cigar-smoking, pot-bellied, old fart. I know he s'pose to be yo' daddy, but he ain't never done nothing for you."

"Mushy right. How you gon' trust somebody who just walk up to you and say he yo' daddy. Hell of a thang," Sam said with amusement. "What else he been telling you."

"Not much," Harvey answered. "Every time I mention Mama, Archie gets this puckered look like he got something real sour in his mouth. He don't never say nothing bad about her, he just don't say much of nothing at all."

"Screw him," Mushy said.

"Yeah," Harvey agreed half-heartedly. "He ain't nobody. Ain't got nothing to offer me, not even a name."

"He offering you a job, boy," Sam reminded him.

"Maybe," Harvey said, "but I ain't seen no school going up nowhere. Could be just talk."

"No, it's true," I said. "Mr. Pace told our class that we're getting a new school. They're going to build it on that land behind the church."

"Hambone mentioned something about it, too," Sam said. "He said they either got to build one or let the Negroes go to school wit' the whites. Wit' a choice like that, what you think they gon' do?"

"So that's settled," Mushy said dejectedly. "Harvey gon' spend his life in Pakersfield being a janitor, working wit' his daddy and living wit' his mama and trying to keep the two from meeting. Hell of a life if you ask me."

"I don't know what I'm gon' do, Mushy," Harvey said. "I don't know that I can sit around here waiting for somebody to build a school. That might take a long time."

"So you gon' marry Carol Sue?" Sam asked.

"I don't know what I'm gon' do."

The conversation died on that note, and Wallace rose from his pallet, stepped into a pair of blue jeans, and went out to the front hall. Tears sprang to my eyes.

Mushy sat up and pulled Judy's basket closer to her, and I closed my eyes and visualized the routine of our household, one step ahead of reality.

In less than a minute, Wallace would return to the kitchen with the night bucket in his hand, Martha Jean following behind him. He would pick up the water bucket, and Martha Jean would open the back door.

"I know something about the midwife," Wallace baited. "Y'all wanna know?"

I opened my eyes and saw him standing there with the two buckets. No one took the bait, and I could not because I was on a higher plane, but low enough to sense we were missing something significant. I closed my eyes again.

Martha Jean would take the only two pots that were not collecting raindrops. She would wait for Wallace, then she would start grits in one pot and water for coffee in the other. After the coffee water was ready, she would warm a bottle for Judy.

My eyes and the back door opened simultaneously, and Wallace was back with the water. I closed my eyes again.

Where's my coffee?

"Where's my coffee?" Mama shouted from the comfort of her palace, and our day had officially begun.

Our mother's presence in the kitchen had an unnerving effect on us. It sent my brothers out early into a pouring rain to loiter at the train depot where they would wait to say their farewells to Mushy. Tarabelle, before she left for work, sailed an urgent plea over Mama's head to Mushy, to which Mushy nodded, ever so slightly, a promise.

"Put that baby down," Mama said to Mushy over the rim of a chipped coffee cup.

The tension in the kitchen was smothering. Edna, Laura, and Martha Jean ate their grits in silence and with synchronized movements—spoon up, spoon down, chew, chew, swallow. I couldn't eat.

The blankets had been rolled, and Mushy sat on one bundle with Judy's basket at her feet. She kept fussing over the baby and would not meet Mama's stare.

"You know that boy's married," Mama said flatly. "You ain't got no business staying out all night wit' no married man."

Mushy said nothing.

"I heard you sneaking in here this morning. I didn't raise my girls for people to be talking 'bout 'em. Ain't you got no shame, Mushy?"

"Mama, I just wanted to sleep on a bed. I ain't used to sleeping on the floor no more," Mushy said. "It makes my shoulders hurt."

"Humph," Mama snorted. "So you just waltz into town and find yo'self somebody's husband to sleep on?"

Mushy glared at Mama, then she balled her hands into fists and pressed them against the roll of blankets. "Richard Mackey is a big, dumb, slow-talking man that I ain't got no need for. If I wanted him, he'd be packing a bag by now. But I don't want him, so let's just drop it, Mama."

"He's a handsome man wit' a good job," Mama said. "You just a slut, Mushy, and a cheap one at that."

Mushy lowered her head, pressing her chin against her chest, then her eyes rolled upward and she said, "How you gon' sit there trying to judge me when I'm the one person know just how low-down and dirty you are? Don't you dare talk to me about sleeping wit' nobody's husband. You know something, Mama? If you was anybody else, I'd get up from here and kick yo' ass."

Mama took another sip of coffee. "Pretend I'm somebody else," she said as she tossed the remainder of the coffee at Mushy's face.

On a crate, as far away from my mother as I could get, I saw the hot, brown liquid depart the cup, linger indecisively in midair, then accelerate in a lopsided flight. It landed in a soundless crash against Mushy's startled face.

I rose to see if coffee had splashed on Judy, and Martha Jean moved frantically toward the basket, but Judy was safe.

Mushy gave a loud gasp, followed by a short scream, then she began to rub at her face with both hands. She rose from the blankets and stormed out of the kitchen, as Martha Jean and I followed.

Mushy snatched her coat from a nail, grabbed her suitcase from the floor, and fled our mother's house with coffee dripping from her hair. I stood on the front porch beside Martha Jean and watched Mushy trudge up the muddy road with her suitcase banging against her leg.

From that moment, and for the next two days, we were forced to listen to our mother's ambivalent sobs as she wept for a child she truly loved—and hated.

seventeen

In my daydreams, Plymouth School stands atop the highest mountain in Georgia. A paved road runs up one side, levels off in front of the school, then runs down the other side, past the football field, and on into oblivion. In reality, my mountain is just one in a series of small hills that, when combined, forms Plymouth.

During the lunch recess for the upper grades, I sat with my daydreams and my best friend, Mattie Long, at the top of the bleachers overlooking the football field. Below us, near the bottom, Edith Dobson and her circle of friends ate their lunches and talked the way they always did, but today, for some reason, they seemed to draw Mattie's attention.

"I'd like to pull her hair out by the roots," Mattie said. "She's having a party. That's what they down there talking 'bout. They been whispering 'bout it all morning. I can't stand her."

In the section of bleachers across from us, Jeff Stallings sat with his elbows resting against the concrete behind him. He seemed to be studying the sky, or maybe lost in a daydream of his own.

"Mattie, what do you think of Jeff Stallings?" I asked, partly trying to pull her attention from Edith, but mainly because I wanted to know.

"He just another nasty ol' boy," she answered. "I think he strange."

"He's smart," I said in Jeff's defense.

"He strange."

"Okay, but do you think he's cute?"

"Boys ain't never cute," she said, glancing over at Jeff. "They s'pose to be called handsome, but I ain't never seen no handsome one."

"What about Harvey and Sam? All the girls think they're cute— I mean—handsome."

"They look like white boys," she said, frowning at me. "That don't mean they handsome. It just mean they got light skin."

Laughter rose from the lower bleacher as Edith and her friends packed away the remains of their lunches. The boys on the field continued to run with their football, but other students were beginning to make their way back toward the doors of the school.

"You like him?" Mattie asked.

I turned once more to glance at Jeff. "Yeah, I guess I like him," I said. "He's always real nice to me."

"Too bad," Mattie informed me. "He's a senior, and he ain't think-ing 'bout you." She reached down into her sock and pulled out a stolen stick of white chalk. On the concrete between our feet, she scribbled, TQ + JS. "This 'bout close as you gon' get to him," she said.

I was trying to erase the initials from the concrete with the sole of my shoe when Mattie nudged me. She glanced toward the aisle, and I turned in that direction to see Edith smiling down at me. I covered the scribble with my shoe.

"Tangy, I'm having a party on Saturday," Edith said. "I'd like for you to come. You can stay overnight if you want."

The heel of Mattie's shoe pressed hard against my toe as she prompted me to refuse the invitation. "I'll have to ask my mother," I said.

"I'm sure she'll let you come," Edith said, "after all, we're almost family. My mother says if your manners are anything like Harvey's, you're welcome at our house any time."

Mattie sat still until Edith and her friends were out of the aisle and back in the schoolyard, then she bumped my shoulder roughly with her own. "Why didn't you just tell her no?" she asked.

"Maybe I wanna go."

"Well, go then. They gon' pick at you. That's the only reason she invited you."

The bell rang, signaling the end of our lunch recess. I sat a moment longer, watching Jeff stand and stretch, then I joined Mattie for our walk back to class. I compared her appearance and my own to that of Edith and her friends. There was actually no comparison. Despite all the washing and scrubbing every Saturday, my blouse was dingy, and the single skirt and two dresses I owned always hung limp and wrinkled on my frame.

Mattie was no better. She had the one dress that would not hold a hem. No matter how often she repaired it, the thread always unraveled and the hem pouched at her knees. The strings in her shoes were broken and knotted into stubs, something I had not noticed before the invitation. She stood about three inches taller than I, and I figured she must have gotten her height from her father, along with the short, kinky hair that she never took a hot comb to.

"I'm not going to the party," I said.

Mattie smiled. "I knew you wouldn't go without me."

I would have gone, though, because I liked Edith, regardless of how Mattie felt about her.

We entered the building through the main doors and moved swiftly across the lobby. It was a large area that served as an auditorium by placement of folding chairs, a gymnasium by removal of folding chairs, and a lunchroom when the weather kept us indoors. Opposite the main doors, at the far side of the lobby, was a small stage with a podium that stood against drawn wine-and-gold curtains. It was where I would stand to give my graduation speech—another one of my daydreams.

After school, I walked with Mattie until we reached her house on Cory Street in Plymouth. Usually, at this time of the afternoon, her mother would be in the side yard taking clothes from the lines, but today she wasn't there. Mrs. Long was the smallest adult I had ever seen. She spent her days washing and ironing clothes, and eating Argo starch straight from the box. Her lips were perpetually white, and she had a lazy left eye as a result of too many beatings. Mr. Long had a reputation of being one of the meanest drunks in Pakersfield.

Mattie's sister, Tina, was standing beside the steps when we entered their yard. She had a thumb shoved into her mouth, and stood with her head bowed. On the porch, Mattie's younger brothers, Lobo and Bennie, were giggling and peering inside the house through a front window.

Tina removed her thumb and glanced up at Mattie. "We can't go in," she said. "Daddy's at it again."

"Drunk?" Mattie asked.

Tina shook her head and shoved her thumb back into her mouth. She was ten—too old to be sucking her thumb.

Mattie raced up the steps, shoved her bothers away from the window, and looked inside. She stood for a minute with her hands on her hips, then she kicked the front door several times, and yelled, "Dogs! Nothing but dogs!"

In Plymouth, the houses were set close to the ground and the porches were small. There were only four steps leading up to Mattie's porch, and I stood at the bottom watching her. Her anger was unsettling and I felt awkward witnessing what amounted to a tantrum. Her hands struck the heads of her brothers in a series of loud slaps, then she grabbed them and roughly pulled them toward the steps.

"Sit here!" she barked. "Don't go back to that goddamn window, or I'll break yo' arms. Y'all know better." She hit them again until they were both holding their heads and crying.

When she stepped back into the yard, I found it difficult to look at her. "I've got to get on home, Mattie," I said.

"I know," she said, and her voice was calm, as if I had only imagined her rage a few seconds ago. "I'll walk wit' you as far as Duluth Street."

As we began to walk, I stole a glance back at the house and saw Mattie's little brothers sitting on the steps watching us, and Tina standing in the yard sucking her thumb. I wondered what Mattie had seen through the window, but I knew better than to ask.

"I ain't going back to school next year," she informed me as we reached the corner of her street and turned onto Lawson Street. "Daddy say I ain't got to, but Mama want me to go. I'm sick of school."

"What will you do if you quit?" I asked.

"I don't know." She shrugged her shoulders. "Get a job or something, I guess."

"I don't want you to quit, Mattie. I want us to graduate together."

She laughed. "What make you think you gon' graduate? I thought you said yo' mama was gon' make you quit."

"I'll find a way to go," I said, and was surprised by the bitterness in my voice, and the anger I suddenly felt toward my best friend.

I made another comparison. I compared Mattie's life to my own. She had obvious advantages, which included a smaller family, two parents, and a mother who encouraged her to attend school. The main advantage, though, was the beatings. In Mattie's house they were fierce and frequent, but only bestowed upon her mother.

"I can't see where it makes no difference," she said. "After you finish school, what you gon' do? You'll get a job doing the same thing somebody doing that ain't never went to school. My daddy say a colored woman ain't shit. He say they ain't good for nothing. Can't do nothing but stand around putting a whole lot of weight on a man."

"We can teach," I said. "And Mushy works in a hospital. There are things we can do, Mattie."

"Mushy don't work in no hospital in Pakersfield. I think my daddy right, so what's the use going to school?"

I fell silent, thinking of the number of people who thought like Mattie. The first-grade classrooms, of which there were two, were filled to capacity every year, but by the time those students reached the seventh and eighth grades, their numbers had dwindled by nearly a third. Each year, the graduating class ranged between ten and twelve students out of the seventy or so who had begun first grade.

". . . so I kicked her in her back," Mattie was saying. "She was sitting there, too beat up and tired to cry, and it made me sick. So I went over and kicked her in the back. I was shame later, but sometimes I just get sick of it."

"What are you talking about?" I asked. I was aware that Mattie had been speaking, but I hadn't been listening to her. She had my undivided attention now.

She stopped walking and turned to face me, then she gave an irritable sigh before speaking again. "I'm talking 'bout my mama, yo' mama, and my daddy. Mama all time saying how Daddy taking her money and giving it to yo' mama. Every time she get mad, she say mean things 'bout Miss Rosie. And every time, Daddy beats her up. Mama don't know when to keep her mouth shut."

"Did you say you kicked your mother?" I asked incredulously. "Mattie, you kicked your mother?"

"Yeah, I kicked her, and it wadn't the first time. I told you I was sorry after I done it, but she makes me sick. If she gon' say all them things to Daddy, she oughta be ready to fight, but she won't even hit back."

"Why does Miss Lucille think your daddy is giving money to my mother? My mother never has any money."

Mattie gave a bitter laugh—a sign that she had not left all of her anger on the front porch of her house. "How she pay the rent then? How she buy food and stuff? And she got all them fancy clothes like some white woman. My mama say half the men in Triacy County pay yo' mama's rent. She say Miss Rosie do nasty, filthy animal things wit' men, and they give her money to do it."

"Then I'm glad your daddy hit her," I said angrily. "I hate your mother."

I didn't truly hate Miss Lucille, but I had said it, and it was too late to take it back. I dropped my books to the ground and stepped back, keeping my gaze on Mattie. I assumed the stance that Tarabelle always took when she boxed with Sam, and I brought my fists up, ready to jab.

Mattie stared at me, then she grunted. "I ain't fixin' to fight you, Tangy. I hate her, too. Leastways, I hate her most of the time."

She resumed walking, glancing back at me several times, waiting for me to catch up. I snatched my books from the ground and followed. After a while we were walking side by side as though nothing had happened. I glanced over and saw that she was looking at me, a half-smile on her face, but I could not return the smile. We reached the library on Duluth Street and Mattie stopped. Neither of us knew what to say to the other.

"Well," Mattie said.

"Well."

"See ya," she said as she turned for home.

"See ya," I echoed.

eighteen

Our first correspondence from Mushy was delivered by Velman Cooper nearly an hour after the post office had closed. He stood on our porch, shifting his weight from foot to foot, holding a white envelope in his hand. There was a broad grin on his face as he nodded a greeting to Mama.

"Evening, ma'am," he said. "I got a letter here for Miss Martha Jean Quinn."

Mama glanced at the envelope in his hand. "You work for the post office?" she asked suspiciously.

"Yes, ma'am."

"Um hum." She nodded her head slowly. "Since when they start delivering mail out here?"

"No, ma'am," Velman said, and gave a short laugh. "I just saw this here letter in the box and thought I'd bring it out."

I placed a finger to my lips, trying to silence him, but he didn't see me.

"How you know Martha Jean?" Mama asked.

"I met her at the post office. You got some fine daughters, Mrs. Quinn."

"Daughters?"

"Yes, ma'am. Martha Jean and Tangy. Oh, yeah, and Mushy."

There was something about Velman Cooper's mouth that had troubled me from the very beginning—from the first time I had seen him. It was a mouth that was too big. It opened and closed before his brain had a chance to warm up.

Mama turned and stepped away from the door, allowing me a clear view of Velman. I tried to warn him with a stare, but he seemed not to get it.

"Bring Martha Jean out here," Mama said.

I found Martha Jean in the kitchen and told her, in a rush of signs, that Velman Cooper was at our front door and we were in a world of trouble.

"Come on over here," Mama said, beckoning to Martha Jean as we entered the hallway. "This boy say he got a letter for you."

I raised my hands to interpret my mother's words.

"Quit that!" Mama yelled. "She know damn well what I'm saying. She done had sense enough to go out and invite this boy to my house."

Velman's smile faded when he saw the terror in Martha Jean's eyes as she approached our mother. He extended the letter toward Martha Jean, but Mama intercepted and snatched it from his hand. She opened it and withdrew a birthday card. Without bothering to glance inside the card, she ripped it and threw the pieces over Martha Jean's head.

"Ma'am, I didn't mean no harm coming out to your house," Velman apologized. "Nobody invited me."

"Why did you come, then?" I snapped, and for the first time he looked directly at me.

His lips formed a circle that blew a long stream of breath into the cold air, as his hands moved nervously about in front of him. My mother stood between us, with her thumb and forefinger pressed into Martha Jean's cheek. Martha Jean's lips were opened and fixed like a gulping fish. Her head bobbed up and down to the flex of Mama's wrist.

"Please, don't do that, ma'am," Velman pleaded. "I'm sorry. I won't come to your house again, but please don't do that."

Mama stepped toward him, pulling Martha Jean with her. "This my child," she said. "I birthed her and she belongs to me. You keep yo' hands off her. You hear?"

It seemed he wanted to say something. He scratched one side of his face and his mouth opened, but before he could form a word, Mama released Martha Jean, gave her a savage, backhand slap across her face, and kicked the door shut in Velman's face.

"Tangy Mae, get the belt!" she ordered.

I stepped into her bedroom and selected the thinnest belt I could find. As I came back into the hall, I could see Martha Jean cowering and retreating. Mama swung with her fists, landing powerful blows on Martha Jean's chest.

"You slut!" Mama screamed. "You goddamn slut! I'll teach you to go out and shame me."

Martha Jean backed into the front room, giving Mama ample space to direct her punches. She aimed for Martha Jean's head. Martha Jean threw an arm up to protect herself, but Mama gripped it brutally and forced it behind Martha Jean's back.

Martha Jean brayed, and arched her spine against the pressure Mama exerted on her shoulder and arm. Effortlessly, Mama wrapped her other arm around Martha Jean's neck and breathed into her ear, "Dumb bitch. You no-good, dumb bitch. I'll break yo' goddamn neck."

I stood there horrified, holding the leather belt, the buckle dangling at my ankles, as my mother and sister struggled in a false embrace.

Edna, crouched in a corner beside Laura, used the knuckles of her hands to wipe away her tears. She either saw or sensed how dangerously close Mama was to trampling Judy. I saw it, too, but feared the slightest movement on my part would be catastrophic. I stood perfectly still while Edna took two small scoots forward, gripped the basket, and pulled Judy to safety.

Mama released Martha Jean. "Goddamn children!" she yelled. "All y'all can go to Hell. I'm sicka worrying 'bout y'all." It seemed she was done with Martha Jean, then suddenly, gracefully, she pivoted and balanced herself on her toes. Her fingers curled and tightened into fists as she landed softly on her heels, and she began to jab. With artistic precision, she opened gashes, loosened teeth, and viciously rearranged my sister's face. Martha Jean collapsed to the floor, and finally Mama snatched the belt from my hand.

I was beyond praying, and had resorted to begging God to help Martha Jean—to stop Mama from hitting her again.

Amen! Amen! God answers prayer. Ain't my God a great God? Hallelujah!

The belt looped through the air in a rush, but instead of striking Martha Jean, it cut into my shoulders, neck, and back. It knocked me off balance. It tangled in my skirt, frustrating my mother, forcing her to change her strategy. She unwrapped the leather from her hand, flipped it over, and brought the metal buckle down on my head.

I did not know why Judy was crying. I was crying from pain, Laura and Edna must have been crying from fear, because they had not been touched. Whatever sounds Martha Jean made were drowned out by our sobs.

"Y'all, shut up!" Mama screamed at us. "Y'all giving me a damn headache."

She sauntered over to an armchair, sat, and leaned back to rest her aching head. We didn't stop crying, though—not right away. Laura and Edna eventually hushed, even little Judy fell silent long before I could. I shed tears of pain, of despair, dry-sobbed from injustice, gave a feeble heave, then finally calmed.

From across the room, my mother smiled at me and slowly shook her head. "Tangy Mae, you oughta be shame of yo'self," she said. "I was two seconds away from giving you something to cry about if you hadn't shut up."

She was still staring at me and shaking her head in disgust when Tarabelle came in from work, then she turned her attention to my sister. "I think we got enough space out in the yard to plant a garden," she said. "What you think, Tarabelle? We can grow our own beans and tomatoes. I'm gon' buy some seeds the next time I'm in town."

Tarabelle did not answer. She gazed at Martha Jean's crumpled form on the floor, then briefly glanced at me, but did not ask what had happened.

We were all quiet now, even Mama. She sat silent for so long it seemed she had fallen asleep with her eyes wide open. Finally, she said, "Well, I gotta finish getting dressed. Tarabelle, you get yo'self together. You gotta make a run wit' me tonight."

"No, Mama," Tarabelle begged. "Please! I'm tired."

God, look down on us. I am in a room where your daughters are weary. They are moaning, and it is a most wretched sound. Can you hear it, Lord? Do something! I never want to shed another tear as long as I live.

"I'll go with you, Mama," I heard myself say, although I had no idea where my mother was going. "I'm not tired. I'll go with you."

In a split second, my mother was across the room and standing over me. I spread my arms to shield Martha Jean, although I knew I was the one in danger.

"Look here!" Mama said.

I glanced up, and she slapped my face so hard that I bit my tongue, and the blood coated my palate and rolled down my throat.

"Who the hell do you think wants you?" she asked.

"Nobody, Mama," I answered truthfully. "Nobody."

nineteen

Martha Jean's face was a horrid rainbow of black lumps and blue bruises encircled by thin rings of lime-green and yellow discolorations. She peered at me from beneath the swollen, black lid of her right eye. Her left eye was closed, puffy, and draining a clear fluid down her cheek. Her upper lip, swollen like a mushroom, blocked the flow of air through her nose and made her breathing sound like snoring.

It pained me to look at her. I think it hurt us all, but each of us expressed our distress in a different way. Harvey paced, and Sam was silent. After they left for work, Wallace mumbled, and Tarabelle said, "Ain't nobody gon' be calling Martha Jean pretty for a long time."

"I'm gonna stay home again today and look after her," I said. "She can't take care of Judy."

"Judy is Mama's baby." Tarabelle said in measured syllables, as if explaining something to a small child. "Martha Jean shouldn't have to take care of her. Mama ain't doing nothing all day 'cept laying up on her ass."

"Will you take her coffee in before you leave?" I asked.

"Nope. I'm late," Tarabelle answered, "and if I can make it

through the rest of my life without seeing Mama, I'll be a happy child." She reached the doorway of the front room, then turned and whispered, "Tan, write Mushy a letter and tell her I'm waiting."

She left, and Wallace gave her some distance before he struck out for school. I took coffee in to Mama, then I fed and changed Judy, got Laura and Edna dressed and fed, and managed to get a few spoonsful of food between Martha Jean's swollen lips.

Martha Jean had remained curled on her pallet all the day before. She hadn't eaten, hadn't even made a trip to the outhouse. Today, at least, she was sitting up, and I noticed that her gown was wet. I cleaned her up as best I could, then helped her walk over to one of the armchairs.

Mama emerged from her room around noon and got her first glance at Martha Jean's face since the beating. She ambled on toward the kitchen, and did not speak to us. Laura sat quietly on the floor beside Martha Jean's chair. I winked at her, and she smiled timidly, as if afraid her smile might attract Mama's notice. I held Judy on my lap, and imagined my mother leaning against the kitchen wall, weeping bitterly for the pain she had inflicted, and promising herself and God that it would never happen again.

Mama had always taught us that we were not to hit each other, and I wondered why she was exempt from that rule. Sometimes I believed she did not mean to hurt us, but could not help herself. She was, after all, the same gentle woman who had once, long ago, taught us to love, and I had learned to love with every part of my being. My love for Martha Jean alone filled my heart to aching.

I was baffled by the ambiguities of my mother's emotions and behavior. She denied and feared God in the same breath. She allowed our actions to shame her, and yet she was void of shame. I truly believed there was something unnatural about her—a madness that only her children could see. My yearning was not to understand it, but to escape it.

"Tan," came her soft voice from the kitchen. "Tan, baby, come here a minute. I need you to do something for me."

With Judy cradled in my arms, I went out to the kitchen. Mama was sitting on a chair, her feet tucked beneath the seat, and an elbow resting on the tabletop. A foul odor—the combination of sweat, caffeine, and booze—emanated from her body and scalp. She reached out to touch me, but recoiled when she saw that I was holding the baby.

"What happened to the dummy?" she asked. "What happened to her? Did she fall down the steps or something?"

I accepted my cue. "Yes, ma'am," I lied. "She fell down the front steps."

"Did you see it?"

"Yes, ma'am."

"Who else saw it?"

"We all saw it. I tried to break her fall, but I couldn't. Harvey went down and picked her up and brought her in the house. We all saw her fall, Mama, but there was nothing we could do."

Mama nodded. "Okay. I ain't blaming you. Y'all just gon' have to be more careful on them steps."

"Is that all, Mama?" I asked.

"Nah, baby. I need you to get them outta here. Take 'em for a walk out toward the country or something. You can do that for Mama, can't you?" She closed her eyes and rubbed her head. "That damn Mr. Poppy coming for his rent today. I ain't got it. I'm gon' have to explain that to 'im, and I can't do it wit' all y'all sitting 'round." She fell silent, and after a long while she said, "I'm gon' tell him to fix them steps, Tan."

Nearly an hour passed before we were on the road. It had taken most of that time to wash dried blood from Martha Jean's face and hair. She hadn't wanted to move, and I couldn't blame her. We started out toward the country, but as soon as we were out of Mama's view, we cut through the grove of trees behind the field and took a detour toward town.

The push broom dropped to the floor with a hollow thump. Velman, his eyes as wide as I had ever seen them, stepped cautiously toward us. He brought a hand up to touch Martha Jean's face, then slowly lowered it to his side. His lips moved, but formed no words.

"I told you not to come to our house," I screamed at him. "I told you the first time you saw us that we were Quinns, but you were so busy listening to your own voice that you didn't hear me. Now look what you've done."

"Hey, what's going on out there?" Charlie Nesbitt asked.

He and Chadlow had come from a back area of the post office and were standing at the counter watching us. Chadlow was tall and brawny, and he loomed about six inches over Charlie Nesbitt. He had dark, wavy hair that was thinning at the top, and dark eyes that always seemed cold and contemptuous. I had seen him sneer and scowl, but I had never seen a true smile grace his rugged features. To the Negroes in Pakersfield, he was an ugly, ugly man.

Judy was heavier than a load of fire logs in my arms. I cradled her in one aching arm, and turned Martha Jean to face Mr. Nesbitt and Chadlow.

"Look what he did to my sister," I said in a voice trembling with threatening sobs.

Charlie Nesbitt studied Martha Jean's face, then nodded his round, bald head in Velman's direction and said, "I reckon this boy knows how to handle his own affairs. Seems to me this here's a private matter. Don't need no meddling from me or nobody else, gal."

Staring down at the counter, I mumbled, "She's my sister."

"What's that?" Charlie asked in a tone intended to humble me.

"She's my sister, sir," I repeated in my most timid voice.

"Don't matter who she is. All I'm saying is you people got to take it someplace else. I can't have you carrying on in my post office. You hear me, Velman? Get 'em outta here!"

"Yes, sir," Velman answered. He lifted the broom from the floor and placed it against a wall, then came to stand beside me. "Come on, little sister," he pleaded. "I know you mad, and it look like you got every right to be, but not in here. Okay?"

We followed him outside and down the walk until we reached his car. All the while, I was thinking how best to cause him as much pain as I felt each time I looked at Martha Jean's face.

"You!" I began, all fired up, but then Edna tugged at my skirt with an urgency that nearly snapped the button at my waist.

"I'm tired, Tangy," she whined. "I gotta number one."

"Me, too. And I'm hungry," Laura chimed in.

I glanced down at the heads of my sisters, feeling that they were conspiring against me for having dragged them so far from home. Edna had tucked her dress between her thighs and was dancing about shamelessly. The closest public facility for coloreds was at least a mile back through town at the bus depot, and by the looks of Edna, I did not think we would make it that far.

Velman, witnessing my dilemma, opened the car door and rolled a window down. He took Judy from my arms and placed her on the front seat.

"Take 'em to the side of the building," he said. "Just keep away from the windows, and don't go near the back. Mr. Nesbitt got some of his buddies up in there. They be opening people's mail and reading it. He don't think I know, but I done seen 'em do it plenty of times."

"Isn't that against the law?" I whispered.

"Must not be in this town," Velman said. "He got the law up in there wit' him."

"Chadlow is not the law," I said, as Edna tugged at my skirt again.

I left Martha Jean standing beside the car, swaying from exhaustion, and God only knew what else. I took Laura and Edna to squat beside the building, all the while expecting Charlie Nesbitt or one of his buddies to come out and shoo us away.

When we returned to the front, Velman was staring at Martha Jean's face with the oddest expression on his own, as if trying to understand the motivation behind such an act of violence. He raised a hand—unsteady and unsure. Gently, he touched her shoulder, and when she did not protest, he embraced her, and the wretched sob that escaped him echoed my own anguish.

When he finally released her and turned back to the post office, he did not ask us to wait. He did not need to. There was no place else for us to go, except home. We waited in his car for nearly two hours, during which time Chadlow and two other men came out of the post office. Chadlow stopped and stared out toward the car, and I thought he was going to come and bother us, but he didn't. He caught up to the other two men, and they all got into Chadlow's car and drove away.

When Velman finally appeared, he slid onto the driver's seat, and without a word, drove west through town.

"Where are you going?" I asked nervously, afraid his rage had made him stupid, afraid he was going to Penyon Road to confront my mother.

"Don't worry, little sister," he said, glancing over at me. "I ain't known for making the same mistake twice. You won't see me back at yo' place unless I'm invited, and I don't guess that's likely to happen. What I'm gon' do is get Martha Jean outta there."

"How?"

"I don't know." He shook his head. "I need time to think."

He stopped the car on Canyon Street, just a little ways up from Logan's store. We got out, and he held Martha Jean for a moment, rocking her against his body.

"We have to go," I said, glancing around to make sure no one saw this man embracing my sister on the side of the road in broad daylight.

"Yeah," he said, slowly releasing Martha Jean, and surreptitiously surveying the whole of Canyon Street. He got back inside the car, started to speak, then shook his head and drove off.

My anger had dissolved; I felt cheated and confused. I ached for the comfort that Velman had offered Martha Jean. She was visibly bruised; my wounds were deeply buried in my soul. No one knew about them. I truly believed Velman would try to help Martha Jean escape our mother's house, but escape was what I desired for myself, as well. I wanted him to love her, but I realized that I wanted him to love me, too.

twenty

On a bright Saturday morning in April, we stripped the newspapers from the windows and allowed the first golden rays of sunlight to enter our dingy dwelling. We bared our arms, legs, and feet, and dug into our chores with enthusiasm. Both the house and the yard bustled with activity. Hambone, Junior, Max, and Skip had come to help Sam and Harvey patch the roof. Mattie had shown up unexpectedly, and Mama had allowed her to stay with the stipulation that she pitch in and help. Mama was enjoying herself, sitting on the front porch, sipping early morning beer, and chatting with Miss Pearl.

Their laughter drifted into the front room where I was busy sweeping and scooping ash into a paper bag. My mother's laughter was music, like chimes in the wind, floating over the motley paradise that Pakersfield had become in spring. I used the broom to sweep my way closer to that sound, and to the sight, across the field on Fife Street, of rosy pink blossoms shimmering on dogwood trees.

My brothers and their friends, sliding sheets of tin across the roof, shook clumps of dirt onto the floorboards, and I gave up trying to clean the floor. I stood in the shadows of the hallway, basking in a warm breeze and my mother's melody—until the squeals of Edna and Laura, romping through the yard, soured her notes.

"Look at 'em, Pearl. I can't trust none of 'em. I don't know when they lying or telling the truth. And I think they stealing from me."

Miss Pearl chuckled. "Rosie, the one thang you ain't gotta worry 'bout is them young'uns of yours. They some good chilluns."

"They was before Mushy came and started turning 'em against me."

"Mushy can't turn 'em against you. You gon' do that all by yo'self. I ain't much on the Bible, but I'm almost sho' it's a sin the way you beat yo' chilluns. Just look at Martha Jean's face. Ain't no need in y'all telling me she fell down no steps neither. You done that, Rosie, just as sho' as I'm sitting here."

"I didn't, Pearl," Mama lied. "Ask any of 'em, they'll tell you she fell down these here steps."

"Yeah?"

"Yeah. It's Mushy done put ideas in they heads. She trying to steal 'em from me. I can't trust Tangy Mae no mo'. Ain't no telling what she be putting in them letters. That's why I went to the post office myself. And guess what? I found out a whole lotta stuff. They got a colored man working at that post office, and ever time he see me, he try to be all nice. He trying to take po' dumb Martha Jean off my hands." Mama chuckled. "And here's another thing, Pearl. Mushy done sent a bus ticket to Tarabelle, trying to get her to run off. Wait a minute, and I'll show you the ticket."

She must have been rising as she spoke because I never had a chance to move out of the hall. I saw one bare, slender leg cross the threshold, then the other. I turned toward the front room, and felt a touch on my head. My head snapped back, and all I could do was follow my head toward the floor, then I was in motion, being dragged by my hair. I blinked and found myself sprawled on the splintered boards of the porch, a toppled mayonnaise jar beside me, cold beer soaking my faded, blue shorts, and Miss Pearl staring down at me.

"You see, Pearl," Mama said. "You see now what I'm talking 'bout. They spy on me, too."

Miss Pearl shook her head and grunted, "Uh, uh, uh. Rosie, you need to buy yo' gals some brassieres."

Above my head tin scraped against tin. I turned my head toward the steps and saw Mattie standing on the ground, looking up, witnessing my humiliation.

"Nah, Pearl," Mama said. "Tangy Mae need to get herself a job. If she grown enough to wear a brassiere, then she grown enough to work. I ain't wasting my money on no foolishness."

With that said, she stepped over my outstretched legs and disappeared into the hallway.

"If I was you, I'd get out there in that yard somewhere," Miss Pearl said, and winked at me.

"You almost got it, didn't you?" Mattie asked, as I cleared the steps. "What'd you do?"

I gave her a "mind your own business" smirk, and kept walking.

Tarabelle was standing beside the washtub with her hands pressed against her lower back. Her fingers were wrinkled from being too long immersed in water. "You done in the house?" she asked.

I nodded. "For now."

"Good. I'm gon' take me a short walk, get this knot out my back."

"Can I walk wit' ya?" Mattie asked.

They walked west on Penyon Road and disappeared past the field and a thicket of trees. I bent over the tub and began to scrub a pair of overalls. Tarabelle had already completed the bulk of the wash—sheets and blankets—and they were hanging on the lines. I tossed the overalls into the rinse water, and glanced up at the roof. Hambone stood at the top of a ladder looking down at me. When our eyes met, he dropped his hammer to the ground and stepped backwards down the rungs to retrieve it.

"How are you this morning, Tangy?" he asked.

"Okay," I mumbled, turning back to the wash.

He came over to stand beside me, purposely pressing his sweaty arm against mine. "You ever heard of a washing machine?" he asked. "You shouldn't have to wash clothes with those pretty little hands."

I stepped away from his sweaty arm and glared at him. "You stink," I said.

A broad grin spread across his face, and he glanced down at my beer-soaked shorts, then he brought his face close to mine. "I don't stink," he said with a short laugh. "What you're smelling is a real man. One-hundred-percent pure man."

"Well, I don't like it," I shot back.

"I'll tell you what, Miss Tangy, you give me a chance and I bet I can make you like it. I know I like what I see."

"You'd better go on now before I call my brothers," I threatened.

"Harvey and Sam?" He glanced toward the roof. "They don't worry about me. They know I'm all right. You know, I've been thinking about taking you out. Maybe to the picture show or up to Stillwaters. I'll even buy you a dress. What color do you want?"

"I don't want a dress," I snapped, "and you know I'm not allowed at Stillwaters."

"That didn't stop you the last time, and as I recall, you had a good time. Why don't you think about it."

My refusal came out as an insult. "You stink," I repeated.

Hambone peeled off the offending T-shirt and tossed it into the wash tub. "How do you expect me to smell when I've been hauling tin all morning?" he asked. "I'm not gonna smell like a rose, Tangy. It's nothing a little soap and water won't take care of."

"Oh, my God!" I whispered, glancing around. "Put your clothes back on."

"Hey, calm down," he said, rubbing a hand slowly across the patch of hair on his chest. "I'll tell you what. You give me a drink of cold water, and I'll get on back to work."

"The faucet's over there," I said, pointing it out to him.

"What? You want me to drink outta my hands? I can't get a glass and a little chunk of ice? I'm working on your roof, and I can't get a glass?"

"All right," I answered with deliberate irritation. "Then will you leave me alone?"

He shrugged his bare shoulders. "Like I said, I'll get on back to work."

He followed me around to the rear of the house where Martha Jean was sitting on a step, dangling a red ribbon over Judy's basket. Hambone paused to admire Judy, and I rushed on off to the kitchen.

Moving as fast as I could, I chopped off two chunks of ice, dropped them into the first jar I saw, and replaced the ice pick in the windowsill. Before I could turn around, though, he was on me. His chest pressed against my back, pushing me against the ice box door, as his tongue made wet circles up and down my neck. His hands squeezed between me and the door, pinching and pawing at my breasts. I held myself as rigid as possible, afraid to scream, afraid my mother would catch me shaming her under her own roof.

Sunlight spilled in through the kitchen window as if God had captured us in a spotlight. I felt embarrassed and as cold as the block of ice beyond the door that kept me from falling. I could hear my mother outside, and I held my breath, thinking she was coming in. She would find me like this, and beat the living tar out of me, then God would send me to Hell, and Satan would burn me up.

"Wallace, where'd you get that thang?" my mother shouted. She was still on the front porch.

"I stole it from some white boys, Mama," Wallace answered. His voice was coming from the yard.

"Did anybody see you?"

"No, ma'am. It was in the alley behind the drugstore. It's new, Mama. You like it?"

Mama and Miss Pearl laughed, then all sound seemed to fade, except for Hambone's panting in my ear.

"Come on, Tangy. Help me out," he said between breaths.

Suddenly, there was a loud noise, and all of his weight fell on me. "Shit!" he cried out. "Shit!"

He stepped back, and I was free. I turned slowly to see Hambone and Tarabelle facing each other. Hambone had one arm raised between his shoulder blades, rubbing his back.

"Why'd you hit me, Tarabelle?" he asked angrily. "You almost broke my damn back."

Tarabelle dropped the milk crate she had used on him, and took a seat at the table. "That's my sister, boy," she said matter-of-factly. There was neither surprise nor anger in her voice. She spoke as if she had walked in to find me stirring grits at the stove, or something else just as mundane.

"You hit me with that crate," Hambone accused.

Tarabelle ignored him. "Tan, we ain't gon' have no blackberries this year," she said. "Somebody done dug up that hill out by the dairy. Ain't nothing now but dirt and holes."

The jar with the two melting chunks of ice stood atop the ice box. I picked it up and gave it to Hambone, then I began to run.

Mattie, Judy, and Edna were on the steps, blocking my path. I leapt from the side of the porch and rushed for the woods, nearly slamming into Martha Jean as she emerged from the outhouse.

I could hear Wallace calling after me, "Tangy, look at my new bike." But I could not stop.

Mattie caught up to me only when there was no path left to travel. I fell to my knees at Mr. Barnwell's fence, and Mattie dropped down beside me.

"What happened?" she asked. "What's wrong wit' you?"

I blurted out the embarrassing details of my experience with Hambone, honestly believing that if I shared it I would feel better. I even told her how I had been afraid to call out for my mother.

Mattie listened, staring down at the ground, and occasionally shaking her head. When I was done, she said, "I told you a long time ago. They can smell the scent when we women. You just lucky nobody ain't came after you sooner than this. They be looking for somewhere to stick they tails. Yo' brothers do it, too. All men do the nasty. They sniff out girls that's done had the curse, then they go after 'em, saying how they gon' make 'em feel good. Saying how they pretty. Telling all sorts of lies 'til they get they tails in her."

"Hambone didn't put anything in me," I said. "I'm never gonna let anybody do that to me."

Mattie laughed. "Then what you worried 'bout? You still a virgin, but he woulda done it if yo' sister hadn't stopped him. You couldn't stop him. Least that's what you said, but maybe you wanted him to do it."

"I didn't, Mattie. He didn't even ask. He just grabbed me and started touching all over me."

"They don't have to ask, stupid. They men. They can do what they want. They all like that."

"I don't believe you, Mattie," I said. "They can't all be like that."

"You name me one that ain't."

"Wallace."

"He just a baby."

"Jeff."

"Jeff Stallings is a sissy," she said. "They different."

"What about Mr. Pace?" I asked.

"He like that, too," she answered. "He just gotta be sly about it 'cause he a teacher." She picked up a twig, snapped it into pieces, and began placing the pieces on the ground. "Yo' sister," she said, "the dumb one, she know anything 'bout the curse?"

I nodded.

"How y'all make her understand things?"

"Martha Jean's not dumb, Mattie," I said. "She can read better than you."

"How you know? You ever heard her read?"

"No. But she understands what she reads. That's more than I can say about you."

"You ain't gotta get smart about it!" she snapped.

"I'm not getting smart," I apologized. "I just don't like it when people call Martha Jean dumb."

"Yo' other sister, Tarabelle, she's pretty," Mattie said. "I like her. She's nice."

"You won't think she's so nice if she hears you calling Martha Jean names."

"Yeah?"

"Yeah."

Mattie stood and scattered the twigs with her foot. "You're being mean," she said. "I'm going back. You think yo' brother'll let me ride his bike?"

I shrugged. "I don't know. He's never had a bicycle before."

She started back along the trail, walking slow at first, then breaking into a trot. I watched her go, and almost before she was out of sight, I saw Junior coming along the trail toward me. I shook my head in disbelief when I saw that he was carrying his satchel. I wondered how much help he had been up on the roof with a bag attached to his body.

He dropped down beside me, looked me in my eyes, and said, "I was standing on the roof when I saw you charge out through here like you were being chased by bloodhounds. Did Hambone bother you?"

I shook my head. "If I told you yes, would you tell Sam?"

He smiled. "No. If there's something about you that Sam needs to know, you'll have to be the one to tell him. Hambone and I are not the best of friends, but Sam likes him."

I nodded. "I don't know whether I like him or not. I don't know him that well, but I don't guess I need to tell my brothers anything."

"Are you sure?"

"I'm sure," I answered.

"Tangy, you're no longer a child. You've grown into a young lady. Rules of the game change as we get older. Sometimes the games aren't fun anymore. Do you understand what I'm saying?"

"You talk in riddles sometimes, Junior, but I think I know what you mean. I listened to that meeting in our backyard a couple of months ago. I thought you were gonna lose everybody with your fancy words."

"Had I begun to speak of Utopia, surely I would have lost them all," he joked, and then his face grew serious. "I'm glad you listened, Tangy. I hope you heard every word that was said. I know you're hungry—so hungry that you will die of starvation if you stay in Pakersfield. I've watched you on the few occasions when I've taught your class. You devour knowledge like a buzzard on a corpse. Forgive the analogy, but that's what I see. There're not enough books on the shelves of all the schools and libraries in this county to feed your hunger. You need more, and you'll never find it here."

"You sound just like Mr. Pace. I don't like it when y'all talk like that, Junior. It makes me feel like y'all gon' hate me if I make a mistake or something."

"We won't hate you. Everybody makes a mistake at some point. Everybody."

"I know, but you just don't understand. I practice hard to speak the way Mr. Pace wants me to speak, but when I come home from school, my sisters and brothers get angry at me for talking that way. If I slip and say the wrong thing at school, Mr. Pace corrects me. Sometimes it embarrasses me when he corrects me in front of other people."

"Don't be embarrassed. It's his job to teach you the right way, but in the end, you won't have to satisfy him, or your brothers and sisters. You'll have to satisfy yourself, Tangy."

"You're talking in riddles again," I accused.

Junior laughed. I laughed with him, and it felt good—like nothing bad had happened that day. If I could keep him talking, maybe I would forget what Hambone had done to me, that my mother had dragged me by my hair, and that I was sitting in the woods in beer-soaked shorts.

"Junior, are y'all still planning to drink from the fountain at the courthouse?" I asked.

"We're still talking about it, but there's a lot of fear and dissension. The sheriff watches Sam every time he goes to town, and that's making us all nervous. Some of the men think we should wait until school is out for the summer so we don't bring any harm to the children. Some think we should take a large group of people with us, and others think we should have as few as possible."

"I think you should take as many people as you can get."

"Well," Junior said, "we're not agreed on much of anything. Harvey thinks we should go on a Wednesday when town is nearly deserted, and now Hambone is trying to run the show. He thinks we should include women and children; others think it should just be the men. Sam doesn't say much at all."

"I think it should be on a Wednesday, and you should take as many people as you can get."

"I agree," Junior said, "but it's up to Sam. We know there'll be trouble, and we don't want anybody to get hurt."

"Tell me about your uncle," I said, "the one they murdered."

Junior's whole demeanor changed. His body stiffened, and the veins in his neck protruded. I was sorry I had brought it up. I was about to apologize when he unfastened his satchel, pulled out a folded sheet of paper, and handed it to me.

"It's a hard thing to talk about," he said, "but I think I can share with you what my heart has to say."

I unfolded the paper and began to read:

Uncle Nathan
Why should I write of teardrops falling
Silently obscuring the timeless craft of a skillful master
Whose fingers traced stained glass of some distant morrow
Ancient souls foretold would never come?
Would that make sense to you?

How would you know that I am thinking
Of Uncle Nathan lightning fast fleeing thunder
Of hooded henchmen spurred on by that man-god Dionysus
Come from Olympus in a pickup truck
To show Uncle Nathan no black man will ever be
As swift as the Great Achilles?
How can I write of morning glories lovingly caressed
By dawn's sweet dew or buds blooming from April showers
And not remember the severed head, protruding eyes
The lifeless body beside twisted vines of morning glories
As torrential rains washed away the blue-black blood
That men bleed when the soft light of dark midnight
Cannot shelter them from murder
As brutal as that
Of Uncle Nathan?

When I was done reading, I said the only thing I could think to say, "It must have been horrible."

"It was." Junior took the paper from me and placed it in his bag.

As he prepared to stand, I touched his arm to stop him. "Junior, I like your writing," I said, "but I want to ask you about those letters you've been mailing out. Have you ever heard from any of those newspapers or from the NAACP?"

He stared at me for a long while. "No. I haven't," he finally said, "but I understand that some things take time. I'm a patient man. Why do you ask?"

"I don't think they're getting your letters. I heard that Mr. Nesbitt lets Chadlow and some of his buddies open people's mail. What if they've been opening your letters and throwing them away?"

Junior groaned and closed his eyes. When he opened them again, he blinked several times, as if in denial. "Oh, my God! Oh, my God!" he repeated. "Are you sure about this, Tangy?"

"I'm sure, Junior. I won't tell you who told me but you're smart enough to figure it out."

And then he was up and racing through the woods leaving me to wonder what he had written in his letters. I sat for a while longer, feeling drained, sorry that my words had been the source of such distress. He needed to know, though, so he could stop writing those letters for other people to read.

I remembered the dirty clothes waiting for me in the tub. I stood, brushed the dirt from my knees, and took the time to read Mr. Barnwell's sign. It was just an old, stupid sign that meant nothing. I picked up a rock and threw it, hitting the board just above the crooked N. The rock striking the wood made a popping sound, then fell to the ground on my side of the fence. The sign did not waver.

Mattie and Tarabelle were sitting on the steps watching me as I came into the clearing. "I ain't washing no mo' clothes, Tangy," Tarabelle called out. "Mama already fussing, saying how they oughta been done by now."

"She oughta wash 'em, then," I mumbled, and continued on toward the side yard.

There was no one on the roof. The ladder, my brothers, and their friends were all gone. Hambone's T-shirt was floating at the top of the tub. I picked it up, holding it between my thumb and middle finger. Without a pause, I walked over to the outhouse, opened the door, and dropped the shirt down the hole.

That day was the beginning of the end of my friendship with Mattie. It was nearly three weeks before I saw Hambone again, and by that time, neither one of us gave a damn about a T-shirt.

twenty-one

Paper fans flapped back and forth in an ineffectual attempt to stir a breeze. Summer was nearly upon us, and as I sat in the choir stand choking on the scent of mothballs emanating from Miss Janie's peach-colored shawl, the fervor of Reverend Nelson's sermon seemed to reach out and envelope Miss Janie. She slumped toward me, and I vigorously fanned her, hoping she would not go into a full faint.

I felt the Holy Ghost rising within me, urging me to sing. I wanted everybody else to feel it, too. If they were unmoved by Reverend Nelson's sermon, I intended to shake them with song.

Reverend Nelson reached the finale of a sermon that had begun nearly thirty minutes earlier with Jacob and Esau. It had somehow wound its way through Huntsville, Alabama, and was now back inside the Solid Rock Baptist Church.

"How many of y'all think God is a blind God?" he asked, staring out at the congregation. "He sees all you do. You can't fool Him, and you can't hide from Him, but you will answer to Him. On that great day, there'll be no hiding place. Great God Almighty!" He leapt across the pulpit and pointed a finger toward the deacons' pews. "Deacon Hall, I found out that night . . . in Huntsville, Alabama . . . well . . . that you can't fool God. Deacon Lawrence, I found out that night that God . . . well . . . ain't nowhere close to blind." He leapt in the opposite direction, waved his handkerchief over his head, dabbed at a trickle of sweat, then scanned the Mothers' Board. "Mother Louise, I found out that night . . . well . . . that God can make you swallow a lie . . . umm-hum . . . before it rolls off your tongue. 'What have you done with your life?'

"Church, y'all don't hear me. I tried to stand up . . . umm-hum . . . face God like a man. 'Look here, God. You done took my mother. Seems like you ought to be telling me why.'"

Reverend Nelson's feet left the floor and he flew toward the choir stand. His gaze came to settle on me. "Sister Tangy," he said, "I was too young to know that God did not have to answer to me. But He showed me that night . . . well . . . on the steps of that church . . . well . . . in Huntsville, Alabama. Seems like He placed a hand on my head, and said, 'Bow down! Bow down! You can't stand up and be a man until you answer to Me.'"

The reverend's hand was on my head like a skullcap, and I felt his touch even after he had flown off in another direction. I glanced up to see him facing the congregation.

"God said, 'Son, I'm about to give you a little glimpse of glory. I'm about to build me . . . well . . . a chamber in your heart.' Great God Almighty! Some of y'all don't know it, but God is busy—building a chamber in your heart as I speak. Welcome Him in, Church. Make Him comfortable."

Freddie Baker swept his fingers softly across the piano keys until Reverend Nelson was seated, then the choir rose, and we began to sing. That was when Sam, Hambone, Maxwell, and little Steve Douglas, a nine-year-old boy from Fife Street, entered the church.

Hambone, wearing blue jeans and a short-sleeved yellow shirt, led the way up the aisle to the pulpit. Sam and Maxwell followed with Little Steve, who wore a pair of cut-off pants and no shirt. He was sobbing, and Maxwell held his arm to keep him from bolting from the church. The disruption brought Reverend Nelson to his feet, and it silenced the choir. Finally, the music stopped.

"We've come here today," Hambone said, spreading his arms to include the others. "We've come here today because it's time. It's time to wake up. We, the Negroes of Triacy County, are gradually being sucked back into slavery, and it's time to do something about it."

"Wait a minute, son," Reverend Nelson said. "This is God's house, and y'all need to respect it."

"We respect this church, and we respect you," Hambone said. "That's why we waited until the sermon was over. I don't think it's gonna hurt these people to listen to me for a few minutes. It won't hurt you, either, Reverend. We're living in a town where Negroes are afraid to walk on the same side of the street as a white man. I think there's something wrong with that, don't you?"

He waited for Reverend Nelson to respond, but the reverend turned to Sam and said, "This is not the time or place. Let us get back to our service."

"It's the perfect time and place," Hambone said. "That's why we're here."

"That's right," Sam said, stepping up to the pulpit. "How long we gotta walk around scared we gon' be lynched for saying or doing something they don't like?"

Charles Hull spoke up from a pew near the back of the church. "They ain't lynched nobody here for years. Why you talking like that, Sam?"

Reverend Nelson raised his hands for silence, then he said to Hambone, "Son, you've been up there in Chicago, and I don't know what they're doing up there, but we're living in peace here. We don't have trouble and we don't want trouble."

Most of the congregation agreed with the reverend, me included. Hambone waited until we had settled down, then he stepped up beside Reverend Nelson. "You're a preacher," he said, "and you don't even know that the gates of Hell surround you. All of you are dragging the gates of Hell around with you every day. It's those gates that keep you from setting foot on Meadow Hill without permission. You drag those gates with you to the back doors of every establishment in Pakersfield. Those gates make you step into the streets to get out of their way. And you want me to believe that you're living in peace?"

"It ain't so bad like you make it sound," said Annabelle Swanson, her voice high-pitched and demanding to be heard. "We all know 'bout you, but we ain't gon' fight your fight. The Good Book tell us to turn the other cheek. We'll get our reward in Heaven."

"You got a reward coming, Miss Annabelle?" Hambone asked sarcastically. "You're getting your reward right now. It's the three-and-a-half cents a pound Mr. Butterfield paying you to pick his cotton. Your ancestors did better than that. They got a shanty, food, clothes, and shoes for picking the white man's cotton. You people are going out the world backwards."

It seemed everybody was speaking at once, canceling each other out. I stepped away from the choir and weaved my way through the crowd blocking the aisle. I saw Wallace sitting with a few of his friends, and I stopped at their pew.

"Have you seen Mattie?" I asked.

"I think she left," Wallace answered. "She was sitting over there wit' Tara a few minutes ago."

Then Sam began to speak, and I stayed where I was to listen.

"Tell 'em what happened to you Tuesday, Mr. Matthew," Sam called out, shifting everyone's attention to Matthew Brogus, a middle-aged man in an ill-fitting, gray suit.

Mr. Matthew stood with his head bowed and his arms hanging at his sides. "Wadn't nothing, Sam," he mumbled. "Didn't hurt nobody."

"What about yo' pride, man?" Sam shouted angrily. "Tell these people how you felt in that store. Tell 'em! Tell 'em how them white boys accused you of stealing. Tell 'em how you felt when they stripped you down to yo' skivvies wit' everybody staring. They wouldn't never do that to no white man. And what'd they do when they didn't find nothing? They just left you standing there naked and feeling like a fool."

"Wadn't nothing, Sam," Mr. Matthew repeated.

"Damn, man," Sam said, dismissing Mr. Matthew with a wave of his hand.

Sam and Hambone exchanged glances, then Hambone said, "We've come here today with bad news. We came to warn you that while you're singing and praying, these white people are busy figuring out ways to get rid of you."

"That's right," Sam agreed. "We came to get Mr. Dobson."

Gerald Dobson pushed his way slowly toward the front of the church. "What do I have to do with any of this?" he asked.

"According to lil' Steve here, they done left you a customer out at Krandike Pond, Mr. Dobson," Sam answered grimly. "They done hung somebody from a tree."

A gasp of disbelief rolled over the pews, front to back. "Are you sure about this, son?" Reverend Nelson asked little Steve.

"I want my daddy," the boy sobbed. "I want my daddy."

It took some time to calm little Steve, and for the child to tell how he had been going out to the pond for a swim, how he had cut through the trees, the way he always did, and had seen the legs first. He had glanced up and seen a man hanging by a rope from a tree.

As the story unraveled, we began to get a picture of the morning's events. Hambone and Maxwell had been out to our house to pick up Sam. They were just leaving and getting ready to turn onto Fife Street when they saw little Steve running through the field and screaming. He had nearly run straight into Hambone's car. Without going out to the pond to verify what the boy had said, Hambone had put him in the car and had driven to the church.

Krandike Pond was about a mile and a half west of our house. It was out in the country near the dairy, and it would have made more sense for Sam and the rest to go out there before they came to the church, but I had a feeling Hambone had insisted on coming to the church first. It gave him the perfect opportunity to use the church as a forum for his civil rights crusade.

Miss Janie Jay finally managed to faint. Too many of the women worked over her—probably because they needed something to do. Most of the men had gathered around the pulpit. I saw little Steve ease himself away from the group and rush outside. Others were leaving, too, and I saw no reason for me to stay. Some man, someone I probably knew, was hanging from a tree. It didn't seem real, and maybe it wasn't. Maybe little Steve had made a mistake. That was all I could think about as I left the church.

Laura and Edna were walking a few steps ahead of me, and I lingered behind, not wanting to answer their questions. A tap on my shoulder startled me and caused me to trip. I turned to see Jeff Stallings.

"I'm sorry," he said. "I didn't mean to scare you, but I guess everybody is a little jumpy right now."

I nodded.

"I saw you leave the church, and I thought I'd walk with you," he said. "Do you mind if I walk with you?"

"You can walk with me," I said. "Do you think there's gonna be trouble?"

"There's already trouble. If what they're saying is true, I don't know what might happen."

"It's awful, isn't it? Are you worried?"

"No. I don't have to worry. No one is going to bother me. I'm invisible."

"You're not invisible," I said. "You might wish you were, but I can see you."

"I know you can, but it takes special eyes to see me."

His tone was as serious as Hambone's had been back at the church, so I stopped walking and stared at this invisible boy who had stopped beside me. He was small-boned and of medium height. He had round eyes and a thin, upturned nose. There was a cleft in his chin, and right at the curve of that chin, the most perfectly round mole I had ever seen.

"Well, I can see you," I repeated.

"You have those special eyes," he remarked.

"My friend, Mattie, she sees you, too."

"Your friend, Mattie, has an evil eye. Of course, she can see me. I wouldn't be surprised if Mattie sees ghouls, and witches, and vampires."

"You don't like Mattie?" I asked.

"I neither like nor dislike her," he answered. "To me she is merely a friend of the prettiest girl in school."

I felt awkward and a little embarrassed. I experienced a tingle of shame in my armpits, and I wanted to scratch, but could not with him watching me.

"I have to go," I said. "My mother is probably wondering where I am."

"I want to make sure you and your sisters get home safely. I'll walk with you," he said.

"We'll be all right," I said, turning to face the road ahead. Laura and Edna were far ahead of me now.

"Tangy," Jeff called as I moved away from him.

I stopped and faced him.

"I'll see you tomorrow," he said. "Maybe we can sit together at lunch. Maybe we'll find out that this is all a big mistake."

I nodded, but the sorrowful feeling inside of me told me that little Steve had not been mistaken. Somebody was dead. Somebody had been lynched.

My mother was not at home wondering where I was. I did not have to wonder where she was, either. Martha Jean would not stop telling me that Mama had left the house with Velman Cooper.

"Make her stop that!" Tarabelle demanded. "If you don't, I'm gon' hit her. I swear I will."

I tried to quiet Martha Jean, but she would not have it. She sailed from the front door to the front window, over and over, pounding her fists against her thighs and signing in choppy, sporadic phrases.

"Mama. Velman. Car," she signed. "Go away. Tell me. Tell me."

"I don't know, Martha Jean," I said aloud, trying to assure Tarabelle that I was doing something. "Sit down, Martha Jean! Please!"

The expression on her scarred and healing face shifted from puzzlement to pain. It troubled me that I could not calm her, but it troubled me more that Mattie was sitting snugly in an armchair watching it all.

"Hurt here," Martha Jean signed, then slapped her chest with the palm of her hand.

"I'm getting outta here," Tarabelle said in a huff. "C'mon, Mattie."

I stood in front of Martha Jean. "Velman bring Mama back. Short time," I signed.

She stopped pacing long enough to read what I was signing to her, then she rushed over to the window again. She studied the road, came back across the room, and slumped down in a chair. She leaned forward, clasped her arms beneath her knees, and began to rock. I explained to her that I would go to the post office tomorrow after school, and I would ask Velman where he had taken Mama, and why. She nodded and continued to rock.

Martha Jean seemed to have forgotten all about Judy, who was awake and lying in her basket. She was such a good baby. She was never fussy and seldom cried. I lifted her from the basket and carried her outside.

In the side yard, Laura and Edna were making awkward attempts at jumping rope. They had changed from their Sunday dresses to shorts, and their bony legs and bare feet kept getting tangled in the ropes. They never questioned the unusual amount of traffic passing our house.

Tarabelle and Mattie came from the rear of the house, cut through the yard, and walked down the embankment to the road. I felt resentment that Mattie hadn't bothered to speak to me. I swallowed my anger and played with Judy until Wallace and his friend, Shaky, came out of the grove of trees west of the field.

"Tan, you shoulda seen it," Wallace exclaimed, coming up to the steps and bending over to catch his breath. "We went out to the pond to see the man that was hanging from that tree. He was still hanging there. I ain't never seen nothing like it before."

"Wallace, you shouldn't have gone out there," I said.

"I wanted to see," he said. "Everybody went. They called the sheriff and Doctor Mathis, but wadn't nothing they could do. Didn't nobody wanna touch him. Doctor Mathis said it looked like somebody had took a baseball bat to him. Said he had a whole lotta broken bones. That's when that ol' mean Chadlow said a nigger musta done it. Sam and them got mad when he said that, and I thought there was gon' be a fight, but the sheriff started making people leave. It's Junior Fess, Tan."

"Junior? Oh, no. Oh, no." Then I asked apprehensively, "Where's Sam now?"

"I don't know. He left wit' Hambone. Sam and Hambone was yelling 'bout Junior being lynched, but the sheriff said it wadn't no lynching. He said it was murder, and he'd arrest anybody he heard talking 'bout a lynching in his town. Me and Shaky hid and stayed to see what they was gon' do wit' Junior. Harvey and Mr. Dobson touched him. They picked him up and put him in Mr. Dobson's hearse."

"Yeah. They oughta be coming by here pretty soon," Shaky said excitedly.

I held Judy closer to my body, and stared down at the road. "If Doctor Mathis didn't touch him, how does he know somebody used a bat on him?" I asked.

"I guess 'cause of the way everything looked backwards on him.

You know. Like his feet was turned so Junior could walk backwards," Wallace answered.

Shaky could not contain himself; he was moving about impatiently, but Wallace looked like he was going to be sick. They had rested long enough for Shaky, and he was ready to be on the move again.

Wallace rushed towards the back of the house. "I'm going to get my bike. I'll be back in a minute, Shaky."

Shaky had settled down and was watching the road by the time Wallace returned, pushing his bike. My brother glanced up at me briefly, just long enough for me to see that his eyes were red-rimmed and watery. He had gone to the backyard, out of his friend's view, to be sick.

"Wallace, did Junior have his satchel with him?" I asked.

Wallace shook his head. "I didn't see it," he said, then he rode off toward Fife Street with Shaky sitting on the handlebars of the bike. Tarabelle passed them coming in the opposite direction. They did not acknowledge each other.

I cried, wetting Judy's tiny body with my tears. I prayed, and waited for my mother to come home. Through my tears, I saw Sam get out of Hambone's car. He stumbled up the bank, and I thought he was drunk, but he wasn't. I saw my mother climb from Velman Cooper's car. Her face was ashen and her eyes were dull. She looked like death struggling up a mountainside.

Never in my life had I heard such rage under one roof as I heard that night. Sam wailed like a strong, full-grown man—the worst sound in the world. Grief and anger wrapped around his chest and sputtered and hissed with his every wail. It seemed to suck the air from his lungs and the blood from his heart. My mother enfolded him in her arms, and together they slumped to the kitchen floor. Sam clutched her shoulders and clung to her as though something inside of her could give him relief.

"My baby, my baby," Mama cried, and that went on for what seemed like hours until Sam's arms fell weakly to his sides.

"They didn't have to kill him, Mama," Sam cried. "They didn't have to kill him. I went and seen how they left him hanging from that tree, and they didn't have to do that. Junior ain't never hurt nobody."

"I know, baby. I know," Mama soothed.

Sam crawled across the floor and curled his body up with his face to the wall. Mama poured herself a teacup of corn whiskey, then she sipped and kept watch over her son. I sat on a milk crate and watched my mother cry real tears. I heard my brother moan.

twenty-two

Although Junior hadn't really been a teacher, everybody at the Plymouth School acted as though he had been. On Monday, after a morning assembly for prayer, it was a quiet day and we weren't required to do much of anything. I wrote a letter to Mushy, and I tried to study, but my mind kept drifting back to the last time I had seen Junior. For me, a busy day would have been better than all of that quiet time to think.

When school let out in the afternoon, I went to the post office to mail my letter. I hadn't thought about Martha Jean, or how upset she had been the day before, until I saw Velman Cooper coming across the post office lawn to meet me.

"I don't think you wanna go inside," he said. "There's a bunch of 'em in there laughing about Junior Fess. Ain't none of 'em claiming they did it, but they ain't sorry he dead."

"You're right then. I don't want to go in there," I said. "I've never seen my brothers take anything this hard before."

"How's Martha Jean taking it?"

"She's okay. She didn't really know Junior. She's more concerned about you. She wants to know what you're doing with our mother."

Velman sighed and stared down at his feet. "Your mother is a sad woman. Even before Mr. Brogus came up to the car and told us about Junior, yo' mama was crying. Kept saying how she don't wanna rear her children here. She wants to get outta Georgia."

"That sounds like a lie." I just didn't believe him.

"Well, lie or not, what I do wit' yo' mama is my business," he said dryly.

"You're right. You and Mama are both full-grown. Martha Jean is the one I'm worried about."

"Why don't you tell yo' sister to trust me, and let's just leave it at that."

"Trust you?" I asked. "Why should she trust you? Look at what just knowing you has gotten her. Martha Jean didn't come looking for you. You chased her, and after I told you she was too young."

"Tell her to trust me, little sister," he pleaded.

"Do you intend to see my mother again?"

He nodded. I walked away from him.

All the way home and on into the evening, I thought about what I should tell Martha Jean. I sat on the front porch listening to my mother, who was trying to talk the misery out of Sam. I imagined she had spent the day talking, until Sam decided he would do anything to shut her up. At least he'd gotten off the kitchen floor and was standing outside in fresh air.

Mama sent Wallace to Logan's store over on Canyon Street to buy Sam a pack of Pall Malls. She talked the whole time Wallace was gone, saying mostly the wrong things.

"Sam, everybody sorry Junior dead, but you been running 'round wit' the wrong people. You don't need to be 'round nobody that people wanna kill."

"Can we talk about something else, Mama?" Sam asked, as he stared out in the direction where Junior's body had been found.

"Sometime you need to talk about what you thinking 'bout, Sam. And I know you keep thinking 'bout that boy, but you can't bring him back. I'm gon' cook up some collard greens, and we gon' take 'em up to Mary Lou and Tannus, say we sorry 'bout they boy, then we gon' put this whole thing behind us."

"Junior ain't even buried yet, Mama, and you want me to put it behind me?" Sam asked. "I done put crying behind me, but somebody gon' pay for what they did to Junior. I'm gon' hurt somebody, soon as I know who the right somebody is."

"Nah, you ain't, Sam."

"What you want me to do, Mama? Just let somebody kill Junior like that, and get away wit' it?"

"I want you to act like you got some sense. I don't want you leaving outta here trying to even no score wit' nobody 'cause you don't even know who killed that boy."

"I got my suspicions," Sam mumbled.

"Me, too," Harvey said, and glanced over at Sam.

"Be quiet, Harvey!" Mama ordered.

"Junior was my friend, too, Mama," Harvey said solemnly.

Mama nodded her head and massaged her temples. "I know, but I want y'all to think about me for a minute. Do y'all know how hard it would be on me if somebody beat y'all wit' a crowbar and strung you from a tree?"

They both looked at her, then Sam said, "I heard it was a baseball bat."

"Maybe it was," Mama agreed. "It was something heavy, something that could break the bones in somebody's body. Now, let's talk about something else."

Nobody spoke. We listened to Laura and Edna playing in the yard until Wallace returned from the store. Mama took the cigarettes from him, ripped open the pack, and persuaded Sam to teach her how to smoke. She coughed, choked, and sucked in breath. After her fifth attempt at inhaling, it became apparent that she would eventually get the hang of it, and I lost interest.

I tugged at Martha Jean's arm, trying to get her to follow me down into the yard, thinking it was a good time to teach Laura and Edna to jump rope. Martha Jean hesitated, pointed toward the house, and cradled her arms.

"Judy sleep," I signed.

Martha Jean finally, reluctantly, followed me down to the yard. I guided Laura to the spot where I wanted her to stand, then Martha Jean and I twirled the rope over her head. Laura did not move her feet until after the rope had hit against her heels. Surprisingly, Edna was better at it, and managed to get two jumps in before getting herself tangled in the rope.

Sitting on the top step with one shoulder pressed against the house, Tarabelle stared down at us. A truck rattled along the road below, and she turned her head as if expecting something or someone. I wondered if I should tell her about the bus ticket Mushy had sent.

"Jump!" I shouted, and twirled my end of the rope. It swept beneath Edna's feet, over her head, and beneath her feet again—six times before a miss.

Up on the porch, Wallace was jumping about excitedly beside Mama's chair. "Let me show you how to do it, Mama," he said. "I know how to do it so you don't cough."

"Boy, who taught you to smoke?" Mama asked between coughs. "Give him one, Sam. Let him show me."

"Can I have one?" Tarabelle asked, then called down to the yard, "Tangy, tell Martha Jean that Judy is crying."

Martha Jean and I made our way up the steps, and the minute we were inside, I signed to her that I thought it best if she forgot about Velman Cooper because he was going to keep seeing our mother. Martha Jean shook her head as though I did not know what I was talking about, then she went over and took Judy from the basket.

Harvey was withdrawn, and refused supper. Mama told him twice, just as she had told Sam, that he needed to put Junior behind him.

"Junior never got a chance to live, Mama," he said. "I don't want that to happen to me."

When we were down on our pallets for the night, Harvey tipped into the front room carrying the kitchen lamp. He hesitated for a second at the doorway, drew in a deep breath, then crossed the short distance of the hall to Mama's room. His voice was a whisper, as he spoke to our mother. There was a moment of complete silence, then Mama screamed.

Tarabelle and I sat up. Sam and Wallace came in from the kitchen. Harvey backed out of Mama's room, and she followed him in slow, menacing steps.

"You stupid son-of-a-bitch!" she screamed. "Is this what I spent my life working for? I raised you, Harvey. I done went without for you, and this how you pay me back?" She was gripping a bamboo cane. "You still my child. I'm gon' beat some sense into you. I'm gon' teach you not to go behind my back doing yo' foolishness."

"Mama, it was time." Harvey pleaded for understanding. "You knew I was gon' do it sooner or later."

"No!" she yelled. "I never thought you'd turn yo' back on me. If you'd thought you was doing the right thing, you wouldna married her behind my back. You woulda tol' me, Harvey."

She spotted the poker propped against the wall behind the stove. She dropped the cane and rushed toward the stove. That was when I cried, "Mama, please don't hit Harvey with that poker!"

Harvey placed the lamp on the table and moved to block her path to the stove but she already had the poker in her hand, and she threw it toward me. It struck the back of a chair and bounced off, hit the top of the cedar chest, and broke the front window pane.

Mama ripped Harvey's shirt and, as he tried to get away, clawed at his back, and damned him to Hell for all eternity. Harvey took his beating like a man until Mama was too exhausted to move anything other than her angry gray eyes.

"I'm leaving now, Mama," Harvey said.

"No," she whimpered.

"Yeah," he said calmly, almost tenderly. "Mama, I don't feel no shame 'bout what I did. I didn't mean to hurt you, but I'm grown."

"I won't let you go. You my baby, Harvey. Don't turn yo' back on me."

"I ain't turning my back on you. If you ever need me, I'll come, but I done took my last beating and it's just time to go. I'm sorry, Mama." He stepped into the hallway, then turned and looked at each of us. When his gaze met mine, he smiled sadly. "Tangy, girl," he said, "this world a awful big place. You can't save everybody in it. Stop trying, okay?"

I nodded, and Harvey turned away. Through his tattered shirt, I saw the marks on his back. My emotions were in turmoil. Already I missed Harvey, but he had just shown me that one day I, too, might walk out of my mother's house—alive.

twenty-three

On the day of Junior's funeral, Wallace stepped on the jagged bottom half of a broken Upper Ten bottle, and left blood all over the schoolyard. Shaky Brown said that Wallace had cut two of his toes off. Tina Long said he was going to lose his foot. Mr. Preston, however, told me that Wallace was going to be just fine, and that someone had come to the school and picked him up.

I wondered aloud as to who had come for Wallace as Mattie and I sat in the bleachers during lunch. Mattie acted as though I had not spoken, talking on and on about Tarabelle. Out of habit, I listened, while looking at Jeff.

"You oughta be shame of yo'self, always watching that boy like that," Mattie commented.

I ignored her.

"I heard yo' brother married the witch's sister," she said.

"I like Carol Sue," I said.

"I ain't said nothing 'bout Carol Sue. I'm talking 'bout Edith, her sister."

"Well, Mattie, he didn't marry Edith."

"Don't get smart wit' me, Tangy," she said. "I don't know what's wrong wit' you lately."

"Me?" I asked, surprised. "There's nothing wrong with me. You're the one who's acting silly. You come out to our house and you never spend time with me anymore. You're always with Tarabelle."

"Tarabelle is more fun. And anyway, I spend time wit' you at school."

"Do you still want to be my best friend?" I asked.

"Not really," she answered. "Best friends tell each other things. You never told me you was sneaking 'round wit' Jeff Stallings."

"That's because I haven't been sneaking around with him," I shot back.

We were glaring at each other when a silence fell over the schoolyard. Students began to line themselves up in the yard and along the sidewalk in front of the school. Mattie and I rose to join them, and Jeff came up to stand behind me. We stood there, silent and humble, paying our last respects to Junior Fess, as the funeral procession snaked along from the church and passed the school.

I glanced between the rows of bowed heads in front of me and saw my brother, Harvey, driving the car that carried Junior's mother, father, and an older sister. Sadness brought tears to my eyes, not because of Junior, but because I hadn't even known Harvey could drive.

Jeff placed a hand on my shoulder as the last car passed. "Are you all right?" he asked.

"Yeah," I answered. Mattie walked away from me.

The silence in the yard became a cacophony as adolescent rage replaced grief, as everyone began to speculate about who had lynched Junior. I walked to the side of the building with Jeff, and began firing questions at him.

"What's going on here?" he asked. "Why are you asking so many questions?"

"Because I don't know much about you."

"Yeah, but slow down, Tangy. You don't have to make it a quiz. We have plenty of time to get to know each other."

"Maybe," I said, "and maybe not. Maybe Junior thought he had plenty of time."

"Is that what this is all about?" Jeff asked. "Do you think you're going to leave school today and drop dead?"

"It could happen," I answered. "I could be walking home and get hit by a car, or a dog with rabies could bite me."

"In that case, I'll walk with you. We can both get rabies and go mad together."

"It's not funny," I said. I was walking away from him when the bell rang, signaling the end of the lunch recess.

After school, Archie Preston caught up to me before I left the building. Archie was a burly, red man—totally and completely. His hair and face were red, and he had freckles covering his face. It was hard for me to imagine him being Harvey's father.

"You need to get your brother's bike from the back," he said. "Shouldn't leave it there all night."

"I can't ride a bike," I said.

"I can." I turned to see Jeff standing there.

I refused his offer, and pushed the bike all the way from Plymouth, through Stump Town, and on home. It was awkward, but wiser for me to push than have my mother see me with a boy. I managed to get home, then I parked the bike behind the house and went inside. I could hear Wallace talking.

"They asked me who to call, Mama," he explained. "We don't have no telephone. I couldn't call Mr. Frank or Miss Pearl 'cause they was at work. I didn't know who to call. That's when I thought about the midwife. Since she's something like a doctor, I thought maybe she could help my foot. That's why I called her."

"Don't you ever do it again," Mama scolded, but her voice was soft, and she touched his head when she spoke. "You don't know them people like I do, and I done tol' you before to stay away from 'em."

"I know, Mama," Wallace said. "If there'd been somebody else, I wouldna called 'em. That ol' woman scares me anyhow."

He glanced at me, and I saw in his eyes that tangled web of deception woven out of necessity. I folded my arms across my chest and stared at him until he dropped his gaze. He was lying, and he was getting away with it.

Mama kissed him lightly before leaving him at the table with his foot propped on a milk crate.

"I brought your bike home," I said. "How's your foot?"

"It hurts. What you think?"

"You're lying, Wallace."

"It hurts," he repeated. "It's my foot. I oughta know."

"Not about the foot. You're lying about the midwife."

"Where'd Mama go?" he asked, glancing over his shoulder toward the door.

"Front porch, I think."

"Go see, Tan. Make sure."

In the front room, Martha Jean was sitting on the floor reading a book, and our younger sisters were napping. I entered the hallway, then doubled back. "Mama where?" I signed to Martha Jean. I did not want to be accused of spying again, which is exactly what I was doing.

Martha Jean pointed toward the front door.

"Front porch," I said, returning to the kitchen.

"Good," Wallace said. "Help me to the back. I wanna see my bike."

He removed his foot from the crate and pulled himself up by bracing his arms against the tabletop. I allowed him to use me as a crutch as we wobbled along toward the back porch. He sat on the top step, and I sat on the edge of the porch with my legs dangling over the side.

"Did you ride it?" Wallace asked.

"You know I can't ride a bike," I answered. I looked at the bike, then at Wallace's bandaged foot. I saw on his other foot the dirty, tattered tennis shoe that he had been wearing since last September. There were two large holes at the bottom, and cardboard had been tucked inside. "Wallace, let me ask you something. Why did you go out and steal a bicycle?"

"'Cause," he answered.

"You stole it from some white boy. What if he had seen you? What if he sees you riding it around? Aren't you afraid?"

Wallace shook his head. "Naw. Can't nobody prove I stole it."

"They don't have to prove it. They can shoot you, or lynch you if they want to. Look what they did to Junior, and he hadn't stolen anything."

"You don't know what Junior did," Wallace replied. "Maybe he stole a horse, or a car, or somebody's money. You don't know. But ain't nobody gon' shoot me for taking some ol' bike."

"All I'm saying, Wallace, is if you were going to steal something, why didn't you take a pair of shoes? That's something you need."

"Aw, shoot, Tan," he whined, "you take the fun outta everything. It's almost summer. I don't need no shoes for summer."

"You don't need shoes at all," I said. "All you need is one shoe. One shoe, Wallace. You can't get anything on your right foot. You're being punished for stealing. God saw you take that bike, and He's punishing you so you can't ride it. Now you can't run, or walk, or ride that ol' stupid bike."

For a moment it seemed as though Wallace was going to cry, but then he said, "Tan, I didn't steal it. I had to tell Mama that. If she knew where I really got it, she'd try to kill me."

"Where did you get it?"

"From the midwife."

"I thought you were afraid of the midwife," I said.

"I was at first, but she ain't all mean like Mama make out. Her husband ain't, either. Tan, I had to see what was scaring Mama so bad. I went over on Selman Street that day after Mama went to the hospital to have Judy. Didn't look like nothing was wrong wit' the house, but I couldn't be sure, and I was scared to get too close. I kept going back every day, looking. One day that ol' woman saw me, and called me. I went to see what she wanted. She remembered who I was and knew everything 'bout me, like she was a witch or something. I started talking to her, and I just wadn't scared no mo'."

I swung my legs up onto the porch, drew my knees up to my chest, and watched Wallace closely as he spoke.

"You shouldn't sit like that," he admonished. "It ain't ladylike."

"Shut up," I said. "How can you worry about modesty? Mama's gonna kill you when she finds out about the midwife."

He flipped a hand nonchalantly, as if to say, I've considered that. "She'll have to catch me first. Mama can't catch me."

I laughed. I dropped my knees and rocked my legs against the porch as I pointed at his foot. "Wallace, a snail could catch you. How are you gonna run with all of that stuff on your foot?"

He stretched a hand down and tugged at the bandages. "If she comes after me, I'll pull this stuff off and run so fast it'll make yo' head spin."

He waited until I had my laughter under control, then asked if I would help him back inside. He draped an arm across my shoulder, and as we approached the door, he reached up and gave my ponytail a timid yank.

"I want you to talk to Miss Zadie," he said. "You'll see, Tan, she ain't so bad. She gave me that bike for my birthday. I didn't even have to tell her it was my birthday. She just knew. Nobody else remembered, except Miss Pearl."

I planted a wet kiss on his cheek, then supported his weight as he awkwardly wiped it away. "Happy birthday, Wallace," I said. "I hope you enjoy your bike."

twenty-four

M en with trucks began to arrive three weeks before Plymouth School was to close its doors for the summer. Wallace was still home nursing his injured foot, and missed the noise of trees going down, the smell of deep earth coming up, the groundbreaking for our new school. It was an exciting time for everybody, but even more so for me. Jeff Stallings had asked me to the prom.

Having rehearsed what I would tell my mother, I entered the house that Thursday afternoon only to find the place deserted. I dropped my books in the front room and went out to the kitchen. Through the window I could see Wallace, Laura, and Edna. Wallace had wrapped his foot in a thin strip of checkered cloth, knotted at the toes. He had the front wheel of his bike propped on the bottom step with Laura and Edna holding it steady while he practiced pedaling.

"Where's Martha Jean?" I called from the window.

"Who knows?" Wallace called back. "Somebody came in a car and got Mama. Two minutes later, Martha Jean was walking up the road wit' Judy. Nobody said nothing to me. They just left me here wit' these two. I ain't staying home tomorrow."

Turning from the window, I picked up my books, and went to sit on the front steps. It was quiet, an ideal time for studying, but I found myself studying the world around me instead of the books on my lap.

Mama had not purchased seeds to plant a garden in the yard as she had said she would, and I did not think anything would have grown anyway. The field would have made a larger garden, but who knew what might grow there, or who it belonged to? It was a place where towering weeds seemed to grow and die in the same breath.

My gaze shifted from the field to the road. I saw Tarabelle turn at the bend and stride briskly toward the house. Tucked under her arm was a bag of something that I assumed Mrs. Munford had given her. She mounted the steps, paused at the door, and removed several items from the bag before dropping a garment on top of my open book.

"Miss Arlisa's expecting," she said before entering the house, and I could not tell from her expression whether that was good news or bad.

I inspected the garment she had given me. It was a straight-cut, long-sleeved, brown gabardine dress with a pink vest. It would need some alterations, but I thought it would make a nice Sunday dress, and I needed one.

A car stopped in front of our house and my mother stepped out. "Y'all come back in 'bout a hour," she said. "We'll be ready." She glanced up and saw me sitting on the step. "Tarabelle home yet?" she asked.

"Yes, ma'am."

Today she was the beautiful, happy mother whom I feared so very much. Her hair was loose and flowing. She wore a yellow dress with a full skirt. Her legs were bare, and on her feet were a pair of flat, white shoes that I had never seen before. She came up the steps, lightly brushed my cheek, and smiled down at me.

"That was Crow," she said, as though I should know who Crow was. "He done come back from New York. Got a pocket full of money. I'm gon' get some of that money for you, baby. Don't you worry 'bout a thing."

She entered the house and immediately began to shout orders at Tarabelle, excitedly. "Get yo'self together, girl. Put on the best dress you got, and tell the dummy to fetch me some bathwater."

I placed my new dress on top of my books and rose to prepare my mother's bath, formulating a lie to tell in Martha Jean's defense if it should become necessary. I carried the tub into Mama's room and found her sitting on the bed checking her stockings for runs.

"I ain't got a decent pair of stockings," she said. "I'll buy me two pair tomorrow. I bet Crow would buy me fifty pair if I ask him."

She reminded me of a spoiled child, not knowing whether to throw a tantrum because of the stockings or jump for joy because of this Crow. I waited until it seemed that joy was winning out, then I spoke. "Your water is warming, Mama," I said. "Do you want me to help you check your stockings?"

She passed half the bundle over to me, and I took a seat beside her on the bed. I stretched a stocking, stuck my arm inside, and turned it to check for snags. Mama tapped a foot against the floor as she concentrated on her task. She was in a good mood—a really good mood.

"Mama, Jeff Stallings invited me to the prom," I said quickly. "Can I go?"

"Jeff Stallings? Ain't that John Henry Stallings' boy? Why he ask you?"

I shrugged. "He just did."

"What you doing, Tangy Mae, the reason that boy ask you? Them people got money. They don't even half speak to people like you."

"He thinks I'm pretty, Mama."

"Nah. That boy ain't said nothing like that. Is he blind?" She removed a stocking from her outstretched arm. "Here's a good one. Don't mix it back wit' the others."

I took the stocking, placed it on her pillow, and waited.

"That boy up to something," she said after a moment of silence. "I don't know what it is, but he up to something. He'll probably be driving that nice car they got. And you mean to tell me he gon' come out here and pick up some skinny, little black girl when he can take anybody he wants? Why ain't he taking one of them Brandon girls?"

"He asked me, Mama."

"Well, if he asked you, then you go. You go and have a good time. And you make sho' that boy bring you home when the dancing over.

Don't play 'round wit' him, Tangy Mae. You ain't the kinda girl he gon' have much time for later. Boys'll play 'round wit' girls like you, but they'll marry one of them Brandon girls. You mark my word."

She got down on her knees, reached beneath the bed, and withdrew a box. From it, she pulled three white brassieres, and placed them side by side on the mattress.

"Here," she said. "If you going out wit' John Henry Stallings' boy, I want you to look decent. Take whichever one you want."

I studied the brassieres, and could see no difference in color, shape, or size. They were all white, cotton, and too small for me. I chose the one from the middle.

"Thank you," I said, and was moved nearly to tears. I pressed the brassiere to my nose and sniffed the faint scent of lilac.

Mama watched me. She stood up, held my head between her palms, and kissed my hair. "Tangy, baby," she said tenderly, "it's just a ol' brassiere. Ain't nothing but a ol' brassiere. Don't cry 'bout it, baby."

"Yes, ma'am," I said, as the tears spilled from my eyes.

I left the room, and returned shortly with her bathwater. I poured the water into the tub while she hummed a tune and laid her clothes out on the bed.

Time seemed to stand still. I kept waiting for Mama to detect Martha Jean's absence, but she never did. When the car returned, she rushed Tarabelle out and followed behind her, glowing with happiness.

I was already awake when Tarabelle tapped the back of my head with the toe of her shoe.

"Stop," I mumbled irritably.

"Well, get up then," she said. "Mama want you to come outside. There's a big, black ape out there wanna have a look at you."

I crawled up from the floor and stumbled about in moonlight, looking for something to put on.

"Here," Tarabelle said, then slipped out of her dress and gave it to me.

Outside, Mama was leaning against a car, talking to someone who was seated inside. I walked slowly down the embankment to the road wondering what was so important that she needed to drag me out of the house at this hour.

"Here she is, Crow," Mama said as I approached the car. "Come stand right here, Tangy Mae." She positioned me in front of the car where I was illuminated by the glare of headlights.

A man stepped from the car. He was as dark as midnight, with large, white teeth that chewed on a matchstick. He was tall—very tall, and muscular. He wore a light brown suit and a brown fedora.

"Damn, Rozelle," he said. "We got us a queen here. A sho' nuff queen."

"You like her, Crow?" Mama asked, beaming with pride.

"If I hadda knowed we could do this," he said, "we coulda stayed together and made a dozen little Crow queens." He stepped closer, towering over me, and brought a hand down to the top of my head. "Lord, if she ain't got my mama's hair."

"I told you so," Mama said. "Didn't I tell you?" She'd had too much to drink. She slurred her words, and rocked unsteadily on the dirt road.

"Look here, Rozelle," Crow said, reaching into his pocket and extracting a billfold, "you go on in the house now. I wanna talk to this gal. We got sixteen years to catch up on."

"Tangy Mae ain't sixteen, yet," Mama said, accepting the bills that Crow offered her. "Don't you keep her out here too long."

"I know she ain't sixteen," Crow responded, staring at me. "We gon' catch up on time 'fo' she got here. I just might tell her a little something 'bout you. How you like that?"

He winked, and Mama tried to wink back, but failed to manage more than a dull blink of both eyes. She stumbled up the embankment, and Crow watched until she was safely on the porch, then he turned his attention back to me and walked me around to a door of the car. As he opened the door for me, Mama yelled down from the porch, "You coming back tomorrow, Crow?"

"Not tomorrow," he answered. "I gotta run up to Knoxville, see my mama. Maybe Sat'day, Rozelle. Maybe I'll see you Sat'day."

There was a man asleep on the back seat of the car. He snored in the ragged rhythm of drunkenness, and I tried to see who he was, but could not because of the way his arm was draped over his face.

"That's Melvin," Crow said, sliding in behind the steering wheel and turning his key in the ignition. "Dorothy probably gon' hit him upside his head wit' something, but that ain't my worry."

"What do you want to talk to me about?" I asked, as the car rolled up Fife Street.

"Don't tell Rozelle, but I thought you was sixteen," he said. "It ain't that you look it or nothing. It's just that I get mixed up wit' the years sometimes. They roll by so fast."

He produced another match from his coat pocket, tossed the old one out the window, and placed the fresh one between his teeth. "Yo' mama is really something," he said after a lengthy silence. "I been knowing her for years. I asked her to marry me once, but she wouldn't do it. You know what she tol' me? She said, 'Crow, I can't marry no man dark as you. I just can't do it.' That's all the reason she ever gave." He chuckled, dry and throaty. "She kinda stuck on that color thang, you know? I was willing to take them babies she had and give 'em a home, but all yo' mama could see was color. She ain't changed a bit, neither. She'd go out wit' me, help me spend my money, have a little fun, but that was all. She didn't want nobody to see her wit' me. She still don't."

"What about him?" I asked, motioning toward the back seat.

"Aw, shoot. Melvin Tate? He ain't nobody."

We reached Market Street where there was not another car in sight. It was strange seeing the town at this early hour of the morning. There was a light on inside the train depot, and crates were lined along the platform, but there seemed to be no one in attendance. I glanced back at the depot as the car thumped across the tracks and turned left in the direction of the flats.

On the back seat, Melvin Tate stirred and pulled himself into a sitting position. He leaned forward across the front seat, placing his head between mine and Crow's. "Hey, Crow. Man, pull over," he said. "Let me outta this damn car 'less you want a wet seat."

Crow swore but stopped the car, and Melvin stumbled out and staggered around to the rear.

"See," Crow said, "I told you he wadn't nobody."

I knew Melvin Tate, and Crow was right.

"How many babies yo' mama got now?" Crow asked, glancing about impatiently and turning on his seat to check on Melvin.

"Ten."

"Goddamn, Rozelle been busy. She wouldn't tell me when I asked her. Said it wadn't none of my business since they didn't belong to me. I had to remind her that she had one belonged to me." He was silent for a moment, then said, "You know what? I oughta leave that nigger out there, but I don't want it to be my fault if he goes to jail."

Melvin returned and managed, with great difficulty, to settle his lanky frame on the back seat. The strong odor of urine followed him inside, and I rolled my window down for fresh air.

Crow turned on his seat and stared at Melvin. "Man, get outta my car," he demanded. "You smell like a damn outhouse. Get out!"

"Come on, man," Melvin pleaded.

"Come on, hell. Get out my car, Melvin. If you wadn't so drunk, you could see yo' house from here. Get out!"

Reluctantly, Melvin crawled from the back seat, and Crow pulled away, leaving him staring after us. Crow turned onto Motten Street and stopped the car.

"I gotta make sho' he gets home," Crow said. "That's his house right up the street there."

I glanced up the street at the row of darkened houses which were identical in structure. A few had enclosed porches, but they all had four wooden steps that practically kissed the sidewalk, and saddle lawns that were mostly well kept. I knew where the Tates lived. I knew who lived in every house on Motten Street, including Skeeter's. Somewhere in the darkness of Skeeter's house was Velman Cooper, a man who was courting my sister and my mother.

"Do you know Skeeter Richards?" I asked Crow.

"I know just about everybody in this town," he answered. "I used to live here. That was years ago."

"I've never heard of you."

"What?" he asked with genuine astonishment. "Rozelle never tol' you nothing 'bout me. Never tol' you how I used to sit for hours just holding you and looking down at yo' face. It's been some years, but y'all oughta remember me. Who yo' mama got you thinking yo' daddy is?"

I did not answer. I could not tell him about my mother and her secrets because I could not explain something I did not understand. Melvin Tate saved me from further interrogation as he staggered around the corner and up to the car, swearing every step of the way.

"I'm through wit' you, Crow," he yelled. "You lowdown dirty mothafucka." He pounded his fists against the trunk of the car and kicked a rear tire before falling to the ground.

Crow laughed, then started the car and pulled away from the curb. On the drive back to Penyon Road, he asked again if my mother had ever told me who my daddy was.

"She never did," I answered, "but the minute I saw you, I knew it was you."

"That's right. It's me."

He parked in front of our house and pressed two bills against my palm. "Here," he said. "Buy yo'self something pretty. Something fit for a queen."

He waited until I was on the porch, then drove off. Under moonlight I looked at the bills in my hand, a five and a twenty. It was more money than I had ever seen in one place at one time in my entire life.

In the front room I knelt on hands and knees, and groped around in darkness for my science book. I hid the money between the last page and the back cover, then crawled over to my pallet.

Tarabelle's voice startled me. "That big ape do you?" she asked.

"Do what? That big ape is my daddy," I said, then I stretched out and tumbled into sleep, spending my riches as I went.

twenty-five

M ama was euphoric in anticipation of Crow's next visit. She was sitting at the kitchen table, sucking on a Pall Mall, getting much better at it. Like the rising sun, she set the mood for the day—light and breezy without a storm cloud in sight. She made a grand production of presenting Wallace with five dollars to buy a pair of shoes. She promised Laura and Edna a trip to Logan's store, and she clapped her hands delightedly when Tarabelle told her that Miss Arlisa was expecting a baby.

"Ain't that funny," she beamed. "Me, too."

Tarabelle glanced at me, and I shrugged my shoulders.

"Mama," Sam said, "I thought you said you couldn't have no mo'. Didn't you tell Mushy you couldn't have no mo'?"

"You see, that's just it, Sam," she said. "That's why I ain't never put no stock in no doctor. Half the time they don't know what they talking 'bout."

"Well . . ." Sam said, and we waited for him to complete his sentence, but nothing more followed. He was at a loss for words, and so was I.

"I think I'm gon' have me a boy," Mama informed us. "Wit'

Harvey gone, we need another boy 'round here." She talked on and on, her lips moving through clouds of cigarette smoke, while we sent messages to each other with our eyes.

Tarabelle went to stand behind our mother's chair. She signed to Martha Jean, "Mama. Baby." She cradled her arms, then jabbed her abdomen twice with a finger. Martha Jean glanced down at Judy, then she stared back quizzically at Tarabelle. Tarabelle jabbed her abdomen again, and understanding registered in Martha Jean's eyes. For a moment, she regarded our mother with somber curiosity, then she rose from the table and left the kitchen with Judy clutched tightly against her chest.

Mama laughed—such a pleasant sound. She challenged Laura and Edna to come up with a name for the baby. "Two candy bars for the one who come up wit' the best name," she said, and Laura and Edna began to toss out names for Mama's approval. When Mama finally decided on the name, Timothy, she made good on her promise, and took the girls to Logan's store for candy.

"I don't like Mama when she happy like that," Wallace said as soon as our mother was gone.

"I don't like her, period," Tarabelle remarked. "How she gon' have another baby for Martha Jean to take care of? It ain't fair."

"I coulda swo' she said she couldn't have no mo'," Sam commented.

"She can't. I just know she can't," I said, but I wasn't really certain. Anything was possible.

I went outside to take clothes from the line. Thoughts of going to the prom with Jeff Stallings began to overshadow thoughts of my mother. There was nothing I could do about Mama having another baby, or even ten more babies, but there was something I could do about the prom. I'd have to buy a dress, and I was looking forward to that. Maybe, after school on Monday, Mattie would go into town with me to shop.

The clothes were inside and folded by the time Mama returned from the store with two very happy little girls, a pair of stockings, and a bag of two-for-a-penny candy. In an atmosphere of serenity, I filled my mouth with sweets and listened to my mother sing as she made herself ready for her date with Crow.

As the hours passed with no sign of Crow, Mama began to make excuses for his delay, saying that maybe he'd had a flat tire or was just running late. She spent the evening watching the road for his car, then she began to berate him, saying he was nothing and nobody, and she didn't care if he came or not. Finally, seated on a chair on the front porch, she spread her slender legs before her, gripped her new nylons, and ripped them to shreds.

On Sunday, after church, Velman Cooper came out to our house and drove away with our mother. When he brought her home late that evening, she was carrying a clock similar to the one she had thrown and broken, and a radio—something we had never owned. She placed the items on the seat of a chair, then she turned to me.

"Where's my money?" she asked. "I know Crow gave you some money. Where is it, Tangy Mae?"

How did she know? I averted my eyes, stared down at my hands, and probably looked guilty, but I said, "Mama, he didn't."

"Don't lie to me 'cause I know he did. Crow all time throwing money 'round like it grow on trees. Give it here, Tangy Mae."

I scanned the room for an ally. It seemed to me that my brothers and sisters were hiding in shadows, dissociating themselves from me. I thought about the money I had removed from the book and tucked into my socks, and I could see my prom dress caught up in a hurricane, whirling away from me. In the eye of the storm, I stood determined. I was not going to give it up, but my mother stepped forward and stood toe to toe with me, breathing a dragon's breath onto me.

My dissolution was swift. My back went limp and my fingers reached down into my left sock where I had hid the twenty-dollar bill. I pulled it out and gave it to my mother. I had been afraid to go for the five because it might not have been enough, and then I would have lost it all.

Mama seemed satisfied. "That's right," she said, fingering the bill. "I knew he gave you something. Don't ever try to steal from me."

"But, Mama," I said, "what about my dress for the prom?"

"You want a dress? Get a job. That's what you do, Tangy Mae. You get a job."

I was not stupid ordinarily, and so I blame my behavior on my desire to impress Jeff Stallings. Desperately, I reached out and tried to retrieve my money from my mother's hand. She clenched a fist around the bill, looked me in my eyes, and began to laugh. I had gotten away with one impulsive moment of impertinence, but . . .

Anger is airborne. It can be inhaled, and once it enters a body it becomes a tenacious blob of blues and browns with tiny speckles of red. It settles heavy in the lungs, making breathing ever so difficult.

. . . I had been infected with anger.

"Give it back, Mama," I wheezed. "It's mine and I want it. I need it."

She stood there toying with the bill, stretching it out, folding it in half, and wrapping it around her fingers. "You don't need shit, Tangy Mae," she said. "Everything you ever needed, I gave you. You remember that. Don't you go getting no big head just 'cause Crow came through town. I mean it."

The gray-eyed witch of a woman stood between me and happiness. I felt, for a fleeting instant, that I might attack her, but not alone. I needed an accomplice, someone strong and vindictive.

"You won't let us have anything!" I shouted. "You take it all. Why do you do that?"

She continued to laugh. It was obvious that I could not reason with her. Anyway, I was beyond trying.

"Tarabelle!" I cried. My hand rose and I pointed an accusing finger at my mother. "Tarabelle, she has your ticket. Mushy sent it weeks ago, and Mama took it. She takes everything."

"What?" Tarabelle's voice came from the shadows, but she did not move to my side. I was left standing alone, pointing a finger at my mother.

Mama bent that finger. The pain radiated along the back of my hand, into my wrist, and up my arm to the elbow, until finally I heard a snap—like a dew-kissed string bean—and the oddest sound crackled in my throat.

twenty-six

F our days passed before Miss Pearl examined my finger and declared it "just a little bit sprained. That's all."

I didn't believe her. My finger was swollen, had a camel's hump at the knuckle, and hurt like the dickens. It didn't matter that I did not believe Miss Pearl; I was indebted to her. How she had done it, I may never know, but she had gone into my mother's room that Friday, and emerged with an invitation for me to follow her.

"Come on, Tangy Mae," she'd said. "You coming wit' me, and we gon' get you a dress."

My dress was new and yellow and frilly and beautiful. I wore white shoes, and white gloves up to my elbows that covered the tape around my *sprained* finger. I felt pretty and shy as I walked, arm in arm, into the gymnasium with Jeff Stallings. Glittering stars and crepe paper moons dangled from the ceiling. The theme was Midnight in the Galaxy. The transformation of the gymnasium nearly took my breath away. Tables had been concealed beneath silver tablecloths that held crescent-shaped candles in crystal holders, and a huge silver dome over a central light fixture cast twinkling stars throughout the hall.

Jeff led me to a table where Evelyn Saunters and Douglas Mayberry were seated. Evelyn, a junior with whom I seldom shared conversation, complimented my dress with a sincerity that made me wish Miss Pearl could have heard. She had spent hours getting me ready for this special occasion, despite objections from her husband that I was too young to be courting.

She had paused in her task to stare at him. "This ain't got nothing to do wit' courting, Frank," she'd said. "This just a few hours in one night in one lifetime. You mean to tell me you don't think ever' one of them children out there deserve at least one good time?"

Reluctantly, he had nodded. "You right, Pearl. They do, but that don't take away from the fact that Tangy Mae awful young for this."

Miss Pearl had given one of her "so what" grunts, then returned to the task of styling my hair into a fancy bun held by pearl-studded clips. The dress, gloves, earrings, and the white shoes with small heels just right for dancing were all gifts from Miss Pearl.

Mama, persuaded by Miss Pearl, allowed me to stay overnight with her and Mr. Frank, where Jeff picked me up. Just like Mama had thought, he was driving his daddy's new car. Before I left for the Garrisons', my mother had spent at least fifteen minutes telling me how I should and should not act on a date. I was not to embarrass her, and I was not to let Jeff touch any part of me, except my hand. What she repeated most was, "Don't let him kiss on you, Tangy Mae."

Mr. Frank had stood at the door with an arm draped over his wife's shoulder. "This a night y'all gon' wanna remember," he'd said. "I ain't saying it's right, but I hope y'all have a good time. You hear?"

We were doing just that. In formal attire and an atmosphere of gaiety, we played at sophistication. We danced, sipped punch from paper cups, and laughed about things we would not have found amusing on any other day. I danced with Jeff over and over again, and I danced with his friend, Douglas.

"You're really something," Jeff said to me when Douglas escorted me back to our table. "I believe you could dance all night. I could sit here and watch you all night, too. But I'm plum worn out from dancing."

For his sake, I tried to sit still; for my sake, I needed to move. He watched me for a moment, then he leaned over and kissed my cheek right there in the gymnasium, under the stars, in front of anybody who happened to be looking, and I didn't mind at all. The kiss wasn't so bad, and how could I refuse it in front of Evelyn and Douglas? How could I say no when I was wearing the beautiful corsage he had given me? I didn't think a kiss on the cheek would embarrass my mother, and for once, I was among people who would not tell.

After the prom, Jeff drove me back to the Garrisons' house, and we sat in the car. For the first time, he brushed his lips against mine, then quickly pulled them away, and I thought his mother must have told him the same thing my mother had told me.

"When will you turn eighteen so I can marry you?" he asked.

I giggled. "In about four years."

He took my hand in his. "Well, that's perfect. That's about the time I'll be done with college. I'll come back through here and take you away with me. We'll go someplace where they don't have red dirt, or cornfields, or cows, or bad storms, or any of the other junk in Pakersfield."

"I kind of like the storms," I said.

"Okay," he said, lightly and agreeably, "we'll keep the storms. I'll just wrap you up and keep you safe."

"Jeff, I'm not afraid of storms. Are you?"

"Well, I don't think afraid is the right word. They make me a little nervous, that's all."

"Then maybe I'll have to wrap you up and keep you safe."

"Show me," he teased. "Show me how you'd keep me safe."

"No." I laughed to hide my embarrassment. "There's no storm tonight. You come on back with the next storm, and I'll show you then."

"It's a deal," he said.

At the Garrisons' front door, under the porch light, Jeff did not kiss me goodnight. He brushed my arm lightly, and winked an eye at me. "I knew you'd be fun," he said. "I knew if I ever got you away from Mattie, you'd be fun."

"Am I?"

"Yes."

"Good night, Jeff Stallings. I had a wonderful time."

"Good night, Tangy Quinn. I did, too."

twenty-seven

The Fourth of July fell on a Friday. God woke up early, before any of us, and painted the sky the softest shade of heavenly blue. He blew a kiss into the air, offering us a gentle breeze against the summer humidity, and when I opened our front door, I saw that He had sent a fearless thrasher to our house. It stood perched atop the weather-worn edge of the porch with its long tail motionless, and it did not fly away, but lingered until I closed the door to keep it out.

We went to the parade in town, and returned to find Mama sitting in the kitchen brooding over nothing that made any sense to me. She wanted Harvey to desert his wife and return to her. I steered clear of the kitchen. Martha Jean had spent her time with Velman Cooper, engrossed in conversation, using signs that were foreign to me. I had experienced a pang of jealously that intensified when Velman reached for Judy and she went to him with the ease of familiarity. Mattie and Tarabelle had walked side by side at the parade, and were off somewhere now, probably in the woods. Sam and Wallace were out with their friends. I felt lonely.

Martha Jean must have sensed my mood. She put Judy down for

a nap, then insisted I join her in the yard. I found myself at one end of a jump rope, twirling for my younger sisters. Halfheartedly, I twirled the rope and watched Laura jump. She was getting better, and jumped sixteen consecutive times before the rope tangled around her ankles. Edna stepped up for her turn, and as we began to twirl for her, an angel peered down on us and shed one giant-sized, humongous tear right in the dirt at Edna's feet. We glanced up at a blue sky and a bright sun that did not add up to rain, but another drop fell, and then another.

Laura began to chant, "The devil's beating his wife. The devil's beating his wife."

Edna joined in, "The devil's beating his wife."

For all of sixty seconds, just long enough to kick up a little dust, the angel wept in quarter-sized drops, but the sun dried the drops on our arms almost as fast as they fell. We began to twirl the rope again, and Edna jumped to the rhythm of her chant.

Suddenly, the twirling ceased at Martha Jean's end. I saw her head lift and tilt slightly as if she'd heard something, then the rope flew from her hand and she cut loose the most bloodcurdling wail. She began to run for the house. My gaze followed her. She had seen Judy, whimpering in our mother's grip.

Mama stood at the edge of the porch dangling our baby sister over the side by one arm. As Martha Jean rushed toward them, Mama swung out once, twice . . .

With my hands to my throat, I waited for a third swing that never came. Mama, staring blankly into space, opened her hand and released Judy. I saw my baby sister sail through the air, flipping and jerking, as she began a descent that took her over the rocky incline and down into the gully.

If there was a sound of impact, I did not hear it over Martha Jean's wails. She teetered for a moment between the bottom step and the yard, then she ran beneath the porch, between the poles that supported the house. Her feet left the ground and she dived down the incline as she raced against death to be the first to reach her baby.

I tried to move, but I could not. I stood there staring at the space where my sisters had disappeared until finally Martha Jean's head came into view. She crawled out of the gully with Judy's lifeless form cradled in one arm, then she sat on the bank and began to rock back and forth. There was no wailing now, only the rustle of leaves as the wind sang through the trees behind the house, a soft mournful hymn.

Mama peered down from the porch. At some point she had lit a cigarette, and smoke, barely visible, rose toward the porch ceiling and seemed to settle as a halo above her head. My hands clenched into fists as I moved, first toward the porch, then down onto the road. I began to run through Stump Town toward the Garrisons' house.

Somehow Miss Pearl and Mr. Frank understood my breathless, broken phrases. She tried to calm me while Mr. Frank telephoned the sheriff.

We rode back to Penyon Road in Mr. Frank's car, and as I climbed from the back seat, I sensed a change had taken place during my absence. Laura and Edna were in the yard where I had left them, Martha Jean was still sitting on the bank cuddling Judy, and Mama was on the porch, but a stillness had settled over the earth. The earlier breeze had dissipated, the humidity had risen to a stifling degree, and we seemed to trudge through quicksand. I saw Miss Pearl lumber up the incline and across the yard toward Martha Jean, and it seemed to take hours for her to get there. When she reached the bank, she dropped to her knees and placed a hand on Martha Jean's shoulder, and the wailing started up again.

Mr. Frank stood in the yard and stared up at Mama. "Rozelle, what's done happened out here?" he asked.

"The baby fell off the porch, Frank," she answered with no remorse or grief in her tone. "She'll be awright. Children fall all the time."

"This 'un ain't gon' be awright, Rosie," Miss Pearl said. "You got a dead baby here. You better come on down from there and see 'bout this."

Mama did not move, not even when the sheriff and Chadlow arrived. Angus Betts strode across our yard, spoke to Mr. Frank, then squatted beside Martha Jean and gently tried to remove Judy from her arms. Martha Jean rocked faster, screamed louder, and held Judy tighter.

Chadlow stood with his arms folded across his chest, staring down at the sheriff, but making no attempt to help. Finally Angus

Betts rose to his feet and came to stand below the porch where he squinted up at Mama. For the longest time he said nothing, possibly did not know what to say. He ran a hand through his dark brown hair, pressed his thin lips into a tight line, then shook his head and sighed.

"All I can do is wait for Morris," he said. "He ought to be here soon. Right now, Rozelle, I don't know if she's dead or alive. Looks like she's dead, but I don't know."

I watched the road for the doctor's car, and finally it rounded the bend. Dr. Mathis got out and came forward with his black bag, a blanket, and the intention of examining Judy. He quickly found that it was not going to be easy. He dropped his bag to the ground and spread the blanket for Martha Jean to lay Judy down. Martha Jean drew away from him, turned her face toward the sky, and let go a scream that caught in her throat and died as a gurgling moan. It must have frightened Dr. Mathis because he stepped back and glanced helplessly at the sheriff.

"Well, Morris, is she dead?" the sheriff asked.

"How the hell do I know, Angus?" Dr. Mathis asked. "I haven't had a chance to examine her yet." He turned to Chadlow. "Come give me a hand over here."

Chadlow moved toward him just as Tarabelle and Mattie emerged from the rear of the house.

"What's done happened?" Tarabelle asked.

"It's Judy," I answered. "I think she's dead."

We watched as Chadlow mimicked the sheriff's gestures and ran a hand through his own thinning hair. He leaned forward and began trying to pry Judy from Martha Jean's grip. He couldn't do it, not even with the doctor's help. He raised a hand, as if to strike Martha Jean, but the sheriff shouted a warning to him, "Chad, I think that girl is hurting enough, and the last thing we need is a ruckus out here."

That was when I noticed the first group of people moving tentatively toward our house. They slowed at the bend, moved uneasily toward the field, and watched from a distance. As more and more people arrived, they began to make their way up to the yard.

"Rozelle, what happened here?" the sheriff asked, exasperated now, holding up a hand to keep the crowd at bay.

"You come on up here, Angus, and I'll tell you what happened," Mama said. "That's my baby down there. I guess if she was hurting, she'd be crying, and she ain't cried, not once."

Angus Betts inspected our steps before placing a foot on them, then he took them two at a time up to the porch. I gathered Laura and Edna and took them with me to sit on the steps. I wanted to hear what Mama had to say.

"Okay, Rozelle, what happened?" the sheriff asked again.

"I don't really know," Mama answered, and began to sob in her rehearsed, refined manner. "I was playing wit' my baby right here on the porch. You know how you do. I was swinging her out, trying to get her to laugh. I don't know what happened. I swung her out that one time and she musta kicked or something 'cause the next thing I knew she was falling. Wadn't nothing I could do."

She was convincing. I thought for a moment that maybe I was mistaken in what I thought had happened. I thought she had thrown Judy from the porch, but no mother could do that, not even mine. Could she?

I saw Harvey push through the crowd, followed by Mr. Dobson, then Sam and Hambone. They surrounded Dr. Mathis, and Sam knelt to touch Martha Jean, but she jerked away.

"This makes no sense," Chadlow said irritably. "There's enough of us here to hold her down and take that baby away from her."

Dr. Mathis and Mr. Dobson agreed, but Sam told them to wait just a minute. Chadlow ignored him, and gripped Martha Jean by her shoulders. Her throat was rested now, and she began to scream all over again. Her screams were such that they caused the onlookers to back away and Miss Pearl to wring her hands and weep.

Sam dived toward Chadlow, grabbed the man by his shoulders, and flung him away from Martha Jean. Regaining his balance, Chadlow turned to see that Harvey and Hambone had stepped up and flanked Sam as they squared off against him now. Chadlow was not in uniform like the sheriff; he had no right to a uniform. He wore cuffed trousers and an open-collared shirt with the tail out. He was tall and burly, but I thought Sam stood a chance against him in a fair fight, only nothing about this fight was going to be fair. Chadlow stared at them for a moment, then he inched his shirt up to expose a revolver that was tucked inside the waistband of his trousers.

I truly believe Chadlow would have shot Sam if the sheriff had not intervened. "Chad, did you come to help me or cause me more headache?" he called down from the porch. "What's wrong with everybody?" He threw his hands up in frustration. "We've got a baby that's either hurt or dead, and all anybody can think about is fighting. Everybody, just move away from that girl! Just move on away!"

He stared down at them, waiting for his command to be obeyed, but nobody moved. Finally he drew his gun and aimed it toward the yard. "Get away from her, or I'll shoot somebody myself."

Now they had an out, where nobody would lose face, and after a moment they took it. Hambone clamped a hand on Sam's shoulder. "Let's think about your sisters, man," he said, and Sam nodded.

The sheriff glared down at Chadlow, and his lips moved, but whatever it was he wanted to say, he kept it to himself. He holstered his weapon and turned back to Mama. "Tell me one more time, Rozelle, why would you swing a baby out from this porch? Didn't you think for one minute that you could drop her?"

"I swung all my children out from here—from the oldest to the youngest. I ain't never dropped a one 'til today. I'd do anything to take it back."

"But you can't take it back, now can you?"

"No, Angus, I can't take it back."

"Well, it's just a mess, Rozelle," he said. "It's just a mess."

"I know." Mama wept.

Softening in the face of my mother's assumed anguish, the sheriff said, "These things happen sometimes and only God knows why. If she's dead, and I pray she's not, I'll need you to come to my office in the morning, but it sounds pretty much like an accident to me."

Down in the yard Dr. Mathis opened his bag and withdrew a syringe. "Angus," he called out, "I'm going to have to give this girl something. That's the only way I'll ever get to examine the baby."

"Do what you have to do, Morris," the sheriff said wearily, "just do it right, will you?"

Mama moved to the very edge of the porch and studied the gathering crowd for a minute or two, then she gave a short cry, swooned, and fell into the sheriff's arms.

"Some of you ladies come see after her, why don't you?" he called down.

I didn't move, except maybe an inch or two to let Miss Janie and Miss Pearl up the steps. I was trying to see what Dr. Mathis was going to do to Martha Jean.

"They say Judy is dead," Wallace whispered. "Is it true, Tan? People saying it all over Stump Town."

Wallace must have arrived while I had been watching the doctor. I hadn't seen him come. I nodded, although nothing seemed real. Judy couldn't really be dead; she was just a baby.

I don't know when Velman Cooper arrived, but I saw him part the crowd and take long strides across the yard. He was still wearing the blue jeans he had worn to the parade and the T-shirt that Judy had nestled her head against. He sat on the ground beside Martha Jean, crossed his legs, and watched as Dr. Mathis tried to get Harvey and Hambone to hold Martha Jean for him. They wouldn't do it, though, and I thought I understood. Martha Jean would have to give Judy up on her own. Chadlow probably would have helped the doctor, but he couldn't risk turning his back to Sam.

Velman began to move his fingers before Martha Jean's face. The onlookers could not hear the words my sister heard, but I understood them all, clearly. "Martha Jean, trust me. Give Judy to the doctor. Will you let her go?"

Martha Jean shook her head, but I could tell by the movement of her elbows that she had loosened her grip on Judy. I could not see her fingers from my place on the step, but she was responding to Velman. I knew that.

"Give her to me," Velman signed. "I want to hold her. I need to hold her. If you let her go, I will take you away from here. I promise. Trust me."

How he intended to keep that promise was beyond me, and Martha Jean must have wondered, too. The minutes passed like hours with everybody waiting to see what would happen, if Martha Jean would pull away from Velman, if Dr. Mathis would have to give her a shot, if Mama would come down from the porch. None of those things happened. Martha Jean must have wanted to trust Velman because slowly she leaned forward and kissed her baby, then she gave Judy over to Velman. An overwhelming sadness consumed me as Velman gave Judy a final kiss and offered her small, still body to Dr. Mathis, and Dr. Mathis, after an expeditious examination, nodded to the sheriff that Judy was indeed dead.

For the first time since her fall, I had a clear view of my baby sister. She looked as if someone had put her to sleep dirty, bloody, and raggedy, with particles of glass clinging to her hair. And I guess somebody had.

My mother, sitting on a chair where the women had placed her, screamed when Dr. Mathis drove away with Judy's body, and Reverend Nelson mounted the steps to console her. He knelt beside her chair and held her hand as he spoke. "It's a great loss, sister," he said. "We're just on loan to this world, and God has a plan for all of us. We have to trust He has His reasons."

"But I don't know what I'm gonna do," Mama cried. "I'm gonna miss her so much. Already my arms feel empty."

Reverend Nelson prayed for all of us, and Mama allowed it. Several people came up to the house to offer their condolences, then they began to ease away from Penyon Road until only the Garrisons and Velman Cooper remained. Miss Pearl helped Mama to stand and walk to the front room, and she told me to get cold water for my mother to drink.

It was late evening when the Garrisons left our house, and Velman Cooper, having remained silent since walking in with Martha Jean, cleared his throat and went to stand before my mother's chair. "Miss Rosie," he said, "I'm taking Martha Jean with me."

"No you ain't," Mama said in a low, croaky voice. "You ain't taking Martha Jean nowhere."

"Yes, ma'am, I am," Velman responded apologetically. "I'm real sorry 'bout Judy, but you been knowing I was gon' take Martha Jean for a long time now. I done taught you to drive, and the car is parked out there on the road. Here's the keys, Miss Rosie." He placed two keys on the round table between the armchairs. "I know I still owe you, and you'll get it, but Martha Jean is coming with me today."

"Look 'round you, boy," Mama said, glancing around the room. "You think we gon' let you walk outta here wit' one of us?"

"Yes, ma'am. I don't think nobody gon' try to stop me."

"Harvey? Sam?" Mama implored.

Sam leaned against the wall and stared at her. His red-rimmed eyes were those of a weary, old man's. "Let him take her," he said. "I can't think about that right now, Mama. Sounds like you done sold her to him anyway for a car."

"It ain't like that, Sam." Mama pleaded for understanding. "It was more than just a car. I got money, too. Can't you see I been buying things for this house—for all y'all. I ain't saying he can't have her. I'm just saying this ain't a good time. What people gon' think?"

Harvey, sitting in the chair beside Mama, raised his head from his palms. "Who gives a damn what people think, Mama?" he asked. "I wanna know what happened to Judy."

"Yeah," Sam agreed.

"She fell, goddamit!" Mama shouted, allowing a bit of her true self to emerge from her folds of pretended sorrow. "Where y'all been? By now everybody in Pakersfield know she fell."

Harvey choked on a sob. "How did she fall?" he asked. "She didn't walk outside. I ain't never seen you touch her, so how she get out there? You ain't never touched her, Mama. Why you have to go and put yo' hands on her today?"

"You hush up wit' that kinda talk!" Mama snapped. "I don't wanna hear it in my house or nowhere else, you hear?" She stared at him and clutched her blouse together, as if it might open to expose her guilt. "All my life people done talked about me. Lies. Always telling lies. I ain't gon' have no child of mine helping spread lies on me. Y'all don't know what I been through. I done gave and gave to y'all, and all I ever got back was trouble."

When she got on the subject of what she had done for her children, it could last for hours. We listened, but as she talked, I moved about the room gathering Martha Jean's meager belongings. Martha Jean seemed to be in a sort of daze, standing on Velman's strength alone, moving with his guidance.

"We're leaving now, Miss Rosie," Velman said, leading Martha Jean toward the hall. "We can sign them papers whenever you want. I understand this ain't a good time, but just whenever . . ."

I expected Mama to leap up from her chair and grab Velman, but she didn't, and no one else tried to stop him from taking Martha Jean. I stood in the doorway and watched them disappear around the bend, and it seemed to me that Velman was carrying my sister on his hip and Martha Jean's feet were dragging against the surface of the road.

The armchairs and the round table had been moved into Mama's room. Folding chairs and paper fans cluttered the front room, and in the center of it all, Judy lay on display in an unadorned pine box.

Laura clung to me throughout the day, threatening to rip the threads at the waist of my dress. She cried for Martha Jean. She would not go near the pine box, and she refused to believe that Judy was in it. She cried until she was hoarse, and I wanted to strike her, to prove to myself that I was incapable of love. Finally, I took her and Edna into the woods, hoping they would find comfort there as I so often did.

I knelt at the fence, and Edna dropped beside me. We began to pray. Laura stood silent until we were done, then she urinated on the ground. With her eyes wide open, she dropped to the ground and stretched there with her feet resting in the puddle she had made, her thumb clamped tightly between her teeth.

I picked her up and carried her back to the house where friends and acquaintances passed through our front room, placed food on our kitchen table, and embraced our mother. Jeff's family, Mattie's family, and so many other families passed through with nods and condolences, and I could not cry for my sister.

That night as we began to stack the folding chairs, a car pulled up on the road, and I went to the door to see who was arriving at such a late hour. From the passenger side of the car, the old mid-wife emerged with a quart-sized jar in her hand. She struggled up the embankment, removed the lid from her jar, and began to sprinkle a liquid into the yard as her voice rose in a shrill chant.

"What is that?" Mama asked, coming to stand beside me. She glanced down, saw the midwife, then staggered back the entire length of the hall. I turned to see her standing in the corner that was reserved for the slop bucket. She was whispering, "No, no, no," and banging her head against the wall, over and over again.

twenty-eight

"Sam! Sam!" Mama called out. "I drove almost to Tennessee yesterday. Went all the way through five counties before I turned around. Next time I'm going all the way 'cross the state line."

Sam waved a hand. "That's good, Mama," he called back. He was in the field with Maxwell and Hambone, using sling blades to clear a patch for Mama to park her car. They had positioned themselves at angles in order to maneuver safely out of reach of each other. Hambone worked the back, Maxwell had the center, and Sam worked closest to the road.

"What you writing there?" Mama asked, turning her attention to me.

"A letter to Mushy," I answered. "It's been a long time." It had been more than three weeks since I had written to Mushy about Judy's death, and she had not responded to my letter, making me wonder if she had received it.

"A letter to Mushy, huh? Let me see it. You better not be saying nothing bad about me in that letter."

Tarabelle stepped out onto the porch. She was wearing blue

pedal pushers and one of Sam's old T-shirts. "It sho' is hot today," she commented, taking a seat on the top step.

"It's summer, Tarabelle," Mama said, forgetting about the letter. "What you want from summer? You want ice all over the place?"

"I want a breeze, Mama. Just a cool breeze," Tarabelle answered, tugging at the T-shirt.

"They sho' making a mess of that field," Mama said. "All I asked for was a little spot to park my car. Hay truck came 'round the bend the other day and nearly hit it. Now Sam got them boys trying to cut down the whole damn field."

I finished my letter, remembering to tell Mushy how we were not allowed to mention Judy's name in our mother's house, as though she had never existed, and of how much I missed my sisters—all of them. Just as I sealed the envelope, the sound of shouting made me glance toward the field. Maxwell had dropped his blade and was running toward the road.

"I bet a snake done got a hold of 'im," Mama said.

Out in the far field, Hambone stood with his blade held over his head, ready to swing. "What happened?" he called. "Hey, Sam. Man, what happened?"

Maxwell reached the road and began beating at the legs of his pants with both hands. Sam squatted to examine the pants, then said, "I don't see nothing, Max. What happened?"

"Rats! Rats, man," Maxwell said, when he was able to speak. "A whole nest of 'em in a hole. I stepped in that motherfuckin' hole, man. I ain't going back out there."

"Just some rats," Sam called out to Hambone.

Hambone eased his blade down and made his way across the field. "Max," he said, "man, you 'bout to give me a heart attack. Running like a bitch from some rats? From some rats, man?"

"Shut up, motherfucka," Maxwell snapped. "One of them damn thangs was halfway up my leg. I'm telling y'all, I ain't going back out there."

"Both of y'all, shut up," Sam said. "Don't y'all see my mama sitting up there?"

Hambone and Maxwell glanced up, nodded their heads at Mama, then in unison said, "Sorry, Miss Rosie."

Mama waggled her fingers. "That's awright," she said, "but y'all gotta get them rats. If you don't kill 'em in the field, they get in yo' house, and I don't want 'em in my house."

Tarabelle stood, tugged at her T-shirt, then walked down to the road. I followed, but stopped short when she marched into the field. I could see her bending and searching through the weeds. We were all watching her when she finally returned to the road.

"Did you see anything?" Hambone asked.

"Yeah," she answered nonchalantly, "one fat, ol' rat dropping a litter."

"Y'all gotta get 'em," Mama yelled.

Tarabelle returned to the house, and I went to see the litter for myself. A huge field rat lay on its side, its gray hairy body pulsating, its long tail curled inside the hole around slimy, little hairless creatures that had slithered from its body. I gagged and backed away, and the eyes of the rodent seemed to follow my every move. Back on the road, I leaned toward the edge of the field, feeling sick to my stomach.

"Don't you faint, Tangy Mae," I heard my mother call down to me. "Don't you dare faint. I ain't going through no mo' of yo' fainting. You had no business going out there no way."

I straightened my back and turned to face her so she could see that I had no intention of fainting. That was when I saw Tarabelle approaching the road again. She was carrying the iron skillet, gripping the handle with both hands as she moved slowly along. She stepped past us and back through the weeds, and my nostrils twitched from the burned, meaty odor of used and reheated lard.

The squeal of the rodent reached us as Tarabelle tilted the skillet and dumped the hot oil. Maxwell swore and hung his head. Sam and Hambone stared silently at Tarabelle as she came back to the road, now swinging the skillet by one hand.

"You just plain hateful, Tarabelle," Mama said.

Tarabelle kept walking. "I thought you said you didn't want 'em in yo' house, Mama. Ain't that what you said?" She returned the skillet to the kitchen, then she came back to the field, picked up Maxwell's blade and, as hot as she claimed to be, began to swing with all her might at the dry weeds.

My mother's expenses were mounting. I would see her
sometimes scraping pennies and nickels together to buy
batteries for her radio, or cigarettes, or gasoline for her car. She paid
the insurance man, the coal man, the ice man, and Mr. Poppy.
When Harvey gave her money, she would buy food or something
nice for herself.

Sam no longer tried to find work, or if he did, he kept it to himself. Mama would tell him that he was too lazy to be a grown man,
then she would turn on me and tell me how I ought to be ashamed
of myself.

Although Tarabelle's housecleaning job provided our only
source of steady income, Mama would turn on her when our food
supply was depleted. "Them Munfords ain't gon' miss a little flour
or meal, or some sugar," she'd say. "You gotta learn to do like I did,
Tarabelle. We need some food in this house."

One morning when my mother had four dollars in her fist, she
announced that she was going to fill her car with gasoline and cross
the Georgia state line. She told Wallace to clean the outhouse, and
she told me to go into town and slip a nice dress from a rack for

Laura's first day of school, then she piled Laura and Edna into the car and drove away.

"She ain't going nowhere," Wallace said, watching as the car moved toward Fife Street. "She can't leave Georgia."

"I think she might," I said. "She seems determined."

"She can't. I know something you don't know. If you help me clean the outhouse, I'll tell you about it."

"Wallace, just tell me. You know I can't help you. I have to go into town and get a dress for Laura."

"Maybe I'll tell you when you get back from town, *if* you make it back." He grinned. "They'll probably catch you trying to steal 'cause you look so scared. You can't look like that, Tan, or they'll know you up to something. Tell you what, you help me and I'll show you how to get that dress without stealing it."

If I could get Laura a dress without having to steal it, I would clean the outhouse and dump the slop bucket for a full week. I told Wallace that, and he sat on the back steps and watched me work. When I was done, he made me promise to keep a secret, then he led me away from Penyon Road and through the streets of Stump Town.

We stopped at a small, white house on Selman Street. My heart raced even faster than when Mama had told me to slip the dress for Laura. I knew where we were without Wallace having to tell me. I followed him through a gate and up to the house. He knocked, and after a short wait, the midwife opened the door. She stepped aside and allowed us to enter a hallway that smelled of age and turpentine.

"Why you bring her here?" Zadie Grodin asked, as she closed the door behind us.

"I had to," Wallace explained. "I want you to tell her everything."

She led us into the living room where we sat on the couch and she took a seat in a chair across from us. There was a Crisco can on the floor beside the chair, and she picked it up and spat snuff into it. "Get me a drink of water, Wallace," she said. "If I'm gon' be talking for a spell, I'm gon' need to wet my throat ever' now and then."

Wallace was obviously familiar with the house. He left the room, and returned shortly with a glass of water. Miss Zadie wet her throat, and brought the glass away from her lips, leaving wet snuff around the rim. My stomach felt queasy. I wasn't sure if it was from the snuff stains on the glass or just from being on Selman Street and in this house. Everything about it felt wrong, from the odors in the room to the old woman's bobbing head and unwavering stare.

"I'm yo' grandma, gal," she said without preamble. "John ain't yo' grandpa, but I'm yo' grandma, awright."

Her words hit me like a blow to my chest. I found myself sinking back into the cushions of the couch, drawing away from her even as I stared at her. My discomfort increased by the second.

"I thought I was barren. You know what that mean?" she asked, and did not wait for an answer. "I was 'round twenty-seven, twenty-eight, I guess, and right pretty. We was living just outside of Nashville, and I was a midwife even then. Menfolks thought I was really something to look at, but I only had eyes for John. He always been enough for me."

She leaned forward, retrieved her can, and spat. There was snuff on her bottom lip that she wiped away with the back of a hand. I noticed a mole on one side of her nose, and when she turned her head a certain way, it was visible beneath a small flap of skin.

"They come for me one night, three of 'em. Say Lillie Sheldon getting near her time. Wadn't 'way from the house good 'fo' I knew I was in trouble 'cause Mister Sheldon didn't act like no man in no rush." She wet her throat, and a long, brown strand appeared in the center of the water and drifted to the bottom of the glass. She seemed not to notice, but I was noticing every little thing about her.

"That Mister Sheldon come at me first," she said, "and it didn't matter none what them others done after that. The damage already been done. They drug me out in a cornfield and stomped me like they was packing dirt." Her foot moved and seemed to grind at something on the floor, either involuntarily or to demonstrate what the men had done to her. "Left me for dead. Never once worried 'bout dying, though, 'cause I knew I had the devil's seed growing in me. Couldn't stand, but I crawled my way back to the house, back to John." She smiled, exposing dirty, brown teeth. "He say I sound like a little kittycat scratching on the do', and he had a good mind not to open it. But he did, and there I was, all broken up so he almost didn't know who I was. Never did heal up right."

My hands rested on my lap, and I glanced down at the finger my mother had broken. The knuckle was disfigured and I couldn't straighten the finger. I thought of my entire body being broken like that, so it would never straighten out again, and I felt sorry for Miss Zadie.

"That baby come into this world white as one of God's clouds and wit' the devil's own gray eyes. It was born a mockin' me, and I knew it. Tried ever'day just to put the tip of my finger on it, but I couldn't. John took care of it, took care of ever'thing."

I sat rigid and quiet. Although I had heard more than I needed to hear, her words seemed to pin and hold me to the couch. I willed Wallace to pull me up, take me out into the fresh air, and tell me it was all a joke, that this old, crippled woman was not our grandmother.

"Let's go, Wallace," I said, louder than I intended. "We need to get on home."

He placed a finger to his lips to silence me, and the midwife spoke right on through my outburst. ". . . when we moved here from Nashville. I'd take a strap to it ever' now and then, but it didn't do no good. Then I took to saying the Bible. 'Honor thy mother' I'd say, and it'd turn them gray eyes on me and be quiet for a spell."

Miss Zadie drained the last of her brown-tinged water. "That's how the devil fool you," she said, as though talking to herself. "No more than thirteen, and done got in a family way. Put the liar's finger on John, and that hurt him bad. Real bad. 'Get outta here and don't come back.' That's what I said." Miss Zadie chuckled, as though something was comical about the memory. "Took on the name of Quinn. There was a policy man used to come by here, had that name. Just a sinful shame. If there's anybody know we kin, they don't mention it to me, and I don't mention it to them. But it ain't right. Me and John getting on up in years wit' all them grand-chilluns and nobody to see after us."

"We can't help you, Miss Zadie," I said. "We're not allowed to come here."

"But you here, ain't you? You want something from me, and I want something from you." Her voice was suddenly strong, and she seemed to shout the words at me.

I bolted. I could feel Wallace trying to hold onto my arm, but I shook him off. I fled from the room and through the hallway. Once outside, I stopped running, but walked with haste away from

Selman Street and from the old woman, with her cryptic insinuations, who needed somebody—but not me.

Wallace was breathless when he caught up to me. He rested his hands on his knees while he caught his breath, then he asked, "Why you run?"

"You should have warned me, Wallace."

"You know you wouldna believed me. I got the money for Laura's dress. Here." He placed a bill in my hand. "You go get the dress. I gotta go back and see after her."

"Why?" I asked. "Why?"

"I just do, Tan. That's all. I just do."

As I walked along, my package tucked beneath my arm, I thought about Laura. Since Judy's death, she had become withdrawn, always quiet, like maybe she was trying to vanish. Mama had noticed it, too. I think that was why Mama had wanted the new dress, something to make Laura smile again.

On the curb outside the bus depot, Jeff Stallings squinted against the sun and watched my approach. "Hey, Tangy. How're you doing?" he asked.

"I'm okay, Jeff. How are you?"

"Okay. I'll be off to Washington in a couple of weeks. Just bought my ticket."

"Well, good luck to you," I said, and stepped down from the curb. I wanted to stay and talk with him; I wanted to go to Washington with him; but I did not want my mother to drive by in her car and see me with him.

Jeff followed after me. "Can I walk along with you?" he asked. "You know, I was really sorry about your little sister."

I shrugged, having weeks ago grown weary from sympathy that did little to ease my grief.

"Tangy, can you meet me somewhere tonight or tomorrow?"

"No, I don't think so. And for what, anyway?"

"So we can spend some time together before I leave. It's a funny thing, but when I was buying my ticket just now, all I could think about was leaving without having a chance to say goodbye to you. And then you came along, walking up the street like it was meant to be. Say you'll meet me. Please."

I shook my head. "I'm fourteen, Jeff. My mother let me go to the prom with you, but I'm not allowed to court."

"How about the fair? Will you meet me at the fair?"

"She ain't gon' meet you nowhere," a voice from behind us said.

I stiffened momentarily, then turned to face Tarabelle. She was wearing her white dress with the tiny flowers, and she held a rolled newspaper in one hand, poised as though she might swat Jeff with it. In her other hand was a bag that I knew contained food, stuff to satisfy our mother. She deliberately stepped between me and Jeff, then kept walking without glancing back. As I rushed to catch up to her, I stole a glance back at Jeff and formed the word "maybe" with my lips.

"What you got there?" Tarabelle asked, after we had walked nearly a quarter of a mile in silence.

"Mama sent me to get a dress for Laura."

"She got money for something like that?"

"She sent me to steal it, Tara."

"Well, how come it's in a bag?" she asked.

Thinking fast, I told the first lie I thought believable. There was no way I could tell her about the midwife. "Jeff let me have the money," I said.

"You gon' tell Mama that?" she asked.

I shook my head.

"Then you better get it out that bag."

I hadn't thought of that. When we reached the top of Fife Street, I removed the dress from the bag, and tucked the bag into some hedge bushes. Tarabelle watched and made little grunting sounds like, "uh, uh, uh," which made me itch with embarrassment.

"I can't figure out how you s'pose to be so smart when you so stupid," she said.

She had saved me from making a mistake, so I kept silent and let her gloat. We turned onto Penyon Road and saw our mother's car parked in the field. Tarabelle slowed her pace.

"Wait a minute," she said. "What you'll do for me if I tell you how you can work and go to school at the same time?"

I studied her face, couldn't tell if she was joking or serious. "Almost anything," I answered, and meant it.

She grunted again. "I'll have to think on it."

"Tell me, Tara, how I can do that?" I asked.

"Well, Miss Arlisa say there's these Whitmans live on Belcher Road in North Ridge. They looking for a girl to work on Wednesdays and Saturdays. Asked me if I knew anybody."

We walked on in silence as I mentally calculated the number of days I would have to miss from school. I could get Mr. Pace to talk to Mr. Hewitt for me, and I could stay after school to catch up on anything I missed. I didn't have the job yet, but I felt that God was smiling down on me, and I was elated.

The house was quiet when we entered. I did not know if my mother had crossed the Georgia state line, but she seemed calm, and she was satisfied with the dress I had gotten. To me, the house and the whole world seemed peaceful. The girls fell asleep almost as soon as they were done with supper, Wallace was his normal self and gave no indication that either of us had been to Selman Street, and when Mama told Tarabelle to get ready to make a run, there was no complaining from my sister. Tarabelle merely nodded.

"I'm seventeen," she announced, much the way one would announce the time. "Today is August twenty-eighth, and I'm seventeen."

A short time later a car stopped down on the road and I watched my mother and sister leave the house, then I stretched out on my pallet and stared at the ceiling, concentrating on ways to keep my world as peaceful as it was right now. Tomorrow I would find the Whitmans' house in North Ridge. I would be mature and charming, and they would hire me on the spot, then Mama would have nothing in the world to complain about.

thirty

Veatrice Whitman was the personification of a cracker in every sense of the word. I found her sitting on the front porch of the worst house in all of North Ridge. The house had once been white with green shutters, but the paint was peeling, and the shutters were dangling. She was surrounded by a dozen red clay pots and a heap of wet earth. Her bare feet and her arms, up to the elbows, were coated with mud. There were smudges of muck on the pink sundress she wore. Her long, blond hair was wet from the recent rain and was plastered to her face and the back of her neck. She appeared to be close to my mother's age.

I approached her cautiously. "Good morning, ma'am. Are you Mrs. Whitman?" I asked.

"I'm Miss Whitman," she drawled. "Could you hand me that spade out there by the rose bush?"

Foolishly, I had worn my best dress. It was now soaked from the downpour. I supposed I appeared to be in desperate need of work. I stepped around holes that had been dug in the yard, picked up the spade, and carried it to the porch.

"It's best to get the dirt when it's raining," Miss Whitman said. "That way you ain't got to water it so much."

"Yes, ma'am," I said. I don't know why I agreed with that, but it seemed the proper thing to do, and I was trying to be charming. "Miss Whitman, I hear you're looking to hire a girl."

"I guess that's right," she said, packing mud into one of the pots, and glancing up at me. "Actually, I don't think we need nobody, but Bakker thinks we do, and it's his money. I been taking care of him all his life and now he thinks I need a rest. Can you beat that? You'd think I was an old woman the way he talks. I'm only thirty-two."

"Yes, ma'am."

She stood, and opened the door with a muddy hand. "Come on, let me show you the house. Bakker just bought it. It ain't much better than the one we moved out of, but Bakker said he had to get closer to town, and he's gonna fix it up right pretty. Said he wasn't gonna spend the rest of his life out on a farm." She laughed girlishly. "I coulda stayed, but he wanted me to come. So here I am."

The mud on Miss Whitman's feet would have made prints had the carpet not been black already from an accumulation of embedded grime. The front room was in a shambles. Lime-green curtains had been tacked over the windows in a haphazard fashion. Clothes were strewn over the couch and chairs. An ashtray, heaped with cigarette butts, stood near the edge of a coffee table which had sustained numerous burns. The house smelled of rot, and as I drew closer to Miss Whitman, I noticed she gave off a faint odor that smelled much like Mr. Frank's dog Squat on a bad day.

On the kitchen floor were broken bottles, empty cans and boxes, and a pot of floating mold. Dirty dishes were stacked on the table and in the sink, and there was not a dishrack or cloth in sight.

"Well, this is it," Miss Whitman said, spreading her arms in a grandiose manner, and I was sure she was pulling my leg. "There's the two bedrooms back there, and the bathroom, and then there's that little room right next to mine. We can't quite figure what to do with it, yet."

Appalled, and trying hard not to show it, I stared at the mess in the kitchen. "Miss Whitman, how long has it been since you've had a girl?" I asked.

"Oh, honey, we ain't never had a girl before. We don't really need one now. Bakker is just trying to be like everybody else, that's all. He got this house for a little of nothing, and now he wants to do things right proper. He told me to hire myself a nigger to get this place in shape and to keep it that way."

"No disrespect, Miss Whitman, but can you afford a girl?" I asked.

"Oh, I don't intend to pay nobody, honey," she answered. "Bakker's gonna take care of all that. He says I'm to offer three dollars a day, and not a penny more. And Bakker says two days a week is plenty. He wants you on Wednesday when he ain't here, and on Saturday when he is." She giggled again. "You can start right here in the kitchen. I would do it myself, but I'm up to my elbows in my flowers."

"Today isn't Wednesday or Saturday," I told her, because I had the impression she didn't know which day of the week it was.

"No, I guess it isn't," she said, "but I'll pay you for today, anyway, and we won't say a word to Bakker."

"Is Bakker your husband?"

"Oh, no, honey. Bakker is my little brother. He got him a job down at the courthouse. He's gonna be a lawyer real soon now."

I stepped over to the sink and contemplated the task before me. *What would you do if you worked all day for a man, and he didn't pay you?* Hambone had asked that question months ago, and at the time it had not applied to me. Now it might. It would take hours just to put the kitchen in order, and I hadn't even glanced inside the bedrooms.

"Pay me first, and I'll do it," I said, in my first act of blatant insolence.

She cocked her head to one side and a frown gouged the space between her brows. Then she stepped into the front room. I was sure she was showing me out so I followed her. She stopped at the couch and searched through a pile of clothes until she found a white cotton shirt.

"Tear yourself a dish rag from this," she said, tossing the shirt to me. "Bakker won't miss it. He'll be able to buy new shirts now. He's gonna be a lawyer." She paused, and our eyes met. "He likes to scare niggers. I won't let him scare you, though."

I stood holding the shirt while she made her way down a short hallway to one of the back rooms. When she returned, she stepped past me, placed three dollars on the cluttered kitchen table, then said, "I trusted you enough to let you in my house. I don't know you, but sometimes you have to trust people."

She brushed past me again and proceeded toward the front porch where she sat on the floor and entertained herself with clay pots and mud. This was my first job, and I had not started it with maturity and charm as I had intended. I didn't feel bad, though, because I did not trust Miss Whitman. Something was wrong with her, although I wasn't qualified to say what it was.

I removed the money from the table and tucked it inside my sock, then I ripped the shirt—really ripped it good—until I had a strip of cloth small enough to work with. As I tackled the dirty dishes, I thought of apologizing to Miss Whitman, but I was sure she would never understand.

thirty-one

My mother's reaction to my job was wide-eyed disbelief. "What the hell we gon' do wit' six dollars a week?" she asked. "That ain't nothing, Tangy Mae. I hear them Griggs, who own the furniture store in town, is looking to hire a girl. I'm gon' take you over there."

"They already hired Becky James," Wallace informed her.

"How you know?" Mama asked.

"That's what I heard."

"Well, I can't go on what you heard. I'm gon' go see for myself. And while I'm gone, Wallace, I want you to clean that outhouse. Damn thing smelling up the whole town, and you ain't done nothing wit' it since some time last year. You oughta know you can't just leave it be in this kinda heat."

Wallace and I exchanged glances. We remembered Mama, just yesterday, commenting on the decent job Wallace had done, and Wallace had accepted the compliment without mentioning it was really I who had done all of the scrubbing. It seemed Mama was preoccupied or forgetful. She barely gave me enough time to comb my hair before rushing me toward the front door, stating that we had to get to East Grove quick before somebody else got the job. Although her car was in plain view, she walked me away from the house as though she had forgotten she could drive.

As we walked, Mama tried several times to engage me in conversation, but I didn't feel much like talking. I was wondering why I could not keep my job with the Whitmans, why we could not compromise. Mama finally gave up on trying to get me to talk, and fell into a monologue about her days working for the Munfords.

"No, it wadn't so bad at all when I think about it," she said. "They was pretty nice to me. Miss Arlisa gave me over half them blankets we still using to this day. Expensive things. When I first started working for 'em, she wadn't fat and she would give me dresses I could wear. And, of course, there was the things I just took on my own. It wadn't like stealing. I mean, if I was there working for 'em, she wouldna begrudged me a cup or two of coffee, so I just didn't drink it there, instead I took it home wit' me. It ain't bad when the missus is gone all day and you got the house to yo'self. There was a time when Miss Arlisa stayed home all day. I remember how tired she used to get from doing nothing. That's when they get mean and start finding things for you to do 'cause they ain't got nothing to do themself."

Mama laughed. "I don't know what it woulda been like if they'd had children. Tarabelle gon' have her hands full. You know, we oughta drop by there when we get done at the Griggs."

It was early morning, but already it was hot and humid. Beads of sweat rolled down my neck and formed on my back and in my armpits while my mother strolled along, seemingly oblivious to the heat. Dark clouds, too heavy and sluggish to float, hung over Triacy County as far as the eye could see. I knew days like this, and we were in for a good storm. It made me think of Jeff Stallings.

We turned onto Oglesbee Street and saw Miss Janie Jay hard at work in one of her flowerbeds. When she noticed us, she leaned against her gate and watched our approach.

"Tangy Quinn, you come early to church Sunday morning," she said as we passed her. "We got two new songs you need to learn, and they ain't easy songs. Brother Freddie wants you to sing lead in one of them. How is it you got that nice voice and can't ever make it to choir practice?"

"I'll come early, Miss Janie," I called, keeping pace with Mama and noticing that the two women had not acknowledged each other.

We crossed the bridge from Stump Town into East Grove, like stepping out of darkness into light. The houses on this side of the bridge were enormous. It was hard to imagine a single family taking up so much space. It was only my third time in East Grove, and my first opportunity to admire the landscape. Assortments of flowers grew in imaginative beds bordering manicured lawns. In one yard a star of white rock held a cushiony mound of colorful chrysanthemums. Across the street from that was a stone walkway lined with zinnias and marigolds. Even with the threatening clouds darkening the earth, East Grove was a kaleidoscope of colors.

Mama came to a halt in front of a two-story red-brick house where the lawn was enclosed by a U-shaped row of neatly trimmed hedges. "I think this is it," she said, and started for the house. I trailed her up the driveway, past a parked car, and around to the back door. There was no porch, only three steps leading up to a cement stoop. I waited on the ground beside the stoop while Mama knocked on the door.

A young male voice greeted Mama through the screen. "Can I help you, ma'am?"

"Morning," Mama began, "I'm Rozelle Quinn, and this here is my daughter, Tangy Mae." She beckoned for me to join her on the stoop. "We hear the Griggses is looking to hire a girl, and Tangy Mae is right good at cleaning."

Almost immediately there was a change in the young man's demeanor. "You're a nigger?" he asked, then yelled back into the house, "Kirk! Dave!" He turned once more to face my mother, and said, "Every five minutes another bunch of you niggers come knocking on this door. What do you think we are?"

Without warning, he shoved open the screen door. The frame of the door caught Mama on one side of her face. She staggered back and sat heavily on the top step, and I saw a crimson teardrop appear at the outer corner of one beautiful gray eye. When I glanced back toward the screen, I saw that the young man had been joined by two others. Their presence did not deter me from what I knew I had to do. I yanked at the screen door. Pain shot through my sprained finger. The youngest Griggs boy attempted to hold the door closed, but he had no grip. The door opened, and I was on him, releasing fourteen years of pent up rage.

For a moment the other two let me get away with it—too startled, I guessed, by the unexpected—then they shoved my prey toward me. "Get her, Donnie," they urged, but Donnie proved to be more talk than action. He was trying desperately to get away from me. I gave up clawing at his face and began to pound the fist of my uninjured hand against his head. That was when the other two came to his defense and began to strike at me. But their blows were without force as the enclosed area of the doorway hindered them. Behind them, I could hear Becky James shouting, "Stop it! Stop it!"

I backed from the doorway and moved down the stoop, then went to stand in the yard beside my mother. Becky was busy trying to calm and restrain the three young men. The one I had attacked looked to be about my age, the other two were older.

"Can't y'all see she just a child?" Becky asked.

"They're niggers," one of the young men said, "and they've got three seconds to get out of our yard."

"They ain't niggers, Kirk Griggs," Becky protested. "They human beings just like you."

Kirk Griggs shoved Becky's arm. Color rose in his cheeks, and he balled his fists. "I think my daddy would agree that I don't have to take this kind of sass from no nigger wench," he retorted.

"And I'm sho' my mama would agree that I ain't gotta take it from no puny little white boy," Becky said. "I'll just get my things, and you can tell yo' daddy to find him somebody else—if he can."

Becky disappeared into the house, then emerged seconds later with her pocketbook swinging from her hand. She was Harvey's age, had entered school and dropped out with Harvey. She stepped past the three young men, then turned back to say, "Y'all can finish cooking, and cleaning that house—if you want. Y'all old enough to do something besides sitting around watching me work."

Becky moved toward the driveway. I started to follow, but stopped when I felt my mother tug slightly at the sleeve of my blouse. Stealthily, Mama eased her feet from her shoes, and turned her head in my direction. Something in her eyes told me to get ready.

The three Griggs boys had moved down from the stoop and were now standing in the yard. The oldest one, Kirk, shouted,

"Now!" They rushed toward us. Kirk went for Mama, Dave went after Becky, and the one named Donnie came straight at me. I could tell from the expression on his face that he wished I would disappear so that he would not have to further humiliate himself. I almost laughed, but instead, I sidestepped his charge and slammed my fist into his back. He went sprawling across the lawn. I followed after him, climbed on top, and held him immobile with my weight while I plucked at his flesh once more with my nails. He cried out, bucked several times, and finally freed himself. He did the right thing after that. He ran for the safety of the house.

Becky was using her pocketbook against Dave. The boy was blubbering and trying to get away, but Becky held onto his arm and kept striking him across his head with a pocketbook that had to have been loaded with more than lipstick and a handkerchief. There was a heavy sound to the blows that landed on Dave Griggs.

Toward the middle of the lawn, Mama was fighting with Kirk Griggs. They were using their fists against each other, and Kirk's were landing with a lot more force than Mama's, but Mama stood her ground. She matched him blow for blow. I glanced about the yard for something to use against Kirk, but saw nothing. Finally, I ran toward them, jumped onto Kirk's back, and sank my teeth into his shoulder. While Kirk struggled to free himself from my grip, Mama stood there momentarily doing nothing, then she raised a knee that connected with Kirk's groin. He groaned, and sank to the ground with me still clinging to his back.

"Let's go!" Mama said. She seemed to be all right, except for a bruise on her cheek and the cut at the corner of her eye.

Becky released the boy she was holding, and she, Mama, and I moved out onto the sidewalk, winded, but walking as fast as we could.

"I was ready to quit anyhow," Becky mumbled. "Four days I been working for 'em, and they been the worst four days of my life, let me tell you. Most folks don't have you working so hard. But them—they gon' get the last drop of blood outta you. All time struttin' 'round that house calling folks niggers like I can't hear 'em. I ain't studyin' 'em."

"Do you think they'll call the police?" I asked.

"They ain't gon' call nobody," Mama said. "You think they gon' tell somebody they let three women beat 'em up like that?"

"That's right," Becky agreed. "That Kirk older than me, and don't work nowhere in the world. Just sit 'round all day being lazy. And they done went out and bought him a car like he just oughta have it. I don't understand white folk, but I know I put a beatin' on that boy's behind like his daddy oughta been doing for years."

Mama stopped to catch her breath, then she laughed. "Wonder why that ol' big, round one come after me?" she asked.

"They planned it that way, Miss Rosie," Becky said, and she began to laugh, too. "I was gon' come help you, but I didn't wanna stop beatin' on that boy's head. That's something I'd been wanting to do for four days."

Becky left us just after we crossed the bridge, and it did not matter that Mama had asked her not to tell what had happened. Becky James would tell. She would tell everybody, and no decent colored woman in Triacy County would ever work for the Griggses again.

"Ooh wee," Mama said as she watched Becky walk off. "I know just what that girl mean, Tangy Mae. Them ain't the kinda people to work for. If the rest of 'em anything like them boys, it's likely they wouldn't even pay you."

She stopped abruptly and pulled at something on her face. The way her hand swept across her skin, I thought maybe she had walked into a spider's web. She checked her hand and brushed it off with the other, then she continued walking.

"I'm glad Janie ain't out in that yard. That woman know she get on my nerves," Mama said. She stopped again and glanced back toward the creek. "That water's got a peculiar odor, don't you think, Tangy Mae? Like a skunk done crawled down there and died. Be nice if a good gust of wind came along and blew that odor into them fancy homes back there."

She brushed at the invisible spider's web once more. This time it was on her arms. "When we get home, I want you to warm me some bathwater. Something's crawling all over me. I wonder if I ain't done picked up something back there at that Griggs house. You know them fancy homes don't mean a thing. Sometimes they got the nastiest folks living in 'em.

"Yeah." She pursed her lips and nodded her head. "There's nasty folks everywhere, coloreds and whites, all over the world. That's why I try to teach y'all to be clean, and that's why I don't want my children traipsing halfway 'cross the world like Mushy done. It ain't bad the way Harvey left, leastways he's still in Pakersfield where he knows what type of people to stay away from."

We cleared Oglesbee Street without seeing Miss Janie, and Mama paused on Chestnut to catch her breath. She rested for a few seconds, then started talking again. "You remember that ticket Mushy sent here?" she asked. "I sat on my bed one night thinking 'bout that ticket. I was holding it in my hand when something tol' me to tear it up. At first I wadn't gon' do it, but seem like something just kept telling me to do it. Finally, I went on and tore it into pieces, and I felt a whole lot better 'bout things.

"The world is changing, Tangy Mae. There was a time when you couldn't find a man to marry a girl if she was dark as you. And I think they probably just drowned po' dumb people like Martha Jean. But it ain't like that no mo'. I think men must be getting desperate or something, but there still ain't no guarantees. You and Edna might have to be wit' me yo' whole life. I don't know. I gotta plan for it, though. 'Cause if it comes to that, it'll be up to you to earn a living for us, and I gotta get you started knowing how."

We walked down Fife Street. The field came into view, then our house, and still Mama talked on. "I hope you understand that sometimes we gotta do things we don't wanna do. Like you. I know you don't wanna come outta school and go to work, but you gotta—ain't no way 'round it."

We reached the house, and Mama plopped down on the bottom step and sent me inside to get her cigarettes. When I came back out, I sat down beside her feeling weary from a day that seemed eternal, although it was still morning. My chest felt light, like something my body needed desperately was floating up and out of me, and breathing only hastened the process. I studied my mother's profile as she puffed on her cigarette.

"Mama," I said, "what's Crow's real name?"

She held the cigarette away from her face as she considered my question, then she said, "I don't know. All I ever knew was Crow. That's all anybody ever called him. Now, get me some bathwater!

And, Tangy Mae, you go on back and work them two days for them people 'til something better come along."

Mama had bathed, napped, dressed, and left by the time Sam came in that evening. Her car was gone, but Sam looked for her in her room anyway before asking, "Where's Mama?"

"She went out," I answered.

"Tangy Mae, did you and Mama go over to East Grove and fight wit' them Griggs boys today?"

"Mama told me not to talk about it, Sam. She said it's best forgotten."

"Mama got a bruise on her face?"

I nodded, figuring he would see it sooner or later.

He nodded, too. "Yeah," he said, "it's best forgotten."

thirty-two

With a cup of water, Pakersfield soil can swallow itself and make a puddle. During an all-day rain, it swallowed my mother's car. I arrived home from the Whitmans' on Saturday afternoon to find Mama pacing the muddy road below our house, swearing and condemning Velman Cooper to Hell for all eternity.

Out in the field, Harvey, Sam, Wallace, Hambone, Maxwell, and Skip Carson were attempting to push the car out of the thick mud and up onto the road. Anybody could see that they were wasting their time. In fact, the car sank a little more with each push.

"It ain't coming out, Mama," Harvey yelled. "We gon' have to wait 'til this rain lets up, and dig it out."

Mama stopped pacing and turned to me. "Will you just listen to that fool," she said, then raised her voice and shouted out, "It's a *car*, Harvey. Drive it out. And don't get none of that mud in it."

"Didn't you already try that, Mama?" Sam asked. "Ain't that how it got stuck in the first place?"

"It got stuck 'cause y'all didn't cut that field right," she answered. "Instead of paying attention to what you oughta been doing, y'all was out there running from a rat. You hadda laid planks like you shoulda done, the damn thing wouldn't be stuck. Now, you shut up, Sam, and get my car outta there!"

"On three," Harvey said, and began to count. They pushed, and all four tires disappeared with a sucking sound, sending mud splattering across the fenders and the hood of the car.

"Well, I just be damn!" Mama spat, placing her hands on her hips, and shaking her head in disbelief.

Out in the field, five young men stood with their arms dangling idly at their sides. The sixth, Maxwell James, held his abdomen and convulsed with laughter. He lifted an arm and pointed to the sunken car, then he leaned forward. Each time he tried to straighten up, his howls would fold him over again.

"Max!" Hambone said sternly. "Max! Shut up, nigger. Ain't nothing funny."

"Damn, man, I'm trying," Maxwell gasped, "but did you see that thing? I mean, plop, man. It just went plop."

Harvey kept his composure. He trudged two steps, then stopped. "Mama, we can't get it out," he said. "We done tried lifting it wit' planks. We done tried pulling it. We done tried pushing it. We . . ."

"We, we, we, we, we," Mama shouted angrily.

At that, Harvey chuckled, then they all began to laugh, hooting and howling in mirth and frustration. Mama stared out at them. Rain dripped from her nose and chin. She slid a hand from her hip, made a fist, and knocked me to the ground.

"Come on, Miss Rosie," Hambone said. "You don't need to hit nobody. We'll come back tomorrow and try again. If there's somewhere you gotta go, I'll take you. How about it?"

"I got somewhere to go awright," Mama said. "I'm going to get Martha Jean. I ain't gon' stand by and let that Velman Cooper swindle me. He can have that piece of junk back."

Pulling myself up from the mud, neither hurt nor embarrassed, I went up to the faucet in the yard to wash the mud from my arms and legs. Mama, muddy shoes and all, stomped over to Hambone's car and opened the door.

"You coming?" she called to Hambone.

"Just give me a minute to get this mud off my hands, Miss Rosie," he said, as he and the others joined me in the yard. "I don't know about taking your mama over there, Sam," Hambone whispered. "What do you think?"

"I think she going whether you take her or not," Sam replied.

Harvey agreed. "Yeah, man. When she makes up her mind to do something, ain't no stopping her."

"I sho' would like to see that boy's face when yo' mama go over there and take his woman," Maxwell said. "What kinda man, you reckon, just gon' let somebody take his woman?"

No one answered. They rinsed the mud from their hands, then Skippy asked, "What time y'all getting up to Greg's tonight?"

"'Bout seven or eight," Sam answered. "They got everything ready?"

"Yeah, man," Skip said, "but they scared. You better make sure you be there."

"I'll be there," Sam assured him.

"Yeah, Sam'll be there," Hambone said. "How about you, Harvey?"

Harvey shook the water from his hands and dried them against the legs of his pants. "I don't know," he answered quietly. "I just don't know about this."

"I'll be there," Max said.

Sam gave him a slap on the back. "I know you will, Max."

Skip and Maxwell went with Hambone, but Harvey did not leave right away. He came inside and dried himself in the kitchen while I prepared supper. Laura and Edna clung to him until he shook them off and shooed them away.

"They miss you, Harvey," I said.

"I know. Any other time I'd be glad to see 'em, but I think I done hurt my back pushing that car."

"Boy, that was really something the way it went down in that mud," Wallace said. "You think we gon' ever get it out?"

"Somebody will," Harvey answered. "I ain't straining my back on it no mo'. Mama gon' have to wait and get a tow truck."

"She ain't gon' pay for nothing like that," Sam said, leaning back on a chair with his bare feet propped on a milk crate. "Mama didn't need that thing no way. You ever seen how she drive? She be all over the road like other people ain't got no business on it. Like the world belong to her."

"It do, don't it?" Harvey asked with a chuckle.

"I don't know about that," Sam said, "but Martha Jean belong to her. I hope Velman don't go acting no fool."

We heard the front door open, then Tarabelle came into the kitchen carrying a newspaper that was drenched from being held over her head. She wiped rainwater from her face as her gaze met Sam's.

"Sheriff's right behind me," she said. "He got that Chadlow wit' him. Asked me if you was here."

"What they want wit' me?" Sam asked, slowly lowering his feet, bringing his chair into an upright position.

"I'm here to arrest you, Sam," Angus Betts answered, stepping into our kitchen with Chadlow on his heels. "Has to do with one of the Griggs boys from over in East Grove. I've got a complaint that you threw a brick through the windshield of his car. Heard you drug him from that car and beat him to within an inch of his life. You know anything about that?"

"He hurt my mama," Sam said, "but I didn't beat him that bad."

The sheriff arched his brows. "Well, that's the complaint I got from Kirk Griggs's hospital bed. That boy says you tried to kill him, and it looks like you did beat him up pretty bad. His daddy is screaming bloody murder, threatening to take matters into his own hands if I don't do something about it, so I'm taking you in. And speaking of murder, a description of you keeps coming up in connection with the death of Tannus Fess. It seems you were the last one seen with him."

"What?" Sam exclaimed, shaking his head as if to clear it. "I didn't kill Junior."

"That may be so, but right now I've got one fellow in the hospital who positively identifies you as his attacker, and I have a witness who says he saw somebody looks like you with Tannus Fess."

Sam rose from his chair and glanced toward the back door. He placed his hands flat on the table that blocked his path, then he glanced at Chadlow who stood with one hand resting on his hip.

"Come easy, son," the sheriff said. "Don't make Chad shoot your knee caps off."

"I didn't kill Junior," Sam protested.

"Maybe not, but I've heard Tannus was last seen with a white boy," the sheriff said. "I don't know any white boys in this county who run around with coloreds. I've spent some time thinking about this, and I keep coming up with you. Now, after this thing with Kirk Griggs, I'm pretty sure I should have arrested you a long time ago. I've seen that bunch of hoodlums you run around with. It's a wonder I haven't gotten you for something long before now."

"It couldna been me," Sam said, his lips quivering as he spoke. "Ain't nobody seen me wit' Junior, and I ain't white."

"No, you're not," Angus Betts agreed, "but it was you, and we both know it."

Chadlow stepped around the table and, with more force than necessary, handcuffed Sam's wrists behind his back, then shoved him toward the door while the sheriff kept watch on the rest of us. I looked at Harvey, waiting for him to do or say something, but he remained unmoving and silent.

"Where's Mama?" Tarabelle asked, after the sheriff had left the kitchen.

"She went to get Martha Jean," Wallace answered. "She's taking her back from Velman."

A short while later, Mama arrived home with Martha Jean, and Harvey broke the news to her. He led her to a chair in the front room, and held her as she sobbed. She clutched his shirt and would not let go.

"Don't leave, Harvey," she pleaded between sobs. "Don't go. You stay here wit' me tonight. I need you here."

"I'll stay, Mama," Harvey said. "I ain't gon' leave you."

"Harvey, do you think I'm being punished for bringing Martha Jean home?" Mama asked, as tears rolled down her face. "I had to fight Skeeter to get her. Maybe I'm being punished. I'd rather have Sam."

"He'll be back," Harvey soothed.

"When?" Mama screamed. "They done took my baby from me. They done took Sam. People trying to take all my babies from me."

Wallace tried to explain things to Martha Jean. She nodded, although her eyes seemed not to follow the movement of his fingers. They appeared hollow, staring out at nothing.

Surprisingly, we were able to eat supper, and as we did, the rain gave a final tap against the roof and hushed.

"Roof holding up pretty good, ain't it?" Harvey observed.

Mama nodded absently, and no one else said anything for a long while, not until Edna announced that she was sleepy.

We settled down, and the house was quiet, but I knew we were all thinking about Sam. He was easily influenced by Hambone, he had a mean streak, and he hadn't denied throwing the brick through Kirk Griggs's car window or beating the boy up. But he never would have killed Junior Fess.

I drifted into a light sleep and was awakened by Tarabelle shaking my shoulder. "Tan, listen," she whispered.

I brought my head up from the floor and strained to hear the low voices coming from the hall. It was Mama and the sheriff.

"Rozelle, I did it for his own good," Angus Betts said. "Do you want somebody to kill him?"

"I want him outta jail," Mama answered. "Ain't nobody gon' kill him. Let him out, Angus, or I'm gon' tell everybody he's yo' son."

"Don't threaten me, Rozelle. I'm trying to help. Bill Griggs cares about his boy the same way you care about yours. He didn't say it to me, but I've been hearing rumors of trouble. He could get a bunch of men together to come out here and snatch Sam from this house, and you know what would happen. I'm trying to keep Sam safe until this dies down some."

"Go to Hell, Angus!" Mama said angrily. "Why you trying to keep him safe? We ain't asked for yo' help. You ain't never claimed Sam to be yo' son, so why you all of a sudden wanna keep him safe?"

"First of all, I'm not convinced that he is my son. All I know is what you told me. I was just a boy, Rozelle, and you had me thinking you were a white woman. Remember that?"

Mama laughed bitterly. "You knew what I was. That's the reason you wanted me. Stop fooling yo'self, Angus. You wanted me then, and you want me now. You can have me if you let Sam go."

"That was a long time ago. That was before I became sheriff, and before I had a wife and children to think about. I don't want you, Rozelle."

"Yes, you do," Mama said. "I can smell wanting all over you, Angus. Let Sam out, and I'll do anything you want."

"Let's get one thing straight," the sheriff said. "I wouldn't dare touch you. You've been with just about every man in this county. I wouldn't take that kind of filth home to my wife."

"By this time tomorrow, everybody gon' know that you my boy's daddy," Mama threatened. "They gon' look, Angus, and they gon' see."

"I've told you once, don't threaten me," he said, his voice heavy with contempt. "If you so much as whisper my name, you'll never see that boy again. You try to remember that, Rozelle."

The front door closed, and I lowered my head to my arms and held myself rigid as Mama stepped into the room. She walked past us and out into the kitchen. "Harvey, wake up!" she snapped. "I want you to run up to Pearl's and get me something to drink. Tell her to send me something. I don't care what it is. I gotta have something to help me think."

thirty-three

Mama was waiting for us at the top of Fife Street when we came from church that Sunday afternoon. "I'm waiting for them Munfords to come home from church," she said. "I want you to go over there wit' me, Tarabelle. I think Mr. Munford can help me get Sam outta jail."

That was plan one, and it didn't work. According to Tarabelle, Mr. Munford had told Mama that he couldn't help her, and he doubted if she would find a lawyer in town willing to take Sam's case. He had suggested she go to one of the neighboring counties to find a lawyer, but even then he thought she'd have to scrape the bottom of the barrel to find someone willing to defend a Negro charged with assaulting a white man. He thought she'd stand a better chance if Sam's only charge had been the murder of a Negro.

Poor Tarabelle had been forced to follow Mama from East Grove all the way to the flats. There Mama had barged in on Harlell Nixon, not at his barber shop, but at the home he shared with his wife and three children. He hadn't been happy to see her, but he had told her that he was sorry to hear about Sam's troubles.

He, however, could not drive her to Atlanta to look for a lawyer. He didn't think his car would make it that far.

On Tuesday evening, after Mama came home from the jail in tears, I suggested she go talk with Mr. Pace, Mr. Hewitt, or Reverend Nelson. "They're educated men, Mama. Maybe they can tell you how to help Sam."

"Educated?" she spat at me. "Junior Fess thought he was educated, and where is he now? I don't need nobody that's too smart for they own good."

I wanted to tell her that any lawyer she found would be an educated man and, hopefully, a smart one, but I knew it was time for me to be quiet.

Several days passed before Velman came to reclaim Martha Jean. He arrived with Skeeter, Red Adams, and a tow truck. They went directly to the field where the sun had baked a mud crust around the tires of my mother's Buick.

Mama, sitting on her porch chair, lit a cigarette and squeezed it between her fingers as she watched them. "I think I'll run up to Pearl's for a bit," she said, but made no effort to move.

Velman pulled a pickax from the truck and began to chop at the dirt around the tires, and Mama rose from her chair to stare down at him. "He don't know what he doing," she said. "He gon' bust my tires wit' that thing." Ordinarily, she would have said as much to him, but she was refusing to acknowledge them until they acknowledged her. She tossed her cigarette butt over the side of the porch and returned to her chair. "What you think they up to?" she asked.

Tarabelle, sitting a few steps below me and Martha Jean, looked up and rolled her eyes. "They trying to get that car outta there," she said. "That's why they brought that truck."

"I know that, Tarabelle. That ain't what I mean. I just wonder why they ain't spoke. They act like we ain't here. That boy ain't even looked at Martha Jean."

"Maybe he decided he'd rather have his car back," Tarabelle suggested.

"I'm going down to help 'em," Wallace said. "You want me to find out what's going on, Mama?"

"Yeah, Wallace. You find out what they planning to do."

Wallace went down to the road, but instead of going out to the field, he climbed into the cab of Red's truck. Mama yelled for him to get out, but it was more to call attention to herself than to get Wallace to obey, and Wallace must have known it. He stayed where he was.

"Boys," Mama said sorrowfully. "That's why Sam in jail right now. They don't listen to nothing you tell 'em 'til it's too late. Leastways, they ain't hurt Sam none, not yet."

"When do you think they'll let Sam out?" I asked.

She ignored my question, and I assumed she had no idea.

Sitting beside me on the step, Martha Jean concentrated on Laura's hair, her fingers working the strands into thick braids. I bumped her knee and pointed, and she nodded, indicating that she had already seen the men.

I propped my elbows on my knees and watched the men as they worked in the field. Velman had removed his shirt, and his bare back glistened with perspiration. I imagined it couldn't be easy trying to remove a buried car from crusted earth, but Velman's agile, flowing movements made the task seem effortless. The sight of him caused my stomach to flutter and my underarms to prickle, and I didn't know why.

Folding my arms across my abdomen, I turned away and focused my attention on Laura's neatly parted braids, anything to keep my thoughts away from Velman. I was beginning to like him. I hadn't at first, when he had seemed pushy and gabby, and when I had thought he was courting my mother. I knew now that he hadn't cared anything about Mama; he'd been teaching her to drive, bargaining with her for the love of Martha Jean. Now he seemed strong and protective, like someone I could depend on.

My mother's grunt of annoyance caused me to glance up. She was frowning and staring down at Velman, who had made his way up to the yard and was standing below the porch.

"Miss Rosie, I need the key," he said.

Mama was slow in doing so, but she reached into the pocket of her dress, then tossed the key down to him. Velman strode back across the road, and Red Adams backed the tow truck into the field. They chained the car to the truck, and on the first try, the car noisily rose up and out of the field. Mama watched until her car was out of sight, then she lit a cigarette, and rocked her body against the back of her chair.

Martha Jean finished braiding Laura's hair, then started on Edna's, and never once glanced up. I think she was staying busy to keep from thinking. That was supposed to work, I knew, but it seldom did.

We went inside and ate our supper in the stifling heat of the kitchen, then returned to the porch where Mama began telling us of her plans to get Sam out of jail. Tomorrow she would go and talk to the sheriff. She would tell him that Sam hadn't killed anybody and hadn't tried to kill anybody. We all knew she had already tried that to no avail. Wallace wasn't paying any attention to what she said. He was reaching out from the steps and snatching fireflies from the air. "That looks like yo' car, Mama," he said, as a Buick turned onto the road.

Mama leaned forward and sighed wearily. "What he want now?" she asked. The car came to a stop, and Velman got out.

Velman entered the yard and stopped at the steps. "I got your car all clean and running, Miss Rosie," he said. "Now we both know it wasn't my fault it got stuck out there, but I got it out for you just the same. I came to get Martha Jean."

"I changed my mind 'bout all that," Mama said. "Martha Jean gon' stay right here where she belong. She too young to be over there wit' you and Skeeter, anyway. People talking."

"Then it all stops, Miss Rosie," Velman said. "It all stops, and I'll have Martha Jean no matter what you say. You can't keep us apart."

"Pretty sho' of yo'self, ain't you?" she challenged, eyeing him with contempt.

"No, ma'am. I'm pretty sure of Martha Jean. And you right about one thing; people talking, but they ain't talking about me and Martha Jean. They talking about you. They talking about what you did to Judy. You a mean woman, Miss Rosie. It don't make no sense to be so hateful."

My mother made a sound like a snake being chopped in half in the middle of a hiss, then she turned on her chair and slammed her fist against the porch wall. It was nearly dark, but I was sure Velman could see hatred in the gray eyes that glared down at him.

"You can be stopped, Miss Rosie," he said. "Don't think for one minute that I don't know what happened out here."

"Shut up!" Mama shouted, then reached a hand up and began to snatch invisible bugs from her nose.

Velman glanced at me, his brows raised questioningly.

I shrugged.

"Bugs," Tarabelle said. "Mama, you want me to fetch you some bathwater?"

"Shut up! I need to think," Mama said, and snatched a bug from her forehead. After a minute or two, she stared once more at Velman. "Give me that damn key. You go on and take that girl. What do I care? People trying to take all my children, but they ain't gon' get 'em all."

Velman stepped between us as he climbed the steps with the key. "Miss Rosie, I can't be going through this," he said. "I don't want you coming back to my house tomorrow or next week saying how you done changed your mind again. This ain't no good for nobody."

When it became apparent that Mama was not going to respond to him, Velman placed the key on the floor beside her feet, then backed away. He crossed the porch to the steps, took Martha Jean's hand, and led her down to the yard. My sister did not even turn around to wave as she followed him up Penyon Road, and this time it was easier for me to watch her go.

"Mama, can I drive yo' car?" Wallace asked, as soon as Velman and Martha Jean were out of sight. "Just down the road a bit and right back? Can I?"

"You can get me some bathwater," Mama said, as she picked the key up from the floor. "Tarabelle, you and Tangy Mae get the house clean. There's something in there."

thirty-four

The school year began on the same day the county fair opened its gates to the Negro population. It wasn't the best of days. I walked to and from school with Laura, who spoke very little going and not at all coming back. We arrived home to find Edna waiting for us on the front porch, and I wondered what it had been like for her alone all day with Mama.

Mama was sitting on the floor of the front room when the three of us went inside. She wore a white dress with purple polka dots. Her shoes were off and her stockings were twisted about her legs. She was drunk. On the floor surrounding her were scattered bills of small denominations. Three five-dollar bills stuck out from the side of her right fist. She raised that fist and shook it at us.

"This here is cursed money," she said. "It ain't no good. Ain't worth the paper it's printed on. Cursed money that the white man won't even touch."

When Tarabelle and Wallace came home, Tarabelle stopped and peered down at the bills. "How much money you got there, Mama?" she asked.

"Don't matter," Mama said. "It ain't no good. It won't get my baby outta jail." Her words were slurred, and her head seemed to favor her left shoulder.

"Is it counterfeit?" Tarabelle asked, reaching down to examine one of the bills.

Mama drew up a leg, then kicked her foot at Tarabelle in a slow, half-hearted effort. "Don't touch it," she said. "Ain't counterfeit. It's cursed. Everything that boy touch is cursed."

"Mama, can we see if they'll take it at the fair?" Wallace asked. "They'll be in another county before they figure out it's counterfeit."

"Ain't counterfeit," Mama repeated. Her head rolled to the right, and she dropped the money from her hand and forced out a sob. "Tangy Mae, I want you to cook up some greens and take 'em down to Sam. Throw about five or six neck bones in the pot. I don't think they feeding him, and they wouldn't let me see him but ten minutes."

"Where you get all that money?" Tarabelle asked.

Mama struggled to her knees, holding onto an armchair to balance herself. "Ain't you been listening to me, Tarabelle? I got it from that damn Velman Cooper. Fifty dollars I got here, and it ain't worth fifty cents. They can't even prove Sam done nothing. I don't understand why they keeping my baby."

"Can I have a dollar of yo' money, Mama?" Wallace asked. "To go to the fair?"

"Is that all you can think about? Yeah, you take yo'self a dollar, and get on outta my sight. And you make sho' it ain't nothing but a dollar."

Wallace picked up a dollar and held it out for Mama to see. "It's just a dollar," he said, "but what about Laura and Edna? Ain't they going, too?"

"Wallace, you trying to tell me all y'all can't ride off a dollar? You take 'em wit' you and make sho' they get a ride. Now, don't say nothing else to me. You oughta be shame of yo'self, anyhow. Tangy Mae, pick that money up!"

I dropped to my knees, gathered the bills together, and gave them to her. With her chin now resting against her chest, she thumbed through the bills and dealt out a dollar to me. "You share this wit' Tarabelle," she said. "All y'all go on to that damn fair and just forget about Sam. I'm his mother. I'm the one s'pose to do the worrying. Gone now, get on outta my sight."

Out on the road Tarabelle kicked a tire on Mama's car. "She coulda took us," she said angrily. "I ain't been in that car since she got it. You'd think she could drive me over to East Grove sometimes, but she won't. And every time I get paid, she right there taking my money."

"I ain't been in it, neither," Wallace said. "It don't matter to me. I'm gon' get my own car and my own house."

"You ain't even got no job, Wallace," Tarabelle shot back. "You done quit school saying you was gon' get one, and you ain't even looked. I wish somebody in that house would do something, besides me. I'm sick of y'all, and I don't wanna go to no damn fair, smelling pig shit and going 'round in circles on some ol' stupid ride."

"Then don't go," I said. "You don't have to go."

"I ain't going." She stopped, flipped a hand in my direction, and said, "Tan, you give me my dollar."

"Our dollar," I corrected.

"My dollar. You think I don't know 'bout that money you hide in yo' sock? You got money, Tan. I'm the one work every day and half the night, and you walking 'round wit' money in yo' sock when I ain't got a penny. Give me my dollar, and I don't wanna have to break yo' arm to get it."

"Here," I said. "Take the doggone thing if it'll make you happy."

"It ain't gon' make me happy. But maybe I wanna strut around awhile wit' money in my sock. Maybe I wanna know how it feels. Huh?"

She snatched the dollar from my hand, and as I glared at her unchanging expression, it occurred to me that she was right. She worked every day and never had a penny to show for it. My anger evaporated.

"Wallace, take the girls on," I said. "I'll catch up to you in a bit."

"Okay," Wallace answered, "but you might not. If I see somebody going that way in a car, I'm gon' catch a ride."

The fairground was quite some distance away, located on a stretch of land between the flats and North Ridge. For the sake of the girls, I hoped Wallace could catch a ride. Maybe later I'd be able to catch one myself, but for now I wanted to talk to Tarabelle. I turned to find her watching me.

"Are you going back to sit with Mama?" I asked.

She shook her head. "Nah. I ain't in no mood to listen to her carry on 'bout nothing. She ain't that worried 'bout Sam nohow. All she worried 'bout is money."

"Well, what are you gonna do?"

"I don't know." She began to walk, and I followed. "I'm so tired, Tan, I don't know what to do," she said. "I feel like I could sleep for a week."

"Go back home. You don't have to listen to Mama. She's probably asleep by now, and if she's not, you can just pretend she's not there."

"How?"

"Just close her out. I do it all the time. I just think of something else until I can't hear what she's saying."

"Yeah? Well, that's easy for you. Everything is easy for you. You ain't got nothing else to do. I got that big fat white lady to worry 'bout. She big as the house, and now she stay home every day wit' me, trying to tell me how to run things. Then she whine and carry on, wanting me to always rub her back. I be washing clothes, she say rub her back. I be washing dishes, she say rub her back. I can't hardly get my work done for all time stopping and rubbing her back. Some people just ought not have babies."

We reached the top of Fife, and continued on. I did not see Wallace, and assumed he had caught a ride. As we neared town, Tarabelle stopped and studied the road, as if deciding what to do.

"Might as well go to the fair," she said. "You gon' be running 'round wit' that boy when we get there?"

"If I see him."

She grunted and smacked her lips in distaste, but said nothing. We reached Market Street, then crossed the railroad tracks and turned north at Erwin in the direction of the flats.

"Wanna stop by and see if Martha Jean wants to come?" I asked.

Tarabelle glanced at me. "Why you scared to be by yo'self?" she asked. "Only time you ever by yo'self is when you reading them books, and even then you make silly faces and talk to yo'self."

"Why do *you* always want to be alone?" I countered. "You never do anything with anybody, except Mattie."

"Mattie. I was wondering when you'd get around to bringing her up. You jealous, ain't you?"

"No. I was at first, but I'm not now," I answered truthfully.

"I knew you was. Mattie is different. She ain't like everybody else who all time laughing when I say things that ain't funny. She know when to laugh and when not to."

"I think she is afraid of you."

"She ain't scared of me," Tarabelle said, then grunted. "She oughta be, though, but she ain't. She the only friend I ever had. All y'all always had friends, 'cept me. I thought something was wrong wit' me. Did you know that, Tan? I ain't friendly like Mushy. I ain't smart like you. And I ain't pretty like Martha Jean. I ain't never knew what I was s'pose to be. Then Mattie wanted to be my friend. She liked me better than she did you. I knew you'd be mad, but I didn't care. It's time for me to have friends, too."

Jack Crothers drove by in his truck, slowed, and asked if we wanted a lift. We declined and continued on, in no rush to get to the fair. We strolled by Skeeter's house and I purposely avoided glancing in that direction. I was captivated by this loquacious side of Tarabelle, by her having taken me into her confidence.

"Sometimes, Tan, I be walking to work and I go by that creek. I be thinking 'bout walking right on out in it. Then I think the water ain't gon' cover my head, and I'm just gon' be wet and look stupid and won't even be dead. You ever think about dying?" she asked. "When Judy died, I wished it was me."

"Why do you wanna die, Tara?" I asked. "I wanna live to get old—older than Miss Janie. I wanna do things."

"Ain't nothing to do. And anyway, I'm too tired to do anything. Sometimes I think I won't take another breath, but then I do, and I don't even know why."

"Maybe you wouldn't feel that way if you could get out of Pakersfield. If Mama hadn't torn up your ticket and you could have left, maybe you wouldn't feel that way."

Tarabelle blew a quick breath through pursed lips. "Shoot," she said, "Pakersfield ain't got nothing to do wit' nothing. I'm glad Mama did it. First, I was mad, but after I thought about it, I didn't even care. I don't wanna go nowhere and live wit' Mushy. She just like Mama. Just like her."

Outside the Tates' house, Miss Dorothy was putting a lot of energy into sweeping down her four wooden steps. She did not wave or speak as we neared her, but glared at us with reproachful eyes.

Tarabelle stepped from the walk and crossed the yard until she was standing at the foot of the steps. She glared up at Dorothy Tate, and shouted, "You mad! You mad 'cause you can't do nothing wit' that ol' drunk husband of yours. I wish you'd come on down here trying to start something wit' me. I'll break that broom over yo' neck. You hear me, Miss Dorothy? I'll break that goddamn broom 'cross yo' neck."

Dorothy Tate slowly backed up the steps, then closed the screen door behind her. She was probably as shocked by Tarabelle's language as I was, but for once, I understood. I remembered the night Melvin Tate and Crow had brought Mama and Tarabelle home. Miss Dorothy must have known about it, too. She held her broom steady, and watched my sister from behind the safety of the screen. I had the impression that Miss Dorothy did not want to fight, but she would if Tarabelle was stupid enough to break through the screen.

I stepped into the yard and grabbed Tarabelle's hand, but she snatched it from my grip, and remained where she was until Miss Dorothy disappeared from the door. Finally, she returned to the walk. She was breathing hard and walking fast.

"Tan, do you know what I do when I go out wit' Mama?" she asked.

"I didn't at first," I said, "but I think I do now."

"Mama think people don't know," she said angrily, "but everybody know. I can tell the way they look at me that they know. They look at me like I'm dirt—like they better not get too close."

We left Motten Street and crossed Atler Avenue, hearing for the first time the sounds of the fair. We stopped at the wire fence that surrounded the grounds, and Tarabelle leaned against a pole and stared straight ahead at the crowd. I glanced along the rows of parked cars, searching for Jeff's father's car.

"I don't think I wanna go in there," Tarabelle said, after a minute of looking. "You gon' be running 'round wit' that boy?"

"I don't have to," I answered.

"I done been knocked up before, fooling 'round wit' men," she said. "Mama took me to Miss Pearl, and she got that baby out my belly wit' a wire hanger. Hurt real bad, too. They made me drink corn whiskey in orange juice. It taste awful—worse than cast'oil. Then Miss Pearl scraped that baby out. Never was no real baby no how—just blood and mess . . . and pain."

Rapid puffs of breath escaped my mouth, and my heart pounded as though I had been running long and hard. My face felt warm, and my head light. I braced myself against the pole, unable to speak. People passed, spoke, and waved with no idea that innocence had sloughed from my body and lay in a heap at my feet.

"How did you know a baby was there?" I asked, when I was able to speak. "I never saw you gain weight or anything."

"You don't get fat 'til later. First the curse stops, then you start to be sick, and you be tired from throwing up all the time."

"Oh," I said, and did not know what else to say.

"You go on now, Tan," Tarabelle said. "I'm gon' stay here 'til I make up my mind what I wanna do."

Disengaging myself from the pole, I tramped slowly along the gravel shoulder beside the fence until I reached the ticket booth, then I glanced back at Tarabelle. She was standing motionless, like a sign of despair mounted to a post, and I could not leave her like that. I retraced my steps.

"Tarabelle," I said, barely above a whisper, "you said you never knew what you were supposed to be. Well, you're brave. You're the bravest child our mother has."

She moved then, and her eyes seemed to bore right through me. "You really think so, Tan?"

"Yeah."

"Okay. You go on now. Go on to the fair."

Moving across earth sprinkled with sawdust, and through air heavy with an assortment of aromas, I stepped out of a babbling crowd at the merry-go-round. Almost immediately someone touched my arm, and I glanced up to see Martha Jean. She was holding a cone of cotton candy and a small stuffed animal. Velman stood directly behind her.

"Hey," he said. "We're gonna get on this thing when it stops. You wanna ride?"

I shook my head. "No. I'm looking for Wallace. Have you seen him?"

"Yeah, I've seen him. He's caught up to me about six times already, asking for a dime. Last time I saw him he was at the Ferris wheel, and the girls are over there wit' Harvey and Carol Sue." He pointed toward the funhouse.

I started in that direction, but he stopped me by placing a strong hand on my shoulder. "Hey, wait a minute," he said. "We're married, me and Martha Jean. Did you know?"

"When?" I asked, surprised that my mother had allowed it.

"Today. We're celebrating."

The merry-go-round stopped, and Velman ushered Martha Jean toward the throng of youngsters rushing for horses.

"Congratulations," I shouted, but I wasn't sure how I felt about the marriage.

I saw Mattie standing at a hot dog stand. When she spotted me, she quickly turned her head, but I approached her anyway and purposely brushed my arm against hers. "Hey, Mattie," I said.

"I ain't talking to you," she said.

"Why?"

"'Cause I ain't got to, that's why."

"I don't want you to talk to me," I said. "I want you to talk to Tarabelle."

"Where she at?" Mattie asked, now turning to face me, and trying to appear angry when we both knew there was nothing to be angry about.

"Out by the fence where the cars are parked. Something's troubling her. I don't know what it is."

"Probably you," Mattie mumbled as she stepped around me, holding a hot dog that was barely visible beneath layers of yellow mustard. She walked off toward the main gate.

For a moment, I stood by the hot dog stand trying to decide which way to go. Finally, I walked the entire length of the grounds, staring up at the colorful, triangular flags flapping in the wind above tents and food stands. Night fell gently over the grounds, and I found myself in a chatoyant glow of swirling, twirling lights. Despite Tarabelle's gloom, Sam's incarceration, and Martha Jean's marriage, I felt strangely carefree. I inched a dime from my sock, and rode the Ferris wheel.

At the top of the ride, I looked down and saw a large crowd

gathering at a game booth beside the root beer barrel. When the ride ended, I rushed toward the gathering. Jeff was in the crowd, staring intently ahead, and I walked over to him.

"Hey," I said. "What's going on?"

"Hey," he said in surprise. "I thought you weren't coming. Hambone's preaching again about the evils of the white man. He's making sense, though."

Hambone's background was a corkboard filled with balloons. It was one of those games where you tossed darts in an attempt to bust a balloon, and Hambone was holding three darts in a hand that was raised above his head.

"Look around you," he said. "They've stored away everything that's worth having, from the lemonade to the game prizes. It's all junk, things they wouldn't dare give to their own kind. Things they intentionally hold until Negro night. Three days they give to the white people before they open the gates for coloreds. I'm willing to bet if you scrape the coating off of some of them candy apples, you're gonna find worms and rot. Hot dogs on stale bread, maggots in the onions. Throw it down! Don't let your children eat it. Don't give these crackers another dime."

"What's wrong wit' you, Hambone?" Harvey asked. He was standing about three feet away from me, and he had the girls with him. "People wait all year for the fair to come. It's the one thing the children have to look forward to. Why you wanna mess it up for everybody?"

"Yeah," Maureen Milner agreed. "I done ate two of them apples and ain't seen no worms. If you so worried 'bout bad stuff, don't eat nothing."

Some people nodded and agreed with Maureen until Hambone brought his hand down, turned toward the corkboard, and threw a dart. It hit a target, and the balloon gave a moderate pop. The man working the booth threw his arms over his head and gasped, causing the crowd to roar with laughter.

"What's funny here?" Hambone asked, spreading his arms and still gripping two of the darts. "Don't you know your ignorance is what's holding you down? As long as you remain ignorant, they'll treat you any way they want. I know most of you have been right here in Pakersfield all of your lives. You don't even realize you're being mistreated. I call that ignorance. Most of you can't even read the newspaper and you won't bother to get someone else to read it to you. You don't know what's going on. You don't even know that the rest of the world ain't like this little backwards cracker town."

"Some of us do know what's going on," Jack Crothers said. "It don't mean we gotta get our heads bashed in 'cause they doing it someplace else. It's easy for you to stand there and talk. You ain't got no children to care about. You get things stirred up 'round here, then you'll go back to Chicago. Leave us alone! If you don't like it here, you oughta leave before you get some trouble started."

"Trouble?" Hambone questioned, then gave a short laugh. "Nigger, you *in* trouble. You just don't know it. You say you care about your children? Is that what you said? Then you need to take a good, long look at that school they building for your children. They're throwing it together with the worst material they could find. Did you know that? When it falls, it won't be on a white child's head. You think about that for a minute."

I could tell by the silence that no one had given much thought to the new school. I hadn't, either. I just assumed it would go up and stand forever like everything else. I saw Harvey glance down at Laura and Edna. He placed a hand on Edna's head before glancing over at Carol Sue.

"Oh, yeah," Hambone said. "You hadn't thought about that, had you? There's something wrong when a man puts all of his trust in another man, especially when that other man don't care if you live or die. The white man don't give a damn about none of us, no more than what we can do for them. And we're doing everything for them."

"What do you expect people to do?" Jeff asked, his voice startling me. I had thought him too reserved to speak out in a crowd.

"I expect you to come together as a race," Hambone answered. "I expect you to stop staring at the ground every time you speak to a white man that ain't a drop better than you. I expect you to be the men you were born to be, and to demand your God-given right to be human."

"We've got wives and children to feed," one man yelled. "Who gon' pay our wages when we go making all these demands?"

"What wages?" Hambone yelled back. "There's not a dozen of you here who can feed your children without your wives going to work. And what is she doing? She's getting calluses on her hands from scrubbing the white man's house, tending his children, washing his clothes, and cooking his meals. I see your wives cutting through town every morning, going to East Grove, Meadow Hill, and some as far as North Ridge. They wash clothes and cook supper for the white man, then you wanna knock them around when they're too tired to have your supper on the table on time."

"I wish some man would come hitting on me when I'm tired," Maureen said. "It'd be the last somebody he'd hit."

A few of the women laughed and agreed with her, but Hambone kept his composure. "That's right, Miss Maureen," he said. "You go on and kill off your man, or let him kill you off. It doesn't matter to the white man. He doesn't care a thing about you. Tomorrow he'll have somebody else plowing his fields and washing his clothes. And while you're at it, go on over there and buy yourself a few more of them apples because I'm telling you, they'll poison you just as soon as lynch you. Have y'all forgot about Junior Fess? They're holding Sam Quinn for his murder, and we all know Junior was killed by white hands. Now, y'all think about that."

A somber mood descended upon us, and even the small children were quiet. The crowd was growing, and Hambone seemed to have everyone's attention now.

"Why don't we see any white faces moving among us today?" he asked. "What's gonna happen if one of us bump against their lily white skin? Not a damn thing, that's what. They think we're animals who're suppose to work for them all day. They let you women touch their babies when you're cleaning smelly diapers, but then you can't sit next to them at the picture show or the soda fountain. Think about that for a minute."

There was no Reverend Nelson to oppose or silence Hambone and, without restraint, he managed to provoke the crowd into anger and action.

"Let's tear it down!" someone shouted.

Hambone raised his arm, then turned and threw the last two darts at the corkboard. It seemed he deliberately missed his target. He shrugged his shoulder and faced the crowd once more. "There're mostly children out here tonight," he said, "so that's not the way we're gonna do it. We need to come together and plan. Now, who's with me on this?"

Hands began to go up as lights began to shut down. Whole sections of the fairgrounds fell into darkness. I saw Wallace and Maxwell move up to stand beside Hambone just as the far section of the grounds, where the Ferris wheel stood, went dark. All music stopped. The funhouse and the fortune teller's tent disappeared into the night.

"Hambone, look!" Wallace shouted.

We all looked. Out of the darkness emerged a nightmare—about three dozen angry white men armed with bats and chains, shotguns and pistols. A tall, thin white man in a plaid shirt and overalls aimed his shotgun at the crowd.

"Awright, you niggers clear on outta here!" he ordered. "And don't drag yo' feet about it."

We outnumbered them eight to one—mostly children. Despite that, we began to disperse and rush for the main gate. I moved along with Jeff, trying to keep Laura and Edna in sight as they hurried out between Harvey and Carol Sue. I could hear Hambone behind us, telling us not to run, not to be cowards. No one listened. We had nothing with which to protect ourselves from bullets and chains.

"This land belongs to the county," Hambone shouted. "We have just as much right to . . ."

A shotgun blast silenced him. The stillness was so abrupt that I thought he had been shot. I glanced back and saw that Hambone was not injured. He was backing slowly toward the gate, flanked by Wallace and Maxwell. There was nothing to prevent the men from killing us. We meant nothing to them. They did not shoot us, but they marched forward with intimidating force.

Cars and trucks began to pull out of the parking lot just as Jeff and I stepped from sawdust to gravel. The men followed us to the gate and stood watching as we scattered for safety. Another gunshot rang out, and I stumbled across the gravel, trembling and feeling weak in my knees. Jeff held me steady and led me between moving vehicles until we reached his car.

I stopped beside the car and yelled for Wallace, knowing he could not hear me over the din of engines and the cries of terror. Tarabelle and Mattie rushed toward us, and Mattie practically dived onto the back seat of the car.

"Let's go, Tangy!" Jeff urged, but I could not move. Up by the main gate, Wallace and a group of young men had armed themselves with gravel and were slinging it at the grounds crew.

"Jeff, look!" I screamed. "They're going to kill Wallace. They're going to kill my brother."

"Shit!" Tarabelle said, as she raced back across the lot toward the gate. It seemed she would be struck by one of the vehicles racing from the grounds, but she made it across intact. Another shot sounded, and the gravel throwing ceased momentarily. Then someone bellowed with rage, a high-pitched battle cry, and the gravel slinging resumed.

Jeff shoved me into the car, then rushed around to the other side and climbed in. Tarabelle had reached Wallace, and I waited for her to grab him and drag him away from the mob. Instead, she stooped and came up with a fistful of gravel. The workers fired again, two shots this time, then raising bats and chains, they began to advance.

"Oh, God! Oh, God!" I sobbed. "They're going to kill somebody."

Jeff stared out at the confusion, then touched my arm. "If they were aiming to kill, somebody would be dead by now," he said. "They just wanna scare us."

The words were barely out of his mouth when one of the men fired his pistol into the crowd, and a body slumped to the ground. Jeff fumbled with the key as he tried to start the car, and I braced myself against the dashboard and tried to suck in enough air to keep from fainting.

Tarabelle and Wallace sprinted toward the car. Jeff had to pry my hands from the dash to let them in. He managed to get the car in gear, and we moved haltingly along, braking for people who were still darting across the lot.

"Anybody get hit?" Jeff asked as he guided the car onto the road.

"Bubba Nash," Wallace answered breathlessly. "Hambone's got him. He ain't dead."

We turned left on Atler Avenue, joining the convoy that was slowly moving west. No one in the car made a sound, other than that necessary to breathe. It was almost too quiet. I stared out the window waiting for the explosion that would kill us all. Jeff dropped Mattie off first, then he drove us to Penyon Road, all the way to our house. As we cleared the bend, I could see Mr. Dobson's car. On the front seat were Harvey and Carol Sue, and on the back were Edith, Laura, and Edna. If Martha Jean and Velman had made it out, then we were all safe. I allowed myself a sigh, and lingered with Jeff while the others went inside.

"Some kind of night, wasn't it?" Jeff asked.

"Yeah. I don't know how it happened. One minute everybody was having fun, and then—"

"—all hell broke loose," Jeff said.

"I want to blame Hambone," I said, "but I know it's not his fault."

"No, it isn't," Jeff agreed. "People are going to say that, but it's not his fault at all. All he did was tell the truth. Maybe he didn't choose the right time and place, but he was telling the truth."

"I know," I said. "Why does it have to be like this?"

"It's always been like this, Tangy. We've just been conditioned to accept it. Now here comes Hambone, wanting to change things and not really knowing how. He's too young, and the older people in this county are not going to back him. His timing is wrong."

"I don't want to talk about it," I said. "I don't even want to think about it. I just want to get away from here. I'd never come back. Are you coming back, Jeff?"

"I'll be back," he said. "In December. I'll come back and find that nothing has changed. Nothing at all."

thirty-five

She was barefoot in a sundress, and her hair hung limp across her shoulders. A cigarette burned between her lips, and her eyes were closed as she swayed to music coming from the radio. She reminded me of my mother.

"Good morning, Miss Veatrice," I said, stepping into the front room.

She opened one eye, and continued to sway. "Hey," she said pleasantly. "I didn't know if you were coming today. That's the Everly Brothers on the radio." She sang along for a second or two, then said, "There's a lot to do today. Bakker's got them boys coming to paint the house. I always wanted to live in a pretty white house. They're gonna patch it up, and Bakker says it's gonna look good as new."

"Yes, ma'am," I said, although I doubted much could be done with the house. "What time are they coming?"

"Should be here soon. I was gonna be a bad girl once, just like Susie in that song. Did you know that? Bakker said it was unbecoming and that he'd disinherit me." She laughed. "He didn't have nothing to disinherit me from, but I didn't want to upset him. I could've been bad if I wanted to."

She followed me toward the kitchen and bumped into me when I stopped abruptly at the doorway. I understood the cluttered table and overflowing sink, but there were paint chips on the floor, broken glass in a chair, and a gooey substance stuck to the top of the stove.

"What happened here?" I asked.

"Oh, honey, we've been doing some work. Didn't I tell you? We're gonna have this old house looking like new."

"What kind of work did you do?"

"Well, let's see," she said, stepping around me. "First off, we scraped these chairs down. We're gonna paint them blue."

"You know, Miss Veatrice, this house would look a lot better if you and your brother picked up behind yourselves."

Her hazel eyes widened with astonishment, and she touched her cheek as if I had slapped her. "That's what we hired you for," she said. "Why are we paying a nigger if we're suppose to clean it ourselves? That don't make sense, honey."

I turned the water on at the sink as her word echoed in my head. I was angry. "Miss Veatrice, do you know there's a difference between calling a person a nigger and a Negro?" I asked.

"Sure, I do," she answered, and explained with such simplicity that my anger dissolved and was replaced by pity. "Bakker says all the Negroes moved north. He says the niggers stayed in the south 'cause they don't have no sense of direction. Oh, look!" She went to the window. "They've come to start on the house."

I peered out the window and saw, of all people, Hambone, wearing overalls and brogans. With him were Maxwell, Russell Tucker, and Mister Leddy. Miss Veatrice started for the back door, and I followed her, my hands dripping water across the floor.

"Miss Veatrice," I said, "don't you go out there calling those men niggers."

"And why not? That's what they are."

"No, ma'am. I know those men and they're Negroes. Try to remember that."

She tilted her head to one side, closed one eye, and stared at me from the other. "I'll call them whatever I want," she whispered, then opened the door and stepped outside. I followed.

"Which one of you is Tucker?" she asked.

Russell Tucker was squatting beside a row of paint cans. He stood when Miss Veatrice entered the yard. "I am," he said. Tucker was in his early forties, and was the type of man who could go from crib to grave unnoticed if he chose. He was of medium height and build with a medium-brown complexion and a soft-spoken voice.

"Bakker says I'm to do business with you," Miss Veatrice said. "Nobody but you. Everything is here for you to work with, and Bakker says you're not to come in the house for any reason. Is that clear?"

"Yes, ma'am," Tucker answered. "I figure we'll start 'round there in the front, on the roof, if that awright wit' you, ma'am."

"Oh, I don't care where you start," Miss Veatrice said, spreading her arms and waggling her fingers. "Just make me a pretty white house. That's all I want. Of course, I work on my flowers in the front, but I guess if I stay out of your way, you'll stay out of mine." She giggled.

Hambone and I exchanged glances. I think he had figured out that Miss Veatrice was a touch simpleminded, but I didn't know how he would respond if she called him a nigger. Maxwell had figured it out, too. He watched her from the top of his eyes, his chin resting against his chest.

"Awright, let's get some of the stuff 'round to the front," Tucker instructed. "Let's get busy."

Back in the kitchen, I listened to the noise of hammering and was comforted by the sound. At noon, when the men took a rest, I went out to the yard and sat on the grass next to Hambone. He had separated himself from the others, as if he'd known I would come. He was stretched out, resting on his elbows, and staring at the house.

"We've got our work cut out for us," he said. "I wonder how this house ever got over here in North Ridge."

"Hambone, I wanna warn you about Miss Veatrice," I said. "She's a little mixed up about some things."

"I already gathered that."

"Yeah, but she might slip up and call you a nigger, and I don't want you to lose your temper and do something stupid."

Hambone sat up and propped his elbows on his knees. He stared at me, shook his head, then grunted. "Let me get this straight," he said. "We've got a twelve-year-old boy shot in the leg, Becky James limping from being struck with a bat, and another boy with a busted arm, and you're worried about whether somebody is gonna hurt some old crazy-ass white woman?"

"It's not like that, Hambone. I'm not worried about her. I'm worried about you."

"Why are you spending your time worrying about me?"

"It's the way you hate," I answered. "It's not right. I believe you'd hurt Miss Veatrice, and they'd come after you. They'd find you, Hambone, and lynch you. You know they would."

"You're too young to be so serious," he said, leaning back on the grass. "You know why I'm out here with Tucker today? It's because I'm getting ready to do everybody a favor. I'm leaving Pakersfield. I'm not washing anymore windows or dishes. I'm not hoeing any more fields or sawing down any more trees. I'm moving on."

"Just like that?"

"Just like that. I figure if old man Leddy can stay sober, we'll finish this job in about three or four days. I'm gonna take my money and split."

I was sitting with my legs tucked beneath me and could feel numbness setting in. I stretched, and Hambone watched. His gaze traveled the length of my legs.

"What are you staring at?" I snapped, remembering my encounter with him in my mother's kitchen.

"You need some shoes," he said. "How long have you worked for these people and can't buy a pair of shoes?"

Apparently Sam had not told him about our mother's arrangements with our pay. I didn't tell him, either. I stared down at my lap and said, "Hambone, I wanna ask you something. When you started preaching at the fair, what did you expect those white men to do? Did you think they were just going to stand around and listen with the rest of us?"

For the longest time, Hambone said nothing. He glanced over at the other men, then back at me. "I don't know," he said at last. "I just know I'm sick and tired of it. I wanna show them that we don't have to take it."

"They could have killed us," I said, "but they didn't."

"No, they didn't. They hurt us, though. You're just a little girl, Tangy. You don't understand that people don't have the right to treat you any old way they want."

"What about you?" I asked, although I hadn't intended to. "Do you have the right to treat me any way you want?"

"What are you talking about?"

"You know what I'm talking about, Hambone. I talking about what you tried to do to me in my mother's kitchen."

"Oh, that," he said. "You shouldn't flirt with people if you don't wanna be bothered. If you remember, you led me to that kitchen. I didn't realize until later that I'd scared you halfway out of your mind."

"Were you blind and stupid?" I snapped.

"If I was, that damn Tarabelle knocked some sight and sense back in me real quick, didn't she? And I haven't bothered you since."

"Because of Tarabelle?"

"Because you weren't ready."

Across the yard, Tucker stood and prepared to get back to work. Down on the front porch, Miss Veatrice packed dirt into a clay pot with her knuckles and never once glanced up.

"What's that she's doing?" Hambone asked, as he helped me to my feet.

"She says she's planting flowers. She does that every time I come, but she never has seeds or anything. I think she's just killing time. What do you think of her brother?"

"I've never met him. He hired Tucker, who asked me if I wanted work."

As we walked toward the house, Hambone asked, "Did I tell you that Reverend Nelson was at my door the other morning before the roosters crowed? Everybody is blaming me for what happened at the fair. I guess in a way it was my fault. I know I feel responsible for Bubba, but he's gonna be all right. I still think people need to wake up."

I slowed my pace, lagging a few steps behind him, then I stopped. He glanced back, as I knew he would. "Were you with Sam when he beat up that Griggs boy?" I asked.

"Did anybody mention my name?"

He went back to work, and I returned to the kitchen and put

supper on the stove. The house was clean now, except the little room next to Miss Veatrice's. Dirty clothes were piled in a corner, and I left them there. I had started out by leaving the wash until Saturdays so I would not have to roam through the rooms in Bakker Whitman's presence, but I had learned that he was not the evil man his sister had made him out to be. He was quiet, studious, patient with his sister, and polite to me.

At two-thirty I left the Whitmans' house. Tucker and his crew were still at work, and I waved to them. Hambone climbed down from his ladder and offered to give me a ride home, which I accepted. On the ride through town he talked about nothing except Becky James.

"If she wasn't stuck on Red Adams, I'm telling you, I'd be talking to her," he said. "That's the kind of woman I need. She's got that something you don't find in most women. She'll stand with you. You know what I mean? She's strong enough to stand there beside you and fight until she falls. That's what she did the other night."

"Well, she's marrying Red Adams, and she's too old for you, anyway," I said.

"Are you kidding? What's a couple of years? Nothing. What am I suppose to do—wait around until you grow up and decide what you wanna do?"

"What you need to do is grow up and decide what *you* wanna do," I answered. "And you don't know how strong Becky is. Sometimes hatred resembles strength."

"You're jealous."

"Okay," I pleasantly agreed, "but if I have to get hit with a bat and knocked down in order to be strong, I'd rather stay a weak little girl."

He was quiet as he turned onto Penyon Road and stopped beside my mother's car, then he laughed. "Get your smart little ass out of my car," he teased. "You're gonna be something else when you do grow up."

"So are you," I said.

I backed away from the car, thinking that Hambone was not as bad as I had thought. I watched him as he shook his head. Then he turned the car around, honked the horn twice, and drove off.

thirty-six

In November, Harvey returned to our mother's house with a change of clothes and not one word of explanation. To my knowledge, Mama never asked him to explain. Harvey had been with us for about three days before Mama even knew he was there. She had been isolated in her room. We had heard her in there screaming Sam's name, or crying, or mumbling to herself, and we had tried not to disturb her. She would do that sometimes—hide away in her room—but she never allowed more than a few days to pass before she would come out with a new plan of how she could get Sam out of jail.

I knew she had spoken to Mr. Frank about helping Sam. I had heard her. Mr. Frank had shaken his head and refused her. "Sam's past the point of bailing out, Rozelle," he'd said, "and I don't know that I would waste my money like that. Given the chance, Sam is likely to run, and anyway, he went down there and just outright admitted he was guilty of attacking that white boy. I can't help nobody don't wanna be helped."

Mama stayed angry with both of the Garrisons for almost a week, but the more she talked to people, the more she heard the same things Mr. Frank had said. Sam, people told her, had been to court and was serving easy time, given the circumstances. He looked good, he was well fed, and no one had laid a hand on him. Mama insisted they were lying. I didn't know what to believe.

Wallace had taken over Hambone's old job of washing windows for the town merchants. Tarabelle dutifully went to the Munfords' and slipped things from their house when she could, in an effort to satisfy our mother. Harvey had stopped going to the funeral home to work, but he went to the train depot almost every day, and most of the time he was hired out.

My most pleasant days, oddly enough, were spent at the Whitmans'. Their house had undergone a remarkable restoration. It was now an unpeeling, spotless white with intact dark green shutters, and I felt more at ease there, to speak and roam about the rooms, than in my mother's house.

In my mother's house, we waited. We waited on her and for her. We waited for change, and nothing ever changed, except our mother's moods. We were sitting and waiting one evening when Mama drove home with Miss Pearl in the car.

"Humph," Tarabelle grunted, as she watched Mama park the car. "She ain't never picked me up from work and drove me nowhere."

"I know," Harvey agreed. "She be sending me all over town and won't even let me drive that car."

"She wouldn't be sending you nowhere if you'd go on home to yo' wife where you oughta be," Tarabelle replied.

"Who you to be saying where somebody oughta be?" Harvey asked angrily.

"I'm me," Tarabelle answered calmly, turning from the window, "and I'm gon' fix Mama. Watch me." She stepped away from the window and sat on the arm of Harvey's chair, then crossed her arms over her chest, and waited.

Wallace and I exchanged glances. We could hear Mama and Miss Pearl laughing as they climbed the stairs. Mama entered the room first, holding a bulky white package in her arms.

"Look what Pearl got for us," she said. "We gon' have a happy Thanksgiving this year. This a turkey from the Skyles Farm. Pearl said it was the biggest one out there."

"Sho' was," Miss Pearl agreed, stepping in behind Mama. "Tangy

Mae, you bring it on up to the house tomorrow and cook it in my stove."

"Here, boy," Mama said, giving the turkey to Wallace. "Put this thing in the ice box 'til tomorrow."

It was two days before Thanksgiving, and once again the fifth grade had chosen the Quinns as their needy family. Tomorrow our principal would deliver twelve boxes to twelve needy families, and we would be presented with the fifth grade's decorated box of canned goods. It thrilled our mother almost as much as it embarrassed us. Mama, who was not one for other holidays, looked forward to Thanksgiving. For me, it was the worst holiday of the year.

Harvey stood and gave his chair to Mama, and Tarabelle eased from the arm and went to stand against the wall near the kitchen, which is probably why Mama sent her to boil water for coffee. I gave my chair to Miss Pearl.

"I don't want no coffee," Miss Pearl said. "Bring me a drink of water. Coffee keep me up half the night."

"You know, Pearl, I was thinking we oughta go up to Stillwaters. You done rode wit' me, now," Mama said. "You know I'm a good driver."

"You kept it on the road, Rosie," Miss Pearl teased. "That don't make you no good driver. I gotta go to work tomorrow, though. I can't be running up to that café."

Tarabelle came from the kitchen and gave Miss Pearl the water she had requested, then she reclaimed her spot against the wall. Mama stared at Tarabelle, as if she knew Tarabelle was up to something.

"Pearl, you lucky you ain't got no children," Mama said. "You can't get away from 'em. Look how they all standing 'round here staring in our mouths."

Miss Pearl laughed. "What you want 'em to do?" she asked. "They ain't got nowhere to go but to bed, and it's too early for that."

"That's what I'm trying to tell you, Pearl. We oughta go up to Stillwaters and see what's happening."

"Rosie, I done worked all day. My feet hurt, and I'm going home."

In the silence that followed, Tarabelle made her move. "Mama," she said, "Miss Arlisa in the hospital. She done went and had herself a big, fat baby boy. When you gon' have yours? Seems like I remember you saying you was expecting, back when Miss Arlisa said it."

There was no mistaking the malice in Tarabelle's statement. She had said she was going to fix Mama, and she had, but she wasn't done.

"Mr. Munford—he just as happy as can be—done went out and bought everything in Pakersfield. He say his boy gon' be handsome and strong. And, Mama, he treating Miss Arlisa just like a queen. He done bought her flowers, and candy, and the prettiest pink robe you ever wanna see. He want me to stay overnight when she come home—just for a week or two. Say he don't want her to have to do nothing."

Mama's lower lip protruded. She reached a hand up and pulled a bug from her face. She brought her feet together and shifted her weight on the chair, then she looked at me. "Get me some bathwater," she said.

"Now, Rosie, I know you ain't fixin' to take no bath 'fo' you take me home," Miss Pearl said. She claimed to have known our mother longer and better than anyone but any of us could have told her that Mama wasn't going anywhere. Tarabelle had fixed her.

Wallace went for the tub while I went for water. We returned to witness our mother snatching bugs so hard and fast that she was abrading the skin on her face and arms.

"Rosie!" Miss Pearl shrieked. "What's the matter wit' you?"

Tarabelle leaned against the wall and watched, and I could not tell if she was satisfied or sorry for the distress she had caused. Mama rushed toward her room, snatching and slinging bugs as she went.

"What's going on?" Miss Pearl wanted to know.

"Bugs, Miss Pearl," I answered. "Sometimes Mama acts like bugs are crawling on her."

"They ain't bugs," Tarabelle said dryly, and I could have sworn her nose tilted about a tenth of an inch. "They ain't bugs. They men. Them is men crawling all over Mama. And she can't pull 'em off, and she can't wash 'em off. There's too many of 'em, and they been crawling on her for too many years. She ain't never gon' get 'em off."

"Tarabelle, why don't you shut up?" Harvey snapped.

"I ain't gon' shut up and you can't make me. If you don't wanna hear me talk, you oughta go home to yo' wife."

"Yeah, that's what I'm gon' do," Harvey said, pulling himself up from the floor.

"That's what you better do," Tarabelle sang out. "You go on where you can beat somebody, they don't shut up when you tell 'em to. 'Cause I ain't Carol Sue, and I ain't gon' shut up. Her daddy gon' kill you, you keep beating her like that, Harvey."

Harvey strode across the room, stood over Tarabelle with balled fists, and glared at her with burning rage.

"Hit me!" she demanded. "Hit me, Harvey! 'Cause I wanna know what it feels like to kill somebody." When he did not strike her, she said, "You ain't shit."

"Tarabelle, you shut up out there!" Mama called from her room. "And bring me some bathwater."

Tarabelle stepped away from Harvey, and his angry gaze followed her movements. "You already got bathwater, Mama," she said.

"It's cold . . . and dirty. Bring me some more."

"Rosie, you awright in there?" Miss Pearl asked. "I can't keep sitting out here wit' yo' chilluns acting crazy. How 'bout you let Harvey drive me on home."

"Harvey ain't driving my car," Mama answered.

"Damnedest place," Miss Pearl mumbled. "Damnedest people. I knew I shoulda took my ass home, and after I done got y'all a turkey." She gripped her pocketbook, and struggled to her feet. "Wallace, you come on and walk wit' me. In case I can't make it, you can run and get Frank."

Wallace obeyed without hesitation, placing a hand at Miss Pearl's elbow, and helping her along as though she was an invalid. Harvey slumped down on the chair Miss Pearl had vacated and stared at the coal stove. His body trembled, and he used one hand to steady the other. Finally, he brought both hands together, placed them over his face, and choked out his frustrations. It started like a sneeze, then grew to ragged broken rales, like pneumonia.

"Don't cry, Harvey," Laura soothed, coming to stand beside him, causing him to cry even harder.

Tarabelle watched, then backed toward the kitchen. At the door, she stopped. "You can't go back, can you, Harvey?" she asked. "Mattie said they had done put you out for beating on that girl. How you gon' be hitting on her in her daddy's house? That was stupid."

I felt neither sympathy nor contempt for my brother. He was just there, in the way, and out of control. I left him sobbing, and went to my mother's room to empty her tub. She was sitting naked on the floor at the foot of her bed, a towel draped across her lap, pulling bugs from her arms and tossing them into the air.

In a voice I had to strain to hear, she said, "Tangy Mae, you tell yo' sister, a man got a right to keep his woman in line."

thirty-seven

Velman stood beside a car that so closely resembled Mama's it could have been hers. It was parked in the church lot on the Sunday evening following the Christmas Program. Velman and Martha Jean did not usually attend the Solid Rock Baptist Church, but they had come for the purpose of watching me sing and the girls recite their Christmas speeches.

"Y'all want a ride home?" Velman asked.

I circled the car, searching for evidence that it did not belong to my mother.

Velman winked at me. "You gon' ride or what?"

I nodded.

"This one ain't mine," he said. "I picked it out, though. This one is Skeeter's. He's not much on driving and I think he bought it for me, but he won't give it to me. Might as well, though. I'm the only one who drives it, except Martha Jean goin' up and down the street." He laughed. "I think Skeeter is scared that if he gives it to me, I'm gon' trade it off for something. He's crazy about Martha Jean, but he says I went about getting her all wrong. I don't even try to explain it to him no more, you know. I did what I had to do, and I'd do it all over again if I had to."

I climbed into the back of the car between Laura and Edna who both wanted a window seat. Martha Jean turned and passed an envelope back to me. I tore it open and began to read a letter from Mushy, saying she was getting married and would be home for New Year's Day. I read the letter four times as the car moved along toward home, then I tucked it under the back seat.

When Velman stopped below our house, I begged him to come inside. "I never get to see Martha Jean anymore," I said. "We can sit in the kitchen and talk."

Reluctantly, he agreed. We went inside to find Mama and Harvey sitting quietly in the front room. Mama warmly greeted Martha Jean and Velman, and told me to get a chair from the kitchen.

"Wouldn't want these springs to rip that suit," she said to Velman. "How's Skeeter doing these days?"

"He's doing all right," Velman answered. "He bought a car. Looks a lot like yours, Miss Rosie."

"Is that right? I always liked ol' Skeeter."

Velman sat down, and Martha Jean removed her coat, hung it on a nail, and went to stand behind him. She looked lovely in a gray-and-white wool dress with white beads hanging from her neck. She seemed uncomfortable, though.

"How you doing, Harvey?" Velman asked, after a lengthy silence.

"I'm doing awright," Harvey lied, and Velman nodded.

I sent Laura and Edna out to the kitchen to change out of their Sunday dresses, then I crossed the room and sat on the arm of Harvey's chair. "Mama, Mushy's coming home for the new year," I said, and signed the same to Martha Jean. "She's going to marry that boy, Curtis, that she was talking about the last time she was home. He's coming with her."

My mother ignored me and said to Velman, "How you come to be kin to Skeeter? On yo' mama's or daddy's side?"

"My mother is his sister," Velman answered.

Mama nodded. "You don't look nothing like Skeeter. I ain't saying that's good or bad, I'm just saying you don't look nothing like him."

Considering the diversity of *her* offspring, I thought that statement was ironic. Velman must have thought so, too. He smiled and
covered it by glancing over his shoulder at Martha Jean.

"I guess yo' mama came from around here then," Mama said. "I
don't think I know her. I never knew Skeeter had no sister. People
move in and out all the time. That's what's wrong wit' the world.
People can't stay still long enough in one place. Me and Pearl been
friends for years. We know each other real good, but you don't find
that no mo'. Now you take Sam, for instance. He was friends wit'
Hambone when they was little boys, then Hambone up and left,
then he come back, and look what it got Sam."

"People don't stay still too long. You right about that, Miss
Rosie," Velman agreed.

"Sho' I am," Mama said. "It gets to the place you can't trust
nobody. One minute you think you know 'em, and the next, you
just have to wonder. Let me show you something."

She went to her room, and returned with an old brown belt
with a heavy brass buckle—her favorite—which she held up for
Velman to inspect. "Look here," she said. "I got this off a man friend
of mine some twelve years ago. It's something when a piece of
leather outlast a friendship, but that's just what this did." She held
the belt higher. "I can trust this when I can't trust nothing else."

Something in her tone jarred me and awakened my hibernating
foresight. Slowly, I rose from the arm of the chair. I saw Harvey open
and close his mouth, and Velman leap to his feet, and Mama dance
across the floor at a side angle, between the chairs and the stove.

The belt snapped, then struck and seemed to wrap around my
head like a tourniquet. A bright orange, the color of pain, seared
my eyeballs. Pain occluded my nostrils and I sucked air in
through my mouth, noisy and panicky. The agony was almost
unbearable. My hands went up to search my skull for an opening,
for a way to let the torment out. "Oh, God! Oh, God! Oh, God!"
I cried, and each time I called His name, my mother struck my
head again until I hushed and bowed to the power at hand.

I could not see her, but I heard her voice close to me, asking,
"How you know what Mushy gon' do? There ain't no letter came
from Mushy, or I woulda been the first to know about it. You
answer me, Tangy Mae!"

"I gave it to her," Velman said. "It had her name on it, and I gave it to her."

"And just who gave you permission to meddle in my business?" Mama asked.

"How many names yo' business got, Miss Rosie?" Velman asked. His voice was loud and angry, and very close to my ears.

I wished they would be quiet long enough for me to still the torment in my head and get my eyesight back. I heard the belt snap again, and I braced myself for another blow.

"Damn!" Velman cried, as the leather connected with his flesh. "Harvey, man, you better see if you can't unglue yo'self from that chair and do something with yo' mama."

"That's enough, Mama," came Harvey's, dull, apathetic voice.

A hand touched me, and I jerked away from it. "You all right, little sister?" Velman asked.

I could not speak or even shake my head in response. He lowered me to the floor, then I felt hands that I knew belonged to Martha Jean place a blanket beneath my head.

"When she having that baby, boy?" my mother asked.

No one answered her.

"I'm talking to you, boy. I said when she having that baby?"

"Who?" Velman shouted.

Mama laughed. "Shit. You just as dumb as she is. You ain't even got sense enough to know you done made a baby. Baby'll probably be dumb, too, but that ain't my worry."

No one spoke after that. There were only the sounds of shoes clicking and thumping against the floorboards, and the opening and closing of the front door.

I must have lain on the floor for hours, dozing in and out of sleep. The pain in my head had eased to a dull throb. I could hear the voices of Laura and Edna in the kitchen, but I did not hear my mother's voice. I tried to sit up and felt a wave of nausea rolling toward my throat. I eased my head back down to the blanket and covered my eyes with my hands. I was afraid to open my eyes, but I had to know if I was blind.

My eyes opened, and I sat up. Sharp pain ricocheted through my head. My stomach flipped and spewed its contents out onto the rolled blanket. On hands and knees, I tried to stand, but found that

I could not. Managing to push the soiled blanket out of the way, I gave in to my dizziness and fell back to the floor.

"Tan! Tan!"

I opened my eyes to see Wallace squatting beside me, and I remembered he hadn't been there earlier. It was dark outside and the kerosene lamp illuminated the room. I was wringing wet with sweat and still wearing my Sunday dress.

"Tan, they done made a mess in there," Wallace said.

"Who?" I groaned. My mouth was dry and I wanted a drink of water. "Who made a mess?"

"Laura and Edna. What's wrong wit' you, Tan?"

"I'm sick, Wallace. Bring me some water."

"Tan! Tan!"

I opened my eyes again to see Wallace squatting beside me again. I was wringing wet with sweat and shivering from the cold. I was still wearing my Sunday dress, but someone had rolled me onto a blanket and covered me.

"You feeling any better, Tan?" Wallace asked.

"I don't know, Wallace. What time is it?"

"It's time for me to go to work, and Mama wants her coffee. Can you get up?"

"It's morning?"

Wallace didn't answer. He helped me to sit up, and I did so without pain or nausea. Laura and Edna stood beside the stove watching me, and I tried to smile at them. I unwrapped the blanket from my legs and rose to my feet.

"I gotta go, Tan," Wallace said. "I put water on the stove for Mama's coffee. You gon' be awright?"

I nodded, and it didn't hurt, but when I took my first step, dizziness stopped me and sat me down again. I leaned forward, holding my head in my hands. The pain returned and jumped about, playing checkers behind my eyeballs.

My mother called for her coffee, and I could not get it for her.

Wallace said, "I'll get the doggone coffee, but when I leave outta here today, I ain't coming back. I'm tired of this."

I told Laura to get me a cold cloth for my head, and I allowed the cool dampness to soak my eyelids, then I tried once more to stand, and the world went dark.

Once, when I was very young, I had a high fever and a chest that was tight with congestion. My mother had lifted me from the floor and carried me to her bed. For the duration of my infirmity, her delicate hands had dampened my fevered brow with a cool cloth, stroked my lips with ice chips, and wet my palate with the delicious juice of a peppermint-flavored orange. She had curled on her bed beside me, attentive to my every stir and groan. She had warmed me in the mingled scents of camphor and talcum powder, then holding my small hand in hers, she had said, "You gon' be awright, baby. Mama's here."

That was the mother that faded in and out of my memory as I reeled in and out of consciousness. The more I tried to hold onto her, the more my head throbbed. Finally, I had to let her go.

thirty-eight

By the time the new year rolled around, Harvey was out of Mama's house and back with the Dobsons, Tarabelle had completed her overnight stint at the Munfords, and Wallace was out in the world somewhere. We had heard nothing more from Mushy, and Sam was still in jail. The weather was colder, the kerosene lamps burned longer, newspapers covered our windows, and soot covered everything else.

Depressed by Sam's many months behind bars, Mama had taken to her bed once more, where she alternated between sleeping and weeping. Things had gotten to the point where she would not eat or bathe. She would get up only to use the slop bucket, then return to her bed. Miss Pearl came over one night and tried her best to stimulate Mama into activity, even offered to accompany her to Stillwaters, but it did no good.

"They coulda done sent Sam away by now," she said to Mama. "There's a hundred things they coulda done, but they ain't. Rosie, you gotta stop worrying yo'self like this. They gon' let him out sooner or later."

Mama said two words to her. "Get out!" They were the first two words we had heard in just as many days.

She told us very little about Sam's legal problems, and I wasn't sure she understood all of it herself. I think in the beginning she had assumed she could use her charm to get him out, but that assumption had proved false. Nothing she did seemed to make a difference.

Sometimes some of Mama's male friends would drive out to the house and blow their horns for her to come out. She would send Tarabelle with them, or tell one of us to make them go away.

It was Hambone who finally got Mama out of bed. What he had to say was so important that he would not be put off. Despite our protests, he went into Mama's room, stood over her bed, and said, "Miss Rosie, I think you better go down to that jail. Becky went to take Sam some cookies Miss Shirley baked for him. She says Sam's been beaten, and somebody laid his head open. Dr. Mathis had sewed his head up before she got there, but she says it looks bad."

"Have you seen him?" Mama asked.

"No, ma'am. If I walk in that jail, they might not let me walk back out."

Mama got out of bed and went straight to the front room wall for her coat. She was still wearing her gown. "Take me over there to see 'bout him," she said to Hambone.

"Miss Rosie, you want me to step outside while you wash up or something?"

Mama twisted her lips and shook her head. "I just want you to take me over there."

Hambone took her, but he was back at our house a few hours later without her. "She's been arrested," he told us. "Sam's not at the jail, and he wasn't at the hospital, either. Nobody will tell Miss Rosie where he is. She went berserk over at the hospital. She was screaming and running in and out of all the rooms. The people at the hospital held her down until the police got there."

I stared at him. "And you did nothing to help her?" I asked.

"What could I do?" he asked resignedly.

"Nothing," I answered sarcastically. "That's why nobody in

Pakersfield listens to you. You can't do anything, except run around getting other people in trouble. You get people in trouble, then you run and hide. Get out, Hambone! Get out of our house!"

Hambone left, and it was the next day before the sheriff brought our mother home. She came into the front room, sat on an armchair, and began to snatch bugs from her body.

The sheriff stood over her and stared down at her. "He's not dead, Rozelle."

I could tell from the tone of his voice that he had been trying to convince her of that on the entire ride home. Finally, he gave up talking to her and turned to me.

"When she decides to listen, tell her that I moved the boy to a jail in Caloona County. He'll be all right there, and it'll give me a chance to find out what the hell happened. Tell her that I've always tried to be fair, and I'll get her boy back to her as soon as I can."

"Will he be dead or alive?" Mama mumbled.

The sheriff did not answer. He looked at her, ran a hand through his hair, then started for the door. I followed behind him on my way out to get the tub, because it was past time for my mother to bathe.

"Sheriff," I said, when we were near the bottom of the steps, "do you still believe that Sam killed Junior?"

"I believe that somebody has been making a fool out of me, and I don't like it," he said. He was facing west, toward the country, staring out as though he could see Krandike Pond through the trees. He couldn't see it from our steps, but I had seen Sam stare in much the same way, like he was trying to see exactly what had happened at the pond on the night Junior was murdered.

"The boy is angry, tough, and stubborn, but I don't know if that makes him a killer. I can't come up with a motive, and yet he's the only suspect I have," the sheriff said, more to himself than to me. When he was halfway across the yard, he turned back and said, "Tell Rozelle that I've always tried to be fair."

I prepared a bath for my mother, but I didn't tell her what the sheriff had said. She wouldn't have listened anyway. She bathed, ate bologna and drank a glass of water, then returned to her bed and slept the day and the night away.

I was glad when the holidays were over and we were back in

school where I felt secure in my surroundings, where Mr. Pace challenged me, gave me hope, and made me dream, but I also wanted to tell him not to expect too much or he might be disappointed.

One day, after the last bell, he stood outside his classroom and beckoned to me as I crossed the lobby. He told me to take a seat, then he sat across from me at his desk. There he studied pamphlets and papers while I studied him. He was a tall, dark, serious man who seldom smiled, but when he did, it was a wide, open smile. His forehead had a slight protrusion that forced his dark brown eyes deep into his face. They were eyes that could silence a classroom with their piercing effect, and cause a disobedient student to break down and weep with shame. They had only shown me kindness and concern.

He pushed the papers aside and glanced up. He seemed uneasy, which was unlike him, and I braced myself for bad news. I was sure he had been delegated to inform me that I was being suspended from Plymouth School for excessive absenteeism.

"I've been looking over college material, trying to decide what to give you," he said. "I think I'll give it all to you and let you make the decision as to where you'd like to go."

I sighed audibly as relief washed over me. Then I considered his statement. It should have been clear to him that I would not be attending college. It was doubtful that I would even finish high school, so why was he enticing me with such unobtainable prospects? I watched as he stacked the papers together, then pushed them to the edge of the desk, within my reach.

"I appreciate this, Mr. Pace, but . . ." I started.

"You will go," he said with conviction. "You'll go on a scholarship because you're earning it. As far as I'm concerned, you've already earned it. I'm aware of the sacrifices you make to come to school, and still you outshine every student here. I've seen your sisters and brothers drop out long before they've even reached my class, but you're determined, whether you know it or not. Tell me, Tangy, where do you see yourself five years from now?"

I closed my eyes, and although Mr. Pace had said five years, I saw myself at my mother's age, working for Miss Veatrice, stumbling over clay pots packed with mud, and living in desolation on Penyon Road. I shuddered.

"What do you see?" he asked.

"I can't see that far, Mr. Pace," I lied.

"I think you can, and you don't like what you see. Go to college, Tangy."

"But what if I don't get a scholarship?"

He laughed as if genuinely amused. "Then I guess we would have to move mountains," he said. "Do you think we're strong enough?"

I looked deep into his eyes, then nodded and reached for the papers on his desk.

"There's one more thing we need to discuss," he said. "And in this, you have an option. When school begins in the fall, a select group of students from Plymouth will integrate Pakersfield High. You, of course, were the first chosen. Mr. Hewitt and I, along with the principal and staff of Pakersfield High, have been in talks with the superintendent of schools. We'd like to make this as smooth a transition as possible. Now, it's not mandatory that you attend. I think you need to give it a great deal of thought. If you attend Pakersfield High, the color of your skin will probably prevent you from being valedictorian, regardless of how deserving you are. You will be harassed, maybe even subjected to physical abuses, but that school will challenge you, Tangy, and you need the challenge. Also, it will increase your chances for winning a full scholarship."

I stirred uneasily, staring down. "My mother will never allow it," I said.

"Nothing is certain, yet," Mr. Pace said. "When and if it happens, we will tell your mother. In fact, I'd rather you not mention it to anyone until we're sure."

I left school that day in a state of anxiety. It was hard to imagine myself inside a building that had never allowed Negroes. In more ways than one I knew I would never fit in, and yet I wanted to go. It would not matter what the white students did or said to me, I would endure. If there was one thing certain about my mother's children, it was our resilience.

thirty-nine

One Wednesday afternoon, I arrived home from work to find my mother curled on her bed and Wallace standing in the kitchen frying bologna for Edna. I was so happy to see my brother that I hugged him as tight as I could. I hugged Wallace until I embarrassed him, and he had to warn me that his bologna was going to burn before I would turn him loose.

"Where have you been?" I asked. "I've been through town every day looking for you."

"I know," he said with a grin. "I seen you, but I hid. I didn't want you trying to talk me into coming back home, but you oughta been able to guess where I was."

The three of us sat at the table and snacked. Wallace informed me that Mama had been to see Sam again. I supposed her depression would hold her in bed for another week.

Laura came in from school and joined us at the table. She was quiet, as usual, and did not seem surprised to see Wallace. For about a minute or two, she nibbled on bologna, then dropped it to the table and looked over at me.

"I forgot," she said. "Tara's outside. She say she can't make it up the steps."

Wallace and I found Tarabelle sitting partially on the bottom step and partially on the ground. We helped her into the house but she barely made it to the front room before slumping to the floor.

"Tan," she moaned, "I think Miss Pearl done killed me this time. It hurts so bad. I think I'm gon' die." She shuddered and rolled over. That was when I saw the blood on her dress.

"Mama!" I shouted. "Mama, you need to come out here. Something is wrong with Tarabelle. Mama!"

It seemed to me that my mother was crawling, like she would never make it to the front room, and I was tempted to step in behind her and shove her along.

"What's wrong wit' her?" Mama asked, staring down at Tara and her blood-soaked dress. "Wallace, you get on up there and wait for Pearl. The minute she gets home from work, you tell her to come straight on out here."

I wet a cloth and began to wash the blood from Tarabelle's legs, but I couldn't get it off. It seemed to be seeping from her skin.

"Is she gonna die, Mama?" I asked.

"Shut up!" Mama ordered, and continued to stand there doing nothing.

"What are we gonna do?"

"I told you to shut up," she said, and this time she knelt and touched Tarabelle's face. Her hand recoiled and she hastily rose to her feet. "Let's get her in the car. I can't wait for Pearl." She called out to Laura, "You run and catch Wallace. Tell him I said to get back here."

I watched my mother go from inanimate to frantic in a matter of seconds. She grabbed a blanket, pushed me aside, and wrapped the blanket around Tarabelle's legs. She began to drag my sister toward the door. I grabbed Tarabelle under her arms and helped Mama carry her.

"I can't let her die here like this," Mama said, more to herself than to me. "That damn Pearl."

We struggled down the steps with Tarabelle between us and had reached the ground by the time Wallace and Laura returned. Wallace opened the car door and helped us get Tarabelle inside.

Her head fell against the window and she did not open her eyes as Mama sped away from the house, leaving us to wait and wonder. Though probably unaware, Tarabelle was getting her first ride in Mama's car.

"What you think is wrong wit' her?" Wallace asked. "You think I should go on and tell Miss Pearl?"

"No," I said, staring at the spot where the car had been. "Miss Pearl will know sooner or later. It's probably her fault." I turned toward the house. "Why did you come back here, Wallace? You were free."

He did not answer me until we were inside, warming ourselves by the stove. Then he said, "Mama came to get me. She found out where I was and she came over there. It was awful, Tan. Mama sat honking her horn in front of Grandma's house. Mr. Grodin saw her from the window but Grandma told me not to go out 'cause she knew Mama wasn't gonna come in. Mama got out the car, though, and started calling for me. She stood out there calling for 'bout an hour. Grandma said, 'Wallace, get me my crystal bowl out the cabinet.' She took the bowl and filled it wit' water from the kitchen sink, then she went outside and I went wit' her. Mama stopped yelling. She sorta backed up against her car like she wanted to run. Grandma kept on walking toward her.

"Mama started screaming, 'Get away from me! You get away from me.' But Grandma didn't stop. She dipped her fingers in the water and sprinkled it on Mama. 'This here holy water, Rozelle,' Grandma said, and Mama fell to the ground, screaming, while Grandma sprinkled that water on her head. Tan, you shoulda seen how Mama was trying to get away, and it wasn't nothing but water."

Wallace shook his head slowly as he stared down at the stove, then he continued. "Grandma said, 'This here water can curse you or bless you, Rozelle. You a harlot. God knows. He can burn a hole in yo' heart wit' this here water. Now, you'd better get on away from here 'fo' I dump the whole thang on you.' Mama started crawling 'round the car trying to get away from Grandma. I didn't know what to do. I wanted to help Mama, but Grandma said, 'Don't touch her, Wallace. She'll ruin you. The demons trying to get out.' I was scared to touch Mama 'cause the demons might get on me. But it was just plain ol' water that Grandma had.

"I helped Mama up, and we got in the car, then she put her head on the steering wheel and started to cry. Grandma went back in the house, and I was worried that she was mad at me. When Mama stopped crying, she drove down to the filling station and bought us some dranks out the machine, then she brought me home and ain't said nothing else about it."

I sighed. "Wallace, do you think the midwife is crazy?" I asked.

"Nah, she ain't crazy. She just mean to people she don't like, and I don't think she likes Mama."

"But Mama is her daughter."

"So what?"

I didn't know, so I stopped thinking about it and began to pray for Tarabelle.

"She ain't gon' die."

That was the news our mother brought home. We did not believe her. We did not believe her because she had returned with a teary-eyed Miss Pearl and enough white lightning to intoxicate a third of Triacy County.

"Tangy Mae, in the morning I want you to go see Miss Arlisa. Tell her you gon' be taking Tarabelle's place for a bit," Mama said. "Just for a bit."

"But what about Wednesday?" I asked. "The Whitmans?"

"I got a week to think on that one. I ain't gon' trouble wit' it tonight. I got enough to worry about."

She sent us to the kitchen with our pallets. I lay with my legs stretched beneath the table as sleep eluded me. From the front room came the sounds of springs creaking in the chairs, the pouring of liquid, low voices, and finally a midnight accusation.

"You almost killed her, Pearl. I thought you knew what you was doing. You ought not get drunk and mess wit' people."

"Rosie, don't you try to put this on me," Miss Pearl shot back. "I wadn't drunk. I told you that girl needed time to heal up 'fo' you took her back out there, but you wouldn't listen to me. It's yo' fault if it's anybody's."

Either I dozed off, or they were silent for a long while because the next thing I heard was Miss Pearl asking, "What'd you tell Dr. Mathis?"

"I didn't tell him nothing. Didn't talk to 'im."

"Well, how you know she ain't gon' die?"

"I don't know."

"Oh, Lord!" Miss Pearl cried. "Don't let that child die. Lord, I'll give my right arm if you see fit to let that child live. She just a child who ain't never ask for none of this. Just a po' innocent little child, Lord."

"Pearl, you stop that right now!" Mama warned.

Miss Pearl tried. I could tell she was trying, but guilt seemed to overwhelm her. "I shouldna done it the first time," she cried. "I tol' you that first time, Rosie. Oh, Lord, have mercy!"

"I done told you to stop it, Pearl," Mama said. "Ain't nobody held no gun to yo' head and made you do nothing."

"I was just trying to help her, Rosie. You the one brought her to me."

Wallace, whom I thought was asleep, whispered to me, "You was right, Tan."

"I know," I said.

"You think Miss Pearl gon' sit in there and cry all night?"

"She might. Did they wake you up?"

"Something did."

"Me, too," Laura whispered. "Why Miss Pearl crying like that? Did Tarabelle die?"

"Go back to sleep," Wallace and I said together.

"I can't," Laura said, forgetting to whisper.

"Shut up in there!" Mama yelled.

We obeyed, and I lay awake until the gray light of day seeped into the room. That night Laura wet her pallet for the first time since last September.

forty

My fifteenth birthday came and went unnoticed by anyone other than myself. For the first time that I could remember there were no white socks in red crepe paper and no sign of Miss Pearl. I did not see her until two days later when she and Mr. Frank brought Tarabelle home from the hospital.

"You gon' be awright?" Miss Pearl asked for the fourth time, as she made Tarabelle comfortable in an armchair. "You shoulda come home wit' me and Frank. You ain't got no business sleeping on no flo'. I done told you that."

"I'll be awright, Miss Pearl," Tarabelle assured her.

Miss Pearl was not convinced. She stood over the chair, patting Tarabelle's hand, rubbing her back, and kissing her hair. "I'm gon' come down here tomorrow after work and wash yo' hair right good for you," she said.

Mr. Frank tugged at his wife's arm. "C'mon, Pearl. She can't get no rest with you carrying on like that."

Reluctantly, Miss Pearl followed him out, and we moved in to surround Tarabelle. She rested her head against the back of the chair and closed her eyes, and I took a blanket from the cedar chest to cover her, then I dropped to the floor at her feet where Wallace, Laura, and Edna were already seated. We stayed that way, saying nothing, until our mother's footsteps sounded on the front porch, then Tarabelle opened her eyes and stared up at the ceiling.

Mama entered the room and leaned against the door frame. "You awright, girl?" she asked.

Tarabelle would not look at her, but she said, "Nah, Mama. I ain't never gon' be awright no mo'."

"What'd them doctors say?"

"Say they wanna talk to you."

"I ain't got nothing to say to 'em," Mama muttered.

"That's what I told 'em," Tarabelle said. "I told 'em you ain't had nothing to say."

"What you mean by that?" Mama asked.

Tarabelle did not answer. She whimpered and groaned, mimicking the melodramatics she had witnessed from our mother over the years. "Tan," she said, "I don't feel good. Spread me a blanket."

I removed the blanket that covered her and spread it on the floor while Wallace helped her to her feet. Mama watched us.

"Is Tara gon' die?" Edna asked, rising from the floor and staring at Mama.

Mama removed a few bugs from her face and arms, then she stepped completely into the room and slumped down on a chair. She sat staring at the coal stove for a long time, then she glanced at me and said, "Tangy Mae, you get yo'self cleaned up. You gotta go wit' me tonight."

For miles, against a narrow dirt road, cornfields and wheatfields raced through darkness, challenging a moon that knew nothing of their existence. It was a full moon that had risen for the sole purpose of watching over me.

Mama stopped the car in the yard of a two-story farmhouse. There were four other cars parked in the yard, and a skeleton of a car standing on cinderblocks beneath a willow tree. I had never been so far out in the country before, and could not say exactly where I was. Through an upstairs window, I could see a human shape pacing back and forth. The rest of the rooms upstairs were dark, and the light spilling into the yard came from the first floor.

"Tangy Mae, there's a man in there that's gonna help us get Sam outta jail," Mama said. "He's a lawyer named Ruggles. I want you to be nice to him, you hear?"

"What do you want me to do, Mama?" I asked, keeping my gaze fixed on the upstairs window. Anxiety was numbing my feet and legs.

"Do whatever he tells you to do. Be nice to him, and tomorrow I'm gon' bring yo' brother home."

Did I care enough about Sam to risk my life as Tarabelle had done? Deep in my gut I knew this was the place that had nearly killed my sister, or at least it had started here, and I wanted no part of it. If there was a choice between saving Sam or myself, I would choose to save myself.

"I don't wanna do this, Mama," I pleaded. "I don't wanna go in there."

"Well, you going, and you gon' do what he tells you to do. Don't you start acting up and shame me out here, Tangy Mae. Now, you come on!"

She stepped from the car, and I tried to open the door on my side, but my hands were shaking too bad to lift the handle. Mama came around and opened the door for me, then she yanked me out by my hair. She did not understand that I was afraid. She thought she had taken care of my fear years ago. But it had slowly grown back.

"Let me have a look at you," she said, fussing with my hair. She ran her hands along the shoulders of my coat, then glanced down at my legs. "You shouldna wore them socks, Tangy Mae, but it's too late now."

"Mama, please don't make me go in there," I begged, as she guided me across the yard.

She stopped abruptly, bunched the back of my coat with one hand, and began to roughly shake me. "You look here," she said. "You gon' do this, and I'm gon' bring yo' brother home so we can be a family again. If you don't do it, Tangy Mae, I ain't got no need for you. I'd just as soon chop you up in pieces and leave you out here in these weeds for the buzzards."

I stifled my protest. She could kill me, leave me out here, and get away with it. She could get away with anything. People would probably think I had run off the way Mushy had done, and they wouldn't even bother to search for me. I would lay in weeds until the buzzards plucked the flesh from my bones.

Moving as slowly as I dared, I followed my mother up five wooden steps and into a large kitchen where a frail, tired-looking woman sat at a table with an infant on her lap.

"Hey, Frances. How you doing?" Mama asked.

"Ain't no need to complain, Rosie," the woman replied. "This 'un yo' daughter, too?"

Mama nodded. "Yeah. This here is Tangy Mae."

"Y'all go on up. He in that last room on yo' left."

"I'm gon' take her on up, then I'm gon' come back down and have a cup of coffee wit' you, Frances," Mama said.

"This ain't coffee I'm drinking," the woman said and winked at Mama.

"Well, whatever it is, I'm gon' have some, too," Mama said, as she nudged me forward and up a flight of stairs.

There were five closed doors and an eerie silence along the corridor. Mama stopped and rapped on the last door on the left with her knuckles, then without invitation she opened it and shoved me forward.

"We here, Mr. Ruggles," she said.

"I can see that, Rozelle. Close the door on your way out."

Mama gave me a warning glance before backing from the room, and I was left with a stranger who sat on a chair and studied me with quiet amusement. When he smiled, he seemed harmless enough, but I clung to the spot where my mother had left me, and did not move a muscle.

"How old are you?" he asked.

My lips quivered and my mouth felt dry. "Fifteen," I croaked. "I'm fifteen."

He was a pale, middle-aged man with a torso and upper arms that sagged like foam sliding down the side of a beer mug. His dark hair, just beginning to gray at the temples, was oily and limp. He wore brown socks, white boxer shorts, and nothing else. He pressed his hands together and leaned forward on his chair.

"Get your things off," he quietly demanded.

When I did not obey, his lips took on an unpleasant twist, and he rose from the chair. "Should I get Rozelle back in here to help you?" he asked.

"Please!" I begged. "Don't do that."

"Well," he said, and nodded his head once, politely.

He returned to his chair and watched as I unbuttoned my dress and pulled it over my head. Tears—the silent kind—rolled down my face. I did not want this man to see my bra, or panties, or any of me, but he would not turn his head. My bra was too small, dingy from too much wear and washing, and the straps were held together by safety pins. I turned my back to him and heard him chuckle.

"Come here!" he ordered when I was standing naked before him. "Come sit over here."

My reflection—a terrified little girl—crept slowly toward me from the windowpane behind his head. In the glass, the girl appeared skinny with mounds of flesh bulging from atop protective hands. I wanted her to disappear, but she just kept right on coming.

"Here. Sit here!" Mr. Ruggles said, patting one flabby thigh with his hand.

Awful, noisy, frightening sobs escaped my throat as he pulled me down onto his lap and closed his pale arms around me. He cradled me and wiped the tears from my face with the back of one finger.

"Don't cry," he soothed. "I'm not going to hurt you."

I wanted to believe him, but the finger he had used to wipe my tears away began to pry between my hand and the breast it hid.

"Don't fight against me," he said impatiently.

But I did fight. Forgetting about my nakedness, I struggled against him until he dumped me to the floor and swung a sock-covered foot onto my belly to still me. His body shifted on the chair, and the chair gave a squeak, then he was on the floor beside me, his hands deep into my hair.

"Don't make me hurt you," he whispered against my ear. "Think about your brother. I can have him free by tomorrow."

At that moment, I did not give one damn about my brother. Mr. Ruggles had straddled my chest, and I was concentrating on how to get his fat, flabby body off of me. I could not buck him off, could not arch my back. My arms were pinned to the floor, and his heavy knees held them there. I was able to move my hands, and I flexed them until they connected with flesh, then I clawed.

He laughed. "If you scratch me one more time, I'll break your little black neck," he said, then gripped my hair like reins and snapped my head sharply forward.

I looked into his eyes and knew he meant it, and I did not want to die naked on a farmhouse floor. Harvey and Mr. Dobson would have to come for my body, and how could I ever explain to them? The sheriff and Chadlow would come and gape at me, and I would be unable to hide my nakedness. Damn!

The fight had left me, or at least Mr. Ruggles thought it had. He eased up from my chest to remove his shorts, and I quickly scampered across the floor. I had reached the bed and was nearly under it when he grabbed my ankle. I kicked with one leg, and he twisted the other. He dragged me from beneath the bed, let go of my leg and seized my hair again, then he sat on the bed and pulled my head up between his thighs. He was breathing hard from his exertion and I could smell his sweat.

"One bite, one scratch, and I'll have Rozelle back in here," he warned, then forced his rigid flesh against my closed, unyielding lips.

"Don't!" I cried, struggling to turn my head. "Please, don't do this to me."

But he did, and I did not bite, and I did not scratch, because the grasp he had on my hair drew my face into a taut mass of pain.

When he was done with me, and I was being sick in a corner, he called my mother into the room. He faced her, and with fleshy hands pressed against a corpulent belly, he reneged on his promise to help my brother, citing my failure to satisfy him. I watched my mother plead with him until I was sick all over again. Finally, he granted her a second chance with the stipulation that I behave myself.

"It'll have to be another night, Rozelle," he said. "Look at her! What man in his right mind would touch her the way she is now?"

After we were home, and my mother had beat me for spoiling her plans, I went out to the back porch, and brushed my teeth and gargled with saltwater.

"What did you do?" Tarabelle asked, as I stretched on my pallet. "Why Mama so mad at you?"

"I threw up."

"Oh," she said. "They made you do it that way. You lucky."

"I don't feel lucky. Why didn't you tell me, Tara?"

"I didn't think you'd ever have to do it. Mama always said didn't no man want you."

"Can I get pregnant?" I asked.

"I think so," she answered. "They do it to you all kinds of ways. I think all them ways can make a baby."

"She says I'll have to go back, Tara. I'll have to go back until that lawyer gets Sam out of jail."

We were silent for a long time, then Tara said, "You wouldn't have to go if Mama was dead."

"But she's not dead, Tara."

"Yeah. I guess it's like Mushy said, 'She ain't never gon' die.'"

forty-one

Night after night, I was taken from my home and delivered to one of the many beds at the farmhouse. One night when I was closed in a room with Harlell Nixon, I worked up the nerve to ask him about Sam. Harlell owned a barbershop, and people talked to him, told him all sorts of things. I asked him if he knew when the lawyer would get Sam out of jail.

Harlell laughed. "Girl, don't yo' mama tell you nothing? Sam doing a year for beating up that boy over in East Grove. That's the way I hear it, and I ain't never heard of no lawyer getting no nigger out when he doing time that a judge done gave him. They ain't never really charged Sam wit' killing Junior, but that don't mean they won't come back and do it later."

"Is that why we need the lawyer?" I asked. "Just in case they charge Sam with Junior's murder?"

Harlell laughed for the entire time it took him to undress. "Shit," he said. "What lawyer anyway? I done tol' yo' mama a hundred times, that motherfucka she giving her money to ain't no damn lawyer."

"What?" I asked incredulously. From the time Harlell pulled me onto the bed and until he finished with me, I asked that one question. "What?"

Every part of my being had been stretched to the limits before my brother was finally released from jail. I had not seen Mr. Ruggles for more than a month, and I wondered what role he had played in the scheme of things—if any. My mother would not say, never mentioned his name.

It was May, and nothing growing on God's green earth enticed or excited me. I felt I could have single-handedly ripped up the roots of the dogwood trees that blossomed on Fife Street. I allowed myself the privilege of anger, had no patience with my siblings, had even thought again of running away, and had made it as far as the four-lane highway before guilt pulled me back to Penyon Road.

I had suffered for Sam's release, and now he came home. I tried not to be angry with him, but I couldn't help it. When I looked at him, he reminded me of a centipede—a creepy, crawly, self-indulgent little thing. He stood in the front room close to the door, commanding our attention. The hair on his face nearly hid his lips, and there was a raised area on his head that looked raw and painful.

"I been cooped up a long time, Mama," he said. "I need to stretch my legs. You got a couple of dollars I can hold 'til I get back to work? I'm thinking I oughta run up and see Harvey for a bit."

"You ain't been home fifteen minutes and already you talking 'bout leaving. I wanna have a look at yo' head, and ain't you got nothing to say to me?" Mama asked, as she gave him three dollars, which was probably all we had. "I don't want you leaving outta here and getting in no mo' trouble, Sam. You know they gon' be watching you."

"For every one eye they have watching me, I'm gon' have two watching them. I ain't never going back to jail, Mama. I just need to be outside for a bit. See things again. We'll talk when I get back. We can talk all night if you want."

Mama chuckled. "Yeah, I guess you do need to stretch them legs. You moving so much look like you gon' break out and dance in a minute."

"Harvey ain't home," Wallace said. "He getting Miss Julia ready for her funeral."

"Miss Julia done died?" Sam asked.

"It ain't bad she died," Tarabelle said. "She was in real poor shape. She looked 'bout bad as you do. You sho' you ain't sick or something, Sam?"

Sam laughed. "Tarabelle, girl, you ain't changed a bit. Ain't nothing wrong wit' me."

"You could stand a shave," Mama remarked, "and before you leave outta here, I wanna know who did that to yo' head."

"I love you, Mama, and that's all that matters," Sam said, as he moved toward the front door. "Don't matter who did nothing to my head."

Mama grabbed his arm, then she studied his face long and hard as if to convince herself that this was the same child who had been taken away from her at the end of last summer. "Is it over, Sam?" she asked soberly. "Are they gonna come back later and say you killed Junior?"

He leaned down and kissed her cheek. "As far as I'm concerned, Mama, it's over."

I followed him to the door and out onto the porch, and I could see Hambone's car waiting on the road. I wanted to yell, "Sam, you've been in jail for nine months. Stand still for a minute! Talk to me!" Maybe I said it aloud; I don't know, but Sam stopped and turned to face me. He took my hand and led me down to the yard.

"Tangy Mae, I heard some things while I was in that jail," he said. "A few people tol' me some awful stuff 'bout you. I wasn't gon' ask you 'bout it 'cause I didn't wanna believe it, but the way you been looking at me ever since I walked through that door, I know it's true. I'm sorry, and that's all I know to say."

I began to cry, and Sam squeezed my hand.

"You go on and cry, Tangy Mae," he said. "You got a reason to cry. When I get time, I'm gon' cry, too."

"How did they treat you in that jail, Sam?"

"Probably better than you been treated. It's hard when somebody take yo' freedom from you, but the sheriff and his deputies was okay. The sheriff in Caloona was awright, too. But Chadlow was something else. Sometimes he'd pull up a chair when wasn't nobody else around, and he'd talk to me through them bars. Tell me how I was gon' fry in the electric chair for what I done to Junior. He would always suppose—Nah, 'imagine,' that was the word he used. He'd say, 'I *imagine* Junior musta squealed like a little girl when you killed him, boy.' Or he'd say, 'I *imagine* it musta took a dozen of you dumb niggers to figure out how to get that rope around that boy's neck.' One day he stuck a broom handle in my cell, started poking and prodding me wit' that thing. I grabbed it and tried to pull him through them bars. Scraped my hands up real good." He opened both hands so I could see his palms.

"I'm sorry, Sam."

"Uh-uh. Nah. You ain't got nothing to be sorry 'bout. I'm the one that's sorry. I'm sorry you had to go through all that stuff you been through. I didn't wish nothing like that on you, Tangy Mae, but when you locked up in jail, you ain't got no control over nothing. And I ain't never had no control over Mama, anyway. I was upset wit' her when I heard, but I knew she was just doing the best she knew how to get me outta that mess I had done got myself into."

I nodded. "I'll be okay, Sam. How about you? How are you doing?"

He shook his head and smiled. "Tangy Mae, I feel like if somebody took mad away from me, I'd be walking 'round empty. I'm gon' tell you what I don't ever want Mama to know. Chadlow let them Griggses in that jail on me—the daddy and all three of them boys. They beat me real good. They didn't kill me, but they shoulda, though."

I watched as he ran down the bank and climbed into Hambone's car, then I returned to the front room where my mother sat with her head resting against the back of her chair. She was happier than she had been in a long time.

"I'm going up to the flats to see Tannus," she said. "I gotta let him know that Sam is free. I gon' let him know that my baby didn't kill his boy."

"Don't do that, Mama," I said. "Mr. Tannus already knows that Sam didn't kill Junior. If you start talking, you'll just get the rumors started again. Some people think Sam is getting away with murder."

"Who saying that?"

"A few people who don't know how close Sam and Junior were."

"Well, I'm gon' put a stop to it," she said.

She brushed past me, raced down the steps and out into the

field. As she drove away, I knew, and thought she should have known, that she would not be able to stop the rumors. She couldn't stop them about Sam, she couldn't stop them about herself, and once they had gotten started about me, she wouldn't be able to stop those, either.

I followed the trail of dust left behind by my mother's car until I reached the paved surface of Fife Street, then I turned right and headed toward the flats. When I arrived on Motten Street, Martha Jean was sitting on the porch swing, looking as though she would explode from the weight of her unborn child. She watched my approach, and smiled slightly when I joined her.

"Velman where?" I signed.

She did not answer, but took my hand and placed it against her abdomen. I allowed my hand to linger for a moment, then repeated my question. "Velman where?"

"He's back up in there somewhere," Skeeter said from behind the screen door. He stepped out onto the porch. "Time for me to get to work. Pretty good the way this thing works out, with Velman getting in before I have to leave. That way Martha Jean is never alone. Don't want her to be by herself when that baby comes."

Skeeter was the same height as Velman, but he was heavier, and about a shade lighter in complexion. He was a handsome man. His eyes reminded me of Velman's. They were small and clear, and right now they were laughing.

"I never would've thought that tiny little girl that Velman brought home would ever get so fat," he teased, and leaned down to tap Martha Jean's protruding navel with his finger tip.

"Baby," Martha Jean signed. "Velman say, fat. See feet, no."

Skeeter laughed, then said, "He right, too, 'cause you sho'nuff done got fat."

"Ain't nothing funny about no fat woman, Skeeter," Velman said lightheartedly as he stepped out onto the porch. He was wearing trousers, but no shirt or shoes, and Martha Jean sent him back inside to dress.

"Well, I'll see y'all later," Skeeter said. "Take care of my girl 'til I get back."

We watched him swagger up the sidewalk, then Martha Jean

pulled herself to her feet, and I followed her inside. Velman was sitting on a chair in the front room, pulling on a pair of socks.

"Little sister, how you say jealous with your fingers?" he asked. "I wanna tell my wife to stop being so jealous."

"I don't know," I answered. "I've never had to use that word."

"Martha Jean's even jealous about Skeeter," Velman said. "It don't make no sense the way her and Miss Shirley be going at it. That woman trying to like my uncle but my wife don't want her over here. Skeeter thinks it's funny, but Miss Shirley don't think it's funny one bit."

I shrugged and sat on the floor beside the coffee table. Martha Jean entered the kitchen.

"She's probably gon' eat something else," Velman said. "I thought Miss Rosie was making fun back when she first said Martha Jean was gon' have a baby. How she know that, you reckon? I hadn't seen no difference in her back then, but I took her on over to Dr. Mathis, and that's what he said, too. It scares me, little sister. I don't know if I'm ready for it."

"You're ready," I said. "There's nothing you can do about it now."

"Yeah, you right," he said, rubbing at a worry line in his forehead. "Hambone was by here again last week. Talking. Always talking. Got me thinking I'm supposed to be mad at somebody, and I don't even know who."

"Sam's out," I said. "You can tell Martha Jean. It'll probably make her happy."

He nodded, settled against the chair cushion, and closed his eyes. "Everything makes her happy," he said. "Sometimes she be moving them fingers all happy-like, and I don't know what the heck she be saying. I got a lot to learn before I can keep up with what she say, but I figure we got all our lives. I be looking at her lately, and wondering if our baby gon' be able to hear."

Velman was so preoccupied with Martha Jean that I was sure he had not heard my news. I repeated it. "Sam came home today. He's out of jail."

"Hey, that's great," he said, opening one eye to look at me. "So the sheriff finally listened to reason?"

Velman had opened the door for me to unburden myself, which

was what I needed to do, but before I could say anything, Martha Jean waddled in from the kitchen, popping the last of a biscuit into her mouth. She settled on Velman's lap as if that was the only place in the room to sit, and he shifted on the chair and supported her back with his arm. He flicked his tongue and stole a crumb from the corner of her mouth, and she buried her face against his neck while he stroked her abdomen. It was an intimacy that negated all existence beyond that chair, and I felt an intruder.

I fought a compelling desire to snatch my sister from the arms I craved comfort from myself. I did not merely want her man; I needed him. He could be my deliverance, rescue me from Penyon Road, mend the broken pieces of my heart and make me whole again. With as much dignity as I could muster, I rose from the floor and went toward the front door, needing to get away from this house and all the things I could not have.

"Where you going, little sister?" Velman asked.

"Home."

"What's the rush? Stay for supper."

My hand was on the door, and all I had to do was keep walking, but I turned around.

"I'm going home," I said bitterly, unable to control my hurt and anger any longer. "Martha Jean can stay for supper. She's bought and paid for. Nobody traded anything for me, and I'm going home."

Rage propelled him across the room. He gripped my shoulders and glared down at me. "Don't you ever say anything like that to me again."

For long agonizing seconds, I could not speak, then my voice eased around the lump in my throat. "I'm sorry," I said. "I didn't mean that." But my mind screamed, *Why didn't you choose me?*

He removed his hands from my shoulders, and composed himself. "What's going on?" he asked.

It was getting late, and I stared out the screen at children playing in shadows along the sidewalk. "Mama used me to get Sam out of jail," I said quietly. "I'm scared, Velman. I'm so scared."

"What do you mean, she used you to get Sam out?"

Settling myself on the couch, I stared up at Velman, then beginning with Mr. Ruggles, I told my story. As I spoke, I could see it all as clearly as though I were suspended above a bed at the farm-house. The terrified girl in the room was someone else. *Not me.* She floated like an impotent ghost. She lay on one bed with a tall man who smelled of garlic. She bowed at another bed for Chadlow, her feet on the floor, her arms pressed against the mattress. She was just a child, really, who collapsed from pain, only to be hoisted up by her mother. Night after night the men came, and the gentle ones were the worst, for they assumed they could coax life into a girl who died each night before they even touched her.

"Damn," Velman whispered when I was done.

"What?" Martha Jean asked. She had come to sit beside me, and her fingers steadily repeated that one word. "What? What?"

"Hurt," I signed.

Velman paced the room, then he stepped toward the couch and I waited for him to say something. His mouth opened and closed. I saw him lift a foot, and the coffee table flew across the room and struck the wall. He followed after the table, kicked it again, then slammed his fist against the wall just above a framed still life of red roses. The roses sprang from their hook and crashed against the overturned table. Martha Jean stared in alarm, but I sat back and watched the destruction. It was futile, yet I understood it was for the love of me.

forty-two

We were awakened in the middle of the night by the smell of smoke and the peal of sirens some distance off in the heart of our city. It was an uncommon sound in Pakersfield, which made it frightening and exciting at the same time. We lit the kerosene lamps and filed out into the night.

"Where's Sam?" Mama asked, a hint of panic in her voice.

"He never came home," Wallace told her.

Mama swore, and her words drifted up into the smoke-filled air. We stared toward the east where I expected to see flames leaping for the sky, but whatever was burning was too far away or too low for us to see.

Miss Pearl arrived early the following morning to tell us that she and Mr. Frank had attempted to go to work and had been rerouted by the police. "Frank went on around through Plymouth, but I told him to let me out," she said. "They say somebody done tried to burn down everything on Market Street. They got barricades up and they ain't letting no coloreds into town. Say they ain't stopping nobody from going to work, just gotta find another way to get there."

"I gotta go to work, Mama," Tarabelle said. "Miss Arlisa gon' get rid of me if I keep staying off."

Mama nodded. "You ain't gotta go through town to get to East Grove. You go on."

"We don't have to go through town to get to school, either, Mama," I said.

She rested her elbows against the tabletop and cupped her hands around her chin. She had a faraway look, like she was staring through me and could see something no one else in the room could see. Finally, she said, "If school that important to you, Tangy Mae, you go on. For all you know, yo' brother could be burned up in a fire, and you standing there talking to me 'bout school."

Tarabelle left almost immediately, but I allowed guilt and indecisiveness to slow me down, which is how I happened to be in the kitchen when Angus Betts and Chadlow stormed into the house. Miss Pearl shrieked, but Mama sat silent, staring with indifference at the gun Chadlow aimed at her chest.

The sheriff was also holding a gun, but his was pointed toward the floor. He glanced about the room, then asked, "Where is he, Rozelle?"

"I ain't seen him," Mama answered. "He didn't come home last night."

"You'd better not be lying to me," the sheriff said, raising his gun slightly. "I've got Marcus and Beck searching those woods out there. If we find him hiding out back there or anywhere near this house, I'm taking you in, too."

"I'm telling you, Angus, I ain't seen him since yesterday."

The sheriff raised his gun and pointed it at her head. "What did you call me?" he asked.

Mama seemed confused. She placed one trembling hand to her throat and stared at him. "What'd I say, Sheriff?" she asked innocently.

He lowered the gun and turned to Chadlow. "You keep an eye on them while I search the rest of the house."

The minute the sheriff was out of the room, Chadlow stepped closer to Mama and said, "He burned down my place of business, Rozelle. That means if we don't catch him, you're gonna owe me. Do you know how I deal with people who cross me?"

My mother trembled with fear. It was the kind of fear she despised, the same kind she had burned from my flesh. Chadlow stared down at her, and she closed her eyes as tight as she could.

There was not much to search in our house, and the sheriff was back in less than five minutes. He holstered his weapon and stared at my mother with contempt. "Rozelle, I don't know where that boy is, but I'll get him. When I find him, I'll make him wish he'd never been born. And don't try to tell me that it wasn't him. He drove through this town throwing Molotov cocktails. Do you know how much damage that can do?"

Mama shook her head. "I don't know what that is."

The sheriff looked at Wallace. "Do you know anything about this?" he asked.

"No, sir," Wallace answered quickly.

"I've got a good mind to just go on and arrest everybody," the sheriff said. "I'm ruined in this town. I stood up for that boy, asked the judge to set him free, to consider he was injured while in my care. I see now that I shouldn't have done that. The Griggs furniture store is gone." He flicked his fingers. "Just gone. The Pioneer Cab Company is rubble, Chad's café was destroyed, and businesses all along Market Street were damaged. The fire started at Griggs's and spread from there. I can't even describe the mess they made on the courthouse lawn or what they did to the water fountain. Ralph was working late at the depot, and he says he saw your boy and some others just before the fires broke out."

Mama wept softly into a dishcloth that Miss Pearl had handed her. She made no effort to deny anything the sheriff had said.

The sheriff watched her for a moment, then he turned to Chadlow and said, "Let's get out of here."

Once they were gone, Mama scraped a mess of bugs from her cheek. Her fingernails left three red marks running from below her right eye down to her chin, and I knew I was not going to school.

"I'm gon' see if they all left," Wallace said, rising from his milk crate.

I followed him out back where we stood on the porch and studied the path between the trees for some sign of movement. There was nothing. Wallace went down the steps and mounted his bike.

"I'm gon' find out what happened," he said.

"Wallace, don't go near town," I said.

"I won't. I'm going up on Plymouth and down to the flats. Somebody knows something, Tan."

I stepped down from the porch, and walked slowly toward the woods. The sheriff's men had invaded my forest, trampled through the underbrush, and disturbed its tranquility. I could feel their intrusion, although they were long gone. I walked in circles, thinking of the price I had paid for Sam's freedom, thinking of Mr. Pace and his plans for my future, thinking of my mother and her bugs.

When I returned to the house, Harvey was on our front porch talking with Mama and Miss Pearl. Mama had stopped crying and was concentrating on the information that Harvey was apprehensively imparting. I eased down on a step to listen.

"I'm telling you, he ain't nowhere in town, Mama," Harvey said. "I been everywhere. The sheriff ain't lying to you. He came up to the house this morning wit' Chadlow, and they searched the whole place. They even searched the funeral home. Ain't nobody seen Sam. It was him and Hambone, Maxwell and Becky. They all gone."

"That don't mean Sam burned nothing down," Mama said. "People all time blaming things on Sam."

"He did it, Mama. Sam was in jail a long time. Every day he probably got a little madder, and he had time to plan this. I'd say Hambone knew about it, too. If Sam didn't do it, where is he? How come he ain't came home? He been outta jail for one day, and all of a sudden half of town burns down. Who ain't gon' think it was him?"

"You know, he got a point there, Rosie," Miss Pearl said.

"Go home, Pearl!" Mama shouted. "You too, Harvey. I don't need nobody 'round me that's against Sam. Y'all don't know that he did nothing."

Miss Pearl rose from her chair. "I'm going," she said. "I didn't believe the sheriff when he was saying Sam killed Junior Fess, but looks like to me he got the right somebody this time."

"He ain't got him yet," Mama retorted.

"Nah, Mama, but they gon' have him soon," Harvey said. "It's just a matter of time." He started down the steps, then stopped and stared out toward the road where Wallace was pedaling for home with all his might. "Look at Wallace. He got some news. Maybe they done caught Sam."

Wallace leapt from his bike and let it fall to the road. He scurried up the embankment. "Miss Pearl!" he called excitedly. "Miss Pearl! Martha Jean done had a baby. Velman needs you to get over there right now. He don't know what to do. Hurry up, Miss Pearl!"

"Lord have mercy. Who caught it?" Miss Pearl asked as she reached the ground.

"Huh?"

"Who caught the baby? Who delivered it?"

"Velman, I guess," Wallace answered. "Ain't nobody there 'cept Velman and Skeeter. Skeeter went to get Miss Shirley, but she too upset 'bout Max and Becky to be bothered."

"Come on, Rosie," Miss Pearl said. "Run me over there right quick, see 'bout this child."

"I ain't going nowhere," Mama said. "I gotta wait for Sam."

"I'll drive you," Harvey offered.

"I'm going, too," Wallace said.

"Me, too," I said, and started for Mr. Dobson's car.

"Tangy Mae, you ain't going nowhere," Mama called down from the porch. "What if I have to run someplace to see 'bout Sam? You gotta be here wit' the girls."

"Get my bike out the road, Tan," Wallace said as he climbed into the car.

"Wallace, what did she have?" I asked. "What did Martha Jean have?"

"A girl."

The car pulled off, and I went down to the road to get the bike, then I went to the back porch to pout in private and to plot a diversion that would get me to Motten Street.

forty-three

They did not wait until the wee hours of the morning to retaliate. The first fire broke out on Tuesday evening long before midnight, but we did not stand gazing into darkness as we had done before. These flames were visible, too high, and too close.

We joined a distressed throng on Canyon Street where hoses had been strung from the two closest houses. We raced back and forth with anything that would hold water, filling our vessels from a faucet in Walter Vanna's yard. We did all we could in a futile attempt to save Logan's store, then stood back and watched as the fire consumed it.

When there was nothing more to do, we began to disperse, then somebody yelled, "Oh, my God! Look!"

Fire illuminated the northern sky. It was far off, but so bright it seemed that all of Plymouth was burning. Walter Vanna, Glenn Henderson, and a few of the other men piled into cars and drove off toward Plymouth. Mama joined some of the women who stood on the wet pavement of Canyon Street to speculate about the distant fire.

Tarabelle grumbled angrily, and I understood why. We were

tired, wet, and reeking of smoke, and it didn't matter what was burning because we didn't have the strength to fight it, anyway. We left Mama and Wallace on Canyon Street, but took the girls with us as we headed for home.

The following morning I left early for work, and because I could not go through town, it took me nearly thirty minutes longer to get to North Ridge. I arrived at the Whitmans' house to find Miss Veatrice blocking my entrance.

"Hey, honey," she said in a pleasant greeting. "I didn't expect to see you today. I'm glad you came, but I can't let you in. Bakker says you can't work here anymore. He says he won't stand for having niggers in his house, not with the way they're acting around here. He says they burned down half the town."

"I had nothing to do with that, Miss Veatrice," I said.

"That's what I told Bakker, but he said it didn't matter. You're one of them, honey, and I can't let you in here. Bakker says if I see you coming, I'm to lock the door, but I didn't think you'd want to do anything to me."

"What could I do to you?"

She giggled. "Why, you could burn my house down. That's what you could do. Only it ain't my house. Did I tell you I'm getting married?"

"That's nice, Miss Veatrice," I said, backing down from the porch.

"Where're you going?" she asked.

"I'm going to school. If I'm not going to work today, then I should be in school."

"They burned it down, you know. Last night they went and burned it down. It's gone, honey. Bakker says they hit all the nigger towns last night. You may as well stay and visit with me because your school is gone."

"I don't believe you, Miss Veatrice. My school is still standing," I said, as my feet touched the ground. "How could anybody burn the school down?"

"Well, they didn't bother your church. Bakker says . . ."

I began to run. I ran away from Miss Veatrice and her little white house with green shutters, then taking a detour around town, I ran along the shoulder of the four-lane highway and kept running until I reached Motten Street and Skeeter's house. I was breathless and bending over when Velman opened the door.

"Hey. Who's chasing you?" he asked.

"Nobody. I came to see my niece."

Holding a finger to his lips to keep me quiet, he led me through the house toward his bedroom. "They're sleeping," he whispered. "Catch yo' breath, and I'll let you peek in on 'em."

Martha Jean's body formed a half circle around the baby, and they both slept peacefully, undisturbed by the world outside. I leaned over the bed, raised the blanket covering the baby, then touched her tiny hand just for the warmth of it.

"I'm an aunt," I whispered.

Velman nodded. "And I'm a daddy," he said proudly. "Her name is Mary Ann."

We tipped from the room, and I took a seat on the couch. "Where's Skeeter?" I asked.

"Up the street with Miss Shirley. They'll be back shortly," Velman said, as he sat beside me. "Miss Shirley's helping out with the baby. Kinda hard when you can't get into town to get things, but we got just about everything we need. Still, I'll be glad when they take them barricades down. The way I hear it, didn't that much burn in town no way—just the furniture store and the Western Auto that's next to it, and that's about all."

"I heard it was more than that," I said. "I don't know what we're gonna do. Half the people can't get to work, and now there's no school."

"You can go to school," he said. "It was the new one they burned down, the one they were building."

"Miss Veatrice told me they burned the school down, and I just assumed she meant the old one. She let me go this morning, said her brother didn't want Negroes in his house."

"Yeah, well, when it rains it pours," Velman said, taking my hand and squeezing it.

"I can't understand why anybody would want to destroy something they've worked so hard at building," I said.

"If Hambone was telling the truth, they didn't put much work into it. Remember? He said they were just throwing it together."

I nodded.

His eyes met mine and he sighed. "Little sister, are things getting any better for you? I wrote a letter to Mushy and asked her to come."

I eased my hand from his and stood up from the couch. "She won't come. And if she does, what can she do?"

"I don't know, but we'll think of something." He stood, too, and wrapped his arms around me. "We'll think of something, little sister."

I pulled away from him. "I have to go."

"Trust me," he said.

"I do," I answered. "That's what's keeping me alive." I winked to let him know that I was teasing when I wasn't teasing at all.

forty-four

The furniture store was a total loss, the two adjacent structures had sustained considerable damage. There was a wide open space where the Market Street Café had once stood, and only a cement slab as a reminder of the Pioneer Taxicab Company. For days we had been locked out of town, not knowing what to expect, and even after the barricades came down, I was leery of Market Street. But my mother needed stockings from the five-and-dime, and she had sent me to get them since, to her way of thinking, it was my fault she had to dress up for a meeting with "them goddamn snooty school people."

"Do I look awright, Tangy Mae?" she asked for the third time as she parked the car on the school lot. "Wonder what this is all about? I bet they gon' ask me if you can come back next year. I already got in my mind what I'm gon' say. You ain't going, and that's final."

I would have asked her why we had come, but looking at my mother, I knew the answer. She had come to flaunt her beauty. It had taken her nearly two hours to dress for this meeting, and she looked absolutely stunning. She wore a brown tunic suit with tiny pink dots and pink cuffed sleeves, leather pumps, and a faille hat with a single pink feather.

We got out of the car, and she held my arm, preventing me from moving forward, as we watched an assemblage of parents and teachers enter the school. It was the presence of four white men entering the schoolyard from the street that caused my mother to reach up and snatch a bug from her lovely face.

"Tangy Mae, what you done went and done?" she asked.

"Nothing, Mama," I answered, but I could tell she did not believe me.

I lingered outside with Edith Dobson and Coleman Hewitt, our principal's son. We spoke to Reverend Nelson as he went in, then we looked at each other questioningly.

"What's this meeting all about, Coleman?" Edith asked.

Coleman was a short, pimply-faced boy, the firstborn of the four Hewitt children. He shoved his hands into his pants pockets and avoided making eye contact with Edith. "They'll tell us when they're ready," he said. "I'm not suppose to say anything until then."

There were three other students in the yard with us: Larry Weston, Philip Ames, and Harold Brandon. They were staring at the charred, skeletal remains of what would have been our new school. Edith nudged me and I followed her across the yard.

"It's a mess, isn't it?" she said. "Daddy says it's not Sam's fault. He doesn't blame your brother at all. He says they kept Sam in jail for no reason, and they can do that to any colored man and get away with it. He says it's time somebody showed them that we're not going to stand for it."

"But somebody could have been killed in one of those fires," I said. "We're lucky no one was."

"Do you think it's over?"

"No. They've let us back into town, but I don't think it's over. I do think people are beginning to see what Hambone was talking about."

"Daddy doesn't think it's over, either," Edith said. "He's afraid somebody's gonna get hurt. He's an undertaker, but he doesn't want people to die unless it's from old age. Mama says with ideas like that he'll die old and poor himself."

"Edith, do you know what this meeting is about?"

"A little."

I heard my name called and I turned to see my mother storming across the school's short wooden porch and nearly tripping over her own feet in her haste to reach her car.

"Come on, Tangy Mae!" she snapped. "Get in the car!"

"What happened, Mama?" I asked, as I raced along beside her.

"What happened? I'll tell you what happened," she said. "You done outsmarted yo'self this time. They sitting in there planning to send you to that white school next year. They say you intelligent, you carry yo'self like a proper young lady, and you the somebody gon' integrate that school." She laughed bitterly. "I ain't buying none of it. They wanna take you away from me. That Mr. Pace of yours always wanted to take you away. I told 'em to kiss my ass 'cause you ain't going to that school. They can find another guinea pig. Them Dobsons feel the same way 'bout they daughter, but they foolish. They gon' sit there and let them people talk 'em into it. Not me."

I was not frightened by the speed or recklessness with which my mother drove. Disappointment had rendered me numb, and I blamed myself for not preparing her. Over the weeks, I could have given her some subtle hints. But I realized that the outcome probably would have been the same.

Mama turned into the Garrisons' driveway and parked behind Mr. Frank's car. "Pearl, you ain't gon' believe this," she said, as soon as Mr. Frank opened the door. "Give me a drink and let me tell you 'bout it. You ain't never gon' guess what them school people wanted wit' me."

Miss Pearl eyed me, then said, "Well, I know Tangy Mae wadn't in no kind of trouble 'cause she ain't the kind to be. I figure they want you to leave her in school another year."

"In the white school, Pearl!" Mama shouted. "They want her to go to the white school. Now you know they must think I'm some kinda fool. They gon' close town down 'cause they say one of my babies tried to burn it down, then they gon' come back and say they want one of my babies to go to school wit' theirs."

"Slow down, Rozelle," Mr. Frank said. "I think them people paying you a compliment. We all know you got a smart girl there. What you think about it, Tangy?"

"She ain't gotta think about it. She ain't going and that's that.

They wanna send five mo' children wit' her. 'Well-behaved children, so she don't have to go by herself,'" Mama said, mimicking someone from the meeting. "Tangy Mae gon' get a job—or starve. She ain't going back to school."

She meant every word she said, but my mother was a liar. I remembered her telling me that people in Georgia did not get hungry, so how could I starve? She had said that I was not going back to school, but I was. I had to.

forty-five

It amazed me that Wallace could come and go as he pleased, and although Mama knew where he spent most of his nights, she didn't make a second attempt to bring him home. Frequently, I caught her watching the road below our house, mumbling Sam's name over and over again, but mostly she just sat on the porch and sucked up the sun.

I spent lazy summer days convincing myself that I no longer loved her, and it occurred to me that I could kill her and my seat in Hell would get no wider or warmer. Remorse sometimes got the best of me; then I prayed for forgiveness for having those evil thoughts.

On the occasions when Mama ordered me to the farmhouse, I went without protest, as did Tarabelle. At first I had objected, reasoning that Sam's freedom should have also freed me, but my mother was an irrational woman who did not have to explain anything to me.

She sat on the porch now, smoking one cigarette after the other, watching Laura and Edna play in the yard. They played chase games and ball games. Laura had not touched a rope since the day Judy died, but at least her smile had returned.

"Della's having a fish fry this evening," Mama said. "That's something we oughta do. We got enough space out there in the yard to hold a lot of people, and we could make some pretty good money."

"We don't have electricity, Mama," I said. "Every fish fry I've ever been to had music playing."

She laughed. "Well, we can get some batteries for the radio. Maybe I'll move outta this house so I can have myself a fish fry." She was talking crazy, but it was lighthearted crazy so I laughed along with her.

"Do you ever think about moving?" I asked.

"Once or twice I thought about it. But then I thought my children was gon' turn out different. I thought by now half of y'all would be working and bringing in money. It's hard on a mother to be disappointed like I been. Just look at what I got outta feeding and raising all y'all. Soon as Harvey could work, he took off. Mushy ain't no good and never was. Sam running 'round trying to burn folks out, half the time I can't find Wallace, and Tarabelle's a fucking bull dyke." She winked at me through her cigarette smoke. "You didn't think I knew that, did you? Hope I'm in my grave befo' folks 'round here figure out what she is. That's one of them curses they ain't got no spell to break."

"What's a bull dyke, Mama?"

"It's a full-grown woman running 'round trying to grow a cock like a full-grown man. Trying to like other women. Don't you know nothing, Tangy Mae? Least ways Tarabelle bring in money. I can say that much for her. I don't know what to say 'bout you, but I know you ain't gon' keep sitting 'round here idle."

Please, God, don't let her start on me, I silently prayed. Aloud I said, "Mama, do you want me to get you some bathwater?"

She nodded. "Yeah. I'm gon' get on up there befo' all the best fish gone. Hope Della got something besides whiting. Got me a taste for some perch."

I readied a bath for my mother, then I joined Tarabelle and Mattie on the back porch. Tarabelle glanced at me, then turned to Mattie. "Mattie, go see if them clothes dry yet," she said.

Mattie rose from her step and walked over to the lines. We watched as she ran her hands along the row of sheets. She didn't say anything, just took the basket that had once belonged to Judy and began removing sheets, folding them, and placing them in the basket.

"Tan, can you remember the first time Mushy tried to leave?" Tarabelle asked.

I nodded.

"Mama had the sheriff go find her, then she beat Mushy and tied her to this rail for a whole week." Tarabelle trailed a finger along the porch rail as she spoke. "Remember? That's why Mushy waited so long befo' she left. She waited all the way 'til she was eighteen so nobody couldn't do nothing about it."

"Is that what you're planning to do?"

"Yeah. I figure ain't nothing nobody can do after that. Mama can't send the sheriff after me, and she can't drag me home like she did po' Martha Jean. Wonder why she ain't sent the sheriff after Wallace?"

"There's no reason to," I answered. "Wallace is still bringing his pay home. When he stops doing that, she'll probably send somebody to get him."

"I hope he stops," Tarabelle said. "I'm leaving here next month. I'm taking me a room at Miss Shirley's. She don't need them rooms now that Max and Becky gone. She said I can have one, and I got me some money saved. You can have some, Tan, if you wanna run off."

"I can't run, Tara. I've thought about it, but I can't leave Laura and Edna. Do you think Mama would make them go to the farmhouse if we weren't here?"

"Yeah. She would," Tarabelle answered bitterly. "And some dog out there would be wit' 'em, too. They wouldn't even care that they just babies."

"That's why I can't leave."

"Well, I can, and I'm going to."

"Does Miss Shirley know about you?" I asked.

"What about me?"

"Mama says you're a bull dyke, that you're running around trying to grow a thing like a man."

Tarabelle made a sound like a sneeze. "To hell wit' Mama!" she said. "She don't know nothing 'bout me, and I ain't gon' spend the rest of my life taking care of her."

"When do you intend to tell her that you're leaving?"

"Never. She'll just wake up one morning and I'll be gone. I ain't gotta tell her nothing after I turn eighteen. I used to hate you, Tan, 'cause you was so smart and I couldn't be. And I used to hate you for staying here even when I knew you couldn't leave. What good is being smart if all you can do is stay here?"

I glanced over at Mattie who had cleared one line and was working her way along another one. I could hear my mother calling me and knew she wanted me to empty her bathwater, but I ignored her. She finally gave up on me and began to call for Tara.

Tarabelle ignored her, too, and said, "Tan, you don't read them books all the time no mo'. How come?"

"They made me dream."

"Bad dreams?"

I shrugged. "Just dreams."

Mattie started toward us with the basket on her hip. I watched her come and wondered if she was ever going to do anything about her hair. It looked awful.

"You wanna go to that white school, don't you?" Tarabelle asked. When I did not answer her, she said, "I want you to go, too. But that's a awful lotta people to have to fight, and you ain't never been no good at fighting."

forty-six

M otten Street drew me outside the range of my mother's voice on those hot summer days—not every day—but just as often as it dared, and sometimes I would take Laura and Edna with me to play hula hoop, hopscotch, or hide and seek. There were days when Mama forbade me to leave the house, but Motten Street would call and I could not resist. I would depart Penyon Road under the pretense of searching for work, and I would spend those days in Skeeter's kitchen watching Mary Ann grow.

Skeeter loved to laugh and would try to make a joke of anything. I sat across from him at his kitchen table as he held Mary Ann on his lap. "Look at her," he said. "She looks like a prune even when she's sleeping. That's why God gives babies a mama and daddy. Somebody gotta think they're cute. You look at her and tell me if you see anything cute."

"You're lucky Martha Jean can't hear you," I said.

"Oh, I tell 'em all the time this a ugly baby. Watch this."

He glanced over at Martha Jean who was washing dishes at the sink. He waited until she turned and he had her attention, then he made a face, raked his fingers across it, and pointed to Mary Ann. Martha Jean smiled, shook her head, and turned back to the sink.

"See," Skeeter said. "She knows. Tell you what, you show me one cute thing on this little prune and I'll let you hold her for a spell."

I walked around the table and stood behind Skeeter to peer down at the baby. "Her nose," I said. "It's perfect."

"Shoot." Skeeter laughed. "You must be kidding. That's Velman's nose. Can't even call it a nose. That's a snout."

"Her hair," I said, anxious to hold my niece.

Skeeter pretended to study Mary Ann's hair, then he looked up at me. "Okay," he said, "I'll give her that. She took hair after her mama." He placed Mary Ann in my arms, then immediately rose from his chair and began to laugh. "Guess you get to change the diaper. That'll probably be cute, too."

"Skeeter," I protested in mock anger.

I didn't mind changing Mary Ann. I liked being alone with her. Her innocence was soothing to me, and I thought I would have liked to crawl inside her, to start life all over again. I took her into her parents' room and changed her diaper, then closed my eyes and held her against my chest until she began to protest.

When I returned to the kitchen, Martha Jean was sitting at the table and Skeeter was shuffling a deck of cards.

"You wanna get in on this hand?" he asked.

"We don't play cards," I answered. "We don't know how."

"Who don't?"

"We don't."

"Speak for yourself. Martha Jean plays. You want me to deal you a hand and teach you how?"

I shook my head. "No. It's too hot to sit in a kitchen playing cards. Why don't we go outside?"

"Who wants to go out there and have to listen to Melvin and Dot going at it like two bulldogs? I'd rather stay in here and be hot."

The Tates had been arguing for close to an hour. By the constant changes in the level of their voices, I assumed they were taking their disagreement back and forth from the house to the yard. It was such a frequent occurrence on Motten Street that most people just ignored them.

"They the strangest two I know," Skeeter said. "All Melvin wants to do is drink all day. I can't understand it. He drinks anything he can get his hands on. It's gonna kill him, too." He held five cards in his hand and studied them, then said, "Here's the funny thing about it. Melvin ain't worked a job in years. Dot gives him the money to drink with, then when he gets drunk, she spends half the night and most of the next day fussing about it. The next morning she gives him money all over again. You tell me what sense that makes."

"Maybe she wants him to drink himself to death," I said.

"That's what I think, too," Skeeter agreed. "But if that's the case, why fuss about it?"

Martha Jean placed five cards on the table and smiled at Skeeter. He looked at the cards, leaned back on his chair, and winked at her. "See," he said. "She beats me about eight hands out of ten."

Martha Jean went to the stove to check on her bread. Still holding Mary Ann, I went over to the back door and tried to catch a breeze. It was humid inside and out, and perspiration made my blouse stick to my back.

"Does Martha Jean ever make sandwiches?" I asked. "It's too hot to be in a kitchen cooking."

"Martha Jean does pretty much what she wants," Skeeter said. "There be days when she won't come near this kitchen. I be so glad when she do that I just come on in here and sit with her. Who you think wanna eat sandwiches?" He tapped his watch and signed, "Work."

"I'll walk with you," I said, turning Mary Ann over to Martha Jean. "I'd better get on home."

Skeeter and I were walking toward the railroad tracks when he spotted my mother's car. I was not where I should have been, and I knew I was caught. The car rolled in our direction, and Skeeter pulled me out of the way just as the front tires hit the sidewalk.

"Get in this car, Tangy Mae!" Mama snapped.

"I thought that was you, Rozelle," Skeeter said lightly, leaning down at her window. "You almost ran us over."

"Go to hell, Skeeter. And get out my way."

She was drunk. She and the entire car smelled of alcohol; it was not a pleasant ride. I found myself pressing my foot against the floor, trying to brake, as the car sped along the streets, barely missing poles, trees, and parked cars.

We had almost made it home when Mama stopped the car on the side of Fife Street. She opened her door and got out. I stared after her but turned my head when I saw that she was being sick right out in the open where people sitting on their porches could see her.

"Disgusting," I mumbled.

She got back in the car and lit a cigarette. I would not look at her, but I heard her inhale, and I smelled the smoke as it circulated throughout the car and drifted out of my window.

"I heard what you called me, and I didn't like it. I didn't like it one damn bit," she said, and attempted to press the burning tip of her cigarette against my thigh. I reached for the door handle, prepared to jump from the car. Sparks flew across the seat, and my mother swore and threw the cigarette from her window.

We made it home safely, and she parked the car in the field like a sane and sober person. She waited until we were inside before she told me why she had come looking for me.

"That damn Mr. Pace was out here today," she said. "What's going on between the two of y'all, Tangy Mae? He say they willing to give you pay if you go to that white school. I asked him how much he was willing to pay, but he wouldn't tell me. So I told him you can't go but he can see you out at Frances's place any night he takes a notion."

"No, Mama, you didn't!" I cried, so mortified by her words that I did not realize I was pulling my own hair until Tarabelle reached out to stop me.

"'No, Mama, you didn't,'" my mother mimicked. "Yes, hell, I did, and I think he left here mad about something. Tangy Mae, I don't want them school people coming to my house." She lit another cigarette. "And you get yo'self cleaned up. You gotta make a run wit' me."

"I've got the curse, Mama," I lied.

She shifted her gaze to Tarabelle. "Tarabelle, get yo'self cleaned up."

"I got it, too, Mama," Tarabelle said and glanced at me.

Mama sat with her chin resting against her chest and said nothing. Finally, her head rose and she said, "Laura Gail, you got the curse, too?"

"What curse, Mama?" I heard my sister ask. "What's a curse?"

Tarabelle and I glanced at each other. We had known, had even predicted this moment in time. "I'll go," I said.

My mother laughed. "You damn right, you'll go," she said. "You think you smart, Tangy Mae, but you the laziest, sorriest something I ever gave birth to."

I went out to the woods and ran the length of the path as hard and fast as I could, then I returned to the house to scrub my lazy, sorry self for a trip to the farmhouse.

forty-seven

"She's dead," Wallace said. "I tried to wake her up this morning, but I couldn't. Harvey and Mr. Dobson already know who she is. I had to tell 'em, Mama. Wouldn't be right, Harvey taking care of his grandma and don't know who she is."

Miss Pearl's hand came up to pat my mother's back. "Ain't nothing worst than being motherless," she said. "Makes you feel like you in the world alone."

"I always been alone, Pearl," Mama said. "Ain't nothing new 'bout that."

Any sadness I might have felt was overshadowed by disappointment. It was as though I had been reading a really great novel when suddenly, right at the climax, I found an entire chapter missing. Now I might never know that significant something that had taken place between the beginning and the ending.

"You can come on home now, Wallace. Ain't nothing to hold you on Selman Street, and I don't want you at the funeral. The less people know, the better," Mama said.

"I gotta go to the funeral," Wallace said, "and I don't wanna come back out here. Somebody gotta take care of Mr. Grodin."

"I can't believe this," Tarabelle said. "Mama, how come you didn't tell us that ol' woman was kin to us?"

"You didn't need to know," Mama told her. "Nobody woulda knew if Wallace hadn't got too big for his britches."

"I'm going to the funeral, too," Tarabelle announced.

"You didn't even know her. Why you wanna go?" Mama asked.

"Just 'cause I can, and you can't stop me. Today is August twenty-eighth, and I'm eighteen. I'm grown."

Mama began to laugh. She stomped her feet against the floor and clapped her hands. It was so bizarre that Miss Pearl's hand ceased its ineffectual consolation and flew to her mouth.

All Tarabelle had to do was pack her things and leave, but she did not do that. She walked across the hall and entered our mother's room, and the sound of scratching, like a big tomcat clawing on planks, reached us in the front room.

Mama sprang from her chair and rushed toward the room. "What you doing?" she yelled. "Get outta here! This is my room."

I had followed my mother. I saw my sister prying up the floorboards with her bare hands.

"I wanna know what's in that box, Mama," Tarabelle said. "Before I leave here today, I'm gon' know what's in that box. What's so important that you woulda killed us all for?"

"Give it to me!" Mama shrieked, and reached for the box that was still attached, by nails, to the floorboard. It was weathered and discolored, but it was the same box that she had put under the house all those years ago.

Tarabelle managed to pry the box from the board and struggled to free the sliding plate. Mama rushed toward her, and as she did, the plate slipped free. Locks of hair, tied together by moldy, withered ribbons, spilled out onto the floor.

"Hair!" Tarabelle cried. "You woulda killed us for hair, you crazy bitch?"

Mama leapt into the air, mindless of the rusted nails that jutted out from the boards. She landed a foot squarely at the center of Tarabelle's back. Tarabelle jerked forward from the blow, but quickly sprang back, turned, and swung a board at Mama's legs. Mama was out of reach. Then, as the board swished past her knees, she moved in determinedly, gripped Tarabelle's hair with both hands, and stepped behind my sister. Tarabelle dropped the board. Her head snapped back and her eyelids fluttered rapidly. Mama untangled one hand from Tarabelle's hair, made a fist, and brought it down with all her strength. Tarabelle's nose seemed to explode, and blood flew everywhere.

Tarabelle was temporarily dazed, but recovered quickly. She twisted her body around and clawed at Mama's arms. She swung a fist at Mama's abdomen that connected but did no damage. She steadily clawed and punched until she brought our mother down with her. Mama, with one hand still entangled in Tarabelle's hair, hit the floor sideways, right over the opening created by the missing boards. Tarabelle's head was yanked forward with what seemed enough force to snap her neck. Fighting for survival, she opened her mouth and sank her teeth into the flesh of Mama's calf. The blood from Tarabelle's nose covered them both.

Mama let go of Tarabelle's hair. She screamed, bucked and kicked, but could not loose herself from Tarabelle's teeth. With her free hand, she reached behind her back and made feeble attempts to strike.

Wallace and I moved forward to separate them. I coaxed and tugged at Tarabelle while Wallace restrained Mama's hand. I managed to get Tarabelle out of the room, and there was Miss Pearl, standing in the hallway, peeling red crepe paper from white socks. She removed one sock from the pair and pressed it against my sister's bleeding nose.

Wallace was breathless when he stepped from Mama's room, but Miss Pearl did not give him a chance to catch his breath. "Take Tarabelle out to the yard," she said. "See if you can't get that bleeding stopped."

Wallace looked at me. "I ain't never coming back, Tan," he said, his chest heaving.

"Eventually, she'll come and get you," I told him.

"She can't," he said, staring at me oddly, as if to say, Tan, I've got another secret.

Miss Zadie was buried on the first Thursday in September when the county fair was in town, the weather was still pleasantly warm and the sky was a clear blue. It did not seen a proper time for death.

Laura, Edna, and I were cloaked in heavy mourning, and it had nothing to do with a grandmother we had never known as such. I think we were mourning the loss of stability. The departure of Wallace and Tarabelle brought a bleak finality to all that remained of our family.

Mama crawled from her bed on that Thursday, went out for a short while, and returned to sit in her favorite spot on the front porch. She unscrewed the lid from a Mason jar and began to drink. Fresh abrasions on her face indicated that her bugs had returned, and I think she was trying to poison them with the spirits she gulped from the jar.

Miss Pearl was the only person who came to our house after the funeral. She sat on the porch with Mama and asked for a drink of water. I placed the last of our ice in a jar and dipped water over it, then took it out to her.

"Thanks," she said, reaching for the jar. "That was a nice service they had for Miss Zadie. Nearly everybody in town showed up. She was well liked."

"They didn't know her," Mama said bitterly. "Was Tarabelle there?"

"Sho' was. Harvey, Wallace, and Tarabelle. Folks was just shocked that you didn't come, Rosie. They got yo' name wrote here on this paper." Miss Pearl reached into her pocketbook and withdrew a folded sheet of paper. "Folks couldn't believe it. They kept asking me, and I just went on and tol' 'em the truth. Ain't no need to hide it now when it's wrote on this here paper for the world to see. Got all yo' chilluns listed here, too."

Mama wept softly. "Who went and done that?" she asked. "That ol' woman dead now. Why folks gotta know 'bout me?"

"I reckon the ol' man done it," Miss Pearl answered, setting her jar on the porch floor, and leaning over to pat Mama's back. "Ain't no need to cry 'bout it, Rosie. She was yo' mama plain and simple. Ain't no denying that."

"She was a liar," Mama said. "Everything she ever tol' me was a lie. That hair that Tarabelle went and spoiled—that ol' woman tol' me I could hold folks wit' that hair. It was just a lie, Pearl. All my babies gone. Everybody I ever loved is gone."

Miss Pearl dropped her hand from Mama's back, and picked up the Mason jar. "Here, Rosie. You take another sip of this and calm yo' nerves. We been friends a long time and I ain't never knowed nobody you loved enough to make you carry on like this."

Mama drained the last of the corn whiskey from her jar, placed the jar on the floor, then turned toward Miss Pearl. "You think I didn't love Sam, Pearl? He wadn't no more than two when I cut his hair, and where is he now? It wadn't s'pose to be like this. All my babies s'pose to be here wit' *me*—not scattered all over the place. I can't even get Wallace to come home, and do you know why, Pearl? It's 'cause that ol' woman peed in a bottle and tol' him to sprinkle it on me if I come near him."

She screamed then, so loud that I jerked back and fell against the door frame.

"Ol' dead woman piss in a bottle," she sobbed. "It'll burn holes in yo' skin, Pearl. It'll make warts grow on yo' face, and that damn Wallace was gon' put it on me. I'm his mother, and he was gon' throw it on me. That hair don't mean shit. All them years, and you seen what happened. You seen Wallace try to fight me."

Miss Pearl gently rubbed Mama's arm. "He wadn't trying to fight you, Rosie. He was trying to help you."

"Who ever tried to help me?" Mama asked, slapping one palm against her chest. "Nobody but you, Pearl. You the only somebody I got in this world. I ain't had no mother. That woman—she dead, but y'all don't know what she was like. She took my hair. I seen her put it in a box, and she said I wouldn't never be able to leave. She was right, too. I can't get outta here. Every time I try, something pulls me back. It's a spell, but it don't work for me. Everybody leaving me and I can't go nowhere 'cause I don't know how to work that spell."

She leaned forward, as if the pain was too much to bear. I found myself moving toward her. I extended a hand and touched her heaving shoulder, then I brought her head to rest against my abdomen.

"Don't cry, Mama," I pleaded. "Please don't cry. I love you, and I won't leave you. You can have my hair, but please don't cry."

Laura came to stand beside me. She placed her hands on Mama's knees. "Mine, too, Mama," she said. "You can have my hair."

"It won't work," Mama sobbed. "All the hair in the world won't work when she didn't tell me how to do it right. She never tol' me nothing. I'm glad she's dead."

Miss Pearl pulled a handkerchief from her pocketbook and dabbed at her eyes. "You ain't glad, Rosie," she said. "You just hurting the way you s'pose to when you lose a mother. It's a sad thing."

Mama leaned heavily against my abdomen and wrapped her arms around my waist. She began to cry harder, and I believed she was grieving for her mother. I knew I felt something for mine. She held onto me until her tears had subsided, then she reached down for the Mason jar and brought it to her lips. It was empty, and she threw it over the side of the porch where it landed and broke in the gully.

"I need something to drink, Pearl," she said. "I ain't got nothing. Ain't nobody left in this house to bring in no money, and I know that man gon' put us out."

"You can get a job, Rosie," Miss Pearl said. "Ain't nothing to stop you from working. I don't know why you ain't married somebody by now. You oughta have a husband taking care of you."

"I'm going to bed," Mama said, as though Miss Pearl had not spoken. She rose unsteadily from the chair and braced herself against the porch wall. "I can't think, and I don't know what to do."

I started to follow after her, but Miss Pearl hooked my arm with her own and guided me down the steps. When we were on the ground, she whispered, "Mushy's in town. I heard it from Shirley that she's staying at Skeeter's house. I don't know how Rosie gon' act when she finds out."

"Are you sure?" I asked. "Why wouldn't she come home first?"

"I don't know, but Shirley ain't got no reason to lie. I just wanted to let you know befo' somebody 'round here lets it slip to Rosie."

I didn't know what Miss Pearl expected me to do with the information, but I nodded, then watched her walk up Penyon Road in the heat of the midday sun, and I thought she had to be the best friend anyone could ask for. She was always there for Mama, but Mama never seemed to be there for her.

Later, as I sat in the kitchen with my sisters forking through peas and rice, my mother called me into her room. She was no longer crying, but her gray eyes had darkened like storm clouds. She stared a me for a moment, then wrapped her arms around herself and began to shake.

"Whose is it?" she asked. "Whose is it, Tangy Mae?"

"What, Mama?" I asked in confusion.

She snatched the pillow from beneath her head and held it to her chest, then she bounced her legs against the mattress. "I know you done got yo'self knocked up," she said. "I went to see them school people this morning—just this very morning—and told them you can go to that white school. You can't do this to me now, not when that school gon' start next week. That Mr. Pace say they gon' pay us what they call a stipend, baby. We need that money, you know we do. How can you do this to me now?"

"I'm not pregnant, Mama."

"I done seen it," she said, as fresh tears spilled from her eyes. "What we gon' do now?"

The curse was with me as she spoke, and I tried to tell her, but she shoved me away. There were no changes in my body, or at least I didn't think there were, but Mama had seen life in Martha Jean's body long before anybody else had. Maybe she saw it in me, too. I sat beside her on the bed, a chasm between us, and my voice echoed in hollowness, "I'm sorry, Mama!"

I did not know why I was apologizing, but it seemed the right thing to do, the only thing to do. She wouldn't listen to me though, and because I could not console her, and she would not explain anything to me, I left her alone to rock the bed with worry.

When the bed ceased to shake and the crying finally ended, I slipped into the hallway and peeked into her room. She was sitting on the side of her bed, her hands moving frantically, pulling at bugs, and I thought for a second that I could see them, too, dripping from her hair, covering her neck, and crawling up and down her arms.

forty-eight

Nobody expected integration to take place, considering the tension that hung over Pakersfield following the fires, but it did. Mama refused my transfer to Pakersfield High, giving up the much needed stipend to retain our dignity. Her reasoning: she would not allow me to parade my swollen belly in front of the town's white folk (although my abdomen was as flat as a board). She had, however, permitted me to begin my junior year at the Plymouth School. For that I was grateful, but I knew the only reason I was in school was because Mama had not quite decided what to do with me.

Every day I came straight home from school and did whatever she ordered. I cooked, I cleaned, I went to the farmhouse. It was in my best interest to abide by her ever-changing rules, and I obeyed them until one October afternoon when I felt an overwhelming desire to see my sister. I summoned up the courage to leave school and go to Motten Street.

Mushy, wearing blue slacks and a sleeveless white blouse, opened the door for me. "Tan!" she said excitedly. "I was wondering when I was gon' see you. Wallace been by, and Tara and Harvey. Harvey say he got him a house up there on Plymouth now. You the only one I ain't seen, and it sho' is good to see you."

She made her way to the couch and stepped behind the coffee table where a opened bottle of gin and a single glass stood side by side. "I'm so bored, Tan. The dancing man still at work, Skeeter out chasing after Miss Shirley, and every time Mary Ann goes to sleep, Martha Jean think she gotta go, too."

"When are you coming out to the house to see Mama?" I asked.

She picked up her glass and finished off the remaining swallow. "You act like you done forgot that Mama threw hot coffee in my face the last time I was here."

"I haven't forgotten, but she's not doing well. Now that Wallace and Tara are gone, and Laura and Edna are at school all day, the house is empty. I think it bothers her."

Mushy poured herself another drink, studied the glass for a few seconds, then glanced up at me and said, "Tan, please don't start talking to me about Mama. Do you know y'all live in the only house in the world ain't got electricity yet?"

I nodded, although I knew it wasn't true, then I eased down beside her on the couch. "Mushy, you do need to go see Mama."

"I done told you, Tan," she warned. "Last time I came here, I didn't know what I was doing. It was like I was running 'round chasing after my own tail. I wound up leaving here sick on rotgut and rain. Not this time, though." She shook her head. "Not this time."

I studied her face, and beyond the mild intoxication I could see a quiet seriousness. "What are you planning to do, Mushy?" I asked.

"I don't want you to worry about it. You just leave things to me. That's why I'm here."

"Mama thinks I'm pregnant," I said. "She's been asking Miss Pearl to get it out, but I don't think there's anything there."

We sat in silence until Mushy reached over and squeezed my hand. In an effort to comfort me, she said, "If you are, Tan, it ain't the end of the world."

"It would be for me. I'd have to drop out of school, and Mr. Pace would hate me. I'd have to stay in Pakersfield for the rest of my life, feeling ashamed of myself. I'm embarrassed enough already, Mushy. I go out to that farmhouse at night and pretend to be a woman, then

I go to school during the day and pretend to be a child. Sometimes I get confused."

Mushy brought her glass to her lips again. She swallowed hard, then said, "Whorehouse, Tan. Call it what it is. It's a goddamn whorehouse, not a farmhouse."

"I don't think I'm pregnant. I think Mama just said that to keep me from going to the Pakersfield High School. I don't think she really cares, or she'd stop making me be with all those men."

Mushy was quiet, and seemed to be considering my statement when Velman came in from work. She abandoned the pain of thinking and offered him a drink, which he refused.

"I'm hungry, not thirsty," Velman said. "What's Martha Jean got fixed in there? I don't smell nothing."

"That's 'cause there ain't nothing," Mushy said. "Come on and have a drink. You gon' need one. I know I do. I done quit my job and gave up my room so I could come back down here. Tan's pregnant, and I believe to my soul Martha Jean is, too. Why couldn't y'all just leave me alone? Why y'all have to keep writing them letters to me?"

Velman bit down on his bottom lip and stared at Mushy. "Martha Jean can't be pregnant," he said. "Mary Ann ain't five months old yet."

"Don't be stupid, dancing man. She can be, and she probably is. She can't stay woke long enough to wash her own face, and she can't butter a piece of bread without puking all over the place. What you think it is?"

The answer to Mushy's question seemed to wait in the bottle on the coffee table. Velman and Mushy reached for it simultaneously, but Mushy was quicker. "Get a glass," she said. "I ain't drinking behind nobody the way pregnancy catching 'round here."

Instead of going for a glass, Velman turned to his right, moved swiftly down the hallway, and entered his bedroom. He came out a few minutes later dragging Martha Jean with him. Her gray dress was wrinkled, her hair was tangled, and she appeared to be sleepwalking. Velman reached out and playfully stroked her abdomen, but she brushed his hand away. She opened her eyes with what seemed like great effort, then she gave him an angry glare and retraced her steps to the bedroom.

"All day she wouldn't talk to me or Skeeter," Mushy said. "I think Martha Jean going through something she don't know how to talk about. She'll get over it, though."

Velman's shoulders visibly sagged as he turned his back to us and entered the kitchen. Moments later I could hear him opening and closing cabinet doors, and slamming pots against the tabletop. I pushed myself up from the couch.

"Where you going?" Mushy asked.

"He has to eat, Mushy, and somebody has to cook."

I found Velman standing at the sink doing nothing, except staring down into the dark, dry drain.

"What's wrong?" I asked.

He stepped away from the sink and ran a hand through his hair. "I don't know," he said. "It's something, but I don't know what it is. I think we missing too many words, little sister. I don't know how to tell her to trust me. I mean, I can make the sign, but it's like it don't mean nothing. She never wants me to leave. I can't go to the filling station or the store without her getting upset. All I can do is go to work, and even then I got a feeling she keeps her eyes on the clock. How do I tell her to trust me?"

"She does," I said. "She does trust you, Velman. She moved here with you, and she's shared a bed with you and had your child. She does trust you."

"That's not trust!" he said. "That's called staying alive. She came out here with me to keep that crazy mother of hers from killing her. You think just 'cause she share a bed with me that she trust me? Don't take this the wrong way, but how many men have you shared a bed with and thought you could trust?"

Through the back door screen came the laughter of children playing outside, and a cool October breeze. Velman ran the palm of his hand across his face and moved slowly toward the door, keeping his back to me.

"Little sister, I . . ." His voice trailed off.

"It's all right," I said. "I know what you meant, but we both know that what you and Martha Jean have is different from what goes on at the farmhouse. She loves you, Velman."

He turned toward me, and the tight, angry expression on his face withered into one of helplessness. "I just wish I could hear her say it. Just once."

For his sake, I became my sister. At least, that's what I told myself. I took a deep breath and stepped forward. Before I could lose my nerve or change my mind, I wrapped my arms around his neck, stood on my toes, and kissed his lips. "She loves you," I whispered. "With all her heart, she loves you. She'd die for you, Velman."

As gracefully as he did everything, he peeled my arms from his neck and stepped away from me, his back pressing against the door frame. "Are those her words or yours, little sister?"

The screen door banged, and I shuddered from the unexpected sound and from the realization of what I had just done. I started after him, but stopped when I saw that he had gone no farther than the pecan tree in his backyard. He leaned against the tree with his back to the house. He was thinking. Maybe he was thinking that he had made a mistake and that it should have been me he had rescued from Penyon Road.

I sighed wistfully, feeling neither guilt nor shame, and stepped away from the door. As I turned, I saw bare feet and the skirt of a wrinkled, gray dress exit the kitchen. I sprinted across the kitchen floor and glanced down the hallway, but it was empty. I shrugged, took a glass from the kitchen cupboard, and returned to the living room.

Mushy's legs were stretched lengthwise on the couch and her back was propped against an armrest. Her eyes were closed. I thought she was asleep, but when I reached for the bottle of gin, she tapped the rim of her glass with a fingernail, and said, "Pour me one, Tan."

"How long have you been sitting here drinking?" I asked. "You're gonna make yourself sick."

"I'm trying to work up the nerve to go see Mama. Everybody keeps telling me how I oughta go see my mother." She gave a bitter laugh. "They don't know I'm trying my best."

"She can't do anything to you," I said. "You're grown, Mushy. Why are you still afraid of her?"

"I'm not afraid of her; I'm afraid of *becoming* her. That's the shit scares the hell outta me. Look at me, Tan. I'm starting to look like her. The other day I was looking in the mirror, and I hadn't had nothing to drink. Not nothing. And it seemed like to me that my eyes was turning gray, and they was starting to slant at the corners. Sometimes I open my mouth and it's her words that come out. I came back to save you, Tan. I'm gon' get you away from her. I'm gon' save you, and Laura, and little Edna."

Mushy babbled on for a long time, giving her drunken philosophy of life. She talked about how she was going to kidnap us when she had enough money. She talked about the sheriff and the FBI and how she was smarter than they were. I listened, but mostly I concentrated on the terrible-tasting liquid in my glass, wishing I had left it in the bottle.

Velman eased back into the room during Mushy's slurred commentary on women. "Just like Lake Erie," she was saying. "It just stretches on and on, seems like forever. Curtis used to take me down to the lake, and I'd study that water. It came to me that women are just like that lake. They do everything to it, but it's still beautiful. I wish you could see it, Tan. They fish from it, throw garbage in it, and sail boats in it, but it's still just as wide and beautiful as ever. That's what women are like, and we ain't gon' run dry. Sell a bit, and five minutes later we just as deep and wet and full as we was before. So what the hell?"

"Damn!" Velman whistled. "What did I walk in on?"

I was relieved that he was able to look at me, and to make eye contact. "Little sister, you mind scrambling me up a couple of eggs?" he asked.

For you, I'd walk on water.

"I don't mind," I answered.

The aroma of sausage and eggs brought Martha Jean out of her bedroom. Mary Ann was cradled in one arm as Martha Jean stopped in the doorway between the kitchen and the living room. She glanced toward Velman, then stepped into the kitchen and faced me with a cold stare. With one hand, she shoved the handle of the skillet. It crashed to the floor and lay upside down, smothering the eggs. She spotted the plate of sausages on the table, and that, too, went clattering to the floor.

I skirted past her and stepped out of the kitchen. Velman sprang from his chair, and even Mushy brought her feet to the floor and sat in an upright position. The three of us stared through the doorway at Martha Jean as she held Mary Ann in her arms and kicked the shattered pieces of the plate with her bare feet. When she was done, she turned and brushed past me, purposely ramming her elbow against my chest. She returned to her bedroom and slammed the door, shutting us out.

Velman slumped back onto his chair and held his head with both hands, and I could hear Mushy mumbling something to him as I cleaned the mess from the kitchen floor. I could not worry about what they were saying. Martha Jean had witnessed my betrayal. She had seen me wrap my arms around her husband, had watched me taste and inhale him. She had looked inside of me and seen the wanting in my heart. But Martha Jean would have to understand that I needed Velman more than I had ever needed anything else in my life. I would have to make her understand.

"Where did he go?" I asked Mushy when I walked into the front room and did not see Velman.

"He went to get Wallace, and I done called Harvey and Tarabelle to come over. We a mess, Tan. We need to be all of us together. We gon' sit down, and talk, and heal. And maybe have a drink or two."

"Mushy, I can't stay over here. I should've been home by now."

"You can stay. Ain't gon' hurt nobody for you to be wit' us for awhile. When you go home, I'm going wit' you. Mama gon' be so happy to see me she won't even know how late it is," Mushy said with mock cheerfulness.

forty-nine

At Mushy's bidding, we all convened at Skeeter's house, but we did not heal. We bickered over insignificant things. We witnessed the cruelest side of Harvey as he berated his wife and drove the joy from her eyes.

Tarabelle puffed on a cigarette, put it out, and lit another. She sighed, shifted on her chair, then finally said, "Carol Sue, you know you ain't gotta take that shit. You got a mama and a daddy you can go home to."

"This my wife, Tarabelle!" Harvey snapped. "What we do ain't got a damn thing to do wit' you."

"That's right," Tarabelle agreed. "It ain't got a damn thing to do wit' me. She the fool 'cause I'd cut yo' motherfuckin' throat if you made my face look like that."

Harvey started to say something else but Tarabelle-the-brave turned her back to him, ignoring him, and said to me, "Did you hear about Mattie?"

"What about her?" I asked, as I kept watch on Harvey from the corner of my eye.

"She got married. Married one of her daddy's friends. A drunk.

He done moved her out there in the country. Next thing you know, she'll probably have fifteen babies and be cockeyed and white-mouthed like her Mama."

"I didn't know," I said. We all fell silent again.

Mushy drank. She sat in a very unladylike manner with her forearms resting against the edge of the coffee table, and her shoulders hunched. She had not spoken a word since Harvey's initial blow to Carol Sue's face. Velman and Martha Jean sat side by side like strangers, neither touching nor acknowledging each other.

Wallace was restless, and paced from the kitchen door to the front door, back and forth, and I noticed how, under my nose, Wallace had grown right over my head. Things had a way of doing that, I supposed. They just grew and grew and snowballed until no one could tell how anything had ever started. My family, people I had known all my life, were turning into strangers. I was at a loss to say why and when it had begun, but it was so.

And, at the end of this dreary evening, Mushy did not return to Penyon Road with me. She called Richard Mackey, who came and took her away from the gloom of Skeeter's house.

Tarabelle was the only upbeat person in the room. She crushed out her cigarette in a dish provided by Martha Jean, then she turned to me and asked, "How's Mama these days?"

"She's doing all right," I answered.

"Bugs still crawling all over her?"

"Sometimes."

"Well, Tan, I'm going to Hell," she announced cheerfully. "I always wondered 'bout that, and now I'm certain. I got it straight from Reverend Nelson's mouth."

"What are you talking about?" I asked, and glanced at the others to see if they were paying attention to Tarabelle. They were.

"You know that 'honor thy mother' thing Mama always be making us say? Remember how they used to make us say it in Sunday School, too, and made us read it on the Sunday School cards. Well, I figured it must be in the Bible, so I asked Reverend Nelson. It's true. He showed it to me, Tan, and read it to me 'cause I couldn't figure it out. It's in Exodus, and it say, 'Honor thy father and thy mother.' I told him I ain't got no father and I already done beat up my mother. He said I need to ask forgiveness from God and Mama or else I'm gon' burn in Hell. I ain't gon' ask neither one for forgiveness 'cause I ain't sorry. Guess I'm going to Hell. What you think, Tan?"

I just stared at her, as did everybody else. Tarabelle lit another cigarette, rose from the couch, and walked out.

It was dark, a little after nine, when the rest of us left Skeeter's house. Velman dropped me off at the turn of the bend on Penyon Road. "I'd go in with you if I thought it would do any good," he said, "but I know it would just make things worse."

I nodded, and silently admonished myself for my stupidity. It hadn't seemed so bad when I'd thought Mushy would be coming home with me, but now I was afraid. I eased my way around to the rear of the house, then slowly pushed open the back door and stepped into the darkness of the kitchen. Holding my breath, I listened for sounds of my mother's presence, expecting her to leap from one of the corners like a jack-in-the-box. My heart raced, sending a pulsating echo through my skull, but nothing sprang out at me. Nothing happened. There was no sign of Mama, and when I dared to breathe, there was no scent of her.

In the front room, I dropped to my knees and reached for the pile of folded blankets. My hand swept across a furry ball, like a small animal, only there was no warmth to this fur, and it did not make a sound. It was light as air and moved freely with the sway of my palm. As I raised my hand, particles of fuzz adhered to my fingers. I rubbed my hands together trying to sense what I had touched. Finally, I threw caution to the wind, and lit the kerosene lamp.

A scream tangled in my throat as I stared in alarm at a floor covered with what appeared to be human hair. I pulled away the blankets that covered my sisters, and both girls awoke, saw me, reached out to me, and began to weep. I wanted to wrap them in my arms, but I could not move. I could only stare at their naked heads. Thin lines of blood had spiraled and dried around the few remaining strands of hair that jutted out from their scalps.

"They said I could have it."

I whirled to the sound of my mother's voice. Either she had quietly slipped into the room, or the pounding in my head had muffled her footsteps. How she had come was irrelevant; why she had come was crucial. In one hand she held a pair of scissors, and in her other a pair of pinking shears.

"I thought you had done run off, Tangy Mae," she said in a weary voice, as she advanced on me at a slow, steady pace. "I can't have no mo' of my children running off. It ain't right. I need yo' hair, and you said I could have it. I done figured out what was wrong. I never had enough hair to work the spell right."

There was no way I was going to stand still and let her butcher my scalp the way she had done Laura's and Edna's. I did not have to think about it. I dipped my shoulders and made a move to rush past her. She stepped in front of me to block my passage, and the pinking shears fell from her hand and clattered against the floor. As she leaned down to retrieve them, I darted behind the coal stove and rushed for the back door. I could hear Laura and Edna screaming, screaming, screaming, but I could not stop.

My feet touched the porch, then I was on the ground. My mind reeled. If I ran for the woods, I would be blocked in by Mr. Barnwell's fence, and God only knew what was on the other side. If I ran for Fife Street, my mother could get in her car and run me down. I knew I had to make a decision. If I continued to stand, frozen, in darkness, my mother would burst through the back door and seize me. Moving by memory, I turned the corner of the house and rushed past the front porch. I would go to Mushy, she would help me. I was moving fast when a voice out of the night calmly whispered my name.

"Tangy Mae."

She was on the front steps, near the ground. I could not see her, but she was there. I heard the snip of the scissors, then I saw the sudden beam from a flashlight, and I heard my mother's feet pounding the dirt behind me as I raced along Penyon Road toward Fife Street.

A ray of light swept across the field, over my head, in the direction of the gully, as Mama searched for me with her flashlight. I thought I could feel the light on my back. In a second her scissors would sail through the air and pierce my spine and I would bleed to death, face down, on Penyon Road. Tears spilled from my eyes, and I fought the impulse to scream. If I screamed and brought shame to my mother, she would kill me over and over again. I ran, reached the top of Fife Street, then hid behind hedge bushes and waited for the sound of my mother's car. After a long period of silence, I rose from the bushes and made my way toward the flats.

fifty

"**M**ama, what the hell have you done?" Mushy shouted.

"All this time you been in town and ain't once stopped by to see me," Mama responded calmly. "Now you gon' step up in my house raising yo' voice at me?"

Mushy sighed, keeping her distance from our mother. "Mama, what'd you do to these babies?" she asked. "I'm gon' get the sheriff out here. You done went too far this time."

"Get 'im," Mama said. "Ain't no law say I can't cut my children's hair. If there was a law against cutting hair, half the town would be in jail."

"It ain't right, Mama," Mushy said. "How they gon' go to school wit' they heads looking like that?"

Mama did not answer. She picked up her cigarettes from the table, shook one loose from the pack and lit it. She leaned her head against the back of the chair and blew smoke toward the ceiling. We stood in silence and watched.

It was five o'clock in the morning, and we had walked from the flats to Penyon Road. I had waited on Skeeter's porch for Richard

Mackey to bring Mushy home. Although Velman wanted to know why I had returned, I would not tell him. I was too ashamed to share with him the price my defiance had cost my sisters, so I had waited for Mushy, who was nearly as much to blame.

We stood in the front room and watched our mother blow smoke rings in the air. Mushy stared at Laura and Edna; I scanned the room for the scissors and pinking shears. Finally Mushy said, "I'm going back up to Skeeter's to pack my things, then I'm coming on home."

Mama glanced up. "You telling me or asking me?"

"I'm asking, Mama," Mushy mumbled. She was wearing the same gray-and-white dress she had worn the night before, only it was wrinkled now. Her eyes were bloodshot, as though she had not slept a wink, and neither comb nor brush had touched her hair.

"Awright then. I guess you can stay for a spell," Mama said.

And it was over—like nothing had ever happened—like Laura and Edna did not resemble plucked chickens. Mushy would move in, make everything right, and we would get on with living. I suspected this peaceful scenario would fall apart at any moment.

fifty-one

Each time I glanced at my sisters, I felt the guilt of disobedience. Mama kept them home from school, and I was glad
about that because the teasing they would have suffered would
have been far worse than missing lessons. Mushy and Mama put
their heads together and decided I should inform Mr. Hewitt that
the girls had tetter. This would justify their absenteeism and explain
their lack of hair.

The relationship between Mama and Mushy was volatile. Mama
could not forgive Mushy for not coming out to the house sooner
and Mushy admonished Mama for her disciplinary tactics. There
were days, though, when I would come in from school to find
them rolling with laughter or planning a night out together.
Sometimes they would compete against each other in an effort to
entertain Laura and Edna with bedtime stories. Those were really
nice days. The bad days were when they pooled their pennies to
buy corn whiskey, or when Richard Mackey came to the house
to take Mushy out, or when Mama pulled at bugs and Mushy's
left eye twitched.

We made it through Thanksgiving Day without incident, but on

Christmas Day, Mama and Mushy had their worst argument ever. It started when Richard bought Mushy a sweater and a watch. He had also given her money, which she had used to buy Christmas gifts. Then Brenda Mackey arrived at our house in a rage, wanting to fight with Mushy. Brenda and Mama had double-teamed Mushy with insults. Mushy handled it well; she had laughed at them both, then gulped down a pint of corn whiskey.

We had been invited to the Garrisons' to bring in the New Year. Mushy wanted to celebrate with Richard, but she told this to me, not to Mama. Mama knew though, and she kept reminding Mushy that Richard was married. Mushy put on her cheerful face, and agreed to stop seeing Richard, but her left eye twitched something awful.

At the Garrisons' house, Mr. Frank opened the door for us, then made himself comfortable on the couch and stared at the television screen as we removed our coats. Laura and Edna rushed over to join him in front of the television.

Mushy purposely hung back in the corner by the coatrack. She waited until Mama was in the kitchen with Miss Pearl, then she whispered, "Tan, I don't think I can stay too much longer in that house wit' Mama. I'm thinking I might go back to Cleveland, and Richard is thinking about going wit' me."

"He's married, Mushy."

"I know. I hear it every day from Mama. Tan, you think Mama ain't never been wit' a married man? She's a hypocrite, that's what makes me the maddest."

I shrugged. It was true. Mushy shook her head as though she could read my thoughts, then arm in arm we went into the kitchen. On the stove, a pot of black-eyed peas sent a spray of steam into the air that mingled with the fragrance of collard greens and candied yams. My mouth watered for just a taste, but I knew the meal was meant for tomorrow.

Mama and Miss Pearl had already filled their glasses from a holiday bottle of Seagram's 7 Crown when Mushy joined them. I sat at the table and listened to the women swap stories about the people in our town. They were able to find so much to laugh about; I wondered who was sitting at a table somewhere laughing at us.

When the giggling trailed off, Mushy asked with a slight smile,

"Mama, when you start getting all that gray hair? I didn't notice it out at the house under the kerosene lamp, but here you can see it real good."

Miss Pearl laughed. "Mushy, yo' mama ain't gon' stay young forever. What you think?"

"I didn't think she was gon' get old so fast, Miss Pearl. You ain't changing."

"We all changing, chil'. I don't get 'round nothing like I used to. Remember, Rosie, how we used to stay up all night, dancing and drinking, then go to work the next day like it wadn't nothing? I can't do that no mo'."

"Ain't no gray in my head," Mama said. "Tangy Mae, you get up and see."

I eased off of my chair and went to stand over her. I barely scanned her hair before I said, "You have a little bit, Mama, but it's pretty."

I wanted to steer clear of any trouble, but they seemed to deliberately pull me in. Mushy sipped from her drink and studied our mother. "I remember when me and Mama could go out together and people thought we was sisters," Mushy said. "They sho' don't think that no mo'."

"Mushy, why can't I just sit here in peace?" Mama asked. "I ain't old. Why you wanna start picking on me?"

"Nah, Mama, I ain't picking. I was just remembering, 'cause we used to have some good times." Mushy turned to face Miss Pearl. "Miss Pearl, you ever been out to the farmhouse?"

"What farmhouse is that?" Miss Pearl asked.

"There's a hundred farmhouses out through the country," Mushy said, "but when you say *the farmhouse,* everybody know where you talking 'bout."

"I done heard about it," Miss Pearl said evasively, "but I ain't never been out there."

Mama was running her hands through her hair, attempting to wipe the gray out, I assumed. She gave a sour grunt, and said, "Pearl, you oughta be shame of yo'self. You the one showed it to me."

Miss Pearl glanced quickly toward the front room. "Be quiet, Rosie," she whispered. "Frank ain't got no business knowing what I used to do. I ain't been out there in years."

Stunned into silence, I stared at Miss Pearl, trying to imagine her at the farmhouse. In my eyes, she was above the transgressions of that horrible place. Maybe she had danced in the parlor, or had a drink or two, and did not know what went on in the rooms upstairs.

"Mr. Frank know all about that place," Mushy said. "Ain't that right, Mama? I musta been 'bout 'leven or twelve when Mama tried to get Mr. Frank to screw me. He wouldn't do it though, and I always respected him for that. He looked at Mama and said, 'Rozelle, you oughta be shame of yo'self bringing that baby out here. Get her up and take her home!' Them was his exact words. I ain't never gon' forget it 'cause he the only man ever came out there didn't jump on top of me."

Miss Pearl placed her glass on the table and folded her arms across her bosom. Her face was tightly puckered as though the Seagram's had suddenly turned bitter. Her eyes were like balls of burning coal as they shifted from Mama to Mushy.

Mushy smiled with assumed innocence. "I always thought Mr. Frank hated Mama," she said. "Just goes to show. Year or so before I left here, you couldn't keep 'em apart. He was all time bringing things out to the house. Bought Mama a dress once that was too fancy to wear anywhere in Triacy County. You remember, Mama?"

The hum of the television reached the kitchen like the swarming of angry bees, and I shivered. Miss Pearl's erratic breathing caused her pudgy arms to bounce against her breasts. She gave Mama ample opportunity to refute these charges, and I willed my mother to deny them, but Mama would not. She made no denials, excuses, or apologies. She picked up her drink, took a sip, and stared defiantly at the woman she had wronged.

Miss Pearl rose slowly from her chair. Tears flowed from her eyes, drenched her cheeks, and turned her angry face a darker shade of black. She balled her right hand into a fist and swung it with enough force to send Mama, and the chair on which she sat, tumbling to the floor.

For a moment, I thought I saw something akin to shame in my mother's eyes, but it was merely the blinking of astonishment. Her head rested on the kitchen floor, and she brought a hand up to touch her face. She was staring up at Miss Pearl when Mr. Frank entered the room.

"What's going on in here?" Mr. Frank asked, glancing first at Mama stretched on the floor, then at his wife, who had both fists balled.

"Let me help you up, Mama," Mushy offered.

Mama brushed Mushy's hand away. "Don't you touch me!"

Nobody touched her. I righted the overturned chair, then backed away. All alone, Mama pulled herself up, and Miss Pearl watched her do so.

"Rosie, we can't never be friends no mo'," Miss Pearl said in a voice so calm it belied rage. "Nobody coulda told me that you'd do something like this to me. I'm coming out to yo' house first thing in the morning, and you gon' give me everything Frank ever gave you. Every stitch of clothes and every penny. Then I don't ever wanna lay eyes on you again."

My mother winced from the pain in her jaw, twisted her lips into a smirk, then snorted indifference through her nostrils. We followed her as she brushed past the Garrisons to retrieve her coat. Mushy and I bundled our younger sisters in theirs, and when we were all ready to leave, Mama paused at the front door. "Here you go, Pearl," she said, shoving Edna forward. "This all I got left belong to Frank."

"Rozelle, you get the hell on outta here!" Mr. Frank shouted.

"I'm going, and don't you put yo' hands on me, Frank. Y'all just take good care of Edna Pearl." She spat the last word at him, and Miss Pearl, standing beside her husband, howled like a mad dog.

Mama let the screen door bang behind her, and I heard Mushy say to Mr. Frank, "If I was you, I'd get Mama for that."

"You get on outta here, too, Mushy," he said. "I heard what you said to Pearl in there. How come you wanna hurt Pearl, somebody ain't never done you no wrong, just to get even wit' Rozelle?"

"You right, Mr. Frank," Mushy agreed. "I'm sorry. But I didn't hurt her all by myself, did I?"

"Get out, Mushy!" Mr. Frank repeated as he reached a hand toward his wife that stopped just short of contact.

Mushy rushed back to the kitchen and returned with the bottle of Seagram's before fleeing from their house. I knew my sister well. She would find a nice, quiet spot, and drink herself into a stupor.

On the television screen, a message read, "Happy New Year," and as I stepped out onto the Garrisons' front porch, the first of the celebratory gunshots sounded in the night, and I saw Mushy staggering away from us and toward town with the Seagram's bottle clutched in her fist.

fifty-two

We stood five minutes outside the Garrisons' door, afraid to knock. Mr. Frank's car was gone, and I wasn't sure anybody was home, still I was afraid to knock. It was our first day back to school following the holiday break, and we had stopped to get Edna.

The door finally opened, and Miss Pearl stared out at us. She was wearing a housedress fastened around her waist with a tied sash that hoisted her breasts up like water balloons.

"Y'all ain't gotta be scared to knock on this door," she said. "Y'all ain't done nothing to me. It was Rosie." Her voice trembled. "What's wrong wit' Rosie, Tangy Mae?"

"I don't know, Miss Pearl," I said. "We came to get Edna, to take her to school."

Miss Pearl stepped away from the door and allowed us to enter. "She's in there in the kitchen, po' thang. Cries herself to sleep. She don't know what's going on, and I don't, either."

Laura rushed off to the kitchen while I stayed in the front room, unable to meet Miss Pearl's gaze. "I brought Edna something to wear," I said. "What are you gonna do, Miss Pearl? I mean about Edna?"

She stood for a moment as though she had not heard me, then she sat down on the couch. "Honey, I don't know. I been woke a solid week trying to think." She chuckled dryly. "Frank done stayed woke, too. He scared to close his eyes. Think I'm gon' do something to him."

"Are you?"

"Nah. I'm gon' make his life miserable for a few more days, and I ain't never gon' trust him no more, but I ain't gon' leave him or nothing. Ain't nowhere to go. I figure Rosie'll come to her senses and tell me Edna ain't really Frank's child. She'll be lying, but maybe she'll tell me that. I keep looking from Edna to Frank, Tangy Mae, and I swear I see Frank's nose on that child. The po' little thang sat here crying the other night, and them was Frank's eyes spilling tears down her little face." Miss Pearl broke down with tears of her own. "I oughta kick myself that I ain't seen it before now."

She wiped her eyes with the palms of her hands, then rose laboriously from the couch and went into her bedroom. When she returned, she was holding two scarves that she gave to me. "Tie they little heads up," she said. "Don't take 'em out looking like that. And when y'all get outta school, you bring Edna on back here. Frank'll come out there to get her if you don't, and I don't want him and Rosie out there fighting."

"Okay," I said, "but I think Mama will probably come up here and get her pretty soon."

Miss Pearl sighed noisily and the water balloons bounced, and I loved her so very deeply and did not know how to tell her.

"We'll cross that bridge when we come to it," she said.

As the months dragged by, neither Mama and Miss Pearl nor Mama and Mushy made any move toward reconciliation, so I, inadvertently, became my mother's best friend. I was her opponent across a faded checkerboard with bottle caps as pieces. When and where she had gotten the board and learned to play checkers was a mystery to me. Maybe she had known how to play this game my entire life, and had only now decided to share it with me. Late into the night we would finish our game, then sit in the tattered armchairs to talk and laugh. We talked about loss, the loss of friendship, the loss of youth, but it frightened me that in the mornings I could not recall what we had laughed about.

Our new and creative mother spun tales for Laura that left the girl begging to hear more, and she confided in me on a level that raised me from child to woman. So sudden was this positive change in our mother that it made us leery of her at a time when we should have been happy. Her bugs became infrequent visitors, but I was constantly on guard for the next blow that would knock me out cold or injure my little sister.

Across the checkerboard one night, I asked Mama when she intended to bring Edna home.

"Edna's useless," she said. "She's just another mouth to feed, and we don't need that right now."

We weren't doing so bad, though. Harvey and Wallace continued to give Mama a portion of their pay, and Mama was teaching her girls to be clever. Each week she drove us into town and told us what to take and how to take it. Laura seemed to have found her niche in life. She stole without trepidation or remorse; I knew I would never be as skillful. I did, however, pilfer seeds from Munford's Hardware Store to plant my mother a garden.

One spring afternoon, I came home from school and cleared a patch of land between the clotheslines and the outhouse, tilled the soil with a splintered plank, then buried the squash and cucumber seeds. Patiently, I watered, weeded, and waited for vegetation to burst forth from the ground, but nothing would grow.

"I told you wadn't nothing gon' grow out there," Mama said to me one evening after I had finished watering the crusted, unyielding plot of earth. "I told you then, and I'll tell you now, seeds was a stupid thing to steal."

She was right, of course, and I was reminded of Miss Veatrice, hands covered in mud and nothing to show for it. Maybe I should have stolen some boards and nails to build myself a bed. That would have made more sense. We had room for a bed now that everybody had left my mother's house, but we couldn't afford one. Funny the way things worked out. Now that I no longer had to share my blankets with Laura, she no longer wet her pallet. Now that Mama did not possess the children she had so desperately wanted to hold onto, she was a calmer, more compassionate mother. I sat on the step next to Laura, feeling serene, wishing all of my siblings could have known this mother, could have known this peace at home, but then my mother spoke.

"Mushy was right, Tangy Mae," she said in a wistful tone. "I'm getting old. Pearl won't even speak to me, people act like they don't want me around 'em, and Chadlow says he'd rather have you than me. You 'bout black as one of them tires on my car, but you younger than me, and I guess that's what counts for Chadlow. He say he coming for you 'round eight o'clock tonight. Don't you go getting no big head, though, 'cause you ain't never gon' be good as me."

With the bravado of an adult confidante, I said, "You're right, Mama. I will never be as good as you, nor do I want to be. Why don't you tell Chadlow that tonight when he comes for you, because I'm not going anywhere."

"Humph," Mama snorted. She rose from her chair, and I thought for sure she was coming to knock me down the steps, but she smiled and winked one gray eye at me before opening the front door and disappearing inside the house.

"You think Mama'll tell me a story?" Laura asked.

"Not right now, Laura," I answered. "I don't think you should ask her right now."

Laura stood up anyway and went inside. I remained on the step, waiting to hear a slap, a cry, or something nerve-shattering from within the house. What I heard was the music of my mother's voice as she sang a lullaby to my sister.

I smiled. A few short months ago, my environment had been predictable, but now my mother's moods were indecipherable, and Laura, whom I had always secretly believed to be a bit dimwitted, was surpassing me in her intuition as to our mother's disposition. Somehow Laura had known Mama to be approachable, or else she was simply starving for the love that was conveyed by fairytales and lullabies.

For a while, I remained outside listening to my mother's voice float out to me. Then, feeling guilty for wasting valuable daylight, I went inside to get my books; there was still at least two hours of study time before sunlight faded completely. Careful not to disturb the intimacy between my mother and sister, I quietly returned to the front porch.

But each time I tried to read, my mind drifted. I thought of Jeff Stallings, who had left Pakersfield and forgotten all about me. I was convinced someone had told him about the farmhouse. I thought about my mother's tirade that had prevented me from attending Pakersfield High School, and of how quickly she had dropped the subject of a pregnancy and an abortion as soon as it was too late into the school year for me to transfer. Mushy had been right about Martha Jean, though. She was expecting her second baby any day now, and even knowing that, I wondered if her husband loved me as much as I loved him. Sam briefly crossed my mind, and I imagined him someplace safe and happy.

I thought of my friends, the students who had integrated Pakersfield High. Their transition had not been smooth. They were shunned by students and teachers and assaulted by adults outside the school building. Twice, black ink had been poured over Edith Dobson's head. Philip Ames had been ganged up on and beaten severely in the boys' lavatory. Each Sunday, Reverend Nelson forced us to share their pain and humiliation. With tears in their eyes or anger in their voices, Edith and the others gave horrific accounts of their experiences, until anger—that had no place in God's house—would burn in my head, smothering me for lack of an outlet.

Lost in thought, I did not hear the front screen open. Footsteps across the porch registered and I glanced up at Mama and Laura, hand in hand, moving toward the steps. They strolled past me as though I was not there, and went down into the yard. A minute later, I saw them coming back with the tub and a bucket of water. Again they passed me without a word. I stared down at my book and forced myself to read.

As dusk slowly crept across the white pages, obscuring the words from top to bottom, I closed the book and went inside. The tin tub stood in the front room, in front of the coal stove, and the water inside had the murky, uninviting appearance of tepid, settling grime. Mama and Laura sat side by side in the armchairs, and I assumed they were playing some sort of game, because Laura was wearing one of Mama's dresses that billowed as she gleefully swung her legs back and forth. Her short hair, that was slowly growing back, had been heaped with pomade and molded to her scalp. Silver earrings weighed her earlobes down, but obviously did not cause her any discomfort because she flashed a smile, showing smeared red teeth between ruby red lips that had no place on a child's face.

"Chadlow is looking to have him somebody young tonight," Mama said, "and that's what I intend to give him. That man can cause me a whole mess of trouble if I don't give him what he wants."

My mother had gone through this elaborate farce to force me to obey her. It was an excellent ploy, and I had to admire her ingenuity.

I peeled off my clothes and stepped into the tepid water of the tin tub.

fifty-three

Martha Jean gave birth to another girl, Valerie. Three weeks later, I was promoted to the twelfth grade. I wasn't particularly thrilled by either event. Mama had the power to snatch me out of school whenever she got ready, and as my old friend, Mattie, had once said, "Girls are useless, so why get an education?" Mama reiterated Mattie's sentiment by saying, "My girls ain't nothing. If it wadn't for my boys bringing us money, we'd be in bad shape. Not one of my girls ever bring one dime to this house." It would have been foolish for me to protest. Bored with staying home, Mama began to drive around Pakersfield stirring up devilment, and I ceased to be her best friend. I became someone who needed to get off my lazy behind and get a job.

Mama connected with an unlikely ally—Brenda Mackey. Together, they harassed Mushy and Richard, and brought confusion to the little house on Echo Road where the adulterous couple had moved in together. People understood Brenda's motives, but they could not understand Mama's. They reproached her for her behavior toward Mushy, yet the same people listened to her malicious accusations as she branded Tarabelle a degenerate who lusted after women and children. Not once, that I'm aware of, did Tarabelle try to defend herself. She went to work at the Munfords', came home to Miss Shirley's house, and allowed the gossip to run its course.

Mama had a friend, people were paying attention to her, and apparently she was once again looking young to Chadlow. Sometimes she would drive her car to the farmhouse to meet him, sometimes he would pick her up in his car, sometimes she would send me with him.

One night late in August when I had been designated to go with Chadlow, he drove me out to the farmhouse and barely glanced at Miss Frances when we entered her kitchen. He was sullen and distant—characteristics I had never witnessed in him before. In an upstairs room, with the door closed, he pressed my head against his chest, and must have felt my recoil because he stepped back and spun me around so that I was facing the bed. To hasten the inevitable, I disrobed and took my place between dingy, white sheets where I transformed timidity and humiliation into emotional numbness—my fortification.

Chadlow momentarily stood in the spot where I had left him. His eyes scanned the room and came to settle on the nightstand where a lamp stood on a lacy, oblong doily. But when he moved, it was not toward the nightstand or the bed, but to the chair where I had placed my clothes. He rummaged through my possessions and lifted a single white sock from the pile, then came to stand over the bed. Fully dressed, Chadlow straddled my chest and pinned my arms to the mattress with his knees, stuffed my sock in my mouth, snatched up the doily from the nightstand, and tied it over my lips.

Panic gripped me. I was used to doing whatever the men commanded of me, but this was different. The faraway look in Chadlow's eyes was terrifying. It was as though he no longer recognized me. I struggled against him, but his weight on my chest restricted my movements and rapidly exhausted me. I gagged as I tried to breathe around the sock in my mouth, then my nostrils took over.

Chadlow eased off of my chest, then I felt rough hands on my body as he flipped me over. With my nose pressed against the mattress and my mouth stuffed, suffocation seemed imminent. I desperately tried to shift my body, slowly realizing that my arms, caught in the grip of a human vise, were extended awkwardly behind my back. My feet, the only mobile part of my body, kicked out against the mattress, then cold metal clicked in place around my wrists.

"Rozelle's been telling me all about you," Chadlow said. He was winded from his struggle with me, and that gave me a smidgen of satisfaction. "Rozelle says you've been giving her a rough time, and that you're lazy, you won't help her out at the house. You've been disrespectful, backtalking your own mother. Now, she tells me you think you're better than everybody else, think you're better than me. Are you?"

With the sock shoved halfway down my throat, I couldn't answer him, but I managed to shake my head.

"You ought to be thrilled that I pay you any attention at all," he went on, "but Rozelle tells me that you don't want me to touch you. Is that right?" He paused, as though waiting for me to answer, then said, "I told your mother I would help her straighten you out. And I will, by God, I will."

It was pure rawhide that cut into my backside, and Chadlow brandished the weapon with expertise. Someone downstairs must have heard the whirr, hiss, crack of the strap as it struck my defenseless body, but if they heard, no one came to investigate. I closed my eyes, twitched and moaned with each excruciating blow, dug my toes into the mattress, and tried to fade away. An inferno roared through my arms, legs, buttocks and back.

After what seemed an eternity, Chadlow ended the beating. He had straightened me out, for sure, to the point where—if I survived this—I would say one last thing to my mother concerning Chadlow, then I would never mention his name to her again.

"I'm gonna let you up now," Chadlow said, "but I don't want to hear one sound from you. You understand?"

I bobbed my head and Chadlow removed the handcuffs. When I tried to move my arms, a soft moan came through my gag. I realized I was crying, and this was clogging my nostrils. Getting the sock out of my mouth was imperative. All the times when, in my naïveté, I had thought death a solution, now fell by the wayside. I wanted the pain to end, but I did not want to die.

"Not one sound from you," Chadlow warned, then ripped the sock from my mouth.

I was so grateful—so grateful for breath—that I would have kissed his pale, rough hands. Instead, I sucked in a mouthful of air and plunged into darkness.

Miss Frances was sitting in a chair at the bedside when I opened my eyes. She was washing my back with water from a basin that stood on the nightstand. She spoke to Chadlow as she worked. "It's a shame you beat this child like this. For what?" she asked. "What she do? These sheets ain't never gon' be no more good. Blood don't wash out that easy. I'm gon' have to throw 'em away."

"I'll pay for the sheets," Chadlow said.

"And this shirt you want me to put on her?"

"I'll pay for that, too."

"You paying for a awful lot tonight. I hope it was worth it," Miss Frances said. "You know Bo don't like this kinda carrying on out here, Mr. Chadlow."

"You watch your mouth when you talk to me, Frances," Chadlow said. "What's done is done. There's nothing you, Bo, or anybody else can do about it now."

Miss Frances fell silent and continued to sponge my back. When she realized I was awake, she asked, in a voice filled with sympathy, "You awright, child? Can you sit up?"

I ignored my pain and pulled myself into a sitting position. Miss Frances wiped my face and bandaged my back with scraps from an old, discolored sheet, then she helped me to get my clothes on. Lastly, she maneuvered my arms into the sleeves of a man's well-worn, brown shirt before leaving me alone in the room with Chadlow.

"I need to see you walk," Chadlow said.

Gritting my teeth, I walked the length of the room without limping or grimacing, because I knew that this was my passport out.

Miss Frances had reclaimed her post at the kitchen table by the time we descended the stairs. I could not remember having ever been to the farmhouse when she was not at the table. It seemed to be the only place she was comfortable. Her husband, Bo, stayed in the parlor where drinking and gambling took place, and I seldom saw him.

Chadlow stopped at the table behind Miss Frances. He lifted a glass from her hand, sniffed the contents, then returned the glass to her. "Room needs cleaning," he told her, as he prodded me along toward the back door.

Footsteps and a woman's giggle could be heard on the back porch. Chadlow shoved me aside as the door opened inward and Leona Wright stepped over the threshold. She was a heavyset woman with a nasty scar that ran along the left side of her face. It was rumored that she had been cut by another woman right here at the farmhouse. Mama had told me about it, and so had Miss Frances. According to them, Leona had won the fight, but after my beating tonight, I wondered if Chadlow's rawhide had actually caused the scar. It was possible.

Leona stepped into the kitchen, glanced at Chadlow, then briefly focused her attention on me. "Damn!" she said. "Y'all getting younger and younger every day. Ain't gon' be no business for me in a minute. Hon,' you ain't nothing but a baby."

"Mind your own business, Leona," Chadlow said, as he guided me by my shoulders toward the opened door.

We had to pause again as Leona's companion entered the room. It was Crow. He stepped past us with a fleeting glance, then took Leona by her hand and started for the parlor.

"It's just a scan'lous," Leona grumbled. "Somebody need to put a foot up Rozelle's ass."

My feet touched the back porch; Chadlow followed behind me and closed the door.

fifty-four

B eside the embankment below my mother's house, I stood waiting for Crow, having decided that if he did not come, he was not my father.

The car's headlights came like cat's eyes out of a long, murky alley—up the dark, narrow road. The passenger door swung open, and Crow's angry, impatient voice commanded, "Get in, Tangy Mae!"

Easing into the car, I clenched my teeth against the pain that rolled in waves from the back of my neck to the bottom of my heels. When I closed the car door, I should have felt safe, but I didn't. I should have been able to cry, scream, do whatever I felt like doing, but I couldn't. "Take me to Velman," I mumbled.

Crow drove slowly around the bend, and accelerated when he reached the smooth surface of Fife Street. "Who is Velman?" he asked, still angry. "Is that another man that's gonna take you back out to that house? Do you need money, sugar? Do you need it that bad?"

"No. You don't understand, Crow."

"Damn right, I don't understand. I gave you money the last time I was here. Ain't no daughter of mine got no business out to Bo's.

If I'da known you was doing that, I'da cut your throat before I left here last time."

"Cut it," I said.

"What?"

"Cut it, Crow. It'll be the first decent thing you've ever done for me. Velman, by the way, is my brother-in-law. He'd never do anything to hurt me no matter what I did."

Crow smacked the steering wheel with his fist, and the horn gave a short, dull beep. "I wouldn't hurt you, either," he said. "I just wanna know what's going on. I'm yo' daddy, Tangy. I wouldn't hurt you."

I thought a daddy would offer love instead of anger. A daddy would soothe me and tell me that everything is going to be all right. A daddy would understand that I am just a child in a grown-ups' world, trying to do what I am told, trying to survive.

"What is a daddy?" I asked. "It's been two years since I've seen you, and then I had to bump into you out there wrapped around Leona Wright. Crow, you didn't even know who I was."

"I ain't perfect, Tangy. I ain't never said I was perfect, but the minute I knew it was you, I came after you."

"Take me to Velman," I pleaded. "Please, Crow, just take me to Velman."

He nodded his head slowly, plucked a match from his shirt pocket and placed it between his teeth. "Where this Velman live?" he asked.

I told him.

It was Velman who opened the door for us. Crow followed me inside, and I introduced him to my brother-in-law, then I gripped Velman's hand. "Where's Martha Jean?" I asked.

"Sleep. It's after midnight, little sister."

"I know," I said, "but wake her up. I need her, Velman."

Crow had taken a seat on the couch, but I was still standing when Martha Jean came into the front room led by her husband.

I stepped up to my sister, and signed, "Hurt. Help me."

She nodded, and I turned my back to her. Over my shoulder I said, "Velman, help me get this shirt off."

"What's that on it?" he asked.

"Blood."

He helped me remove the shirt and the blouse beneath it. Slowly, carefully, he peeled away the bandages, then profanities rapidly spilled from his lips. "Damn! Shit! What the hell . . . ? I'm gonna call Mushy."

"Why do you think Mushy is the answer to everything?" I calmly asked.

"Because you do. You always have."

I shook my head. "No. I think you're the answer to everything. That's why I'm here and not over on Echo Road."

"Well, I'm not, little sister. I'm not the answer to anything. I don't know what to do wit' yo' back. It looks like . . ."

I closed my eyes and braced myself, but words failed him. When I opened my eyes, Martha Jean was standing in front of me. Her hands were raised in a gesture of helplessness, and tears rolled from her eyes.

"What?" she signed. "What, Tangy?"

"Help me."

On the couch behind me, Crow was stuck in a single phrase. "Oh, my God, sugar! Oh, my God, sugar!"

Velman gave me three aspirins and a glass of water. I swallowed the pills, then lay on the floor where Martha Jean could properly clean my back. Martha Jean tended my wounds with a care and gentleness Miss Frances did not possess. It wasn't that I didn't trust Miss Frances. But I believed her bandages, torn from discolored sheets, were contaminated with sin and decay.

Velman squatted on the floor beside Martha Jean. He didn't touch me, but as he watched his wife work on my back, he said, "You need to see a doctor, little sister."

"No," I answered, "I need sleep."

"You shoulda been sleep hours ago," he said angrily. "This stuff's gotta stop. You can't keep going through this. You oughta be home, asleep, wit' no reason in the world to be scared and beat up. It's after midnight."

"That a hint?" Crow barked, when obviously it was not intended to be.

Velman rose from his crouched position beside me, taking my comfort away. "Nah, man," he said, "it ain't no goddamn hint. I ain't got to hint in my own house. If I want you outta here, I'll just tell you to get yo' ass out."

"Bad little nigger, ain't you?" Crow snarled. "If you so bad, and you suppose to care so much about my daughter, tell me how come she all messed up."

"Maybe 'cause she ain't never had no daddy to help her out," Velman retorted.

"Please!" I groaned. "Please, don't argue." Flat on my belly with my head resting on folded arms, I could not see them, could only imagine their frustration and anger. "Please!"

There was silence in the room, except for the dribble of water as Martha Jean wrung out the cloth she was using. Velman finally came back to squat on the floor beside me, but tension lingered in the air, as stifling as August humidity.

"How was Detroit, Crow?" I asked, hoping that his reply would transport us away from Pakersfield, away from the wounds on my back, away from the bloody water in Martha Jean's basin.

"I never made it to Detroit," Crow snapped. "I been in Pittsburgh. Shoulda stayed there."

Martha Jean's cloth touched a spot on my back that caused me to howl with pain. It was so severe that I scooted away from her and sat upright on the sheet.

"I'm calling Mushy," Velman said, alarmed.

He started for the telephone, but Crow shot him a scornful look, and said, "This how you handle business, man? You gotta call for a woman?"

Velman stopped, turned to face Crow. "Hey, man," he said, "this ain't *my* business. Ain't nobody pimping my daughter all over Triacy County. And I got two daughters. But I'm man enough to stay put and see about mine. Let's hear you say that. And while you running all over the place, from Detroit to Pittsburgh or wherever the hell you go, do you sleep on a bed? Your daughter been sleeping on a floor all her life. My daughter's in there in a bed. So don't you talk to me 'bout no business, motherfucka. And while you sitting there trying to be mad about something, you oughta be taking her to a doctor."

It seemed to me that Crow did not move, but he must have. In the blink of an eye he was off the couch, around the coffee table, and standing over Velman with an opened switchblade gleaming in his grip.

"No!" I screamed, then half crawling, half stumbling, I threw my body between the two men—my heart, my father.

Martha Jean had eased toward the center of confusion. She stood next to Velman with a hand on his arm and a quizzical expression on her face. Velman touched her hand, patted it softly, then retreated toward his bedroom.

"Shit," Crow hissed, as he folded the switchblade and slipped it into his pants pocket. "You gon' stay here, sugar?"

My voice was shaky when I answered him. "No. I have to get home to Laura."

"Well, I'll wait for you out in the car. Hurry up and get dressed."

Once Crow was out of the house, Martha Jean did not ask me about the confrontation. She simply spun me around and began to heap salve onto my wounds. She did it in a hasty fashion with none of her earlier tenderness. I assumed she was anxious to get to Velman, to comfort her man.

I was wearing one of Velman's shirts over fresh bandages when I climbed into Crow's idling vehicle. Crow shifted gears and sped away from the curb. "You want me to take you to a doctor tonight?" he asked.

"No," I answered. "I just want to go home and go to sleep."

As we crossed the railroad tracks in town, Crow leaned toward me, so close I could smell the tip of the fresh match he was chewing. "Out at Bo's, who was that man, sugar?" he asked.

"Chadlow. He's the law in this county."

"He's a dead man."

fifty - five

The school year began with more turmoil than Triacy County had ever known. The integration of Pakersfield High by five students last year had caused a minor ruckus, but nothing in comparison to the large-scale warfare of the second year, with the addition of two dozen Negro students. The *Pakersfield Herald* called it "an invasion of Negroes," but in our communities, it was called a step toward equal rights. By the end of the first week of school, seven Negro students and twelve adults had been arrested. There were injuries on both sides, and Wallace, though not a student anywhere, was right in the thick of it all. His picture appeared on the front page of the newspaper. In the picture, Wallace, with an angry scowl on his face, was brandishing a baseball bat, although his target had been conveniently left out of the shot.

Hysteria ruled the county. It spilled over to Plymouth where a night raid resulted in broken windows at our school, and manure heaped across the walkway leading to the main door. Some speculated it was the work of a few young whites, but I didn't agree because Negro students were being chased home from school by grown men in cars and pickup trucks. We stopped going to school and once again stayed away from town, fearful of what might happen.

Finally, it was decided that all schools in Triacy County would close down for one week while meetings were held to determine a course of action. On that Saturday, Reverend Nelson stood beside Mr. Hewitt, our principal, and bitterly announced to the congregation that desegregation in Triacy County had been temporarily suspended. All Negro students would return to the Plymouth School.

"Separate but equal will be the Triacy County motto for as long as we allow it," Reverend Nelson said. "I don't agree with it, and I'm sure most of you don't, either, but I'm asking you today for just a little more patience. Now, I know you're all aware of the town meetings we've been attending all week, and there were some things said in those meetings that angered me, and probably would have angered most of you. After a while, I had to stop listening and start praying. You know, when you're talking to God, you can't hear all the evil that sinners around you are talking. If you don't believe me, try prayer for yourself. It's a wonderful thing. I'm gonna turn this particular meeting over to Mr. Hewitt, but before I sit down, I just want to say to you the same thing I said at the town meeting. Before we can hope to have even one drop of harmony in this desegregation process, those 'white only' signs must come down. How can we expect black and white children to get along at school when they can't even drink from the same water fountains where God's water flows freely?"

We applauded our agreement as Reverend Nelson took his seat and Mr. Hewitt stepped up to the podium. He unrolled his speech and began to read.

"We are all aware of the May, 1954, Supreme Court decision that declared segregation in public schools unconstitutional," he read. "Therefore, an unconstitutional deed is being perpetrated by the Board of Education and the elected officials of this county."

People who had never set foot in the Solid Rock Baptist Church before were crowded in. They filled every pew and every inch of standing space. My mother was not one of them, but Crow sat beside me. We had listened intently to the words of the reverend, and now we were trying to concentrate on Mr. Hewitt's speech.

"We are being asked to take a huge step backwards in our struggle for fairness," Mr. Hewitt said, "but this is only a short-term setback. I regret having to say this, but the time is not right for this movement in Triacy County. Aggression on our part can only make a bad situation worse. What the town council has proposed is the completion of the new school here in Plymouth. The way things stand, it is the best possible solution."

An angry din rose from the pews, and I waited for a Junior Fess or a Hambone to rush up to the podium to set my principal straight, but no one moved. Beside me, Crow lowered his chin to his chest and slowly shook his head.

"Sugar," he said, "stand up and ask that nigger if he got that shit from them pissant rednecks."

"No!" I protested. "You ask him."

"I can't bring attention to myself, and anyway you know how to ask it better than me."

For a moment, I just sat there staring at Crow, but as the crowd's disgruntlement subsided, I rose from my seat. Before I could open my mouth, though, someone else in the church said, "Excuse me, Mr. Hewitt, but was that a decision agreed on by everybody? I mean, did you, the reverend, Deacon Hall, everybody agree?"

Mr. Hewitt looked out over the gathering and nodded his head. "It was the decision of the majority," he answered solemnly, then rolled his papers and abandoned his speech. "This is their condition for the release of nineteen Negroes being held in the county jail. I'll listen to any one of you who is willing to sacrifice them for a hope. I, for one, am not willing."

He waited to see if anyone would step forward to protest. As we left the church, Crow leaned down and mumbled in my ear, "This a messed-up town. Shoulda been called Passivefield."

Crow remained in Pakersfield, rooming with Melvin and Dorothy Tate. He had made the healing of my wounds a priority. Everyday he would pick me up from home or school and take me to Mushy on Echo Road, or to Martha Jean on Motten Street, so that my sisters could treat the gashes on my back. For my sake, Crow and Velman had formed a fragile bond.

Mama knew Crow was in town because I had told her, and

because he pacified her with monetary tidbits brought by me or Laura. Once or twice, she had seen his car when he came to pick me up, but she had not gone down to the road to talk with him, and he had not gone up to the house to talk with her. He wanted to, though. I could tell by the way he stared past me and up toward the porch each time he came to Penyon Road.

One afternoon at Skeeter's house, after Martha Jean was done putting fresh bandages on my back, Crow said, "I don't guess you been too happy, sugar. I don't understand yo' mama. The Rozelle I knew was always laughing and full of fun, just like yo' sister, Mushy. I loved Rozelle once, but she wanted herself a man with light skin and good hair. I know this ain't got nothing to do with you, but I'd give my right arm if I could go back and change some things."

I signed to Martha Jean that once upon a time Crow had been in love with Mama. Martha Jean didn't even smile, just gave him a pitying glance.

"I swear, for the last few weeks, I been trying to understand this shit," Crow said. "I don't understand it. I ain't never heard of no mama doing the kinda things y'all say Rozelle do."

Crow was obsessed with Mama. He watched our house at night. He didn't know that I knew, but I did. Sometimes, late at night, I would see his car parked in weeds at the turn of the bend. I don't think Mama was aware that she was being spied on. She wouldn't have liked it.

Laura was sitting on the floor playing with Mary Ann and Valerie. Mary Ann could walk now, and she kept moving little blocks from one area of the floor to another. She was teasing Laura by offering the blocks, then taking them away. Laura managed to divide her attention evenly between the sisters. She cradled Valerie and cooed to her; she switched blocks with Mary Ann and giggled with her.

I still thought of it as Skeeter's house, although it was now occupied only by the Coopers. Skeeter had moved in with Miss Shirley right after Valerie was born. He had done it out of love for his nephew; Velman was easy to love. They were all easy to love. As I watched Mary Ann shift her blocks around, I felt the serenity of the house. Martha Jean also appeared relaxed as she watched her daughter toddle about, but Crow, insensitive to our need, obsessed about Rozelle, until, lo and behold, he talked her up.

She drew our attention by scratching on the screen door, then without invitation, she opened the door and stepped into the room. "I knew you was here, Crow," she said. "I been waiting on you to come up to the house to see me. What's taking you so long?"

Crow cleared his throat. "Rozelle, I'm here to look after my daughter. I don't want you coming in here upsetting her."

"Shoot!" Mama said. "I can't upset Tangy Mae. She the one upsetting me."

"That ain't the way I hear it," Crow said.

"How you hear it, baby?" Mama asked, as she swaggered seductively toward the couch where Crow was sitting beside me. "You need to come wit' me, let me whisper a thing or two in yo' ear."

"I ain't here for none of that, Rozelle," Crow replied curtly.

Undaunted, Mama winked at him. "You always here for that," she said. "I'll be waiting for you outside by yo' car. You hurry up now. I ain't gon' wait too long."

She pranced from the room like a pretty, painted pony, and Crow kept his gaze on her every prance of the way. When she was out of sight, he reached into his pocket, withdrew a match, and stuck it between his teeth. I studied him, wondering if he realized that Mama had not spoken a single word to her daughters or granddaughters.

Crow slowly rose from the couch, and I reached for his arm. "Don't go," I said.

"Won't take but a minute," he said but I noticed he did not look at me. "I'm just gon' get rid of her so she don't come back in here bothering you."

He was lying, of course. Lust was written all over his face. I turned my head and met Martha Jean's gaze, as the door opened and closed, delivering my father into the arms of my mother.

Crow came the following day to drive us from school to Mushy's house, and I rushed to his car before Laura could make her way from the back of the school building where the third-grade classroom was located. As soon as I was in the car, I asked, "Did you screw her?"

Crow laughed. "What kinda question is that for you to be asking yo' daddy?"

"She's got the clap, you know."

The smile vanished from his face, but he held my gaze. "What you know about clap?" he asked.

"Crow, I'm not a little girl. You know what I've been doing. I should know something about it."

He removed the match that had been dangling on his lip. "Shit!" he barked angrily, staring at the match as though it was somehow to blame. "Why didn't you tell me this yesterday?"

"I didn't have time to tell you anything. As soon as Mama came and whistled at you, you went running like some old dog."

"Watch yo'self!" he snapped.

He meant for me to be quiet, but I could not resist saying, "I am watching myself. That's why I'm not the one with the clap."

He glared at me and was about to say something else when Laura came skipping up to the car, then his face softened and he laughed. "Ooh wee," he said, shaking his head, "you know you got a smart mouth."

Crow drove us to Echo Road with Laura chattering on and on about how she had spent the day with Edna. "They didn't have no teacher. And they all came to our room. And we had to share our desk with them. And Edna sat with me all day. And it was fun, Tangy. Is Miss Pearl Edna's mama? Edna say Miss Pearl her mama and Mr. Frank her daddy. Is they, Tangy?"

"Are they," I corrected.

"Well, are they?"

Crow stopped the car in front of Mushy's house, and as I let Laura out, I said, "Tell Mushy to explain it to you."

We watched as Laura walked the short distance to Mushy's front door, then Crow said, "When Mushy gets done wit' yo' back, send Laura over to Melvin's to get me so I can drive y'all home."

"We can walk," I said.

"I'll take you."

"Why? So you can see Mama again?"

"Nah. I don't wanna see Rozelle. I'll take you 'cause I wanna make sure you get there awright. Mushy told me yo' back don't seem to be doing no good. I don't want you walking no more than you got to, and I got to run up to Tennessee tonight. It'll be a few days before I get back through here."

"Are you coming back?" I asked.

He nodded.

"Did you give Mama any more money, Crow?"

"Yeah. A little."

"Tarabelle says Mushy is just like Mama. Do you think she is?"

He did not answer right away. He seemed to mull over the question before saying, "They both like to have a good time. That's about all. Mushy cares about people, and that makes her different from Rozelle. Yo' sister drinks a little too much, but this a messed up town. It'll make you drink or lose yo' mind."

"Yeah," I agreed. "Sometimes I think I'm losing my mind."

"You too young to lose yo' mind. You just a little girl, sugar, and you don't even know it."

I smiled at that because we both knew that I hadn't been a little girl for a long time now. I had reached for the door handle, preparing to get out, when Crow touched my arm.

"Something I wanna talk to you about," he said, before I could get out of the car. "Martha Jean is a sweet girl, and I see the way you be looking at her husband. You know you gotta quit that, don't you? I be watching him, too. He ain't gon' keep refusing you. He ain't gon' be able to. And yo' sister—she ain't gon' keep forgiving you."

I settled back on the seat, closed the car door, and turned to face my father. "But I want him, Crow," I said. "I want Velman." It was the first time I had admitted it aloud to anyone, and the confession gave me a sense of relief.

"What would you do wit' him if you had him?" Crow asked.

"I don't know," I answered truthfully. "I've never had to think about that. I guess I've always known I'd never have him."

"Leave it alone, sugar. He's happy wit' yo' sister."

"I know, but I'll die without him."

Crow chuckled. "You won't die, sugar," he said. "Believe me, you won't die." He leaned over and kissed my forehead. "There was a time when I loved Rozelle like that. I couldn't do much of nothing for always thinking 'bout her."

"She doesn't even know your name."

"What?

"Mama," I said. "She doesn't know your name. I don't, either."

He sat up straight, reached into his shirt pocket, and removed a folded sheet of paper and a match. He stuck the match between his teeth, and gave the paper to me. "Clarence Otis Yardley," he said. "That's my name. My mama always knows where I am. If you ever need me, she'll know where to find me."

I opened the folded paper. There were five twenty-dollar bills lying atop the name, address, and telephone number of his mother.

"This is goodbye?" I asked.

Crow shook his head. "When it's goodbye, I'll say goodbye."

I got out of the car, and Crow leaned his head toward the passenger window.

"Yo' mama really got the clap?" he asked.

"Time will tell," I answered, although I didn't think my mother had anything, except a bad case of lunacy, for if she did, I surely had it, too.

fifty-six

For weeks, I would get up during the night, peer out the front door, search the dark field for Crow's car. It was never there, and I did not see him, but I continued to feel his presence. I had even been by the Tates' house to ask if they had seen him. He had vanished without the promised goodbye. Through Thanksgiving, Christmas, and New Year's Day, I kept waiting for Crow to pop up at our door and say, "Hey, sugar, you knew I wouldn't forget about you." But he never showed up.

Mama complained about not having any money, and several times I was tempted to give her the money I had stashed with Martha Jean for safekeeping, but I subdued the impulse. Sometimes the bugs would come back to annoy Mama, but she would drink corn whiskey and swat the bugs away.

One evening while Mama, Laura, and I were sitting in the kitchen, Mama asked, "How's yo' back, Tangy Mae?"

"It's healing," I answered.

"I had a little talk wit' Chadlow 'bout what he done to you," she said. "He wants to see you. He says he wants to apologize, and that he's got something special for you."

"I don't want anything from him."

"Just let the man apologize, Tangy Mae. That ain't gon' hurt nothing."

I sat at the table, staring across at my mother. I had promised myself that I would mention Chadlow's name to her only once more in my life. I sent Laura out of the kitchen because the time was now.

"Mama, you scraped the bottom of the barrel to find Chadlow," I said calmly. "He doesn't like your children, and I wonder if he even cares anything about you. He's a mean man. One day he might hurt you the way he did me. I hate what you've made me do, and as soon as I'm old enough, I'm moving out of here."

"Humph," she grunted. "You ain't moving nowhere, Tangy Mae. You too lazy to leave here. Who you think gon' let you stay wit' them when all you wanna do is go to school, go to school, go to school. But when you leave, *if* you leave, I'll still have Laura, and I can always go back and get Edna. You say one more thing to me, and I'll pull you outta that damn school tomorrow."

"Do you love me, Mama?" I asked, did not wait for an answer, afraid to hear what she might say. "I love you. I get angry with you sometimes, but I've always loved you. I just don't like what you've made me do. When I was younger, the children would tease me because I went to school smelling like pee. They don't tease me anymore, but now I think they can smell the stench of that farmhouse all over my body. Behind our backs, people call us sluts, Mama. You, me, Tarabelle, and Mushy. Mr. Pace has changed, and Mr. Hewitt tolerates me only because he has to. At school, mostly everybody stays away from me. So pull me out if you want. I might quit and save you the trouble."

My mother stared at me and snatched a bug from her nose. She worked her tongue across her bottom gum the way her mother used to do with snuff, then she said, "The way they treat you at that school, Tangy Mae, do it stop you from learning how to read, and write, and count up yo' numbers?"

I shook my head and smiled. "No, Mama. It just makes me try harder to be the best student there."

"Humph." She grunted as she rose from her chair. "You know, I really miss Pearl. You oughta go up there tomorrow and tell her I'm sorry for hitting her. Did I hit her or did she hit me?"

Without waiting for an answer, she went off to her room, and left me sitting there thinking about Miss Pearl and wondering if she would forgive my mother, thinking about school and wondering if I should quit with less than four months left to go, thinking about Laura and Edna and wondering what their lives would be like after I left Pakersfield.

Laura returned to the kitchen and drew me away from my thoughts by announcing she was hungry. We decided on peanut butter and crackers, and although the evening was chilly, we took our snacks out to the front steps. Maybe twenty minutes after we were done licking peanut butter from our fingers, Mama came out of the house and moved down the steps past us. We watched her climb into her car and drive west toward the farmhouse.

A few seconds after Mama's car was out of sight, I heard a rustle in the thickets on the road side of the gully. As I watched, a figure sprinted across the road and into the field of weeds. Had Laura not gripped my thigh in alarm, I might have thought the figure a figment of my imagination, it disappeared so fast. We rose from the steps and quietly hurried inside, barely escaping the lights that rippled through the weeds and glinted across the front of the house.

There was little I could do to ensure our safety, as the front door was weak and had no lock. I thought of dragging one of the armchairs to the door, but then I thought if someone was after us, they wouldn't have gone into the field. They could have gotten us while we were sitting on the steps.

Laura was clinging to me, crying, and my heart was hammering so loud that I almost missed the sound of a car. I peered out the front door and saw the tail end of a black car heading west, the same way Mama had gone. I would have sworn it was Crow's car if Crow, the liar, had not been long gone from Pakersfield. I tried to calm myself, realizing it was my anxiety that was causing Laura so much distress.

"There's no one there, Laura," I said, and opened the door wider so that she could look out. "Look! Whoever it was is gone now."

It took a while to get her settled down enough to fall asleep, but she finally did, and I sat in an armchair to watch over her. No one had ever come to our house to cause us harm, and there was no reason to believe anybody would tonight. I kept reminding myself of that until I was able to think pleasant thoughts. I thought of Velman Cooper, and of what Crow had said to me. Crow was right. Velman would never belong to me, and I did not want to see Martha Jean unhappy. Why did I need Velman anyway? What had he ever done for me? Nothing, except stand up to my mother—and win. But he had won Martha Jean, and not me. I would stay away from Motten Street. I would forget about Velman Cooper if it killed me.

I felt myself leaving fear behind and heading toward self pity. I tried to shake it off, finally deciding to sleep it off. As I rose from the chair to change for bed, I heard a car on the road again. It passed our house and kept going.

Martha Jean was changing the bandages on my back only twice a week now, and I no longer asked Mushy to do it. I thought the bandages were unnecessary, but Martha Jean insisted I keep them on, and since I could not see what my back looked like, I decided to respect her opinion. I removed my blouse and checked the back of it for signs of blood or drainage before dousing the kerosene lamp. With my nightclothes on, I unrolled my blankets. But I had barely settled on the floor when I heard a crash outside that seemed to shake the foundation of the house. Laura awakened with a shudder, and I drew her to me to calm her down, then together we went to the porch to investigate.

My mother's car had struck the embankment below the house. As we watched, the car shifted into reverse and the front end came free of the embankment and bounced several times as it settled on the dirt road. It stood idling for a second or two, then it veered to the left and accelerated. For a moment, it seemed to hang in midair before crashing into the field.

The car door opened, and a huge, white bird came flying out from the front seat. As it drew closer, I realized it was my mother. She was wrapped in a white sheet that fluttered in the wind as she half ran, half stumbled out of the field and across the road. The abandoned car idled nosily, and a wisp of its exhaust vapor was captured in the beam of red tail lights.

Hurriedly, I went into the house, lit the kerosene lamp, and returned to the porch. Mama had reached the yard. She was naked beneath the sheet and her feet were bare. She rushed up the steps and brushed past us, and I could hear a gurgling sound coming from her throat. There was blood on the sheet, a splatter of blood on her face and neck, and a lot on her chest.

"Mama, what happened?" I screamed, but she would not answer me.

She used the sheet to wipe at the blood on her chest. In the hallway, she turned in circles as though she had lost all sense of direction, then she lurched toward her room. Laura and I followed behind her. I drew close to examine her injuries. There was so much blood that it seemed her chest had been slashed open. Laura cried, and I held my hands to my ears to make it all go away.

Finally, my mother spoke with a humming, nasal sound, "Get the tub. Get the tub. Get the tub, Tangy Mae."

Relieved, I snatched the flashlight from the kitchen shelf and raced outside for the tub. I took it inside, then rushed back to the yard for water. Out in the field, Mama's car was still idling nosily, and I turned it off. When I returned to Mama's room with the water, she was kneeling in the dry tub, rubbing at her chest with the palms of her hands. I dumped the entire bucket of cold water into the tub but Mama did not shiver. Laura gave me a cloth, and I began to gently wash away the blood from my mother's chest. She did not struggle against me nor try to help me. When the blood was gone, I saw no injuries at all.

"What happened, Mama?" I asked again.

She would not speak, and when I tried to help her from the tub, she would not move. Exhausted from straining to lift her up, I sat on the floor beside the tub and tried to talk her out of the cold water. She would not budge, and finally, I got the basin and dipper, and began to scoop the water out.

Laura drifted off to sleep, leaving me alone to care for Mama. I fed the fire in the fireplace with bits of kindling and coal, covered Mama's back with a blanket, then used the bloody sheet she had worn home to soak up as much water as I could from the bottom of the tub. Lastly, I brought hot coffee to her and held it to her lips. She managed two sips before clamping her mouth closed.

It was near daybreak when a siren breached the silence around us. I made it to the door in time to see the sheriff's car zoom past our house heading west, the direction from which Mama had come. I was frightened enough to rouse Laura and send her to get Miss Pearl.

"Rosie, you talk to me!" Miss Pearl demanded. "What's wrong wit' you? What's done happened?"

It had taken Miss Pearl the longest time to reach Penyon Road because at first she had not thought there was any emergency. She had taken the time to feed Laura and Edna, and send them off to school. Laura had only told her that Mama would not get out of the tub. Miss Pearl had to question Laura at length before she understood that Mama had been in the tub all night, and that she had come home covered in blood.

"I almost didn't come out here, Tangy Mae," Miss Pearl said. "I ain't even spoke to Rosie in more than a year. What in the world done happened?"

"I don't know, Miss Pearl, but I sure am glad you came."

"Well, let's see can't we get her outta this doggone tub. She gon' catch her death of pneumonia as cold as it is in here."

We gripped Mama beneath her arms and tried to pull her from the tub. She was stuck though, as if she had been cemented to the bottom. Each time we pulled, we lifted tub and all. Miss Pearl finally lubricated her hands with cooking lard and rubbed it on Mama's knees, feet, and every part of the body she could reach within the confines of the tub, and when we tried again, Mama came loose.

We heaved her onto the bed, and she lay there hollow-eyed, stiff, and speechless.

For several minutes, Miss Pearl sat on the bed beside Mama and tried to coax her into telling us what had happened, but Mama was like a dead woman with wide open eyes, and her body remained rigid the whole while we worked to get a dress over her head and her arms into the sleeves.

"We gon' have to get Doctor Mathis out here," Miss Pearl said. "I don't like the looks of this, Tangy Mae."

I nodded, and went into the front room to get dressed. I had changed from gown to clothes, had my coat in my hand, and was in the hallway near the door when Mama spoke. Her voice had the quality of a frightened child just awakened from a nightmare.

"Pearl," she whimpered. "Pearl, I knew you'd forgive me."

"I'm here, Rosie. I need you to tell me what happened," Miss Pearl said.

Still holding on to my coat, I eased back into my mother's room. She was lying flat on the bed with her eyes open, just as she had been for the last hour or so, but now her right hand was groping the air for something unseen.

"Junior came," she whispered. "You remember Junior, don't you, Pearl? Junior Fess? He came in through the window and cut Chadlow's throat."

A frown creased Miss Pearl's brow as she stared at Mama. "Rosie, Junior been dead for nearly three years now."

Mama sobbed and her body twitched on the bed. "I know, Pearl. I know," she said. "Chadlow killed him. Now Junior done come back and killed Chadlow. He came in through the window. I seen him."

Miss Pearl glanced in my direction and rapidly waved a hand toward the door. I knew she wanted me to rush to get Dr. Mathis, but I was transfixed.

"Rosie, how you know Chadlow killed Junior?" Miss Pearl asked.

Mama seemed barely able to get the words out. "I was wit' him when he done it," she whispered. "He beat Junior wit' a crowbar 'til Junior was all broke up in pieces on the ground, but he wadn't dead. Chadlow coulda stopped. He coulda stopped, Pearl, but he wouldn't. He made me help him hang Junior from that tree. I didn't wanna do it, I swear I didn't. Junior was begging me to help him. 'Help me, Miss Rosie. Please, Miss Rosie, don't let him kill me.' But Chadlow had done made up his mind, and wadn't nothing I could do."

"Oh, my God!" Miss Pearl groaned, and stepped away from the bed.

Mama's groping hand now reached toward the sound of her friend's voice. "Don't leave me, Pearl. It wadn't my fault."

Miss Pearl came over to where I had braced myself against the bedroom wall. "You know you can't repeat a word of this, don't you?" she asked.

With downcast eyes, I nodded. I couldn't even look at the woman who had delivered me into the world. Miss Pearl held me tightly to her chest, and we both wept. Across the room, Mama never turned her head in our direction. She relaxed her hand, made a gurgling sound, then she lay still—perfectly still.

When Angus Betts arrived at the house, Miss Pearl and I were still in Mama's room trying to decide what to do. Miss Pearl had feared Mama would blabber her tale to the doctor if he came out, and now here was the sheriff.

Angus Betts stepped into Mama's room with the intention of questioning her, but he could not rouse Mama from her stupor. "How long has she been like this?" he asked.

"'Bout a hour," Miss Pearl answered.

"She tell you that Chad is dead?" the sheriff asked. "I talked with Bo and Frances. They claim nobody else was at the house, except Chad and Rozelle. They say they heard screaming, and by the time they reached the room, Chad was dead and Rozelle took off running, screaming about ghosts."

He leaned over the bed, examined Mama's eyes, lightly slapped her cheeks, but she did not respond. "It's a mess," he said, "but we know Chad wasn't killed by a ghost. Sooner or later somebody has to talk. How long you say she's been like this?"

"'Bout a hour," Miss Pearl repeated.

"How the hell did she drive a car all the way down a dark road in this condition?" Angus Betts asked, more to himself than to us. "For all I know she may have been the one who killed Chad." He studied Mama's body, her open, hollow eyes, the rise and fall of her chest, then he turned to me. "Help me get her in the car," he said. "I'll take her over to the hospital. Morris is still out at Bo's seeing after Chad."

fifty-seven

We were not sure what was going to happen with Mama, I told Laura when she came home from school. The news of Chadlow's murder was all over town by now, and if Mushy or the others wanted to know more, they would have to come to me. I had not been out of the house since helping to carry Mama out to the sheriff's car. I had spent the day thinking of how I would prepare Laura for the changes I knew we had to make.

For the second day in a row, we took peanut butter and crackers to the front steps. More traffic than usual moved back and forth on the road, and Laura watched the road with interest while I watched her. She was nearly nine. I wondered if I was mature enough to repair some of the damage Mama had done to her. I knew I had to try.

"Laura, do you know it's wrong . . ." I began, but stopped when she turned to face me. Her proudest moments were when she lifted items from the stores in town to please our mother. Admonishing her for stealing was not the way to start. I was guilty of the same thing and of so much more. Perhaps I wasn't the right person to address my sister's morals, but I could think of no one else. Laura liked fairytales. Maybe I could start with a fairytale, tell it with sincerity, tell it enough times that she would believe it to be true.

"What?" she asked.

Forcing a smile to my lips, I said, "Do you know where I was born?"

"Right here," she answered, "in this house."

"Nope," I responded lightly. "I was born in a paradise—a beautiful paradise—beneath the sprawling branches of a live oak tree. You were born there, too. My first remembered sight was of morning glories climbing the boards of a white picket fence. My first remembered sound was the melody of our mother's voice singing a lullaby."

Laura propped her elbows on her knees and listened with curiosity.

"Mama's hands were soft and had the fragrance of Jergens lotion," I said. "Do you remember that fragrance, Laura?"

She shook her head.

"It doesn't matter," I said. "One day it'll come back to you—it'll all come back, Laura—the way we rolled down grassy slopes over sweet grass and four-leaf clovers, and how we ran barefoot over earth as soft as sand, and chased butterflies under a golden sun and fireflies under a silver moon."

In the fading daylight, my sister smiled at me. "Was Miss Pearl there?" she asked.

"Yeah. She would come in the evenings, especially during the winter. She would stand in front of the coal stove, and sing to you. She didn't bring white socks back then. She brought little frilly dresses and pink bonnets."

"We had a coal stove in Paradise?" Laura asked skeptically.

I laughed. "We didn't stay in Paradise all the time. Sometimes we would come to this house."

"I don't wanna know about this house. Tell me about the Paradise."

"Well, there was a pond with crystal clear water. The water was so clear that we could see all the way to the bottom. On the bottom there were violet, emerald, and ruby rocks that sparkled in the sun. The earth would stop revolving just so the sun could shine down on that pond. Sometimes we would leap into that cool water and feel it tingle all over our bodies. You let the water flow between your fingers and toes, then you would laugh, and your laughter was contagious."

"What's contagious?" Laura asked. "I don't think I ever knew how to swim, Tangy."

"You didn't swim. We kept you afloat just so we could hear your laughter."

Laura rested her head on my lap. "What else?" she asked sleepily.

"Sometimes Harvey, Sam, and Wallace would go all the way to the far side of the pond, and they would come back with fish. While they were gone, the rest of us would stroll the grove of trees and fill our baskets with walnuts and pecans, apples, peaches, and pears."

"I think I know where that Paradise was," Laura said. "It was behind our house, and the gully was the pond. Is um right, Tangy?"

"Am I right," I corrected. "Maybe that's where it was. The where isn't important. The important thing is how much fun we all had."

Laura yawned. "Can we go back there one day?" she asked.

"I hope so, Laura," I answered. "I'll tell you more about it tomorrow. Right now you need to go in and get ready for bed."

She didn't want to move, but I kept nudging her head away from my lap, until she finally got up and went inside. I stayed on the step staring up at a moon that was not the silver moon of my fairytale. I was thirsty from the peanut butter and crackers, and a little chilly from the cool March night, but unlike Laura, I could not move. I had to wait and hear what the voice out of the night would say to me. For the last few minutes of my fairytale, I had known he was there.

He said nothing, so I whispered, "Please, don't say you did it for me."

"I did it for you." Crow stepped out of the darkness at the side of the house. "I did it for you and because it needed to be done. Don't make me lie to you, sugar."

"Mama thinks it was a ghost, and now she can't even speak. You nearly scared her to death."

Crow said without a trace of sympathy in his voice, "She's lucky to be alive." He sat on the bottom step and looked out toward the road. "You know I gotta leave here, don't you?"

"No one knows it was you," I said.

"Rozelle looked me straight in my eyes just as I cut that man's throat. Seems like she wanted me to do it. Held her screams 'til I was out the window and halfway cross the yard. But it's just a matter of time before she talks."

"I wish you hadn't done it, Crow."

"Nah, sugar, you glad I done it. You knew I was gon' do it. You'll forgive me for putting you through this, but you wouldn't never forgive me if I'da left here without doing something."

"You're wrong, Crow. I thought you were already gone. I never expected you to come back and kill anybody. I guess I don't want to believe that my father is a murderer and my mother has been frightened out of her mind, because where does that leave me?"

"I don't know where it leaves you," he answered. "I hope it leaves you safe. You shouldn't be so quick to judge others, but I guess I am a murderer. A murderer is a murderer whether he kills one or one hundred, and I'd kill a thousand for you. So where does that leave you, sugar?"

I stared down the steps at the moonlit face of my father. Tears sprang to my eyes. "Loved?" I asked. "You don't even know me, Crow."

"I know my blood runs through yo' veins. I know the hurt I felt when I saw yo' back. I didn't know I could hurt like that for anybody, except my mama. Whether you believe it or not, Tangy, I do love you. And if you gon' sit there and cry for somebody, don't cry for that dead man. Cry for me—or Rozelle."

"I'm not crying," I lied, "but I don't think I could love anybody enough to kill for them."

Crow sighed deeply. "Yeah, you could," he said. "That's one of the reasons I came back. You give yo' heart like it's water. You need to keep enough of it to love yo'self. Now, tell me you wouldn't kill for that Velman."

My mouth opened and closed. I thought about it, then said, "Maybe I'd die for him, but I don't know that I would kill for him."

"Humph," Crow grunted. "That's the easy way out, sugar. But let's just say I had died for you, who woulda stopped that man the next time around?"

No one had ever stopped Chadlow before, so I had no answer for Crow.

He stood. "I left my car parked in some bushes over on Canyon," he said. "I better get on outta this ol' messed up town before somebody catches me. Rozelle could be telling them white folks about me right now. You take care of yo'self, sugar. And don't lose my mama's number. She always knows where I am."

He started across the yard, and as I watched him go, I felt cheated and betrayed—as if he had given me something special, then had quickly snatched it back.

"Crow," I called.

He stopped, turned, looked up at me.

"I think I could kill for you," I said.

"I hope not," he said, as he started to walk again.

"Crow."

He stopped once more.

"If you ever come through this messed up town again, don't look for me," I said. "I won't be here, but your mother will always know where I am."

fifty-eight

Crow had been wrong about Mama. She had not been talking. In fact, she had not so much as mumbled a single word since being carried away from Penyon Road nearly a week ago. Mushy and Tarabelle came out to the house, pretending that they didn't care what happened to Mama, but they did care. They asked too many questions not to care.

It was Wallace who had the answers. "They sending Mama to a hospital in Milledgeville," he told us. "It ain't really no hospital. It's an insane asylum. They say Mama crazy outta her mind."

"I knew it!" Tarabelle exclaimed. "I always knew it."

"What's Harvey saying 'bout all of this?" Mushy asked.

"He say it's the best thing for her," Wallace answered. "She don't even know him. I went to see her, and she don't know me, either."

"Maybe it is the best thing," Mushy agreed. "Tan, you and Laura get y'all's things together and come stay wit' me 'til we know how long Mama gon' be gone. Where she leave the key to that car?"

"Don't mess with her car, Mushy," I said. "You know she doesn't allow anybody to drive it."

"If I can find that key, I'm gon' mess wit' it," Mushy said. "We can be using that car. If y'all help me find that key, we gon' ride straight on back to the flats in that car, and there ain't a damn thing Mama can do about it, and since she can't talk, there ain't a damn thing she can say about it, either. Now is it?"

I relinquished the key, and as Mushy took it from my hand, she said, "Y'all gon' be staying wit' me and Richard. I ain't gon' have nobody turning up they nose 'bout nothing I do, so, Tan, you can leave all that kinda shit right here on Penyon Road."

She and Wallace went out to the field to start the car, but Tarabelle stayed to watch me and Laura as we shoved our clothes inside paper bags. "Mama still got that box of hair under the floor in her room?" she asked.

"I don't know," I answered.

Tarabelle went out to the kitchen, then came back through the room with a hammer in her hand. When she crossed the hall and stepped into Mama's room, I turned to look down at Laura who seemed to be on the verge of tears.

"Do you understand what's happening?" I asked.

She nodded slowly. "They sending Mama away somewhere 'cause she crazy, and we going to stay with Mushy."

"It's still here," Tarabelle called from Mama's room. "I'm gon' dump it out. I knew she was crazy when I first saw this shit."

By the time I reached the bedroom, Tara was standing with the empty metal box in her hand. She had dumped the hair into the hole made by the missing floorboard. "Well, that's that," she said, then glanced around the room as though she wanted to destroy something else with the hammer. "Tan, you oughta take some of Mama's clothes to wear to school. She got all this nice stuff she done bought when she ain't never bought us nothing." She dropped the hammer and the box on Mama's bed, and began to pull dresses from the line of ropes that held Mama's clothes.

I sorted through Mama's dresses as Tara pulled them down but I said, "Tara, Mama's not dead. She's just in the hospital for a while. She'll come back and look for these things, and I'll be the one she'll be angry with. You won't know anything about it."

"Well, it's up to you," Tara said. "You can keep right on looking like Twiddle Dee Dum for all I care, but I hear that when people go off to one of them crazy hospitals, sometimes they don't never come back. So you can take these things and wear 'em, or let 'em stay here to dry rot. It's up to you."

I shoved most of the dresses into a paper bag, then helped Laura to do the same with her things. When we were done packing, Tarabelle, much to my chagrin, used the hammer to knock the shelves from the walls of Mama's room. She busted the radio and the windup clock, broke the windowpane, and ripped the mattress to shreds.

All I could do was think *what if.* What if Mama started to talk today, and they sent her home? What if she walked in, saw this mess, and went crazy all over again? But what if I tried to stop Tarabelle and she turned the hammer on me?

The noise of her destruction brought Mushy and Wallace back into the house. They surveyed the damage, then Mushy looked at Tarabelle, and asked, "Did you have to do this?"

"I had to do it," Tara answered.

Mushy nodded. "Let's get outta here."

Wallace drove the dirty, banged-up car away from Penyon Road, and at my insistence, we stopped by the Garrisons' to inform Miss Pearl about Mama.

"That's one woman sho' done had it hard," Miss Pearl said. "Everybody in this town done been mad at her at one time or another, but they can't stay mad at her long."

"You been mad at her for more than a year. That's a long time, Miss Pearl," Mushy said.

"Nah, Mushy. I was mad at her for 'bout a week or two, then I started to miss her, but I wanted her to come to me to say she was sorry. She never did, but that's Rosie for you. I don't care what nobody say, she always done the best she could by y'all. Ain't too many women, young as she was when she first started having babies, coulda kept all y'all fed, clothed, and under the same roof."

"You don't know what she's like, Miss Pearl," Tarabelle said. "I tried to tell you a long time ago, but you wouldn't listen to me."

"Nah, now, don't you tell me I don't know what she like. I knew her before any of y'all was born. She was thirteen, and her mama had done threw her out the house. Rosie swore she wouldn't never put none of her babies out wit' nowhere for 'em to go, and she never did. Now, I know y'all might think it's wrong what she done to little Edna here, but Rosie knew what was best, and she knew what she was doing. She just didn't know how to do it right. How could she know when she ain't never had nobody to teach her nothing? Edna is Frank's child, and he shoulda been taking care of her from the day she was born. All y'all got a daddy that ain't never done nothing for you, and y'all walking 'round here blaming Rosie that's done the best she knew how. How come y'all ain't blaming them daddies?"

"Who is my daddy, Miss Pearl?" Tara asked. "Tell me who he is. I wanna hate him, but I don't know who he is."

"You listen to me, Tarabelle!" Miss Pearl said firmly. "You ain't got no need to hate nobody. You a grown woman. And you know why you grown? It's 'cause Rosie done all she could to get you there. Do you hear what I'm saying to you?"

"Yes, ma'am," Tara mumbled, then clutched the bodice of her dress with both hands and pulled until the dress began to rip. I understood that she was trying to release the confusion from her chest when actually it was in her head. I felt it in my chest, too, that Miss Pearl was so right and yet so very wrong.

"We gotta go, Miss Pearl," Mushy said, beckoning for Tarabelle first, then the rest of us.

Gripping Edna's hand as though she feared we might try to kidnap our sister, Miss Pearl followed us out to the porch. "Y'all pray for Rosie," she told us.

Mushy stopped abruptly and whirled around to face Miss Pearl. "Pray?" she asked angrily. "You want us to pray for yo' precious Rosie? We ain't gon' do it, and you ain't gon' make us feel bad 'bout nothing. Tara got a right to know who her daddy is, and if you know, you oughta tell her. I love you, Miss Pearl, and I respect you, but don't you say nothing else to us today. Just let us get in this car and go on 'bout our business. I mean it! Don't you say another damn word to us."

Five of my mother's nine living children rode away from the Garrisons' house in silence. No one expressed what they were feeling, but I thought we were all angry and also maybe a little guilty for being ungrateful. We had memories, however, that would help us to get over these feelings. We knew things that Miss Pearl would never know. And I knew things that I hoped the others would never find out.

fifty-nine

Echo Road lay parallel to the railroad tracks. Each time a train passed by, the house would vibrate and the noise of the locomotive would drown out all other sounds in the universe. It was a sharp contrast to the silence of Penyon Road, but it was wonderful. Laura and I shared a bedroom and a bed. We had electricity, indoor plumbing, and a stationary bathtub. Laura had other children to play with, though she seldom did. Sometimes she would walk around to Martha Jean's house, or stay outside alone until dark.

The drawback to our living arrangements was our proximity to the stores in town. Laura would sneak across the tracks to steal whatever she could conveniently get her hands on, usually things that could have been bought for less than a quarter. One day she stole Velman's watch from Martha Jean's living room. Unbeknownst to the Coopers, I returned the watch and tucked it between the cushions of the couch.

Richard Mackey worked at the Pakersfield carpet mill along with Mr. Frank. He provided well for Mushy, and she made sure we did not want for anything, so I was bewildered by Laura's constant need to steal. My fairytales were not working; finally, I had to tell her outright that it was wrong for her to steal.

"Mama didn't think it was wrong," she responded.

"But it is, Laura. If you get caught, you can go to jail. Tell me you won't do it again."

"Okay, if you say so," she said with a smirk that made me want to strike her.

I was losing Laura; I didn't know how to reach her. In the few short weeks since our move to the flats, she had taken on a personality that completely baffled me. She was meek one day, defiant the next. She wouldn't study. She was failing third grade, and no Quinn had ever repeated a grade, not even Tarabelle.

Mushy took more interest in me than she did in Laura, and when I tried to discuss Laura's behavior with her, she said, "Let her be a little girl, Tan. She ain't never had no freedom being stuck out there wit' Mama. She'll outgrow all them things you think is wrong wit' her. Just give her some time."

Time was something I could give to Laura—and patience—I could be patient with her. After all, I was not without fault. There were times when I would walk around in a daze, so deep in daydreams that I was unaware of my surroundings. I would be Martha Jean—happily married to Velman with two precious little girls in a home I could call my very own. My daydreams were not always pleasant, though. Sometimes I would see myself as my mother, locked away in an insane asylum, unable to think or speak, trying to regain my voice, trying to break free.

In reality, our time on Echo Road was an endless celebration of life. Richard and Mushy seemed to love everything and everyone, and at any given moment, friends, food, music, and booze could fill their house in a party that lasted for hours. Harvey and Carol Sue would stop by on the weekends, and sometimes Wallace and Tarabelle would come over.

There were other nights when Richard's wife, Brenda, would come to Echo Road. She would stand in front of the house and shout for Richard to come out to her. Often her shouts were drowned out by a passing train or the music from inside, but we always knew she was there. One night when there was no music or trains passing, Brenda threw rocks at the house while she cussed

Richard and Mushy loud enough to get the attention of everyone on the street.

After controlling her temper for as long as she could, Mushy angrily faced Richard. "Go on wit' yo' wife," she said. "I ain't gon' fight her for you, Richard. I already done proved I can beat her, so it don't make no sense for me to go out there and do it again. You go on wit' her and stay wit' her till you decide what you wanna do."

"I wanna be wit' you, Mushy," Richard said. "That's why I'm here."

"Well, then get rid of her!"

"How? Tell me how to get rid of her, Mushy," he pleaded, and his face was puckered as though he might cry.

"I don't know, Richard. She's yo' goddamn wife. Go get her ass from in front of my house! Take her home, and stay there wit' her 'til y'all work things out."

Reluctantly, handsome, slow-talking, big-footed Richard Mackey, the good provider, went out to face his wife. He didn't take anything with him, and I assumed he would get rid of her and come back in to Mushy, but after a while I saw him walk off down the street beside Brenda.

"Mushy, what are you gonna do?" I asked.

"About what?"

"About Richard. He's gone."

Mushy laughed. "So what?" she asked. "That's one silly-ass man if I ever saw one. Tell the truth, Tan. Ain't he?"

"He's the one with a job," I explained. "We can't buy food or pay the rent."

"Tan, if it's one thing I learned from my mama, it's how to pay the rent," Mushy said, and winked at me. "I don't know why you worrying 'bout it anyway. Richard'll come crawling back by tomorrow. We'll be okay."

Less than two hours later, Richard returned, begging Mushy to forgive him. I lay on the bed beside Laura, and once again fell into my habit of judging people. Richard Mackey was a pitiful excuse for a man. He was like so many other men in Pakersfield who were unfaithful when things were good, and who fled when things were bad. In my opinion, Velman Cooper was the only decent man in Triacy County. I truly believed that.

It was May 11, 1961—a month before I would have a well-earned diploma in my hands—when we received two visits from the Pakersfield police. They had picked Laura up that morning for stealing key chains from the five-and-dime. They brought her home, gave her a stern warning, and released her to Mushy. Mushy's reaction was to ball a fist and knock Laura to the floor. While Laura sobbed in sorrow over being caught, if not in remorse, I resorted to fairytales again. I bit my tongue to keep from saying, *I told you so,* and I spoke of a paradise from the past.

Later in the day, while Laura was outside playing, hiding, or doing whatever she did when she was alone, another policeman arrived.

"What she steal this time?" Mushy asked wearily.

"I'm here about Rozelle Quinn," the policeman said from the other side of the screen door. "We thought you folks ought to know that she'll be home on Monday."

"Uh-uh." Mushy shook her head. "Home where?" she asked.

"We're bringing her here. You are her daughter, aren't you?"

"Uh-uh," Mushy repeated. "Y'all can't bring her here. Ain't y'all suppose to take her to jail or something?"

"Is she better?" I asked.

The policeman glanced at me. "All I know is that they're sending her home," he said, before disappearing from the screen.

"What the hell am I supposed to do now?" Mushy asked as she slumped down on the couch next to Richard. "Tan, call Harvey and them. Tell 'em to come on over here so they can decide what to do wit' Mama, 'cause she ain't staying here wit' me and Richard."

"Now, baby, she is yo' mama," Richard began. "We can make room. We can . . ."

"Be quiet, Richard," Mushy whispered. "You just don't understand."

I made the calls, then went out to the kitchen to fry chicken and make potato salad and lemonade. Miss Pearl had always said that people couldn't make rational decisions on an empty stomach, and we had some serious decisions to make.

They came: Tarabelle, Wallace, Harvey with Carol Sue, Martha Jean with Velman and the babies. We ate, and tossed responsibility out with the chicken bones. We were unwilling to sacrifice much for the woman who had given us life.

"I don't even know why y'all called me," Tarabelle said. "Y'all know I stay wit' Miss Shirley, and she ain't gon' let Mama stay in her house."

"I went through a lot to get Martha Jean away from Miss Rosie," Velman reminded us. "I didn't go through all that just so I can take Miss Rosie in and start all that mess again. We can't do it."

Finally, Harvey weighed in. "Carol Sue 'bout to have a baby. I don't know what happened to Judy, but I know I don't never wanna come home from work to find our baby dead in no ditch. We can fit a small bed in here in that room wit' Tangy Mae and Laura. I'll buy the bed tomorrow."

Wallace spoke up. "I been seeing after Mr. Grodin. He's sick, and he needs somebody to help him, but if I gotta make a choice between him and Mama, I'll go wit' Mama. I'll move back out to the house and look after her."

"I'll move back, too," I said. "I don't want to take Laura back out there, but I'll go."

"You gon' quit school, little sister?" Velman asked. "You this close to graduating, and you gon' quit? Wallace gotta go to work, and somebody gotta be there with Miss Rosie."

"Tangy Mae, you ain't gon' quit school," Harvey said. "And anyway, when's the last time any of y'all been out there and looked at that house. It's a mess, and we ain't been paying no rent on it. Mr. Poppy might not even let Mama move back in there. I say we get a small bed and put it in that room wit' Tangy Mae and Laura."

Mushy had not touched her food, nor had she spoken a single word. After the others had departed with the assumption that Mama would move in with us on Echo Road, Mushy rested her head on Richard's shoulder, and said. "I knew this shit was gon' happen. How long I gotta pay for being born first in this damn family?"

sixty

They had cut her hair at the hospital, and it was growing back with specks of gray amidst reddish-brown—a motley mane. Her skin was ashen, her eyes were dull, and her face had the lifeless expression Tarabelle had once worn. She could walk—thank God—but when she opened her mouth to speak, it was not to us, but to herself.

She would sit in the kitchen staring into space for hours, then fall asleep on the chair. Not once had she slept on the bed that Harvey had bought for her. We spoke to her in high and low tones, but we never knew exactly what to say. We bathed, clothed, and fed her, because she would do nothing for herself. Almost immediately upon her arrival, Angus Betts appeared at our door to question her about the death of Chad Lowe, but he could get no information from her.

Often Mushy would pull a chair up beside Mama and pour them both a drink of corn whiskey or whatever else she happened to have in the house. But Mama would not hold a glass and Mushy would have to pour the drink into her mouth.

Once I heard Mushy say, "You done spent yo' whole hateful life calling Martha Jean dumb. Who the dumb one now? You can't even wash yo' own ol' nasty behind. I don't know why they didn't keep you in that hospital."

Mushy tried to pour more of the whiskey down Mama's throat, but Mama gagged and coughed until finally I said, "Stop, Mushy. Don't make her drink that stuff."

"Shut up!" Mushy yelled at me. "I told you before you came here not to turn yo' nose up at nothing I do. If I get her drunk enough, maybe she'll go to bed. How we suppose to rest at night when she sitting up here like something dead. Who knows what the hell she might do. Tan, you able to go in there and sleep like it ain't nothing, but I ain't had no sleep in days, and I'm tired."

Mushy didn't think Mama could hear her, but I thought she did. I watched Mama, and noticed that sometimes her hands twitched, or her clouded eyes would clear long enough to watch Laura's movements in a room. She fixed on Laura with the demeanor of a cat ready to swoop up its prey, but never for long, and Laura never seemed to notice.

On Saturdays and some days after school, I would take my mother's hand and walk her out to Penyon Road, trying to spark some remembrance, trying to restore some life into her dull eyes.

One day when I had walked her through the woods beyond the old house and through the house itself, she raised a hand to my chin and tilted my head skyward. "Sam," she said, and her face broke into an open, loving smile. "Sam."

"Hey, Mama," I said in that fleeting moment before she was lost to me again.

When I told the others about it, Tarabelle asked, "You think she ever gon' be right again?"

"It's possible," I answered. "She remembered Sam."

"I wanna take her out there the next time, Tan," Tarabelle said. "Maybe she'll remember me. She's my mama, too. I'm gon' fix us a picnic lunch and take her out there one day next week."

My life continued, not much altered by Mama's return. I went to school and church, then came home and tried to give Mushy a rest. Mushy's life had changed drastically. Her friends no longer crowded the living room for impromptu parties. She was angry with the world and mean to everybody in it. Sometimes poor

Richard would be forced to go and spend a couple of nights with his wife until it was safe for him to return home. Under the influence of booze, Mushy was managing to get a few hours sleep each night, but it was never enough.

She woke up one morning and yanked me out of sleep and out of bed in the same motion. "Mama's gone!" she shouted. "She ain't nowhere in this damn house. We gotta go find her."

We went door to door, and woke up nearly everybody in the flats, but nobody had seen our mother. Mushy finally decided to take the car and search all over town, starting with the house on Penyon Road. I was to stay in the flats with Laura in the unlikely event Mama returned there.

We gave the house, the front and back yards, a final search before Mushy hurried out to the car. She had just turned the key in the ignition when a black-and-white police car turned onto Echo Road and stopped behind her. The policeman who got out and opened the rear door for Mama, told us that he had spotted her pacing the ground below the platform of the train depot.

"At first I thought it was somebody waiting for the next train," he said, "but the next train is not due for another two hours. When I saw who it was, I brought her on home."

"I don't live here," Mama protested.

The policeman ignored her. "Y'all need to keep a better watch on her," he scolded. "Another time of day, and she could've been run over by a train."

Mama was barefoot and still wearing the nightgown I had dressed her in before going to bed myself. She struggled as we tried to help her inside the house, and Mushy roughly shoved her forward.

"I don't live here!" Mama shouted. "I wanna go home."

When we had her inside, Mushy collared her, wrenching her gown around her with such force that they nearly bumped heads. "Look here, Mama," she hissed, "I ain't gon' be hunting all over town for you, and you ain't gon' be embarrassing me by leaving outta here half naked. This is where you live. You don't like it, and I don't like it, but that's the way it is. So sit yo' ass down somewhere and stay put!"

"Mushy, don't . . ." I started.

Mushy released Mama and turned on me. "Tan, you gon' graduate next week, and I'm happy for you. You'll be the first one of us to get that piece of paper, and when you get it in yo' hands, I want you to get the hell out my house. I don't want you back here turning up yo' nose up at nothing I do." She fanned one hand as though shooing me away. "I just want you outta here. You can take Mama, take Laura, take Richard, too. All y'all just get the hell away from me."

In the silence following Mushy's outburst, we heard the trickle of urine dripping to the floor as Mama wet herself and everything within a six-inch radius. "Oh-oh," she said in a child-like sing-song. "Oh-oh."

Mushy threw herself on the couch, turned her rear end toward the ceiling, and covered her head with her hands. I sent Laura off to school, then took Mama into the bathroom and gave her a bath. When I had her dressed, I went back to the front room to check on Mushy.

She was sitting up on the couch with a Mason jar of corn whiskey in her hand. "Tan, I'm sorry," she said. "I don't want you to leave. I wouldn't never put you out."

"You're tired, Mushy," I said. "I know you wouldn't put me out, but I think you meant it about me turning up my nose at things. If my nose turns up, I'm not aware of it."

She tried to smile. "It's a look you get all over yo' face whenever I do something you don't like," she said. "It makes me feel small, like you think you so much better than me. I got a right to get angry. Everybody got a right to get angry, even you. If you don't let it out, it'll eat yo' insides up."

"So will corn whiskey," I said, and regretted my words even before they were out of my mouth.

"You see?" she asked. "You see what I mean?"

I did see, didn't like it, and didn't have time to apologize for it. Maybe after school, after I got my diploma, I could work on the tilt of my nose, the expression on my face, and my use of words that made Mushy feel small. My priority at present was to finish my last few days of school. I left Mushy with her feelings, and took mine with me as I walked to Plymouth.

Mama was gone again the following morning, and this time Mushy went straight to the train depot and brought her home. Mama had already soiled her gown, but she seemed not to notice. As I watched her sitting at the kitchen table, I thought I saw the stoic expression on her face change to a devious one, and twice I was sure I saw her stick out a leg and try to trip Laura.

The next time Mama slipped out of the house, we did not go out to find her, and eventually she came back to the house on her own. Another morning it was Tarabelle who brought her home.

"Y'all better do something 'bout Mama," Tara said. "Do y'all know she had done walked all the way 'round to Miss Shirley's, and was standing out in the street yelling 'Tarabelle, Tarabelle, you's a bull dyke, Tarabelle.' How come she can call me names, but act like she don't know I'm her daughter? I think Mama pulling y'all's leg."

Mushy, who was so sleepy she could barely keep her eyes open, waggled her fingers at Tarabelle. "Take her on back around there wit' you, Tara," she mumbled. "I need some sleep."

"You know I gotta go to work, Mushy. I ain't gon' lose my job fooling 'round wit' Mama," Tara said. "I'm trying to help out. I told you I'll watch her while you go see Tan get her diploma, and I'm taking her on a picnic. That oughta be enough."

My mother would not watch me graduate from high school. It wasn't such a bad thing because she had never thought much of education, but all of my life I had pictured her being there. She stood beside me in Mushy's living room, seemingly staring at nothing though I felt she was observing everything. I took her hand, led her to the kitchen, and fixed her a cup of coffee.

"Mama," I said, "if you're gonna keep going out in the mornings, you need to put on some clothes."

There was no response from her, and I picked up her cup to allow her to sip her coffee when I was almost certain she could have held the cup herself.

Mushy was asleep on the couch when Laura and I left for school. We walked in silence through the flats and up the hills toward Plymouth. As we neared the school, I asked Laura how she felt about Mama being home.

"I don't know," Laura answered. "How come she pee on herself like a baby?"

I changed the subject. "Laura, Miss Hollis has told me that you're not going to be promoted to the fourth grade."

"I know," she said. "I'll be with Edna next year."

"How would you feel about going to a different school in another town?"

"Wit' Edna?"

"Just you."

"No," she said. "I wanna be wit' Edna."

"Even if it means moving back to Penyon Road and living in our old house with Mama?"

"Will you be there wit' me?" she asked.

"No, Laura, I'd like to leave here. I don't ever want to live in that house again."

We reached the school before she could ask me the whys and wherefores of my plans, which had not been completely thought out. I had one hundred dollars and an address, both provided by Crow. I had common sense, and I would have a high school diploma. Those things would have to be enough for whatever I decided to do.

At home that night, I had a most serious conversation with God. I did not try to bargain, nor did I send up a request for anything ridiculous, although I was reminded of the time when I had asked Him to dry up my tear ducts and those of my sisters. He hadn't done it, and tears slid from my eyes as I prayed. My prayer was a jumble of messages that I felt He understood. I thanked Him for every breath I had ever taken in my lifetime, even the ones He had forced into my lungs when I had thought I wanted to die.

"Lead us not into temptation, but deliver us from evil," I prayed, and stilled my lust for Velman Cooper, though I had sinned already. "Forgive me."

I asked questions, expecting no answers because God did not have to answer to me, but I wanted to know if I could honor my mother from a distance. Would that be all right? Would guilt consume me if I abandoned my family? Was I mature enough to raise Laura the way He would have me do? Was there someone else better suited?

"Snip the tip of my nose so that it remains unchanging in the presence of my sister. Soften the words that spill from my tongue, and make me less judgmental. I cannot cast a stone; I can only ask forgiveness. I want to leave Pakersfield so bad, Lord, that I'm blind to nearly everything else. Help me to see. If it is Your will that I stay here, then You will have to give me a sign. Amen."

I dried my eyes, shifted my body closer to Laura's, and allowed her soft breathing to lull me toward sleep.

"*I have lightened your burden, removed stumbling blocks from your path,*" I thought I heard a voice whisper. I listened for more, but heard only my sister's breathing. An early dream? An active imagination? And if my path was clear and my burden lighter, did that mean I should stay or leave?

arabelle intended to kill two birds with one stone. On my commencement day, she arrived at our house at noon with a picnic basket covered with a flower-patterned dishcloth. "Y'all got Mama ready to go?" she asked as she entered the house.

"We trying to get ready for Tan's graduation," Mushy informed her. "You can get Mama dressed."

"Damn," Tara mumbled, and placed her basket on the floor beside the couch. "I gotta watch her for y'all, and get her dressed, too? Where she at?"

"She back up in there somewhere," Mushy answered. She was standing behind me, fastening the back of my dress, while I stared at myself in the mirror. "You pretty as a picture, Tan," she said. "I'm so proud of you."

"Thank you, Mushy," I said. "I don't think I would have made it without you."

She winked at me. "You was born to make it. You done spent yo' whole life talking 'bout that one piece of paper. I can't wait to see it."

On the couch, dressed in a pink dress, white socks and black shoes, Laura sat patiently waiting for us to finish dressing. From our bedroom came the voice of Tarabelle encouraging Mama to put her arms into the sleeves of a blouse.

"Maybe I better go help her," Mushy suggested.

Mushy went into the bedroom, and Tarabelle came out. I don't know why Laura missed the cues—Tara's voice coming and Mushy's going, the click and the clump of footsteps passing each other—but she did. When Tarabelle stepped into the front room, Laura was on her knees beside the couch rummaging through the picnic basket.

"You little thief!" Tarabelle shouted as she charged toward Laura. "You steal anything that ain't nailed down."

"I didn't take nothing, Tara," Laura cried, and moved swiftly out of harm's way. "I was just trying to see."

"See what? What this damn basket gotta do wit' you?" Tarabelle snatched the basket up from the floor. "Everybody in this town talking 'bout yo' little roguish ass. Ain't nothing in the world worse than a thief," she said, then shouted toward the bedroom, "Mushy, you better hurry up and send Mama on outta there before I change my mind, 'cause I'm gon' have to hurt Laura out here. Little, low-down, dirty, thieving-ass, mangy dog."

Laura sniffed her fingers, glanced down at her dress, then fled toward the bathroom while Tarabelle took her basket and went to wait on the front porch for Mama. I still stood in front of the mirror. A train thundered down the tracks behind the house, the house vibrated, and my reflection rippled in the glass. Soon, I thought. *Soon.*

It was beautiful, breezy, sunny, a perfect day for a graduation, and I wasn't the least bit nervous. We were leaving the house at twelve-thirty for a one o'clock ceremony, so I wasn't rushed, and although I had not written a valedictory speech, I knew exactly what I would say. I felt calm as I adjusted the garters on my stockings and stepped into my shoes. Glancing at the mirror once more, I thought I looked nice—real nice. My warped finger was not on the hand that would reach for my diploma, but on the hand that would shake Mr. Hewitt's. The scars on my back were hidden beneath a lovely, new dress, and the brand on my leg was barely discernible through nylon stockings.

My mother stepped into the living room, briefly glanced in my direction, and winked an eye that did not appear nearly as dull as it had a week ago. I realized that the movement of her eye must have been involuntary. But it winked again, before she stepped across the threshold.

I watched my mother walk up the street behind my sister. Mushy had offered to drive them to Penyon Road, but Tara had insisted on walking, so they strode like strangers, with Tara several paces ahead.

"Who woulda ever thought Mama would be so pitiful?" Mushy asked as we left the house for the Plymouth School. "I keep thinking 'bout how she used to be and how she is now. I know she still sick 'cause if she wadn't, she'd be going on and on 'bout me living wit' Richard, and she ain't said nothing yet."

"She's coming around," I said. "Every day she seems to get better. Even her eyes look clearer."

"Maybe," Mushy agreed.

We rode in silence for a while, and were midway up the last hill when I asked, "Mushy, if I wasn't here, and Mama got better, would you let her take Laura back to Penyon Road to live?"

"I guess I would," she said. "I don't know how I could stop her. Laura is Mama's child; she ain't mine."

As the school building came into view, Mushy asked, "Tan, you planning on leaving here?"

I nodded. "Yeah."

"When?"

"I don't know. Maybe later this year or next year."

"You gon' leave me stuck wit' Mama? I came back down here to help you, now you just gon' leave me stuck here?"

Mushy parked the car on the school lot, and turned to glare at me, waiting for an answer.

"I'm sorry, Mushy," I said. "I wanna leave Pakersfield. I thought you'd understand."

"You selfish, Tan," she said solemnly, shaking her head as though I had disappointed her. "We all done got dressed up today to come see you graduate 'cause we care 'bout you, and we proud of you. We thought you'd get a job and help take care of Mama. Me and Richard done took care of you for these last few months, and this how you say thank you?"

"Thank you," I mumbled as I opened the car door to get out.

We walked across the schoolyard side by side, but not together at all. Mushy, I was sure, was craving a drink of whiskey. It seemed to be her solution to anger and frustration—her coping remedy. Although, sooner or later, she would have to face the inevitability of my departure, I blamed myself for my timing and for putting a damper on a day that should have been special.

Friends and neighbors stood in small groups, enjoying each other's company while waiting for the start of the graduation ceremony. We were greeted cheerfully, and responded somberly, as we made our way to the main door.

"We gon' be here all day 'til it gets dark?" Laura asked.

"Probably a couple of hours," I answered. "You'll have plenty of time to play with Edna, if that's what you're worried about."

"It won't be dark?" Laura asked.

"No, Laura, it won't be dark," Mushy answered irritably. "Why you keep asking that?"

"'Cause why Tara need lamps?" Laura asked. "Mama don't let us turn on the lamps 'til it's dark."

Mushy halted in her tracks and glanced down at Laura. "What you talking about?" she asked. "You know Tara ain't gon' stay out there all day wit' Mama."

"Tara ain't got no food in her basket," Laura answered. "She just got something that smell like kerosene, and a box of matches to light the lamps."

"Shit!" Mushy whispered. "She gon' set the damn house on fire. Tan, I'm gon' drive out there before she do something stupid. I'll try to make it back in time to see you graduate."

"I'm going with you," I said. "Laura, you go inside and wait for Harvey or Martha Jean."

"Don't tell Tara that I told," Laura pleaded.

We saw the smoke and flames even before we turned off of Fife Street onto Penyon Road. Mushy, gripping the steering wheel, was swearing so fast that it came out as a chant. I was praying much the same way.

As we rounded the bend, we saw a shower of sparks drift down from the burning house to land in the field. Almost immediately, a small area of dry weeds began to burn. Up on the hill, smoke swelled from the broken window of Mama's room and through the front door. Angry, orange flames blazed through the walls of the house and licked at the tin roof.

"Damn! Damn!" Mushy shouted. She stopped the car and shifted into reverse. "I can't park next to the field."

She was backing the car toward Fife when I glanced up the hill once more and saw my mother standing in a cascade of cinders. Her arms were outstretched as she whirled around like a child enjoying a spring rain.

"Let me out, Mushy!" I cried. "Stop the car! I think I see Mama."

Mushy braked the car on the gully side of the road, and we both jumped out and raced toward the doomed house. The fire department did not cross the city line, and even if they did, they wouldn't have been able to save anything. The room where I had spent the nights of my youth was no more. It had caved into the gully. Fire climbed the back wall of what had once been the front room, and the coal stove had dropped and rolled down the incline to be halted midway by burning rubble. Mama's room, the hallway, half of the front porch, and all of the front steps were standing, but teetering toward collapse.

The smoke was frightening, and I could feel the intense heat from the fire as I scurried up the bank and into the yard. Mushy and I reached Mama at the same time, shouting the same thing, "Where's Tara?"

Mama whirled in a world that revolved around her. Around and around she turned until I gripped her shoulders and brought her to a standstill. It took a few seconds before her eyes focused on me, and all the while Mushy and I were asking where Tara was.

"Where's Tara, Mama?" I screamed once more.

Mama pointed toward the remains of the house. "She up in the house somewhere," she answered calmly.

"No!" Mushy cried. "No, Mama!"

Across the road, the field was now burning out of control. I knew there was a possibility of embers igniting the foliage surrounding the gully, and if that happened, we could be trapped in blinding smoke. Even knowing that, we stayed where we were.

With tears streaming down her face, nearly hysterical, Mushy patted a hand against her chest, above her heart. "I don't believe my sister is in there," she cried. "If she was in there, I'd have that bad feeling right here. I don't feel it."

I knew exactly what she meant, and I didn't feel it, either. "Take Mama out of here," I said. "I'll look around back for Tara."

Mushy nodded and tried to move Mama toward the road, but Mama wouldn't budge. "Come on, Mama, I gotta get you outta here!" Mushy shouted, tugging Mama by an arm.

Confident that Mushy would get Mama to safety—even if she had to hit her over the head and drag her away from the fire—I rushed toward the backyard, keeping as far away from the house as I could. Flames feeding greedily on dried lumber did not yet reach out into the yard, but I was cautious. I quickly scanned the rear of the house where wood crackled and crumbled at the kitchen's corner, and the overhanging branch of a honey locust smoldered.

Tarabelle was nowhere, yet she had to be somewhere—down in the gully, under a bush, long gone from here—anywhere, except in the hell that was burning in front of me. I called out her name but got no answer.

I could see the rear wall of the house shifting beneath the roof. I stepped back along the path that led to the woods, putting distance between me and a charred wall whose fall in some direction was imminent. It roared as it separated from foundation and roof, then struck the ground, sending burning embers flying through the air. The roaring increased; it was the metallic cry of disintegrating tin.

Smoke, that had been drifting upward, now streamed out over the gully and toward the woods. My eyes watered; my throat itched, and when I tried once again to call Tara's name, I began to cough. I stepped off of the path toward the outhouse, not quite ready to end my search, heading for the small space between the outhouse and the woods that would lead me safely back to the side yard and down to the road.

Someone had turned on the faucet in the yard. Water sprayed from the spout and hit the ground, sending a muddy stream cascading like blood, down the bank and onto the road.

Through the smoke, I saw stick figures coming toward me. "Is there anything we can do?" they asked.

If there was anything to be done, I would have done it.

I shook my head in response to their questions, and I was suddenly struck with that feeling of loss that neither Mushy nor I had felt earlier. Down on the road, Angus Betts and one of his deputies stood staring up at the burning house. They had come without my knowledge, without a siren, as though they had known there was no help to be given.

"Mushy tells me your sister is in there," the sheriff said.

I nodded, and kept walking until I reached the spot where Mushy was waiting with Mama. I climbed onto the back seat, but for the longest time Mushy did not start the car. She stared straight ahead through the windshield, as though she expected Tarabelle to leap from the fire and smoke unharmed.

Behind us, on Fife Street, the Pakersfield Fire Department was hosing down the field on the city side of the line.

sixty-two

Mushy had not known a sober second since returning home from Penyon Road. Richard Mackey stayed with her, consoling her. The siblings came—stunned and silent in their grief. Reverend Nelson arrived to exonerate the soul of Tarabelle Quinn for every sin she had committed in her lifetime. He bowed his head, raised a hand, and asked that her spirit rest in peace. How? I wondered. Was he not the same man who had condemned her to Hell for all eternity because she failed to honor a mother who knew nothing of honor? I was bitter.

Miss Pearl wept noisily, and Mattie stood in the living room silently shedding tears. Mr. Hewitt and Mr. Pace arrived to offer their condolences and to deliver my diploma to me. I would rather have had my sister.

I took the diploma into my room, stared at it, thought of how quickly it could go up in smoke. Finally, I tucked it inside a shopping bag that contained a change of clothes for me and Laura, then I went to the back porch and waited for a train to come along and fill my head with a roar that would obliterate all anger and pain.

Mushy stumbled out onto the porch and leaned on the banister beside me. There were puffy bags beneath her bloodshot eyes, her cheeks were flushed, and she could barely hold her head up.

"Tan," she said, slurring her words. "I'm just gon' come right on out and say this 'cause I can't keep it in no longer. Mama killed our sister. While you was all up there in that smoke and stuff, I was down in that car wit' that devil bitch, asking her what the hell happened. Took me a long time to get it outta her, but I got it. I sho' nuff got it."

Mushy dropped to the porch, held onto the rail, closed her eyes, bowed her head. "She say Tara told her to take a rest from her long walk. She was tired, so she done it even though the bed was all tore up to pieces." Mushy cried, pounded her thigh with a fist. "She saw Tara pouring gasoline all through the house, could smell it, so she got up, got the matches, and went to the front door. Says she lit a match and threw it. Just walked on out the damn house and left my sister in there to burn."

While I stood there staring straight ahead, a train whistle screamed in proxy. No sound came from me, but the roar and rumble of the locomotive filling my head were exactly what I needed.

Long after Mushy had crawled her way back inside, I remained on the porch, waiting for more trains to pass and shake up the world. *Sam, where are you? There's a place filled with sorrow in my heart, and you're not there. Where are you?* I prayed for Sam, then I prayed that Tarabelle was in Heaven with Judy, and knew nothing of the fires burning in Hell.

I cried on the porch until darkness hid me. When I was able, I walked into a quiet house to see my mother, sitting on a kitchen chair, Mushy and Richard, both passed out from drink, and Laura, curled up on our bed asleep. I kissed my little sister, checked my shopping bag, then returned to the kitchen.

I didn't really know what to tell my mother, but I knew I needed to say something. So I said, "Mama, I know you're sick, and I'm sorry, but I think you know exactly what you're doing. You didn't have to kill Tara."

"She was trying to kill me, Tangy Mae," Mama said without emotion, without looking at me.

"You need to understand that you've placed yourself in the hands of the same children you taught to honor you. I'm afraid they might honor you the same way you've honored them, and we both know that's no good. Tara wanted you to love her, but I don't think you ever did. Since she died, my thoughts have been selfish ones. I think of all the chances I had to tell her I loved her, and I never said it. Now that I want to say it, she can't hear me."

I waited for my mother to respond, but she said nothing.

"I'd like to say that I love you, Mama, but I can't say it today. I'll just say that I'm trying hard not to hate you. I'm trying to understand."

"Get away from me, Tangy Mae," she whispered.

"I'm going," I said, and turned to leave the kitchen, but I stopped in the doorway, and turned to look at her. "Mama, do you remember how Junior Fess came through that window and frightened you?"

She did not answer me, but I saw her back stiffen as though she knew what I was going to say.

"What do you think it's going to be like when Tara comes back for you?" I asked. It was the cruelest thing I had ever said.

"Tangy Mae, if Tarabelle comes back, she'll come as a fireball," Mama said. "That's what she was the last time I seen her."

I never slept that night. I watched the clock, and awakened Laura at four o'clock in the morning. She was sleepy and confused as I helped her to dress. We slipped past Mushy and Richard who were still asleep on the couch, then with a shopping bag between us, we walked up Echo Road, crossed the tracks, and made our way through town toward the bus depot.

As we stood in the dark outside the depot, Laura asked, "What happened to Tara?"

"I'm not sure," I answered, which was the truth.

We climbed onto the five-thirty bus out of Pakersfield, and Laura took the window seat. It was fine with me. Over her head, I could see familiar landmarks passing in the dawn. Goodbye, so long, farewell.

"Where're we going?" Laura finally thought to ask.

"We're crossing the Georgia state line," I answered.

She turned from the window, studied the high backs of the seats, and glanced down the narrow aisle. The bus yielded at the train tracks, and over Laura's head, through the dirty window, I saw our mother. She was pacing the ground in front of the platform of the train depot. Her arms were folded across her chest as she marched back and forth, seemingly without purpose. She stopped, glanced at the bus, straight up at the window where we were seated. I was sure she could not see us, yet it seemed she could.

I did not want Laura to see her and take that memory with her. I placed a hand on my sister's knee, and quickly asked, "Laura, do you remember where I was born?"

She nodded. "Yeah. You was born in a paradise beneath the sp-sp-sprawling branches of a live oak tree."

The bus rattled across the tracks. "What else?" I asked.

"Your first remembered sight was . . ."

The Darkest Child
Readers Guide

1. As the book opens, does Tangy Mae truly believe her mother is dying? If she does, how has she remained so innocent? Would things be different today? How is the loss of Tangy's innocence reflected in her telling of the story?

2. How is the hierarchy that Rozelle establishes among her children of "white," "Indian," and "Negro" shaped by her own experience as a light-skinned black woman, as well as America's history of colonization and slavery? Do you believe that racism based on skin tone persists today? How does its role differ within and outside of minority communities?

3. Rozelle has been brutal to her children, but she has never killed one until she throws Judy from the porch (Chapter 27). She is convincing when she tells the sheriff it was an accident. Why does Tangy momentarily refuse to believe her own senses? When she thinks, "No mother could do that, not even mine. Could she?" who or what is she questioning?

4. What affect does Rozelle's appearance have on her mental condition? What benefits does she derive from her beauty, and conversely, how does it harm her? What is the difference between her current treatment by white society and the treatment she would be accorded if she "passed" as white?

5. What do you believe Rozelle's reasons are for having children? Do you think she would have used "the pill" if it had been available? Rozelle says of Judy's birth, "It broke something inside me they can't fix. Had to take it out . . . said I couldn't have no mo', and all I got was a darkie." What might this have to do with Judy's untimely death?

6. How is Mushy different from her mother? How did she manage to leave the family to go to work in Cleveland? Did the experience really change her? Is Tangy Mae right to judge her for drinking? Why has she returned to Pakersfield?

7. Do you think Junior Fess could have proceeded differently and still been true to his ideals?

8. Was the burning of the town's stores by Sam and his friends an act of protest against racism, an impulsive response to Junior's murder and Sam's incarceration, or a combination of these and/or other factors?

9. Why does the Sheriff deny Sam as his son? Knowing Rozelle's history, do you believe that Sam is, in fact, his son? Is there ever any indication that the Sheriff cares for Sam?

10. Tangy Mae's adolescence coincides with the last decade of Jim Crow and the start of integration in schools. She mentions in Chapter 55 that the county's decision to integrate high schools is reversed in the second year due to violence. Do you think Tangy Mae would still have benefited from being part of the inaugural integrated class?

11. Tarabelle tries to murder her mother. Why is she so much angrier with Rozelle than the other children? Is she justified in her anger? What do Rozelle's feelings seem to be for Tarabelle?

12. Despite her mother's constant disparagement and the pain she has had to endure, Tangy Mae retains her strength and ambition. How has she been able to survive and retain her humanity? Is she right to leave at the end of the book, or could she have done something else? Why does she bring Laura with her?

Continue reading for an excerpt of Delores Phillips's
unfinished sequel to *The Darkest Child*,
Stumbling Blocks

Chapter I

" I wanna get off this bus." Laura, restless from miles of riding, eased forward on her seat as though preparing to stand.

"Sit back!" I said. "The driver's not gonna stop to let you off, and where would you go anyway?"

She blew a long, dissatisfied sigh, then slowly leaned back and stared once again from the window. After a few seconds of watching her, I closed my eyes and tried to get some much-needed rest. I couldn't remember the last time I had slept, and I felt drained. I was nodding off when Laura's voice startled me.

"Is Tara my fault?" she asked. "Am I the reason she's dead?"

I opened my eyes. "No, Laura. She died in a fire, and it wasn't your fault."

"But I told," she said. "I told 'bout her havin' the matches. She was mad at me, but I didn't take nothin' outta her basket."

"She knew that, and I don't think she was angry with you."

"I don't know," Laura said doubtfully as tears oozed from her eyes and slid down her face.

"It'll be all right," I soothed.

She cried in silence for a while, then leaned her head against the bus window and closed her eyes. A copper-colored complexion made Laura one of our mother's Indian children, as Tarabelle had been. Laura and Tara had never been close, and Tara's last words to her had been in anger. I watched my sister through sleepy eyes. Her side profile revealed slightly parted lips, a small narrow nose, almond-shaped eyes, and dark, satiny lashes that were now wet with tears. It was hard to believe that her hair had grown to its present length when she had been nearly bald a year ago, but it had, and I would need to comb it before we reached Knoxville.

Laura was a thief, just as Tara had said. I didn't like it, but she was what she was. Mama had taught her to shoplift from the stores in Pakersfield, and Laura had learned it well. I think she'd had to prove that she could do something to please our mother. At first, she had stolen out of necessity under Mama's guidance, but it gradually became a game to her, a challenge of sorts. She had wet her pallet until she was six years old, but she had finally stopped, so I had to believe that she would eventually stop stealing. I reached over and touched her as she dozed, then I dropped my hand onto my lap and closed my eyes again.

I drifted into a fitful sleep with trepidation. What would life be like with a grandmother I had yet to meet? What troubled me most was the fact that she had no idea we were coming. Telephone calls and mail service out of Pakersfield were ill-advised for anyone aiming for discretion. It was inevitable that I would flee Pakersfield, but I questioned whether I had been right to snatch Laura and bring her along. I tried to assure myself that there had been no other option. Sometimes, solving a problem is as simple as moving from one place to another. I envisioned our move as playing a game of checkers, moving pieces diagonally forward, trying to avoid being captured, trying to avoid crowning an opponent a king. I never wanted anybody to rule over my life again.

No longer a child, though not yet considered a full-grown woman, I had placed myself in the position of an adult, now responsible for Laura. Being full-grown would bring many changes. It would mean that I could make my own decisions, like the one that had placed me on a Greyhound bus. In eight months I would be eighteen, and it was past time that I got to know my father. I wondered if I would ever be able to call him Daddy. It didn't matter. I had already decided that when I reached Knoxville, I would no longer be a Quinn. I would take my father's last name and become a Yardley. If my mother ever found out, she'd never forgive me, but forgiveness had never been one of her attributes.

It was my birthright to bear some of my mother's traits. I did not inherit her beauty or cruelty, and I prayed to never be marked by her insanity. At her best, melodious laughter flowed from her like spring in perfection, giving life to everything within its reach. At her worst, her soft hands turned violent against her children, spiteful words spilled from her tongue like the harsh coldness of winter, and her dark side would manifest as hallucinations. Bugs that no one else could see would crawl all over her. She would scrape her skin raw, and still could not rid her body of those bugs.

With a solemn expression, and in a dry tone, Tara had once said, "They ain't bugs. They men. Them is men crawlin' all over Mama. And she can't pull 'em off and she can't wash 'em off. There's too many of 'em, and they been crawlin' on her for too many years. She ain't never gon' get 'em off."

For sure, there had been plenty of men in my mother's life, and in my own as well. Although nothing was crawling on me, I felt myself squirming in my seat, struggling to wake up, trying to shake the vivid memories of my mother and her bugs.

I didn't know where along the highway we were when my eyes finally opened. My heart began to race as my blurred vision caught the sight of ghosts drifting along the aisle and hovering overhead. They were my sisters, Tarabelle and Judy, both murdered by our mother's hands. Judy seemed to purposely plummet toward my seat. I stretched my hands out to catch her, but she was like a gentle breeze, barely grazing my fingertips as she passed by. And Tarabelle, sad, confused Tarabelle, stared down at me with dead, black eyes. She never parted her lips, and still I heard her say, "You always been silly, Tangy Mae. You can't catch Judy now. You shoulda caught her when Mama threw her off that damn porch."

I couldn't, Tara. It all happened so fast. I couldn't.

"Humph," Tarabelle snorted, and then she was gone. My ghosts vanished and were replaced by guilt.

As though sensing my discomfort, Laura turned in sleep to rest her head against my arm. She, at least, was real, and I needed her close to me. That was not why I had brought her along, though. I had brought her to keep her safe, and because I could not bear the thought of leaving her behind to be passed from man to man at the farmhouse. It had happened to me and to my sisters before me. It was not by choice, but by our mother's will. I could not stop her.

Sometimes I think I am at fault for all of the horrible things that have happened in our lives. Culpability must be acknowledged, so that I do not repeat my past mistakes. I am not the oldest of my mother's children, nor do I know much about life, other than what I have learned from books. I was valedictorian of my senior class, while none of my siblings had made it past the sixth grade. Intelligence countered by defenselessness offers no rewards, though, and I have always been weak. Had I been stronger, more vigilant, Tarabelle and Judy might still be alive. I should have screamed to the world from the high porch of our house on Penyon Road, "Help us! There is something terribly wrong with our mother. She is going to kill us all." Instead, I did nothing.

Rozelle Quinn. Often I have rolled my mother's name across my tongue, trying to get a taste of what she is, who she is. She is a beautiful woman with a cream-colored complexion, high cheek bones, dimples, and gray eyes. Her beauty attracted men who planted their seeds and moved on before the harvest. Of my mother's ten children, I wonder if she can pinpoint all of the fathers, say to them without a doubt, "This is your child."

I was fourteen when I first met my father, Crow. That was three years ago, back in 1958. It was nighttime in the center of a dirt road. He loomed out of and blended into the darkness. He was a tall, muscular man with a broad nose and a matchstick dangling from the corner of smiling lips. He said I had his mother's hair, and he called me a queen. I was happy that someone as dark as me had come along to claim me. He believed he was my father, and I knew without a doubt that I was his child. To this day, I don't think my mother knows or cares that his given name is Clarence Otis Yardley. All she knows him by is Crow.

People often say that a man spit a child out when the child looks so much like him. Foolishly, I had studied the faces of the men in Pakersfield, trying to deduce the fathers of my siblings.

When I was young, I searched for a man who could not hear with the intention of making him Martha Jean's father. No man would have divulged paternity, though, because no man spit her out. She is the spitting image of our mother, with her dimples, gray eyes, and light complexion. She came into this world deaf, eleven months before me.

I imagine it must have baffled Mama—what to do with a child who could not hear the storms raging beneath our roof. Every child has to learn, and so Mama taught her. She taught Martha Jean obedience by embedding an ice pick in her hand, and once again I did nothing. I was six at the time—only six—but that's a feeble excuse. When Mama traded Martha Jean to Velman for an automobile, I resented it because I thought he should have bartered for me. I stole a kiss from him once and tried to fool myself into believing that it was for the sake of my sister. She could not, but I could, voice love for him. He called me "little sister," though, and made it clear that was all I'd ever be.

My list of transgressions is long. It is my fault that Mushy returned from Ohio to Georgia. She came back to help me, and now I'd left her there in Pakersfield. Mushy once asked the question: "How long I gotta pay for being born first in this damn family?" I had no reply then, but I should have said, "We've all paid a high price." It would not have answered her question, but it would have expressed my understanding. Mushy, whose real name is Elizabeth Ann, had not been there when Mama wrapped a leather belt around my head and bent my finger to the point of breaking. She had not been there when Mama had taken me to the farmhouse, where I swallowed the semen of men while they swallowed my spirit. Mushy is eight years older than I, so I had not been there for her when her young body had been bartered for cash in haylofts and back rooms. I think Mushy was serious when she told me one day, in a joking tone, "If it's one thing I learned from my mama, it's how to pay the rent." Maybe that was how Mama got Mushy started. I don't know what she did or said to Tara, but she forced me into pleasing men under the obligation of getting my brother, Sam, out of jail. If I ever see Sam again, I will say, "Sam, you look white because you are the son of a white man." I think he needs to know that the man who locked him away, stole nearly a year of his life, is his father. I found that out one night by eavesdropping on the sheriff and my mother.

I slipped away from Pakersfield with memories, my high school diploma, a shopping bag of belongings, and the resolution that Laura's childhood would never be like mine. If I found my grandmother hostile in the face of our unexpected arrival, my backup plan was to at least get her to tell me where to find my father. In the past, Crow had been free to travel anywhere he pleased. Now, since he had killed a man for me, he couldn't return to Pakersfield. "A murderer is a murderer whether he kills one or one hundred," Crow had told me, "and I'd kill a thousand for you." It is no wonder that I've seen ghosts. I am the progeny of murderous parents. At this point in my life I just wanted to put that all behind me, find Crow and let him be a father to me before I totally outgrew the need for one.

Chapter 2

Laura had slept for most of the trip, and was ready to be on the move as soon as we stepped from the bus. I didn't know what annoyed me more—placing call after call to my grandmother's residence to no avail, or trying to keep Laura in sight while I placed my call. I spotted her across the lobby, begging pennies and nickels from strangers. By the time I made my way across the room, seized her, and brought her back to the pay booths, all the telephones were in use.

Inwardly seething, I gripped Laura's arm and gave her a stern warning. "Look, Laura," I said with mounting frustration, "you don't know where you are, you don't know these people, and you don't beg." She began to cry and struggle against me, which caused me to tighten my hold on her.

"Leave me alone!" she yelled in the midst of sobbing. We were attracting attention, which we didn't need, but it seemed to be Laura's purpose.

It occurred to me that Knoxville might be like Pakersfield where all destinations were within walking distance. Holding on to my sister and a shopping bag that had begun to rip, I made my way out of the depot to the street, where I approached a taxicab.

"Where to?" the driver asked.

More than a ride, I wanted directions. "How far is Booster Street?" I asked.

The driver, a heavyset, middle-aged man, blew a half-whistle, half-sigh. "Booster Street is up on Roanoke Pike," he informed me. "I'll tell you before you start, whether you use me or another driver, the fare is extra to go up there."

From the money that Crow had given me, I still had all but what I'd paid for the bus trip. I was anxious to meet my grandmother, and even if she wasn't home, I knew that I would rather wait for her at her house than at the bus depot with Laura becoming more and more agitated. "How much more?" I asked.

"Buck and a half."

The ride took us across a bridge, where a few pedestrians ambled along the walkway. Laura had calmed down and was holding a hand from the window to catch the passing breeze. After numerous stops and turns, we crossed an intersection of small shops, then continued on past a cemetery, and several minutes later we were riding by a tobacco field. At the foot of a steep hill, the driver stopped and let the car idle for a spell. "Roanoke Pike is up there," he informed me as he pointed toward the hill. "That's Moon Road. It's a rough road, and when we start up, you'll see why the fare is extra."

He shifted gears, and the car rolled so slowly toward the hill that I got the impression he was giving me the chance to change my mind, but there was no choice other than to forge ahead. I was observant of the landscape along the route even as I listened to the driver grumble and swear as rocks kicked up underneath the car. Before and behind us was the dirt hill dotted with stones and ruts, and on each side of the car was a wall of trees. More dust than air blew in through all four windows, and the heat inside became uncomfortable. With each ping of a stone and bump in a rut, I was sure that the driver was tallying an even higher fare.

We reached the crest of the hill and turned left at a boarded-up corner building. Old signs of cigarette and cold drink advertisements were dangling but still attached to the building that I assumed had once been a store. As we turned the corner, our driver slowed and finally stopped. "This is it. Forty-two Booster Street," he said. "Another dying section of Knoxville."

Green paint gave way to brown, or vice-versa, on the exterior walls of the single-story house where he'd stopped. The house had a screened-in front porch and twin red rose bushes at each corner. As I stepped from the taxi, the first thing I noticed was the lack of sidewalks and driveways along the street. Dust hung high and gravel crunched beneath our feet as the cab pulled away and we headed for the house.

Laura summed up the paint situation. "Somebody ran outta green paint," she said with a frown. "We gon' be stayin' here?"

I nodded and said, "I hope so."

A graveled path led us to the steps where the sound of a television traveled through the walls and out into the yard. I knocked, waited, then knocked again even harder. After several knocks with no response, I took Laura with me and ventured around to the rear of the house. Nobody was in the yard, but a large, gray cat was stretched on the top step. It watched us, showed no fear, and did not move until we were nearly upon it. I peered through a window in the door and saw no signs of activity, but knocked anyway.

"I know somebody in there," Laura grumbled as we moved back along the side of the house to the front. She was hungry and thirsty, and wanted to go home.

"Try to be patient," I said. "She can't have gone too far, or the television wouldn't be on. She's old. Maybe she's taking a bath or something and can't get to the door right away."

Directly across the street were two vacant houses, but there were others along the row that appeared to be occupied. To our left was another empty house with grass growing high in the yard, but in a shabby yellow house to our right a little girl stood at a window looking out at us. When I waved to her, she disappeared from the window, but at least I knew that somebody lived in and was at home in that particular house.

Each time I crossed the front porch to knock at my grandmother's door, I would tell myself it was the last time, but it wasn't. We sat on the front steps as bees drifted out from the rosebushes and buzzed around our heads. Early on, I had been comforted by the fragrance of the freshly mowed lawn and the presence of a pickup truck out on the street. They and the little girl next door indicated that we were not isolated in the neighborhood, but I felt lost and alone, like I had made the worst mistake of my life. What if night caught us out here with nothing to eat and nowhere to sleep?

I watched my sister swat at a bee hovering near her face. Childish frustration prompted her to remove one of her shoes to bat at the bee. I warned her that she was going to get stung, but she wouldn't listen. She hopped around from the steps to the ground, swinging at the bee. To my surprise, she caught it in an outward swing, knocked it to the ground, then squashed it into the gravel with the shoe.

"You got lucky," I told her.

With one patent leather shoe in hand, she started toward one of the rose bushes. "I'm gon' get 'em all," she said.

"No, you're not. You're gonna come sit on this step and leave those bees alone. If you don't bother them, they won't bother you."

"They started it," she sulked, and moved on toward the bush.

I had enough on my mind already without having to worry about Laura getting stung by a bee. Rising from the step, I moved swiftly to catch her before she could disturb the rosebush and trigger a swarm of angry bees.

There was a window just above the rosebush. On tiptoes I could possibly peer inside, but not without bumping against the bush and inevitably getting stung. Maybe my grandmother had already seen us from one of her windows, I thought. We would be strangers to her, and she was probably cautious about opening her door. If she would just show herself, come to a window, I would tell her that I was her granddaughter.

We sat on the steps again and I looked for the girl at the window next door, but she hadn't reappeared. Because Laura was angry with me, she had seated herself on the top step, as far from me as she could get. I allowed her to pout while I tried to strategize my next move, in the case that my grandmother never came to the door. I would have to go to the house next door, ask to use the telephone, and call a taxi to take us back to the bus depot. I told Laura my plan. It was enough to bring her to sit down next to me.

"You think they'll give me somethin' to eat?" she asked as she pointed toward the yellow house.

"I don't know, but we can get something when we go back to the bus depot," I answered. The thought of going back to Pakersfield gave me a helpless feeling, like everything that I had done to free myself had been in vain. Nobody had abandoned me, and yet that was how I felt as the hours passed with my muttered prayers.

Our salvation appeared in the form of an elderly man who came along the street pushing a lawnmower. He wore overalls and a plaid shirt with hanging threads from where the sleeves had been ripped off. He had a cinnamon-colored complexion, and thin, salt and pepper hair showing from beneath a pushed back straw hat. He hoisted his lawnmower onto the back of the pick-up truck, then he turned toward my grandmother's house. "Hey," he called out to us. "Where'd y'all come from? I just cut this grass 'bout a hour ago, and y'all wadn't here."

As hours go, he was badly mistaken. We had been on those steps long enough to watch the sun shift in the Tennessee sky, long enough to think that my grandmother must surly have caught sight of us by now and decided that she could not be bothered.

"We're looking for Francine Yardley," I said.

The man glanced at the shopping bag beside my feet. "Y'all got somethin' there for her?"

"No, sir. I'm her granddaughter."

"Her granddaughter? Well, I'll say." He came up to the steps. "Did y'all knock?"

"Yes, sir. Several times."

"A hundred times," Laura mumbled.

"I'm Percy Hudson, a friend of Francine's," the man said as he mounted the steps between me and Laura. "Y'all come on."

He pulled a chain of keys from his pocket and within seconds had opened the front door. From my spot on the porch, I watched him turn the television off, and the sound that had been both a comfort and an annoyance was finally silenced. Over and over he called my grandmother's name, and I was thinking that maybe she really wasn't at home. Finally, Mr. Percy Hudson called out to us, "I told y'all to come on in. She in here on the couch."

More than anything I had wanted to look presentable when my grandmother saw me for the first time. I had worn my best dress—a bright green one with short sleeves—and a pair of white pumps, but wind and dust blowing through the open window of the taxi had wrestled with my hair, the bus seat had wrinkled my dress, and I knew that my face was shiny with perspiration. I held onto our shopping bag with one hand, used the other to smooth down my hair as best I could, then drew in a deep breath to calm myself.

Laura and I entered the house to see a dark, large-boned woman either dead or asleep on a flower-patterned blue couch. Her head was on an armrest and her legs were stretched across the cushions. Her left leg, from ankle to knee, was wrapped in an opaque bandage, and she wore a floral-printed purple dress that clashed with the pattern on the couch. Sitting on the coffee table in front of her were a cane and an empty water glass.

Mr. Percy had moved to the space between the coffee table and couch. "Francine!" he shouted as he leaned to shake her. After several shakes he straightened his back, then turned to face us. "She'll be awright when she wakes up if y'all wanna wait that long. It's them darn pills the doctor give her for pain. They ain't no good for her. I done told her that."

I thought he had given up on my grandmother when he stepped around the table to stand in front of me. "Clarence told her last year that he had a daughter, so I reckon that must be you," he said. "She ain't said nothin' 'bout you comin', though."

"I wanted to surprise her," I said.

"She'll be surprised awright," he said as he moved through a doorway where I could see a kitchen table and chairs. When he returned he was holding a wet towel. He winked at me. "Cold water," he explained. "This oughta do it."

He went back over to the couch and plopped the towel over my grandmother's face. Her head turned as though trying to free her face of the towel, and her bandaged leg twitched a little. "Francine!" Mr. Percy shouted impatiently as his hand worked the cloth across her face.

He could have been smothering her for all I knew, but he was getting results. She was beginning to stir. Her hands reached for the cloth, and finally Mr. Percy let her have it as he stepped away.

My grandmother's eyelids fluttered and opened a crack. "Earlene?" she questioned drowsily. "Is that you, Earlene?"

"Wake up, Francine," Mr. Percy commanded. "It ain't Earlene. These girls say they ya' grandchillun. Wake up now!"

"I'm woke," she mumbled, then brushed her dress down over her knees to prove it. She made the full opening of her eyes suspenseful, like something that might never happen. Her head turned slowly back and forth against the armrest, toward the window and away from the window. Her eyelids tightened, fluttered, smoothed out, tightened again, and finally opened.

"Ma'am," I'd said before her eyes could close again, "My name is Tangy Mae, and this is my sister, Laura."

"Who?" she questioned in a hoarse voice.

"Tangy Mae," I repeated. "I'm Crow's daughter."

"Lord, have mercy," she mumbled as she continued her struggle toward alertness. "Percy, get me a drink of water."

Mr. Percy picked up the empty glass from the table and stepped back into the kitchen. When he came back, he placed a glass of water on the table and picked up the discarded towel. "Here, Francine. Wash ya' face right good. You need to wake up. You been takin' them darn pills again, ain't you?"

She ran the cloth across her face, took a sip of water, then cleared her throat. "Where'd y'all come from?" she asked.

"Pakersfield, Georgia," I answered. "Crow gave me your address and telephone number."

"Lord, have mercy," she repeated softly, and shifted until her back was against the armrest. "If he gave you all that, how come you didn't let me know you were coming? Y'all done caught me looking a mess. Let me get up from here." She slowly maneuvered her body into a sitting position. The fabric of the armrest had left indentations in her face, and light from the window made the lines appear deep. "You say you Clarence's child?"

"Yes, ma'am."

She had a round face, Crow's broad nose, and thick, graying hair braided like a crown around her head. Strands of hair were sticking up in places, and her eyes were puffy from sleep. She did indeed look a mess. Actually, she portrayed the mannerism of an intoxicated person barely able to hold her head up. Squinting through puffy eyes made her appear angry as she leaned forward for a better look at me. "Child, you look just like my sister, Earlene. All anybody gotta do is look to see," she said. "Don't you see it, Percy?"

"Yeah, Francine. I seen it when she was out there on the steps. That's how come I brought 'em on in here."

"Well, I gotta call Clarence to make sure," she said as she struggled to slip her feet into a pair of black loafers. She picked up her cane and tried to stand, but she was still a little too sluggish.

Chapter 3

"Just take your time, Francine. And yell out when you ready for me to help you over to the telephone," Mr. Percy said before he led me and Laura out to the kitchen. "That's the bathroom right there, in case y'all need to go," he informed us.

The bathroom door and the back door nearly kissed each other at the rear of the large, busy kitchen. There were two large windows behind a square wooden table that seated four, and a short window above the kitchen sink. All of the windows were draped in yellow curtains to match the green and yellow wallpaper. Against the wall that separated the kitchen from the front room was a wringer-washer, and on each side of the washer were metal hooks that supported an array of pots and pans. Just past the end of the table was yet another doorway.

"I reckon y'all gon' be sleepin' in here," Mr. Percy said as he moved toward the dark room. "I'm gon' open the window to air it out."

In the front room, my grandmother had heard enough to say, "Hold on, Percy! We don't know these girls. Don't put them nowhere until I talk to Clarence."

Of course she needed to verify that we were who we claimed to be. Still, I was tired and hungry. It was getting late, and I didn't need the burden of trying to make alternate arrangements. Seeing the immediate droop of my shoulders, Mr. Percy shook his head. "Uh-uh. No need to look so worried," he whispered. "What you need to do is go in there, get your bag, and bring it in here. While you're out there, I want you to take a look at the biggest picture hanging over the television. That's Francine's sister, Earlene. Died about ten years ago. When Francine get them eyes fully open, ain't no way she gon' wanna let you leave this house."

His words had a calming effect, and I eased into the front room where my grandmother was dilly-dallying with her cane. Laura was ahead of me, and as she snatched up the ripped bag from the floor, it finally disintegrated and spilled the contents beside the coffee table. My grandmother didn't make a sound. She wasn't fully awake, but I thought she was almost there. Laura and I gathered the items from the floor, and I took the time to look at the photograph of Earlene before stepping back into the kitchen.

"What'd you think about the picture?" Mr. Percy asked. "It's like looking in the mirror, isn't it?"

I didn't think so, but I smiled and nodded agreeably. The woman in the photograph had a narrow face, a thick ponytail draped over one shoulder, and a closed-lipped smile. I guessed if I stared long and hard enough, I might find some resemblance, but I was more interested in seeing myself in a different light than comparing myself to a relative. With our belongings held tightly against our chests, we fell in behind Mr. Percy to see where we would sleep.

An awkward step down from the kitchen led into a small bedroom that had no door. He pulled a hanging string to light the room, and we were able to see a single window with white Venetian blinds, a closet, a full-sized bed, and a four-drawer dresser. On the dresser was a framed snapshot of Crow. He was wearing an army uniform, and he had an arm wrapped around a short, attractive woman.

Standing beside me, Mr. Percy opened the top drawer and crammed its contents into the bottom one. "Y'all can use this drawer for now," he said. "I'm thinking y'all gon' be here for the whole summer, so just move things around when you need to. Clarence won't mind."

"Per-cee," came a broken cry from the front room, and never had I seen an old man move so fast. Fearing that something was wrong, I also rushed for the front room. What we witnessed was Miss Francine gripping her cane and teetering at the edge of a cushion, very close to tumbling off. Mr. Percy reached her and secured her by bracing a hand firmly against her shoulder. I got on her other side of her and did the same. Together we were able to slide her back onto the couch.

"I wanna call Clarence," she mumbled.

From my position beside the couch, I caught sight of Laura sneaking through the kitchen. She was out of my view for only a moment before I saw her again. In her hand was an unwrapped deli pack of bologna, and she was already nibbling on a slice. *So be it*, I thought. *She's hungry, and I have the money to pay for it if it comes to that.*

Because my grandmother kept insisting on using the telephone, we helped her up. Her cane made a tapping sound against the hardwood floor as we made our way slowly across the room. With one loud grunt, she seated herself at a telephone table that resembled a school desk. She squeezed the bridge of her nose, closed her eyes, and for a moment sat there doing nothing.

"You shoulda stayed on the couch, Francine!" Mr. Percy said. "You still halfway sleep."

"I ain't sleep, Percy," she said in an even tone. "I gotta call Clarence."

She woke up enough to place a person to person call to Detroit, Michigan. After a long pause, I heard her say, "Hey, Clarence. Nothing's wrong. I just called to let you know that your daughter is here with me. Didn't call or nothing; just showed up. Hold on and I'll let you talk to her, but don't stay on too long."

"Hey, Crow," I said as soon as the receiver was turned over to me.

"Hey, sugar," came his pleasant voice. "What you doin' in Knoxville?"

"Looking for you. I wanna see you, Crow."

"I wanna see you, too, but I just left there. I'll be back in maybe two or three weeks. I'm glad you there to help Mama out. I worry 'bout her wit' that bad leg and all. How you talk Rozelle into let-tin' you go to Knoxville?"

"I didn't," I answered softly.

"What you mean, you didn't?"

"I finished school, Crow," I said. "I have my diploma."

"Listen to me, sugar," he said, "Do Rozelle know where you at?"

"Not really," I answered, "but I'll tell you all about it when you get here."

"I'll be there soon as I can," I heard Crow say just before my grandmother's hand reached out and took the receiver from me.

"Do that sound like your daughter?" she asked into the tele-phone, then nodded her head. "I knew it was. She looks just like Earlene for the world."

They talked for about a minute longer, and I gathered from my grandmother's responses that Crow was asking about her injured leg. She said her goodbye, then glanced up at me. "When it's long-distance, you get on, say what you gotta say and you get off," she informed me. "Long-distance calls cost too much, but while we're at it, I guess I should let you call your mother."

A moment of dread gripped me, but then I thought, *Tangy, you're smart enough to know that you don't call the person you're running from to tell them where you are.* "She doesn't have a telephone," I responded and glanced toward the kitchen at Laura, who had finished eating and was now flicking the balled deli paper across the table.

My grandmother nodded her head in understanding. "There's a lotta people don't have telephones, but can't you call somebody to let your mother know you made it here safe?"

"She'll probably use somebody's telephone to call us," I lied. "If she doesn't, I'll call somebody."

"Francine, I got two mo' yards to cut, then I'll be back," Mr. Percy interrupted. My grandmother gave an exasperated sigh.

"Percy, you know you ought not to be out there cutting grass at this time of day. How many times I gotta tell you that?"

Mr. Percy smiled. "Girl, stop worryin' 'bout me. How you know what time it is when you been layin' up in here sleep?"

She waved a hand in dismissal. "Since you looking for some-thing to do, just gotta have something to do, why don't you run down to the restaurant and get these children something to eat?"

"Well, awright then," Mr. Percy said. "You want me to help you back over to the couch befo' I leave?"

"Not now," she said. "I'm gon' sit right here and talk to my granddaughter."

"Keep an eye on her, will ya?" Mr. Percy asked.

As soon as the door closed behind him, my grandmother dropped her hands onto her lap, closed her eyes, and fell asleep again right there at the telephone desk. *Welcome to Knoxville that's not really Knoxville at all*, I thought to myself.

Chapter 4

Although we had very little conversation with Miss Francine, I considered our first week on Roanoke Pike a learning experience. We had a chance to freely roam and explore our new lodgings and neighborhood. We dared to leave Booster Street and walk a five-block distance. What we saw were more vacant houses than occupied homes, three pedestrians who nodded in greeting, and two stray dogs that paid us even less attention than we paid them. There was a boarded-up elementary school with a playground that was cluttered with cans, paper, and other debris. It was a blighted and nearly abandoned neighborhood, and quite disheartening for a new start in my life.

The other thing that discouraged me was the lack of reading material in my grandmother's house. I had yet to see a single book or magazine. The television stayed on most of the day, but neither Laura nor I had an interest in television. Mr. Percy came to the house every day to see that my grandmother was all right and whether we needed anything. Laura and I tried not to disturb Miss Francine, and we eagerly awaited Mr. Percy's daily visit.

Rising early was the best way to catch my grandmother

relaxed and with a few words to spare. She would have cold cereal and a pain pill with orange juice for breakfast, then she would make a telephone call to a woman named Betty. After ending her conversation, she would turn on the television and retire to the couch.

One early morning, she blinked me into focus at the breakfast table and flatly stated, "You're Clarence's daughter."

It wasn't a question, but I responded just the same. "Yes, ma'am."

"Call me Granny," she said, then nodded her head toward Laura. "Both of y'all. I wanna hear how it sounds. You can't be walking around here calling me Miss Francine when you're supposed to be my grandchild. Maybe I won't be in so much pain now that y'all here to help me out."

It was obvious to me that my grandmother couldn't do much. She nursed her injured leg and kept it wrapped in a bandage for warmth, despite the fact that her house was mostly closed up and stuffy. Although her bedroom was near the front of the house, just off the front room, I would sometimes hear her crying during the nights. Her sobs had the resonance of despair that I began to associate with the settling of the house.

In due time, I was sure I would get to know my grandmother, but while she slept I had already determined a few things about her. Her refrigerator and cabinets were well stocked, although when she took a notion to eat, the food usually came from the restaurant.

Each weekday evening between four and five, Mr. Percy would arrive at the house. Once I knew his routine, I knew to get a cold, wet cloth and a cup of hot tea, then pester my grandmother until she was awake enough to speak a few coherent words. On the days when my schedule worked, the house would blossom with activity, laughter, and conversation. When it did not work, disappointment would show on Mr. Percy's face and he would either wake her himself or allow her to sleep longer.

One day he came in to find me trying to wake her. "Let her be," he said. "I saw Maggie Mundy's girls out in the backyard when I drove up. Did y'all meet 'em yet?"

"No, sir," I answered. "We've seen them, but we haven't actually met them."

"No better time than now," he said. "Francine ain't gon' like it, but y'all can't stay in here guarding this house day in and day out."

Granny had no back porch to mention, and no rails to hold onto. The back door opened to a short wooden platform with seven narrow steps descending between the expanse of exterior walls. A garbage can stood at the foot of the steps, and a small shed had been built near the rear of the yard. Wire fences separated her property from the neighboring houses, and a green metal lawn chair stood against one of the fences. Curled on the chair was the gray cat.

We headed toward the Mundys' house, and through the wire fence I could see two little girls in a sandbox laughing and squishing dirty sand between their toes. They were both dressed in navy blue shorts and sleeveless light blue tops with emblems of Mickey Mouse stitched in on the front. They watched our approach, then quietly drifted toward us. A moderately tall, thin woman stepped out onto the back poach just as Mr. Percy raised a fist to knock. "Mr. Percy," she exclaimed, "What brings you over? Leon ain't home from work yet, but he oughta be here soon."

"I came to introduce Francine's granddaughters to your girls," he said. "This one is Tangy, and the lil' one there is Laura."

"My girls told me they thought Miss Francine had company, but you know me. I didn't wanna go over there being nosy." She turned, opened the door, and yelled back into the house, "Sylvia, come on out here for a minute." The girl stepped outside and Miss Maggie prompted us to make introductions all around. Her six-year-old twins, Kay and Kathy, were not identical, but they were both chubby little girls with shoulder-length hair. Twelve-year-old Sylvia resembled her mother. She was tall and thin with short hair and the first signs of acne dotting her face. To my surprise, Laura joined the twins as they returned to the sandbox.

"You gotta be Crow's daughter to be Miss Francine's granddaughter, unless she been keeping' secrets," Miss Maggie said.

My mouth opened to respond, but she never stopped talking. She reminded me of a sound—a pop, in fact. Everything about her was quick—the way she moved, the way she spoke, and the way her thoughts seemed to tumble over each other.

"Yeah, you Crow's all right," she said with a smile. "You favor him. I was sweet on him once, but we wadn't no good for each other. I needed me a man that would stay put, and Crow wadn't never gon' do that. Leon was the kinda man I needed. He works over at Alcoa," she chattered on. "You might see him out in this yard sometime, but mostly he's up in the house gettin' on my nerves. You know, a man can get on your nerves worst than a child sometimes. If you love 'em, you put up wit' it, and you don't never let 'em know. That's the way I see it."

"Mama, you left the meatloaf in the stove," Sylvia interrupted in a surly tone. "You want me to take it out?"

"Are you hungry, Sylvia?" Miss Maggie snapped. "Don't say nothin' else to me 'bout that damn meatloaf. It ain't gon' burn."

Sylvia rolled her eyes behind her mother's back, then she glanced at me. She stepped from the porch just as a car pulled up in front of the house. A stout, middle-aged man climbed from the car with a brown grocery bag tucked beneath one arm. As he drew closer to the backyard, I could see that he had sideburns, and a thin mustache over full lips. "Daddy, Daddy, Daddy," the twins yelled as they bolted toward him, leaving Laura alone in the sandbox.

"How you doin', Leon?" Mr. Percy asked in greeting.

"Comin' from hot to hot, Mr. Percy," the man answered as he disengaged himself from the twins and shoed them back off to the sandbox. "You want a cold one?"

"Not right now. I gotta get on back over to the house and check on Francine. Just came over to let her granddaughters meet your girls."

Mr. Leon draped an arm over Miss Maggie's shoulder, and I couldn't tell if it was out of affection or just to hold himself up. He looked like a tired man. My impression of him was that of a man who sought to be cordial when he was about to drop from exhaustion. Miss Maggie led him into the house, and Mr. Percy made his way back across the lawns.

I was about to follow him when Sylvia stepped closer to me. She looked me up and down from my ponytail to my blue canvas shoes, then said, "Let's go over to your yard befo' Mama come back out here talkin'. You ain't old enough for Mama to be tellin' her business to," she said.

We had almost reached the fence when Miss Maggie opened the screen door and said, "Tangy Mae, if y'all gon be here for a while, y'all might wanna go to church wit' us some Sunday. What you think?"

"I don't know," I answered. "Granny wants us to wait until her leg is better so we can go with her."

"Shoot," Miss Maggie huffed, "Ya soul'll rot in Hell waitin' on Miss Francine."

"See what I mean?" Sylvia whispered as she paused to rub the cat that was still stretched on the lawn chair. "Go home, Fred," she commanded. The cat didn't move, but out on the street I saw Mr. Percy drive away in his Plymouth.

Sylvia and I settled on Granny's back steps, and I had a view of Laura through the fence. She and the twins had moved from the sandbox to a swing set, and Miss Maggie was passing popsicles out to them. This was absolutely the best day we'd had since our arrival. The Mundy family was friendly, and Laura was having fun for a change.

"I used to come over here and help Miss Francine when she first broke her leg," Sylvia offered, "but she didn't like the way I did things. I guess you'll be helping her now."

"I will," I admitted.

"So how long y'all gon' stay?"

"I'm not sure yet."

Sylvia stood and tugged at the hems of her pink shorts, then she glanced up toward Granny's back door, and said, "Well, I can tell you right now, Miss Francine ain't gon' like nothin' you do."

"She hasn't complained about anything so far," I said.

"That's 'cause you just got here, but just wait; you'll see. What she be doin' up in there all day?"

"Mostly resting, but she's probably up by now," I said as I also glanced toward the door, hoping that the prospect of Granny being up and moving through the house would prompt Sylvia into talking about something else.

"I knew she didn't go nowhere 'cause she won't leave this house," Sylvia said. "She even had my mama watch this ol' house when she went to the doctor. She need to get up. Her leg ain't hurt that bad."

She had finally managed to get on my nerves, and I gave her a reproachful look. "How would you know," I asked.

Unmoved by my disapproval, Sylvia shrugged and said, "When Jeremy Blackmon broke his leg, he was back in school in no time. He didn't lay up all these months like Miss Francine doin'. My mama say Miss Francine go for bad. Ya daddy go for bad, too, but my daddy ain't scared of 'im."

Sylvia was only twelve. I had to remind myself of that in order to quiet my mounting anger. If I revealed my true annoyance, I might alienate the only person I had met in Knoxville who was even remotely close to my age. Changing the subject, I asked, "Is there a store or library anywhere close to here"

"Shoot," she said. "Ain't nothin' close to here, and you have to go all the way down to Vine to get to the library. Mr. Leary sell candy outta his house over on the next street, but he gon' be movin' soon."

"Why is everybody moving?"

"'Cause we gotta. I think they puttin' a highway through Roanoke Pike. That's what my daddy say, and everybody gotta move."

"My grandmother, too?"

She nodded. "Everybody. We movin' in August, and Mama worried that there ain't gon' be nobody to come to the twins' birthday party next month." She counted on her fingers the few children that remained on Roanoke Pike. As she rattled off the names, I was trying to recall if Granny had mentioned anything about moving. I was sure she hadn't. There were no pictures coming down from the walls and no boxes to be packed.

About the Author

Delores Faye Phillips was born on September 26, 1950 in Centersville, Georgia (just north of Atlanta), to Lennie and Annie Ruth Miller. She grew up in nearby Bartow County, the second of four siblings. Her mother, who worked several jobs, read poetry to her children every night, and even wrote occasionally herself—she was published just once, in *True Story* magazine. The Miller children spent two years in Detroit, from 1959 to 1961, but returned to Georgia after their father passed away. There, they continued their schooling. Though formal integration was supposed to take place in Georgia in the mid-1950s after the *Brown v. Board of Education* ruling, it didn't happen before Phillips's mother moved the family to Cleveland in 1964.

Phillips had always known she wanted to be a writer, putting her pen to paper from a very young age, but eventually followed in her older sister Linda's footsteps, training to become a nurse. Between long career stretches as a practical nurse, Delores Phillips was an advocate for battered women at the Center for the Prevention of Domestic Violence in Cleveland. She married her husband, Charles Phillips, in 1983. He passed away from cancer in 1988.

Still harboring her dream of becoming a writer, Phillips went back to school and obtained her Bachelor of Arts in English at Cleveland State University in 1994, after which she began her seminal work. *The Darkest Child* initially began as a long-form poem, written over a period of four years. Given that it was several hundred pages by the time Phillips completed it, she decided to reshape it into a novel.

The Darkest Child was published by Soho Press in January of 2004 to critical acclaim. Phillips went on an extensive tour for the book's release, visiting schools, bookstores, and women's groups around the country. Her family, who knew her as an introvert with a fear of public speaking and flying, was surprised to see her take to audiences at readings and speaking engagements. Phillips felt honored to travel to Chicago to receive her first award from the Black Caucus of the American Library Association (BCALA).

Even after the novel came out, Phillips continued to work full-time as a nurse in the Northcoast Behavioral Healthcare System in Cleveland, which remained her home city until she passed away in 2014. She was at work on a second novel at the time of her death.

Phillips's poetry has been published in *Jean's Journal*, *Black Times*, and *The Crisis* under the name Faye Miller Knox. In addition to her siblings, she is survived by her daughter, Shalana, and 15-year-old granddaughter, Mikaela, both of whom are writers. She is remembered as a go-getter who loved family, friends, comedy, and laughter.

About Tayari Jones

Tayari Jones is the author of the novels *Leaving Atlanta*, *The Untelling*, *Silver Sparrow*, and *An American Marriage*. Her writing has appeared in *Tin House*, *The Believer*, *The New York Times*, and *Callaloo*. A member of the Fellowship of Southern Writers, she is also a recipient of a Hurston/Wright Legacy Award, a Lifetime Achievement Award in Fine Arts from the Congressional Black Caucus Foundation, a United States Artist Fellowship, an NEA Fellowship and a Radcliffe Institute Bunting Fellowship. *Silver Sparrow* was named an American Booksellers Association #1 Indie Next Pick and an NEA Big Read Library selection. Jones is a graduate of Spelman College, University of Iowa, and Arizona State University. An associate professor in the MFA program at Rutgers-Newark University, she is the 2017–2018 Shearing Fellow for Distinguished Writers at the Beverly Rogers, Carol C. Harter Black Mountain Institute at the University of Nevada, Las Vegas.